LEGION'S LADIES

A soft scratching at her sitting room door interrupted Eleanor's musings.

She climbed down from the high old four-poster, drew her wrapper around her and hurried into her slippers. She opened the door and stepped back agog to discover instead the Earl of Wright leaning against her door frame. "May I have a word with you, Miss Howard?" he drawled languidly, his eyes roaming over her in what she felt to be a most unnerving fashion.

"It is the middle of the night!"

"Well, no, actually it is merely eleven."

"But I am not—most certainly even you must know a gentleman does not—oh! Go away."

"I did not come to ravish you, m'dear, if that is what you're thinking."

His dark, sparkling eyes seized her own and held them, and they stood speechless for what seemed an eternity. Eleanor felt her heart leap in her breast, and it pounded so loudly that she thought surely it must echo all the way down the corridor. She knew at last that she must tear her gaze from his or sink down into his very soul. "Please," she gasped, a maddening warmth rushing over her.

ZEBRA'S REGENCY ROMANCES DAZZLE AND DELIGHT

A BEGUILING INTRIGUE (4441, $3.99)
by Olivia Sumner

Pretty as a picture Justine Riggs cared nothing for propriety. She dressed as a boy, sat on her horse like a jockey, and pondered the stars like a scientist. But when she tried to best the handsome Quenton Fletcher, Marquess of Devon, by proving that she was the better equestrian, he would try to prove Justine's antics were pure folly. The game he had in mind was seduction—never imagining that he might lose his heart in the process!

AN INCONVENIENT ENGAGEMENT (4442, $3.99)
by Joy Reed

Rebecca Wentworth was furious when she saw her betrothed waltzing with another. So she decides to make him jealous by flirting with the handsomest man at the ball, John Collinwood, Earl of Stanford. The "wicked" nobleman knew exactly what the enticing miss was up to—and he was only too happy to play along. But as Rebecca gazed into his magnificent eyes, her errant fiancé was soon utterly forgotten.

SCANDAL'S LADY (4472, $3.99)
by Mary Kingsley

Cassandra was shocked to learn that the new Earl of Litton was her childhood friend, Nicholas St. John. After years at sea and mixed feelings Nicholas had come home to take the family title. And although Cassandra knew her place as a governess, she could not help the thrill that went through her each time he was near. Nicholas was pleased to find that his old friend Cassandra was his new next door neighbor, but after being near her, he wondered if mere friendship would be enough . . .

HIS LORDSHIP'S REWARD (4473, $3.99)
by Carola Dunn

As the daughter of a seasoned soldier, Fanny Ingram was accustomed to the vagaries of military life and cared not a whit about matters of rank and social standing. So she certainly never foresaw her *tendre* for handsome Viscount Roworth of Kent with whom she was forced to share lodgings, while he carried out his clandestine activities on behalf of the British Army. And though good sense told Roworth to keep his distance, he couldn't stop from taking Fanny in his arms for a kiss that made all hearts equal!

LEGION'S LADIES

Judith A. Landsdowne

Zebra Books
Kensington Publishing Corp.
http://www.zebrabooks.com

To Fay, the Daughter of My Heart:
Thank you for every moment shared.
You are loved beyond measure!

ZEBRA BOOKS are published by

Kensington Publishing Corp.
850 Third Avenue
New York, NY 10022

First Printing: November, 1996
10 9 8 7 6 5 4 3 2 1

Printed in the United States of America

One

Colly Shepard shivered in the bitter November night and stared at the shrouded windows of the house in Mayfair. A timid gentleman, of slight build and mild mien, he was nevertheless astoundingly obdurate in the service of the Duke of Ware, so he gathered his wits about him and approached the front door, prizing the knocker with vicious abandon. "I have come," he announced to the tall, gaunt butler who confronted him, "to speak with the Earl of Wright. You will say that Colly Shepard awaits his presence."

"His lordship is occupied," announced August Congreve in a sonorous voice that fit admirably with his skeletal form.

"You will deliver my message nonetheless," ordered Shepard so sharply that a look of disbelief inched across Congreve's countenance. Shepard stalked past the butler into the entrance hall and looked about. "I will wait in there," he declared finally, turning into a parlor where a fire blazed and taking a determined seat upon the edge of a Louis XIV chair.

Congreve, who recognized a servant when he saw one, had not offered to take the man's greatcoat, hat, or gloves. Thoughts of evicting the windblown, travel-worn individual bodily nibbled at Congreve's mind, but the mention of Wright's name brought second thoughts. One could never tell to whom the Earl of Wright might wish to speak. With solemn steps Congreve mounted the staircase, puzzling over the best way to go about interrupting the earl and Miss Lily and still keep his head upon his shoulders.

* * *

Lily Lipton, whom Wright had gifted with the house in May-fair four years earlier, wrapped her soft, sweet-smelling arms around Wright's damp chest and nibbled at his dark, wet curls as he finished his bath. She knew perfectly well that he had spent the afternoon at White's raging against the Corn Laws, though she had not the least idea why. And she had had a hot bath waiting for him when he came to her, because he was always so grumpy when he had spent the day arguing and he was ever so much nicer once he had lazed in the water for a while. She helped him to dry himself and wrapped a towel about his waist, and he pulled her gently against him, kissing her golden curls and her pale brow and each lovely eyelid tenderly. He swung her up into his arms and carried her toward the silk-hung hideaway of their bed. Congreve rapped upon the door of the sitting room. "Damnation," Wright growled, setting her upon the bedcovers. "Stay right there, Lilliputian. I shall go and strangle whoever it is and return immediately."

Lily giggled.

Wright stalked to the sitting room door and swung it inward. Congreve, his face a mask of indifference, announced that a person named Colly Shepard had forced his way into the front parlor and demanded the earl's presence immediately.

"What? How the devil did he know to come here?"

"I am afraid I cannot say, sir."

"No, well, say I shall be right down, Congreve."

"Yes, my lord."

Lily pouted prettily, traipsing daintily into the room, "Can't you just tell him to wait for you at Wright House, Josh?"

"No, Lily. Be a good girl and fetch my breeches. If Colly Shepard has sought me out here, there is good reason for it."

Jocelyn Elders, the Earl of Wright, dropped the towel and hurried into his small clothes. With a very kissable frown upon her pretty lips, Lily handed him his shirt and helped him shrug into his coat. Wright ran his fingers ruthlessly through his tousled curls in lieu of his missing comb, slid his feet into his shoes and, abandoning waistcoat and cravat, planted an encouraging smooch on the tip of Lily's bewitchingly upturned nose. "Do not run off, Lily love. I shan't be long. Go warm the sheets for me. That's an angel."

The earl had not laid eyes upon his nephew's valet for at least six months—sometime in May, when he had gone to Ware's estate in Sussex to help celebrate the duke's birthday.

"Colly? What is it?" he bellowed as he bounded down the stairs and swung into the parlor. He came to an abrupt halt. Never had he seen Ware's valet so pale and frightened. "No, don't get up, Colly. Congreve, fetch us some cognac."

The earl's disarray immediately convinced Shepard that he had interrupted a romantic encounter. Had he been less upset by the news he carried, he would have blushed clear to his toes to think of it. But he had no time for such nonsense now, and though he willingly accepted the glass Congreve offered him, he breathed a sigh of relief when the butler at last departed.

"Now," drawled the earl, sipping at his own glass, "what's this all about? No one's ill?"

"No, my lord, not ill. The duchess—is missing, my lord."

Wright, who had just settled into a wing chair, jolted to his feet, cognac sloshing over the side of his glass. "What? No, never mind, Colly, " he roared as the little valet jumped up to mop the cognac from his coat for him. "How could Jenny go missing? Why? Where is Jessie?"

"His grace is safe at Willowset, my lord. We were to spend the Christmas season there. Her grace set out ahead of us. She does not like to travel as slowly as one must with the duke, you know. And when we arrived, we learned that her grace and Miss Tynesbury had not."

"Tynesbury was with Jenny, then? Who else?"

"Glenby Oakes drove, my lord, with Nelson beside him and Gregory and Carson as outriders."

"And they are all missing?"

"Yes, my lord."

"How long?"

Shepard studied the gentleman before him carefully. He had wished to notify this dangerous and quite extraordinary brother of the duchess immediately. But the Reverend Howard had taken charge at Willowset and forbidden the staff to bring the matter to the earl's attention. The staff had finally secretly combined forces to help Shepard slip out and make his way via the mail coaches as far as London.

"How long, Colly?"

"T-two weeks, my lord."

Wright, who had been glaring into the grate, spun around, and Shepard flinched at the fury in his eyes. "Two weeks? My sister disappears and I am not to know of it for two weeks? What, are you snowed in at Willowset in November?"

"There were, ah, complications, my lord."

"Yes?" The earl's brow rose slightly as he awaited Shepard's explanation.

"There has been a search, my lord. It was done most discreetly, of course, but—"

"Under whose direction? What, Colly, are you afraid to tell me? Why was I not notified? Does Grimsby know? Paxton?"

"N-no, my lord. That is, I do not think so. Though certainly they will receive word shortly. It was Reverend Howard's suggestion to keep the thing as quiet as possible."

"Howard!" Wright spit the name into the midst of the small parlor, then paused, a grim and foreboding calm enveloping him. "Am I to understand that Howard has taken charge at Willowset?"

"He had come to meet the duchess upon her arrival, my lord."

"I see."

"He is, after all, one of the duke's guardians."

"Indeed. One—of four. Does Jessie know?"

"No, my lord. Mrs. Bowers and I have told him that his mama has gone to visit his Aunt Althea and will return shortly."

"Well, at least that imbecile Howard has not got Jess all in a pucker. Is the coach outside, Colly?"

"No, my lord. I did not come in the traveling coach. I came by—public conveyance."

The earl's brow lifted again. "Am I to understand, Colly, that Howard had not even the decency to send you to me in the duke's equipage? Or that he did not send you to me at all?"

Shepard sank back down into the Louis XIV chair and reached for his cognac, afraid to answer. He took a long swallow as the earl began to pace. Wright fought to bring his sense of outrage under control. Shepard, after all, was not the person he should like to horse whip. "He did not send you to me at all, eh, Colly? Well, I appreciate that you had the audacity to ignore him." He reached into his coat pocket, produced some of the ready and placed it into Shepard's hand. "Take a hackney to Wright House and wait for me there, Colly. Tell Harry Cross to hitch the bays and saddle Tugforth. Say he and Tibbs are to accompany us to Willowset and we leave tonight. How are the roads?"

"Wretched, my lord."

"No matter. We shall manage. Will you pack for me? Tibbs will have enough to pack his own gear, for I shan't be far behind you and I have no wish to dawdle."

"Most certainly, my lord."

"Good. Off with you, then. I have a matter to conclude here."

Lily extended both arms to Wright from between the sheets as he entered the bedchamber and he went straight to her and dropped onto the edge of the bed. "Sorry, sweetings, not tonight," he murmured. "Tonight, my dear, you have the bed to yourself."

"But Josh—"

"No, Lily. I must go. For considerably longer than a day or two, I fear."

"Where?"

"Where?"

"Can you not tell me? Is it a secret, then?"

"No, of course not. I am off to visit my nephew for a bit is all. I know you will not pine for me, sweetings," he grinned, tugging one golden ringlet.

Lily sighed. "You think that I will take advantage of your absence to invite other gentlemen to my boudoir and that is extremely unfair of you, Josh. I would never do such a thing."

"No, of course you would not." The earl leaned forward to kiss the pouty lips lightly. "I am only teasing."

Lily's arms went around his neck and she clung to him for a brief moment. Then she set him free and slipped out of the bed to help him finish dressing properly. "Where is the duke?" she asked nonchalantly, buttoning Wright's waistcoat as he fiddled with his cravat. "In Sussex still?"

"No, they've gone to Willowset. Though why anyone wishes to winter amid those confounded cliffs and moors, I can't imagine. Come and give me another kiss, Lilliputian. I shall miss you."

Lily looked up into the handsome face and crossed her eyes at him. "Oh, la, sirrah, will you really?" she trilled with a little dip of a curtsy. "I am overwhelmed."

"Stubble it, m'dear," Wright laughed, pulling her into his arms and crushing her against his chest, messing his neckcloth in the process. When he released her, she was breathless. "Be good, won't you, Lily," he whispered. "I *shall* miss you."

Even with Harry Cross on the box and Wright mounted alongside, the small party found themselves encumbered and inconvenienced and thwarted at every turn by the state of the roads and the bitterness of the weather. A snapped axle, a broken wheel and an exceedingly aggravating trip into a ditch kept them warming themselves before one or another of the public room fires at the various inns. And Wright, who would have switched teams as often as necessary to make better time, discovered his bays and Tugforth so far superior to anything available at the posting houses that he chose to bide his time while his own cattle rested.

In the end, it took them three days to reach Dorset and another two hours to make their cold, soggy way to the village of St. Swithin's and from thence to the great stone and timber edifice of Willowset. It was old Burton, his great gray eyes flickering with relief, who stripped the earl of his sodden greatcoat, hat, and gloves and hustled that gentleman up to a set of chambers on the second floor where a fire blazed in the grate and a single glass, accompanied by a crystal decanter of brandy, sat upon a cherrywood table beside a wing chair pulled as close as possible to the hearth. No sooner had Wright noted the readiness of the chambers than three footmen appeared with hot water to fill the hip bath that stood ready in the adjoining room. "Expecting me, were you, Burton?"

"Indeed, my lord." The butler, who had been in the employ of the Dukes of Ware in one capacity or another for over fifty years, nodded. "Every day since Mr. Shepard's departure. We none of us doubted you would come. I thought, however, that you would prefer chambers in the main house rather than occupying your suite as there are no other guests."

"The Reverend Howard?"

"His presence is always likely, my lord, but he has had the good grace not to request chambers here. He was with us earlier in the day but has departed."

"Good. Tibbs and Shepard and Harry Cross are as cold and wet as I."

"They are all of them being attended to, I assure you, my lord. I shall stand in Mr. Tibbs's place, if you will permit it." Distracted by the arrival of his luggage, Wright merely nodded as Burton helped him to shrug out of his coat and then sat him down and removed his muddy Hessians.

Tibbs, assured by the first footman that his earl was in good hands, gratefully accepted his own chance for a hot bath and clean clothes. "I thought," he sighed, easing into the tub and letting the water send the chills he had suffered the last three days to the right about, "that we might not be so eagerly welcomed. Shepard seemed to think the Reverend Howard is in control of Willowset."

"Only when his magnificence is present and we are pretending to bow to his will." James grinned, scooping Tibbs's wet garments from the floor. "The moment he disappears, his commands are significantly disremembered. I shall deliver these to Mrs. Hornby, along with the earl's and Mr. Cross's, and see that Sandy takes polish and brush to everyone's boots as well. You need not hurry, Mr. Tibbs. Burton will valet his lordship for you this night. He will do an adequate job of it."

Harry Cross, though he had to be forced to abandon his horses to the care of the duke's grooms, was nonetheless thankful for a warm room, a hot bath, and the luxury of changing into clean, dry clothing. "I disremember ever feelin' as cold an' dismal as I have the last few days." He sighed as the hot water sloshed over him. "Been a while, eh, Whitson?"

"A while," agreed the duke's head groom, whose chambers over the stables Harry was to share. "Legion still in top form?"

Cross laughed. "Does he hear you calling him that, he'll be showing you what form he's in."

"He'll not be hearin' me, though it's a damned suitable appellation for the gen'leman."

"Loads of blokes call him Legion behind his back, Whitson. But only one was ever brave enough to do so to his face."

"Aye," Whitson nodded, passing Cross a glass of homebrewed. "My duke."

"Your duke," Cross agreed, raising his glass in salute. "God bless 'im; may he rest in peace."

"Which 'e will," Whitson nodded thoughtfully, "now Legion's come to 'er grace's aid."

The Earl of Wright drew a deep blue satin robe about him,

slipped his bare feet into a pair of bedroom slippers and tugged a silver-backed comb through his wet curls. "How is it, Burton, that I have been in this place a full thirty minutes and not been pounced upon by His Nibs? Do I dress for dinner or not?"

"Not, I think, my lord. There is no one expected."

"Not Howard?"

"No, my lord. Only yourself."

"I shall dine in the nursery then, shall I?"

"His grace will be delighted. He does not in the least expect you and has been playing at highwayman all afternoon in the home woods. Mrs. Bowers was able to catch the scamp only a few moments before you arrived, and being such a formidable and notorious character as he is this day, I doubt but she has just barely got him set into his tub."

Wright chuckled as he slipped off the robe and donned buck-skin breeches and a collarless linen shirt. "Did Charlie play at highwayman in the home woods as well, Burton?"

"Never, my lord," Burton grinned, locating a pair of Hessians from amid the almost unpacked luggage. "I believe Master Charlie's fantasies ran more to knights and dragons."

"And I wager he was always the White Knight or King Arthur. Charlie would never have been the villain."

"Heavens no, my lord. But then, he never had the pleasure of your acquaintance at that age."

Wright sent Burton a penetrating glance from beneath fine black brows, saw only a smile in that gentleman's eyes and smiled back. "Not as fortunate as Jessemy," he drawled, and left a chuckling Burton behind him as he started for the stair-way to the third floor.

Charles Jocelyn Stuart Jessemy Brenford, Duke of Ware, a reg'lar rum one, up to every rig, with more bottom than a thousand million of the King's Guard and more heart than the bravest of the bravest of all highwaymen, planted one of his captors a facer, slipped through the other's grasp and, scaling the walls of his Bastille, dashed buck naked through the open doorway and into his fierce and magnificent Uncle Josh. The surprised earl closed his arms around the wet, soapy little body, scooped the boy up and burst into chuckles. "I say, Duke," he laughed, planting a kiss on the scoundrel's nose, "you are making wretched work of my clothes, you know."

"Uncle Josh!" shouted the rascal, throwing his arms about that gentleman's neck and cuddling happily against him.

"Very sorry, I'm sure, my lord," said a voice from the doorway. "Escaped the tub, he did."

"Not for long," Wright replied.

"No, Uncle Josh! No! I am scrubbled up enuf!"

"Ah, but you are not rinsed off or dried, are you? And now we are both covered in slimy old bathwater."

The engaging giggle that met this observation set Mrs. Bowers and a young woman swathed in an apron much too large for her to smiling, though Mrs. Bowers did so with a certain degree of hesitation. One never knew, after all, what mood the earl might be in. She was well aware of the hours he had ridden through the grim drizzle, the mud, and the wretched cold. His eyes, however, shone down upon her and he winked broadly. "Ogre though I am, I'll not eat you today, Bowey," he declared, "though I cannot promise for tomorrow, can I, Duke?"

"Uh-uh," agreed the child, gleefully shaking his soaking ringlets and splattering water everywhere. "Ellie, Ellie," he shouted, his bright blue eyes falling upon the young woman, "this here's my Uncle Josh!"

The young woman's fine hazel eyes glanced upward into the earl's silver-flecked, nearly black ones, and her lips parted in a startled gasp at the sheer beauty of them.

Wright looked away from her on the instant. In three long strides he carried the little duke back into the tiny chamber, plunked him heartlessly into the tub, seized one of the waiting water buckets and sloshed its contents over Jessemy's head, announcing that the child had indeed been scrubbed enough and now there was an end to it. He dried the boy off, wrapped him in a tremendously large towel and carried him into the nursery sitting room, where he sat with him on his lap before the fire and brushed at the wet, unruly mop of golden curls with the tiny brush Bowey handed him. "Now we are hungry," Wright announced, bestowing a kiss upon a damp ear.

"Starvin'," declared the little duke.

"Famished!" encouraged the earl.

"Rav'nous!"

"Voracious!"

The child opened his mouth and closed it again. "I don't know no more, Uncle Josh," he whispered as quietly as he knew how, which was not quiet in the least and made both women grin.

"Hungry enough to devour a bear," whispered the earl.

"Hungry nuff to deflower a bear!" shouted the duke triumphantly, and Wright went off into whoops of laughter.

An incredibly pretty blush rose in bright patches to the porcelain cheeks of the young woman Jessie had called Ellie, and managing at last to smother his laughter, Wright set his eyes on her once again. "Do not be embarrassed, sweetings," he said charmingly. "He is only five, after all. I am sure the bears are safe for another few years at least."

Mrs. Bowers gasped and flew to the young woman's side. "Oh, Miss Eleanor, I am sure I don't know where my mind has flown."

The earl's eyebrows rose questioningly. "Miss Eleanor?" He stood with the boy in his arms. "I have made a dreadful mistake, Jess," he announced to the giggling duke. "Your Ellie is not a new nursery maid."

"No, my lord," agreed Mrs. Bowers hastily. "May I present to your lordship Miss Eleanor Howard? She is the Reverend Howard's sister, you know."

"No, I did not know." The earl frowned, bowing gracefully despite an armful of wiggling boy. "A pleasure, Miss Howard."

Eleanor, mesmerized by the remarkable eyes, made him a dignified curtsy. "The pleasure is mine, your lordship."

"What a clanker," Wright declared, "though I admire such determined good manners."

"Miss Howard helped me to search for his grace," offered Bowey, "and since Colly was not to be found, she was kind enough to help with his bath as well. He is a handful, your lordship, when confronted with a bath."

Wright noted immediately the words "Colly was not to be found" and concluded that this young lady was not privy to Colly's trip to London. "Then I must offer you my gratitude and my apologies, Miss Howard," he drawled. "My gratitude for your service to Bowey and my apologies for failing to recognize your breeding." He took his eyes from Eleanor and boosted the duke a bit higher in his arms. "I think we must both dress more appropriately, Duke, since there is a lady present."

"Oh! No!" said Eleanor. "I do not stay, your lordship. In fact, you must excuse me this very moment." She scrabbled to untie the strings of the apron Bowey had loaned her. "I am certain Martin must be wondering where I am." Blister the man, she thought, as Wright's bold, teasing gaze came back to her, flustering her more. "Sit down, do," she urged him. "You must not stand upon ceremony with me."

"Oh, but I fear I must, Miss Howard, or your brother will have one more transgression to lay at my door."

The little duke's fingers tugged at one of his uncle's curls. "What's a tran'gressin?" he asked with a tiny scowl.

"Anything we do that Reverend Howard does not like, rascal."

Eleanor's mouth popped opened in protest, but he overrode her as he placed Jessie into Bowey's arms. "Take this chap away, Bowey, and snuggle him into his night gear, will you? I shall escort Miss Howard to the front door. Or must I escort you all the way home?" he asked, as Bowey and the duke disappeared. "No," he answered himself, "I don't feel that much of a gentleman. I will give you the loan of a carriage, however."

"I am perfectly capable of finding my own way out, my

lord," mumbled Eleanor, seizing her reticule from a cricket table near the windows. "And I came in my own carriage."

"Then I bid you farewell, Miss Howard," Wright drawled, opening the door. "Be certain to tell your brother that I have arrived. He will be interested to know."

Martin Howard's eyes narrowed as he frowned over the last of the blackberry tarts that marked an end to dinner. He rose silently and signaled Eleanor to follow him into the parlor. "Now," he said, as he saw her settled on a striped silk settee and sat across from her, "what did that villain say to you? You may tell me with every confidence, Eleanor. I am well aware of his scurrilous manner, and nothing he said will surprise me."

Eleanor, hoping to disguise her sudden nervousness, reached for her knitting and began to ply her needles. "He only asked me to inform you that he had arrived, Martin. He was quite gentlemanly." Her hazel eyes studied her work intently. She knew perfectly well that the earl had not been gentlemanly, but she could see Martin was already angry. Eleanor had never lied to her brother before and so was loathe to do so now, only she did not wish to upset him further by revealing the earl's nonchalant attitude toward her. "Did you not expect him so soon?"

"I did not expect him at all," muttered Howard.

"But surely, with his sister missing—"

"I gave orders he was not to hear of it," growled Howard, pounding one hand down upon the chair arm, "and when I discover how word reached him—"

"You gave orders? You, Martin? At Willowset?"

"I am his grace's guardian, Ellie. I have a responsibility to the boy. It is unfortunate enough that he must be raised by a bird-witted mother without compounding the problem by placing him under the influence of a monster like Wright."

Eleanor dropped a stitch. Her eyes darted to Howard's scowling countenance. "But surely the man has a right to know of his own sister's disappearance!"

The Reverend Howard pouted, his wide red lips turning downward and his eyebrows meeting across the bridge of his nose. "Do not think badly of me, Ellie. If it were any other man, I should have sent word on the instant."

Eleanor's eyes returned to her work. She could never, of course, think badly of Martin. Yet Jessie had been so happy to see his uncle. Her mind wandered back over the scene in the nursery. No, she was not mistaken; the Earl of Wright was a welcome presence in Jessie's world. And it had appeared to her that Jessie was a welcome presence in his uncle's world as well.

"I think, Martin," she murmured, without looking up, "that you misunderstand the earl. He is not, I suspect, a thoroughly pleasant gentleman, but surely he loves his nephew and sister."

"If such a man can love," muttered Howard, "which I doubt. I do not want you to go to Willowset while he remains in residence, Eleanor, unless I am with you. It would not only be most improper but dangerous."

It was the word *dangerous* that Eleanor could not expel from her mind, not even as she lay cuddled beneath the pile of quilts on the bed in her brother's guest room. Each time she closed her eyes she saw Wright's improbable eyes staring at her, and his strong, determined jaw, and his broad shoulders covered only by a damp, clinging linen shirt. She had never seen a gentleman before sans coat and waistcoat and cravat, and the mere thought of the form-fitting buckskins sent her pulses to racing feverishly. What on earth was the matter with her? If Martin said the man was dangerous, she would do best to believe him and dismiss all thought of Wright from her mind. But she could not. What sort of dangerous was he? How could anyone so handsome, so obviously kind to children, so interesting, be dangerous? She giggled to herself as she remembered the earl's definition of *transgression*. He had meant to offend her brother, she knew, and she had been insulted herself then, but when one actually thought about it—it was funny and true. A great many of her transgressions had been exactly something she had done that Martin had not liked. And Martin would not like this, either, she told herself, twisting onto her side and staring into the glowing coals of the grate. I must desist immediately and go to sleep. But it was a long while before visions of the Earl of Wright, handsome and haughty, funny and intimidating, faded from her mind and she was able to lose herself in dreams.

Two

Glenby Oakes had been coachman to the Duchess of Ware for three years. He had accepted that position at the urging of the Earl of Wright, to whom he owed a sizable debt of gratitude. Powerful, stocky, with a fierce visage and an enormous black beard, the intimidating Oakes had been farmer, soldier, highwayman—and three days from the gallows when the fervent, defiant earl had taken his case directly to the House of Lords and won the man's freedom. That action had damned Wright farther than ever in some very influential minds but had brought forcibly to the attention of many others the plague of poverty and despair under which a large number of returned British soldiers struggled. It had also turned Oakes from an embittered veteran into a loyal champion of the man they called Legion. But at the moment Glenby Oakes was silently cursing the man.

He understood that Wright lived in constant anxiety over his sister's welfare. He understood that the little duchess had more hair than wit and stood in need of protection. He understood that everything the Earl of Wright did concerning the beautiful Jenny was for her security and benefit. But he did not understand why the earl had waited until they were almost to Willowset to send him word to take the duchess on to the Elders's estate in Yorkshire instead. This morning the suspicion that he had been cozened was stronger than ever and, as he sat down to breakfast in the kitchen, his brow creased in thought.

"Tell me, ma'am," he said, accepting a glass of ale from

Mrs. Simon who, with her husband, had been caretaker at Elders Rise for the past ten years, "did 'is lordship mention to you anything about expectin' him?"

"No, no," replied that estimable woman with a shake of her head. "Will ye have some kidneys, Mr. Oakes? Niver a word in the message about expectin' 'is lor'ship. Only the little miss—the Duchess of Ware, I means. Terse, it were. Not much like 'is lor'ship ta write so brief an' to the point. Not a word 'bout Casper's sciatica, which he usually do inquire after."

"Was it sealed? The message, I mean."

Casper Simon came alert at the far end of the table.

"Aye," Mrs. Simon replied, taking a chair midway between the two men. "Came in t'post, ye know. Sealed an' franked it were like usual, weren't it, Casper?"

"Ye reckon Legion's in some scrape?" Casper Simon asked, a spoonful of poached egg on the way to his mouth.

"Well, his lordship's got a lot of coves what don't like 'im," Oakes sighed. "An' I'd not be surprised but there be a few of 'em might threaten her grace, knowin' how close they be. But I don't ken why Wright should send us 'ere and not turn the rest of our party in a like direction. Nor I ain't near to understandin' why we've not heard a word from 'im since."

"Perhaps," suggested Neville Nelson, taking a seat across from Mrs. Simon and helping himself to biscuits and tea, "one of us ought to ride to London and inquire his motives."

"Yer daft," drawled Casper Simon. "Las' person inquired inta Legion's motives be conversin' wi' the worms this day."

"Still," Oakes grumbled, "ain't any o' this makes sense. The duchess ought not be stuck away out 'ere with only Peggy ta support her. Leastways not for all this time. An' it ain't a bit like the earl to let 'er languish without sendin' word every now an' then. Three years I've worked fer the man, an' there ain't a week gone by when 'er grace didn't be receivin' letters or presents or flowers from 'im. Suspicious is what I'm becoming."

Peggy Tynesbury was herself beginning to doubt the earl's

good sense in sequestering his sister at Elders Rise in the chill, wet weather of late November. Rise lands stretched for miles in all directions dismal and sodden, broken only by the home woods and the moors. No longer farmed, the fields lay fallow, and even the bit of society and civilization once provided by the tenants was extinct. The roads, if not yet impassable, were at the very least forbidding, and the thought of a trip to the nearest village was more intimidating than enticing. Peggy placed the final hairpin into the duchess's thick blond hair and smiled at her angelic countenance in the beveled mirror. "There, your grace. All finished." She went to gather the gray wool, long-sleeved, high-collared morning dress into her arms and helped the little duchess into it.

"I wish we were at Willowset," Jenny sighed. "At least it does not rain every day. I am so terribly bored, Peggy. I cannot think what to do. And it isn't fair of us to put so much extra work upon the Simons."

"It has only been two weeks, your grace. And Oakes, Nelson, Gregory, Carson and I have been helping with the housework and the stables. Of course, it is not like having an entire staff at one's disposal."

"T—two weeks? Has it been so long, Peggy?"

"Indeed, your grace."

"Oh, dear!" The duchess's hand went to her sweetly pink-tinted cheeks and her thick, dark, curling lashes blinked in bewilderment. "I never did think he meant me to be away so long. We cannot stay much longer, Peggy, truly we cannot. Joshie will hear of it and soar up into the boughs."

Tynesbury, who was busily buttoning her grace's dress, looked up quickly at the words. "Pardon me, your grace?"

"Yes, of course, Peggy. For what?"

"No, ma'am; I meant, I think I misunderstood what it was you just said."

"Oh. What did I just say?"

"That—that the earl would hear of it and be upset?"

"Yes, quite so. He will, you know. He does not like anyone to come here when he is not in residence."

"But your grace, it was the earl sent us here, was it not?"

"Oh! Yes, of course it was! I had forgotten."

The look of perplexed innocence in the big blue eyes and the slight trembling of the lovely cupid's lips, aroused Peggy's suspicions immediately. Having filled the position of abigail to Lady Jenny Elders from her first foray into society at the age of seventeen, through her brief but happy marriage to the Duke of Ware, and for the three years following the duke's death, Peggy was well aware of the potential problems that specific look on the duchess's face signified. Much more companion than servant, and caring a great deal for the younger woman, Peggy took the duchess's hands into her own and led her to a window seat where she sat cozily beside her. "Tell me, dearest," she murmured. "I know something is wrong. I can see it in your eyes."

"I am not supposed to tell anyone," replied the duchess with a tiny shake of her head. "It is a secret. Francesco said so."

"Francesco?"

"The Marquis di Roche."

"Not that dreadful Italian person?"

"He is not dreadful!" declared the duchess passionately, tugging her hands from Peggy's comforting grasp. "You sound exactly like Joshie! Francesco is wonderful and handsome and kind, and he cares very much for me."

Peggy, who had accompanied her grace on several saunters through the park in the presence of di Roche, found herself inclined to argue this assessment but declined to do so in hopes of discovering more about the present situation. "Perhaps I have misjudged the gentleman, then," she said in a conciliatory tone which instantly restored Jenny's faith in her. "Can you not tell me, dearest, what secret you share with the gentleman? I can see you are upset, and perhaps I may be of help."

Jenny's wide, guileless eyes studied Peggy hopefully.

"Have we not been friends for ever so long, your grace?"

"Yes, you are my very best friend, Peggy. Joshie says it is perfectly all right that you are. He says that I may be friends with anyone I like."

"But friends must trust each other, dearest. Can you not trust me enough to tell me what secret you share with the marquis and why it disturbs you?"

"Oh, it is not the secret that disturbs me," replied the duchess. "It is—it is what I did."

"And what did you do?"

"I—I wrote notes and signed Joshie's name. And I pressed Papa's signet ring into the sealing wax to make everyone think they were real. And—and I franked them, too, just like Joshie does. I know I should not have done it Peggy, but it was the very best way I could think of to come here instead of going to Willowset."

Peggy took a deep breath and attempted to look unconcerned. "Did you wish to come to the Rise so badly then, your grace? I am sure you only needed to ask his lordship and he would have opened the house to you. He loves you very much, you know, and would do most anything in the world to please you."

A single tear fell glistening to one of her grace's porcelain cheeks. "Francesco said I could not tell Joshie where I had gone. He said it would ruin everything."

"I see," Peggy nodded, her mind rapidly calculating the possibilities at the foundation of such a scheme.

"Only I did not think I must be away so very long," sighed Jenny, dashing the tear from her cheek with the back of her hand. "Francesco promised to come and fetch me immediately if our plan had succeeded."

"And what was your plan, dearest? Had it something to do with his lordship?"

"Well, Joshie is so very fierce, you know. All the gentlemen are afraid of him. And he has taken the most unaccountable dislike to Francesco. And we thought—"

"What did you think, your grace?"

"That—that if I were to be kidnapped and Francesco to rescue me and bring me safely home, then Joshie would be grateful to him and like him and not keep us from—from getting married."

Peggy's exquisite brows rose in amazement. "You wish to marry the Marquis di Roche?" she asked, stunned.

"Oh, yes. Very much."

"But, your grace, you barely know each other."

"I know him much better than anyone supposes," declared Jenny. "Charlie and I stayed with him at his villa on our marriage trip. And we have met him since, too. And when he heard that my darling Charlie had d-died—"

"He came to England to seek your hand?" asked Peggy, agog.

The lovely blond head nodded.

It was not inconceivable. Jenny was a perfect gudgeon but also beautiful, gentle and, in her extreme innocence, remarkably appealing. In her first Season she had won a plethora of masculine hearts, and the earl had been driven to distraction by constant offers for her hand. That an honorable gentleman should fall under her spell even after her marriage and spend years languishing in silence and adoring her from afar, romantic as it might seem, was a distinct likelihood. "But you are a widow, your grace, and may choose whom you like. You need not obtain the earl's permission to marry this gentleman."

"Yes I must too," replied Jenny emphatically. "Joshie will be very angry if I marry someone he does not approve, and he will never wish to see me again. And I cannot live without him, and so I said to Francesco. And that is why we made the plan."

At that precise moment the gentleman who shuddered every time Jenny referred to him as Joshie and without whose filial love she could not survive, was in the midst of a tirade aimed at the head of the Reverend Martin Howard. Accustomed to

see in Wright an eerie, rigid and freezing wrath, Howard was
nonplussed at the seething passion that confronted him in the
library at Willowset. He cringed in the leather-covered chair
and his hands tightened on the chair arms. He was sorely
tempted to rise and leave the room, but fear that one of the
ornaments upon the mantelpiece would connect with the back
of his head before he managed to close the door kept him in
his place. In the main drawing room, across the hall and four
doors down, Eleanor blushed at the invectives that reached her
ears, and her bewildered eyes sought those of Mrs. Bowers,
who had brought Jessie down from the nursery floor to visit
her. Harry Cross, stepping into the main hall from beyond the
servants' door to inform the earl that one of the bays had taken
ill from their journey, did an immediate about-face and took
himself directly back to the stables. In Wright's chambers on
the floor above Horace Tibbs raised his eyes beseechingly to
the ceiling mural and prayed, "Please, God, don't let his lordship kill the fool."

His lordship was having considerable difficulty in not killing
the fool and so set the strong, efficient hands that ached to
come together around Howard's neck to hurling anything within
reach. "Of all the insufferable, interfering, self-righteous
prigs!" he thundered, the crashing of a crystal decanter against
the library door punctuating this epithet. "You sanctimonious
evangelist! You prunes-and-prisms parson! You stiff-rumped,
dog-eared, flea-bitten maggot!" A china pug dog shattered off
the back wall; a miniature of the former duke whizzed past
Howard's ear and crunched into the books behind him; a bright
red Venetian vase exploded into dazzling shards against the
edge of the huge oak desk.

Howard's eyes widened in fear. He was not a cowardly man.
Nor was he foppish, effeminate, or a dandy. He was, in fact,
as tall and powerfully built as the earl, and an excellent boxer
besides. But he was experiencing a considerable number of
conflicting emotions, one of which was sheer terror. He opened
his mouth to protest, and the dazzling white glint of his teeth

made Wright want to slam his fist into them and knock them down the reverend's throat. Instead he turned away and pounded his fists into the rough-hewn stone of the fireplace, splitting his knuckles open and spattering blood over the hearth. Howard blanched. Wright stared, dumbfounded, his diatribe forgotten. In one fluid movement Howard left the chair, pulled the bellpull and went to open the library door. "Ellie," he shouted down the hall. "Come here! Quickly!"

Eleanor rose immediately, as did Mrs. Bowers, but the little duke ran the fastest down the hallway and dodged through the door between the reverend's legs. "Uncle Josh," he gasped, coming to an abrupt halt, "you are hurted!"

The earl could feel his fingers swelling, especially the one that was encircled by his signet ring. "Jessie?" he began, but the little duke had already turned fiercely away and was stomping toward Howard.

"You hurted my Uncle Josh!" exclaimed Jessie, hands on hips, staring up into Howard's scowling face with a scowl of his own. "Go away or I will tell Bowey and she will paddle your bottom!"

In spite of everything that had gone before, the words sent Wright off into whoops. Howard's scowl disappeared beneath twitching lips that parted and gave way to a chuckle.

"You will not laugh when Bowey takes 'er switch to you," the duke threatened soberly.

Eleanor and Mrs. Bowers, followed immediately by Burton, entered the library just as the duke's hands balled into tiny fists and he struck a perfect pugilistic pose before the reverend. "I willn't wait for Bowey," he declared. "I will punch you myself."

Wright doubled over in laughter.

"Your grace," cried Mrs. Bowers, "cease and desist this instant!"

"Bowey," the little duke announced gravely, standing his ground, "this vill'nous scallion has hurted my Uncle Josh an' maked 'im bleed!"

All eyes went instantly to the earl, who was just then straightening up and wiping tears of laughter from his eyes with the back of one battered hand.

"You maked 'im cry, too, you dabbed egret!" Jessie exclaimed and punched the Reverend Mr. Howard in the thigh, which, luckily, was as high as his grace could reach.

Wright swooped down upon Charles Jocelyn Stuart Jessemy Brenford from behind and caught him up into his arms.

Mrs. Bowers took the boy from his uncle's obviously aching hands and carried the resisting little duke from the room.

Burton, having assessed the situation fully, had already summoned and sent one footman rushing to the icehouse, another to the kitchen and a third to the earl's chambers in search of Tibbs. "You had best sit down, my lord," he drawled in the earl's direction.

"Indeed," agreed Eleanor wholeheartedly. "Martin, give me your handkerchief." She seized the large square of linen from her brother and, kneeling beside Wright's chair, began to dab the blood from his hands. "How did this happen?" she asked quietly. "Did Martin do it?"

"Not likely!" growled Wright, who winced as she examined his ring finger. "Broken," he muttered, looking at it over her shoulder.

"Well, I should think so," drawled Howard. "Any fool who would pound his fists into a fireplace might expect—"

"You are just lucky, Howard, I did not pound them into your teeth, which is where they itched to go!"

"Be quiet! Both of you!" ordered Eleanor. "Burton, I think you must send someone to St. Swithin's for the doctor."

"No," Wright protested quietly, his eyes wandering over the thick chestnut hair caught into a twist at the back of Miss Howard's lovely neck. "That will not be necessary. Harry Cross can splint them up well enough. Do not fuss, Miss Howard. I am not like to die," he muttered. "If you do wish to be of some assistance, you might consider removing your brother from my sight. His presence is making me decidedly nauseous."

Eleanor's gaze left his hands instantly and her mouth opened in protest, but the words died on her lips as she found herself caught in the perplexing glitter of his compelling eyes.

"Please, Miss Howard, take him away," Wright pleaded. "I shall be forced to do him severe bodily harm if you don't."

All the way back to her brother's house Eleanor questioned what had happened in the Willowset library. "The man is irrational," Howard declared. "He belongs in Bedlam. I actually feared for my life in that room, Ellie. Any moment he might have seized the halberd from above the mantel and sent it at my head."

"To keep such news from him, for any reason, was cruel, Martin. I know you do not consider it so, but the duchess is his sister and she is missing. Any gentleman would have been angry."

"Yes, but Ellie, you did not see him. He had not the least concept of his own actions, I assure you. He destroyed everything within his reach and then, for no reason, turned and swung both fists against the hearth as if he would kill someone. And no sooner was it done than he stopped and stared at his battered hands as if he had no idea how they had gotten into such a condition. And when his grace entered Wright roared into the wildest laughter. The man is a lunatic, and he must be kept from endangering Jessemy at whatever cost. I shall write to Paxton and Grimsby immediately. I cannot think what possessed Cousin Charles to make that devil one of Jessie's guardians."

That devil was stout-heartedly suffering the ministrations of Tibbs and Harry Cross, Colly Shepard, and even Mrs. Bowers as his hands were cleaned and examined and packed into ice. "There's two fingers broken far as I can tell," offered Harry Cross, sipping a cup of coffee. "We'll give 'em a while an' see can we get the swellin' out o' 'em afore I try splintin' 'em up."

"They ain't bleedin' no more, Uncle Josh," noted Jessie, studying the bowls of ice containing his uncle's hands with great interest.

"No, my blood has frozen to a stop," agreed Wright sociably. "Bowey, what is a dabbed egret?" Wright's exotic eyes sparkled at the nanny.

The good woman blushed. "He meant to say damned ingrat," she sighed. "He has tried to say it before. I cannot think where he learned such an expression."

"From Mr. Reverent Howard," the duke announced. "I hearded him say it las' week when he was talkin' to Burtie."

Wright laughed. "Well, I think you must not say it again, scoundrel, not until you are grown. Your mother will not like to hear you use such language."

"Where is Mama, Uncle Josh? Is she still visitin' Aunt Althea? Ain't she never, ever, comin' home?"

"Oh, I expect she will arrive sooner or later," drawled the earl. "She will most certainly not wish to miss me, will she?"

"Uh-uh," the duke acknowledged with a shake of his fine golden ringlets. "Mama's always happiest when you're here."

Burton's calm, imposing figure appeared at that moment to stand directly before the earl, a sealed envelope in his hand.

"Late for the post to arrive, no, Burton?"

" 'Tis not the post, my lord. 'Twas delivered by Bob Kinsley from the Crossroads. Found it upon the bar in the public room."

The earl's gaze drifted from Burton to the duke and back again. He raised a questioning brow, and Burton raised a brow in return. "Jessie, old chap," Wright said, "do you think that you and Harry Cross might look for some sticks to splint my fingers? You need Jessie's help doing that, don't you, Harry?"

Harry Cross nodded. "Sure could use a pair of young eyes. Got to be just the right size sticks, and straight as well."

"I will gets my jacket and my boots on right away, won't I, Bowey?" Jessie responded eagerly. "An' my cap, too, 'cause it is drizzlin' ag'in." The boy hurried into the hall, followed by a silent Mrs. Bowers and Harry Cross, who looked back over his shoulder at the note in Burton's hand.

"You'll need to open it and read it to me, Burton. No, don't go, Tibbs, or you either, Colly. If my suspicions are correct, the contents of the thing will concern all of us."

Burton broke the seal. His cool gray eyes scanned the page. "It is a ransom note, my lord," he informed the earl grimly. "The writer demands one hundred and fifty thousand pounds for the return of the Duchess of Ware."

"And I'll wager no one at the Crossroads can identify the individual who placed the thing on the bar, eh?"

"No, my lord," Burton sighed. "I thought to ask, you know, when Kinsley delivered it, but no one knows who 'twas left it."

"Does it say where we are to deliver this sum?"

"It says merely that you will be contacted again, my lord."

"And it is addressed specifically to me?"

"Yes, my lord. Personal, it says, Lord Jocelyn Elders, Earl of Wright, Willowset."

The earl pulled his hands from the ice chips, leaned back in the chair and closed his eyes. "Why," he asked quietly, "did no one deliver this to me in London? Or why did they not deliver it to Howard? Why wait for two weeks until I arrived in Dorset? If Colly had not come to fetch me, would the note have been delivered at all? We learned that Jenny stayed at the White Rose the second night, Burton. They know her well and are sure of the date. And a fellow at the Wagoner's saw the coach on the main road driving north near Brinsby early the following morning. They should have come through St. Swithin's near noon, but no one can be found who saw them."

"They needs must have left the main road between Brinsby and St. Swithin's then," Tibbs asserted.

"But they did not," offered Burton. "We searched, you know. Had Whitson and the grooms riding every track between Brinsby and St. Swithin's. Knocked on every door. Spoke to every living soul old enough to speak, and not one saw the coach or the outriders or even a lady resembling her grace."

"So, what do we conclude?" the earl sighed. "That my sister was abducted in broad daylight by a villain who could somehow swallow a traveling coach, coachman, guard and two out-riders, plus Tynesbury? Absurd. We are missing something obvious."

"What, my lord?"

"I don't know, Burton. It is sitting there staring me in the face, but I cannot quite comprehend it. You don't suppose Martin Howard is at the bottom of this, do you?"

The remark received an audible gasp from all present.

"No, I expect not," the earl answered himself with a scowl. "The man's an officious, self-righteous, meddling fool, but I doubt he would kidnap Jenny. Wouldn't last five minutes alone in the same room with m'sister."

"Shush, do not you dare roar and stomp about, Glenby Oakes, or I will lay a frying pan along the side of your head." Peggy Tynesbury folded her arms across her bountiful breasts and glared at Oakes as he sank into one of the chairs in the staff's parlor. "It is not her grace's fault. She only did as she was told by the man she loves."

"Well, b'god, I don't see how she done it. 'Twas Legion's handwritin' an' Legion's seal."

"No, but it wasn't, Glenby." Peggy settled herself on a cassock beside the glowering coachman and laid one hand upon his arm. " 'Twas her ladyship writing in his lordship's hand. He taught her to do so himself. I remember, now that I think on it. Spent hours, he did, coaxing a smile from her and begging to know what had made her unhappy. An' when he learned she had overheard several young ladies making sport of her behind her back for her lack of wit he set about to find something she might do which no other young lady could. He only thought to make her happy, you know. He taught her ways to look at someone else's writing and see what made it different from her own, and then change her own to match it. Made a game of it, he did, and taught her so well that even he could not tell which was his writing and which her grace's."

"An' the seal?"

"She pressed her father's signet ring into the wax. The earl gave it to her the day their father was buried, as a keepsake. The one his lordship wears is merely a copy. I should have known!" declared Peggy suddenly. "I knew she held the signet ring; I knew she could copy Lord Wright's hand, but I—I had not the least suspicion. The earl is so unpredictable, and I did not think it odder than usual that he should send us to the Rise. I wish I had thought to question it at the time! What should we do, Glenby?"

"Do y'mean aside from takin' 'er grace across m'knee?"

Peggy grinned. She knew an empty threat when she heard one. Glenby Oakes was as fond of her grace as a man might be without falling head over heels in love with her. "Yes, you big lout, I mean aside from taking her across your knee."

"Well, I expect as we ought ta drive back to Willowset—if we kin work our way through the bogs these roads've become. Ah, lord, Peggy," he sighed, crossing one leg over the other, "do ye realize we have gone an' abducted ourselves?"

Three

Two days after her brother's confrontation with Wright, on a cloudy, blustery afternoon, Eleanor, dressed in her oldest wool round gown beneath a fur-lined cottage cape of forest green, her hands encased in kidskin gloves and her feet well protected from the muddy street by heavy walking boots, strode purposefully toward a cottage on the west side of the square in the village of St. Swithin's. She carried a wicker basket containing blackberry jam, a freshly baked rhubarb pie and several loaves of bread and intended to deliver these to the Widow Dish who, at the moment, was not feeling quite the thing. The cottage was neat and clean and well tended, reflecting in its ancient whitewashed stone and carefully thatched roof a prudence and pride readily apparent in the lives of all the residents of St. Swithin's. Here existed none of the economical poverty nor the poverty of the spirit that so pervaded the larger cities. Eleanor, who had grown to young womanhood in just such a place as this, saw nothing extraordinary in the attitude and the aspect of the village. She was quite accustomed to walking streets unaccompanied, to expect pleasant greetings from people she met and to take for granted the safety of her reticule and of herself.

The gentleman who approached Mrs. Dish's home from the opposite end of the square, however, was unaccustomed to all of these things. In white whipcord breeches, hightop black boots and a lined nankeen hunting jacket with a Belcher kerchief tied rakishly about his throat, Tugforth's reins dangling negligently over one shoulder and a brace of dressed rabbits slung over Tugforth's saddle bow, the Earl of Wright ambled along in a daze. He knew where he was bound, having visited Mrs. Dish before, and therefore he expended little thought upon the direction of his feet. Instead his mind probed and pondered the peace and prosperity of the village in the hope of discovering what lay at the bottom of such serenity.

Born and raised in the rough and wild lands of northernmost Yorkshire, where his dogs to this day coursed sixteen point buck and wild boar, where the likes of Stubby Jack Grove and Bloody Beecham and Captain Jason Fate still ruled the roads, where no one spoke to you without purpose nor smiled at you without desire, and all clung tightly to their purse strings and their womenfolk, Wright had found the transition to the streets of London during his school days easy enough to make, but all his attempts to feel acceptable in the village of St. Swithin's had proved failures. Wrapped in awe of the tiny society around him, he strolled directly into Eleanor, knocked her off-balance and barely caught her before she toppled over Mrs. Dish's little picket fence.

"Well, of all the——" began Eleanor as she juggled the basket on her arm to keep its contents from spilling out.

"I beg your pardon, ma'am—Miss Howard," the earl sputtered, releasing her gingerly from his grasp now she was firmly upright again. "I'm afraid I did not see you."

Eleanor's chin lifted. "I tend to think, my lord, that I am a large enough woman to be seen by everyone," she said regally, and was immediately startled by the brilliant light of laughter that shot into Wright's eyes.

"Well, you ain't a mere slip of a thing like Jenny, Miss Howard, but I hardly think you ought to refer to yourself as a *large* woman. Are you bound beyond this gate?"

"Indeed." Eleanor stared admiringly at the wind-whipped dark locks that curled in wild disarray around his sharply chiseled face, and the rippling of the muscles beneath his jacket as he leaned forward to unlatch the gate and hold it open for her, and especially the lean, taut, powerful thighs that strained against the tight whipcord breeches as he stepped out of her way.

"Ma'am?" Wright drawled, a smile twitching at his lips. "You will enter, will you not, when I have passed inspection?"

A distinct warmth rose to Eleanor's already wind-tinted cheeks, and she whipped her gaze away from him, hurrying through the gate to the front door of the cottage. By the time Mrs. Dish answered her knock Wright had lifted the rabbits from his saddle bow and come up behind her.

"Eleanor, my dear, and Josh, come in."

Eleanor, startled to discover the earl directly behind her, hesitated, considering whether she might change her plans and simply leave the basket. It was bound to be an uncomfortable visit with Wright present. A slight push from behind, however, sent her stumbling across the threshold. "Oh!" she gasped, turning around to scowl at the earl.

"I *am* sorry, Miss Howard," he murmured soberly. "Tripped."

Mrs. Dish smiled and took Eleanor's basket. "How kind of you to come, Eleanor. Josh, will you take this to the kitchen?"

"Certainly, madam," the earl replied, reaching for the basket handle.

"Oh, my, what happened?" Mrs. Dish exclaimed, noticing the earl's ungloved hand, a splinted finger very apparent.

"A minor altercation with a fireplace. I have got another one that matches," he added proudly, like a little boy, and held his other hand up for her inspection. Eleanor was appalled to see the splints and the deep bruises that stained those strong hands. "Shall I stoke up the fires, Melinda?" he asked, tossing the rabbits over one shoulder, taking the basket in his other hand and strolling off toward the back of the little house as if he had lived there his entire life.

"Please do," Mrs. Dish laughed, helping Eleanor to slip out of her cape and setting her gloves upon the sideboard. "Come and warm yourself before the fire, dear. I am so pleased to see you again. You must tell me how you do, and your mother and father as well. You have not visited St. Swithin's for such a long while."

Eleanor allowed herself to be settled next to Mrs. Dish on a worn but elegant sofa before the parlor fireplace, where a blaze burned brightly. She longed to ask the elderly lady what put her upon such informal footing with Wright, but refrained from doing so. Instead she attempted to draw from the woman the details of her illness and discover if she was recovering as fully as she appeared. They were quite involved in conversation when the clinking of tea cups reached Eleanor's ears and she turned to see the earl, a tray balanced unsteadily in both hands, coming across the brightly braided rug toward them.

"I put the rabbits in the oven, Melinda. You ought to check on them in thirty minutes or so," he said, setting the tea things on a low table before the two women. "I hope I made this correctly. Miss Howard, I think, is certainly in need of some, having walked all the way from the vicarage."

Eleanor's mouth opened in surprise at his thoughtfulness, but she closed it quickly, hoping the gentleman had not noticed.

"Thank you, my dear," Mrs. Dish smiled. "Sit down now and join us."

"Another time, perhaps. I cannot leave Tug standing long in this weather. One of my bays is down as it is. Miss Howard," he said, with a curt bow in Eleanor's direction, "a pleasure to have seen you again."

"Do you know the earl well?" Mrs. Dish asked, pouring the tea as Eleanor heard the outside door open and then close behind him. "He is a remarkable gentleman."

"I—we have only met a few days ago. Martin does not—"

Mrs. Dish handed Eleanor a teacup and took a little sip of her own drink. "I know the reverend is not fond of Josh. He calls him Legion, you know, behind his back."

"He calls him what?"

"Legion. But then, all the men do. Do you not remember in

the Bible when the Lord told the demon in that poor man to say its name, and it said 'we are Legion'?"

"What a perfectly dreadful thing to call anyone! Does Lord Wright know? Oh, I am ashamed to think Martin would do such a thing! The earl is a good friend of yours, is he not, Mrs. Dish? He seems at home here."

The elderly woman, her round face serious, gazed for a moment into the fire. When she looked back to Eleanor a small tear glistened in the corner of one eye. "He will always be welcome here," she murmured. "Josh done me an exceptional service, but I cannot tell anyone of it."

Wright, hoping for a private word with Mrs. Dish when Eleanor left, rode Tugforth to the edge of St. Swithin's and left him in the care of the hostlers at the Crossroads while he waited in the public room of the inn. A glass of home-brewed in his hand, he rested his boot heels upon the rail before the hearth and let a wing chair swallow him up. A day earlier he had questioned every employee of the inn about the ransom note, but they could tell him nothing, so he did not attempt to question them again. He was missing something obvious, he knew, but he could not seem to alight upon what, exactly, he had overlooked. What he did alight upon was the enchanting pink blush that had ridden high upon Miss Howard's cheeks when he had caught her studying him and called her on it. She was so very innocent that she hadn't had the least idea how to reply to his teasing. Not that he found innocent maids compelling. He definitely did not. Still, there was something that intrigued him about Miss Howard. It would be interesting to get to know the woman. She had very pretty eyes. And she appeared to have a mind as well, though he was not yet convinced of it. Enough! he told himself. He ought to be pondering Jenny's whereabouts, not Miss Howard's attributes.

He steered himself back to the problem of his sister's abduction and downed what little ale remained in his glass. He would not, of course, pay the ransom. Anyone who knew him at all would know that. Therefore her abductors did not know him. Highwaymen? Had it happened on the Great North Road he would not have doubted it, but it had not. The nagging feeling that he was overlooking something returned and made him shift uneasily in his chair. Bob Kinsley appeared as if by magic with another glass of home-brewed. "Anything else I kin get ye, my lord?"

"No, thank you, Kinsley."

"The boys, they was wishing for me to tell ye how we all be sorry that the little duchess come up missing like. An' if there be anything we might do, why—"

Kinsley stuttered to a halt as Wright's startling eyes fell full upon him. He had tried for a number of years now not to let this particular gentleman or these particular eyes disturb him. He had not yet succeeded.

Kinsley's hesitation pierced Wright to the quick, confirming his notion that the men would never accept him as a friend, and the earl immediately turned his gaze away. "I thank you, Kinsley," he drawled, in a voice as chilly as the weather. He guessed his tone would convince Kinsley that he was dismissed from any further attempts toward neighborliness and groaned inwardly to see he was correct.

Wright downed the home-brewed, set the glass and a stack of coins on the table beside him and left the room. He cursed himself for a fool all the way to the stables, mounted Tugforth and rode like the devil to the rear of Mrs. Dish's little cottage where he dismounted, led Tugforth into a timber shed and proceeded to unsaddle the animal, rub him down and place a warm blanket over him. He carried the horse a portion of oats that he kept laid by and lugged a bucket of water within reach—all of this in an attempt to dislodge the feelings of exclusion that Kinsley's slight and unintended hesitation had brought about. When he had done all he could think to settle the horse he closed the shed door and stalked into the cottage kitchen, no longer caring whether Miss Howard had left the premises or not. The smell of the rabbits roasting in herbs and spices calmed him somewhat, and he ceased to mutter under his breath, pulled up a ladder-backed chair before the fire and straddled it, resting his chin on his crossed arms.

Mrs. Dish and Eleanor discovered him a short time later. "Josh!" the elderly woman exclaimed. "What has happened?" Hurriedly she lit a taper at the hearth and set about lighting the kitchen candles until the evening's darkness was swept from the pleasant little room. The earl, to Eleanor's chagrin, did not rise at their entrance, nor did he answer Mrs. Dish's cry. He did not even look at them. Mrs. Dish gave one of the broad shoulders a pat, checked on the rabbits and directed Eleanor where to find dishes and utensils. "Josh," she said lightly, "you will dine with us, so you must climb up out of your sulk by the time the rabbits are done."

The earl made not the least effort to acknowledge her words, but Mrs. Dish ignored that and maintained a steady stream of innocent chatter as she warmed the loaves and prepared side dishes to accompany the rabbits to table.

Memories of Martin's references to Wright's mental insta-bility rose to the forefront of Eleanor's mind, and she stepped cautiously around the man. She had no idea where he had come from or what he might do if he were disturbed and she did not wish to find out.

"Oh, don't pay Josh the least mind," Mrs. Dish declared when she noticed Eleanor's nervousness. "He's buried himself away. He does when he's seriously bothered, but he'll return to us shortly, for I'll not allow him to persist in't." When at last all was in readiness Mrs. Dish produced a bottle of claret and set it upon the cast-iron sink. "Josh, come uncork the wine."

The earl appeared to awake into the present and crossed to the sink. Eleanor heard him murmur, then chuckle. "I expect we must enlist Eleanor's aid then," Mrs. Dish laughed. "Eleanor? Uncorking wine, it appears, is beyond Josh's ability."

"Oh, the splints!" Eleanor exclaimed. "I had forgotten!" She joined them at the sink and found Wright looking down at her, his eyes alive with mirth.

"Now you will be sure I'm mad, Miss Howard," he chuckled. "I had forgot the splints myself until I attempted to put my fingers, round this bottle neck."

Sharing the small meal around the oft-scrubbed kitchen table brought a cozy informality that charmed Eleanor, who had never done such a thing before in her life. Her father might be a vicar, but he possessed, like Martin, substantial wealth, and though his wife and daughters might minister to the sick and the poor of the parish, at home they were waited upon by a large staff. Though Eleanor expected conversation would dwindle in Wright's presence, it proved wickedly amusing instead, the earl being singularly adept at mimicking London's fashionable fribbles and imparting frivolous gossip in their own voices and with their own gestures, much to the ladies' delight. Mrs. Dish urged him on to imitate more and more of the elegant beaux whose names she had only heard or read in the papers, and he did so with relish, at the last declaring in the voice of the Prince Regent that if he ate one more fork full of the wonderful rhubarb pie, his stays would undoubtedly burst.

"Oh, no," gurgled Mrs. Dish, wiping tears of laughter from her eyes, "does he truly wear those dreadful things?"

"Whalebone." Wright nodded soberly. "Creak every time he bends. Everyone pretends not to notice. Foolishness. But there you are—we are all foolish about one thing or another."

Eleanor's gaze flew to the finely chiseled face. "Not all are foolish, my lord. Martin is never foolish about anything."

"Is he not? No, I expect you are right. Your brother, Miss Howard, may be the only exception to the rule. Do you know that your eyes turn golden when you laugh, like honey?"

"My lord?"

"You ought to laugh more, Miss Howard. But then, I expect you do when you are with Jessie. He's exceeding fond of you, you know. Says you have come to play with him every day since he arrived at Willowset—until I turned up. I have been severely harangued by the brat for keeping you away. Have I been keeping you away? I do not mean to do so."

The eyes that had sparkled so vibrantly moments before abruptly became dark and brooding. Eleanor almost gasped at the rapidity and severity of the transformation. Only Mrs. Dish's hand settling upon her own in warning kept the sound from her lips. "Shall we leave you to your wine, my lord?" the elder woman asked quietly.

"No, ma'am, I think not." The earl gained his feet and tugged his chair before the fire, took Mrs. Dish by the arm and led her to it. "You will sit here and observe while Miss Howard and I do the washing up. You must do the actual washing part, Miss Howard," he added, carrying the pot of water that had been warming over the fire to the sink, "but I shall manage to dry them and see them stored in their rightful places."

Eleanor spent the next fifteen minutes in a state of hilarity as Wright, his eyes once more aglow, charmingly terrorized Mrs. Dish. He juggled her best china clumsily, built towers of her teacups and wineglasses, played music upon her pots and muttered "Oops!" every now and then just to see that she was paying attention. "There," he sighed, restoring the last of the pots to its rightful hook, "now I may return to knowing nothing of kitchens."

"How do you come to know your way around a kitchen at all?" Eleanor asked, drying her hands upon her apron. "I don't think Martin even knows dishes must be washed. He never acknowledges the fact. And to tell the truth, I have not done them very many times myself."

"That, Miss Howard, was evident," Wright drawled with a swift, teasing glance. "I, on the other hand, was set to the task often in childhood. Exile to the kitchen was standard penance at the Rise. I often thought such a unique punishment had to do with the fact that my father and the cook were having an *affaire*. Do close your mouth, Miss Howard, before something inedible flies in. I take it your father never thought to seduce your cook?"

"N-no," stuttered Eleanor, a blush rising to her cheeks.

"Well, but then, your father is a vicar, my dear, and my father was a barbarian." Wright offered her his arm and then offered Mrs. Dish his other and led them down the hall and into the parlor. He added a log to the fire and prodded the low-burning embers into a brighter blaze, then rested his arm along the mantelpiece. "Have you a way home, Miss Howard? I shall be more than happy to escort you."

"Martin is sending the carriage."

"I see. Then I will say what I have come to say and take my leave. Melinda," he hunted carefully through his pockets and produced a folded letter, "Mary and Joyce send their love, and this. She wrote it hurriedly, for I was in a rush to be off, but they are both well and happy."

Mrs. Dish took the letter and clutched it tightly. "I can never thank you enough, Jocelyn."

"No," drawled the earl arrogantly, "you never can." And then his face broke into smiles and he stooped to kiss the soft rouged cheek. "I must go before the staff at Willowset think I have been kidnapped as well."

"Kidnapped!" exclaimed Mrs. Dish and Eleanor together. "Oh, my goodness," Eleanor rushed on. "Martin told me that the duchess was missing, but I thought she had gone on a visit, forgetting to leave word. Are you certain she has been kidnapped?"

"My sister has more hair than wit, Miss Howard," replied Wright softly, "and might well have gone off on her own, but a ransom note has arrived at Willowset."

"Oh, Josh, is there nothing we can do?" asked Mrs. Dish. "Perhaps someone in the village has seen or heard something."

"No—Kinsley delivered the note but can't say who left it, nor can anyone else. I expect I shall hear from the villains again shortly. They will want their money, after all, and have not left word how I am to deliver it. I must be going, Melinda. I thank you for the dinner. Miss Howard." He bowed correctly in farewell and left the room.

Eleanor listened as he made his way out through the kitchen door. "How dreadful," she said then. "He must be horridly worried. Surely he will pay the ransom."

"He will pay with the tip of his sword or a pistol ball through the heart," replied Mrs. Dish. "Whoever took Jenny will rue the day they thought to do so."

Arturo Francesco Luciano Tivoli, Marquis di Roche took a very deep breath, grabbed his leg with both gloved hands and pulled with all his might, which action sent him reeling backwards, his boot sucking up out of the mud and his bottom plunging down into it. Unable to control his temper one instant longer, a string of strident Italian epithets flailed the dank, vile air. His curricle had overturned, his horses had run off, and he had labored for the past twenty minutes to fight his way out of the bog into which he'd been thrown. Luckily the moon had finally risen, so that he could see where the road lay. Unluckily, between himself and the road lay fifty feet of mud, slime and swamp. "Damnded Inglese roads!" roared the marquis, wobbling once again to his feet. "Always where they should being they nots and where they nots being perfidy!" Di Roche swiped the sleeve of his many-caped greatcoat across his brow and cold globules of mud transferred themselves to his forehead and from there oozed icily into his eyes and down his face. Sputtering as the slime crossed his lips, he searched wildly through his pockets for his handkerchief. In triumph, he tugged the large square of muslin from his breeches' pocket only to find it soggy with swamp water and rapidly absorbing the mud from his hands. In sheer rage he threw the thing from him, ran his filthy fingers through his hair and once again attempted to stomp through the bog to the road. The gluttonous quagmire sucked hungrily at every hard-fought step. He reminded himself, especially when he stepped into a hole that brought the foul-smelling muck up to his hips, that this thing he did for the love of the beautiful Jenny. *"Bella,"* he muttered. *"Mia bella,* for you onlies these I doing. Bah! A pox be on these Legion! Only such a one would choosing to lives in such vile place as these!"

At the precise moment that di Roche set his foot upon squishy but comparatively solid roadbed, Jenny stood in the main hall of the Rise, the front door open wide, staring up at the sky. "I think the rain has stopped at last," she informed Peggy, who stood looking up as well. "We shall be able to leave tomorrow if it doesn't rain, don't you think?"

"Gregory will ride out tomorrow, your grace. But I hardly think Oakes will venture forth with the coach. The roads will still be impossible with such a heavy vehicle."

"Oh, but we must, Peggy. Something has gone very wrong. I know it has, or Francesco would certainly have come for me by now. You don't think Joshie has discovered our plan and done something terrible, do you? He would not shoot the marquis, do you think?" The great blue eyes stared woefully into Peggy's.

"If the earl believes your Francesco has abducted you, your grace, he will shoot the man," Tynesbury responded. "But if he discovers the plot and so knows it was all a hoax, I expect he will not. He will draw the marquis's cork for him, is all."

"Oh, we must get to Willowset, Peggy. We absolutely must. Francesco will not stand to have his nose bloodied and will challenge Joshie to a duel, and then—and then—"

"And then the Marquis di Roche will no longer present a problem," finished Tynesbury in a ruthless drawl. "Why you could not simply confide in his lordship and explain that you loved the man, I cannot understand. Your brother wants only to see you happy."

"No! Joshie detests Francesco and will forbid me to have the least thing to do with him. You did not hear him, Peggy, when he discovered I had gone to Vauxhall in Francesco's company. He was intolerable. He called my darling a fribble and a damned libertine and swore to have the marquis's liver on a plate."

Tynesbury's lips twitched. She had no doubt that the earl had said precisely those words. "But you know how his lordship is, your grace," she said reassuringly, taking the duchess's arm and escorting her back into the warmth of the front parlor. "Sometimes he growls and rages at the least little thing. If you were to tell him you truly loved this Italian person, he would attempt to be more sensible about the matter. He is not an ogre, after all."

"But he is most disconcerting and everyone is afraid of him, especially Francesco, because Charles told such awful clankers about Joshie when we stayed in Italy."

Tynesbury chuckled. She could well imagine the tales the late duke would have told about his infamous brother-in-law. The Duke of Ware had had the most unruly sense of humor and had reveled in his association with Wright and the opportunities for outrageous bouncers that that relationship provided him. "I shall tell Oakes, your grace, that you wish to leave as soon as possible. Perhaps the roads are not as impassable as might be expected. Glenby is the finest coachman in all England, you know, and might drive almost anywhere at any time."

It was Jenny's turn to smile and she did so widely, a glow filling her sweet countenance. "You are in love with him, aren't you, Peggy? I have thought so for the longest time. He is such a very romantic figure—so tall and strong and fierce. And he is so very kind as well."

Tynesbury's fine eyes lit and she giggled girlishly. "Next to his lordship, Glenby Oakes is the most extraordinary man in England," she declared, "and I have told him so."

"Have you, Peggy? What did he say?"

"That I am a thoroughly misguided romp."

Mrs. Simon, at that moment entering with the tea tray, was invited to make a cozy third before the fire, and the conversation extended to irrefutable truths of love, the impossibility of understanding a gentleman's mind and the dismal quality of existence in the hinterlands once the summer has flown. While the spectacle of a duchess sharing tea with her abigail and housekeeper would have raised innumerable eyebrows amid the London *ton,* none of the women gave it the least thought. It was and always had been acceptable at Elders Rise for the barriers of class to fall from time to time and the bonds of common human experience unite all. Mrs. Simon had just begun to expound upon the necessity for all men, especially the Earl of Wright, to discover the love of a good woman when she was interrupted by a frenzied barking and howling of the earl's hounds and a wild pounding upon the front door. She rose immediately and hurried into the main hall, but Mr. Simon, rushing from the kitchen, called to her to let the door to him. "For ye niver know what sorta cove might come swoopin' down out o' the wilds in the dead o' night, m'dear," he declared. "An' 'tis best they see that men are present." With that he stalked to the door, opened it and was immediately jostled aside by a half-frozen, mud-covered Marquis di Roche, attempting to avoid the sharp nips of two of the earl's hounds.

Four

Neville Nelson entered the kitchen at Elders Rise laden with muddy, foul-scented clothes and a harassed look upon his florid countenance that sent Glenby Oakes off into whoops of laughter.

"Stubble it, Oakes. I ain't finding this particularly amusing. Dash it all, if the man don't think someone's goin' to clean this mess!"

Oakes leaned back in his chair and laughed all the harder. "B-better b-build a b-bonfire fast," he stuttered around gasps of hilarity.

"Aye, and so I'm gonna do does the bloody furriner like it or not. Gonna have to find him somethin' else to wear, though. Can't take the man back with us buck naked."

"Eh? Who's takin' 'im back with us?" Oakes asked, raising a bushy eyebrow. "Not I, m'dear. I ain't about ta let 'im ride in a closed coach wi' her grace all the way back ta Willowset."

"Tynesbury will chaperon."

"I ain't about ta let 'im ride with Peggy neither. I got enough worry thinkin' how ta explain ta Legion why I drove ta the Rise. Can't let on her grace cozened us, can I?"

"No, but we can't leave the man here, Oakes. Not naked we can't. You think he'll fit into any of the earl's kit?"

The mere thought sent Oakes back into whoops.

The marquis, however, was far from laughing as he stepped from his bath, toweled himself and wrapped one of the earl's dressing gowns around him. His teeth had stopped chattering.

Casper Simon had been good enough to lay a fire for him and Mrs. Simon had rushed to make up the bed in the rose and white bedchamber in the east wing and from somewhere the servant called Gregory had produced the satin robe but nothing else.

Worn to a frazzle, Francesco stared wearily about him. The room held little in the way of amenities. Only one candle sat in a holder upon the bedside table. There was a worn brocade wing chair before the fire and a remnant of carpet on the cold hardwood floor. There was no sign of a brandy decanter or even a teapot—which Francesco would certainly have welcomed—nor were there draperies across the windows nor paintings upon the walls. No clothes press, no armoire, no escritoire, not even a footstool. A great draft blew in around the windowpanes and encouraged him to climb immediately into the bed to keep warm. Which he most certainly would have done, had he been given anything to sleep in. He could not sleep in the earl's robe; it wrapped around him twice and was sure to strangle him in his slumbers. Muttering, he spied a bellpull and tugged it angrily. The wide rose and gold silk cord came down in his hands, bringing part of the ceiling with it. *"Santa Maria!"* he exclaimed dodging quickly out of the way of falling plaster. "These Inglese, they being barbarians!" He threw the bellpull to the floor and stomped angrily into the hall, shouting for servants.

Glenby Oakes appeared fifteen minutes later to find the marquis huddled before the fire carefully feeding the blaze from a meager store of tinder. "Cold, eh?"

Francesco jumped clear out of the chair at the unexpected voice. Oakes studied the smaller man, a wry smile nudging at his lips. "Her grace found these in the earl's wardrobe," he explained, tossing the clothing he carried onto the bed. "Doubt they'll fit, but ye might give 'em a try-on. My guess is ye'll drown in 'em."

A scowl furrowing his brow, the marquis walked to the pile of clothes and rummaged through them. "The leetle duchess, she is for me wait?" he asked, tossing one after another of the earl's garments aside.

"Nope," Oakes replied. "The duchess's in the west wing tucked up fer the night. Ye oughta climb inta bed yerself afore the fire dies and ye freeze solid—or afore the ghost begins ta walk."

"Ghost?" asked Francesco, ceasing to rummage through the clothes.

"Ghost." Oakes nodded. "Abigail Andrews. Murdered in 'er bed a long time ago. Husband done it. Lady's bin threatenin' the men at the Rise ever since."

Francesco's deep brown eyes widened perceptibly.

"Lucky for ye she didn't find ye in the bog. Drown ye, she would ha'. Drowned two coves we know of. Likes plaguin' Legion, but 'tis the others what she takes 'er revenge upon, an' leaves the earl t'clean up 'er mess. Does she notice a fire burnin' an' a candle lit, might be as she'd be curious enough ta see who was visitin'. Git in the bed quick is what I say, an' fall asleep so as not to draw no attention."

Francesco, whose experience of ghosts was gleaned solely from gothic romances, gulped visibly and once again began to rummage through the clothes Oakes had brought. "There ees here not the night-sleeping shirt," the marquis sighed finally. "He has not, the Legion, one such?"

"A nightshirt?" Oakes tugged at his beard thoughtfully. "Well now, I reckon he don't, come ta think on it. Never seen 'im in one. Never seen Tibbs pack one neither. Tell ye what, yer lor'ship. I'll go fetch ye one o' Casper's. Back in a minute, eh?" Oakes dashed out into the hallway and down the back stairs, chuckling gleefully under his breath. When he reached the servants' quarters and related the look on the marquis's face at the tale of Abigail Andrews, Nelson, Gregory and Carson collapsed with laughter and Simon, snickering, went merrily in search of a clean nightshirt for the bedeviled little man. Tynesbury, who entered with Mrs. Simon at that moment, asked to be let in on the joke and frowned impatiently as Oakes related it to her.

"Glenby Oakes," she declared, "you ought to be ashamed of yourself. Has not the poor man suffered enough without your filling his mind with Abigail Andrews?"

"No," replied Oakes, grinning.

"Bad enough to force him to sleep in the east wing, without you taint the poor gentleman's mind with tales of haunts," scolded Mrs. Simon. "You are worse than schoolboys."

"Well, now, an' ain't it kinder ta tease the cove than ta draw 'is cork?" Oakes asked, winking at Peggy, "which I bin longin' ta do since I heerd o' this plan o' his and her grace's. It's sure the duchess ain't ta blame, for she don't know no better, but that chap deserves a bit o' hardship. Pro'bly got Legion tearin' his hair out by now."

The Earl of Wright was not, in fact, tearing out his hair but running his fingers through it distractedly as he paced the floor of the Blue Saloon at Willowset. Visions of Jenny in grave peril made him curse himself for a fool at not being able to uncover her abductors' trail. His mind went over and over again the information that had been gathered. He walked to the rosewood sideboard, poured himself a brandy and slouched into one of the chairs. Glenby Oakes, he reminded himself, had been driving. And Glenby Oakes would not allow any harm to come to Jenny. Unless the man was dead, whispered a tiny voice from the other side of his brain. He groaned at the thought and took a swallow of the fiery liquid. If Oakes was dead, if Nelson and Carson and Gregory were dead as well, then all fell upon Peggy Tynesbury's shoulders, and strong and capable as Tynesbury was, she was not like to be able to protect herself and Jenny from bully-ruffians. Not that she wouldn't try. Wright cursed himself for a fool and slumped deeper into the chair. A moment later he straightened and set his glass upon the side table. "North," he murmured with suppressed excitement as he rose from the chair and tugged at the bellpull. Burton, just passing the doorway, entered solemnly.

"Yes, your lordship, is there something you wish?"

"Burton, damnation but it is so simple!"

"What is simple, my lord?"

"I must have Tug saddled immediately."

"But, your lordship," Burton said stoically, as the earl shrugged out of his red satin smoking jacket and scrambled to untie his cravat in the middle of the saloon, "it is after midnight. We are not in London, my lord. There is nowhere to ride *to* at such an hour. This late in the year, even the public room at the Crossroads will be closed."

"No, but Burton, I know what we have overlooked. Tell Harry Cross to saddle one of Charlie's hacks for himself. I shall be down in five minutes." Leaving his jacket upon the arm of a chair and his neckcloth hanging from the mantelpiece, Wright hurried past Burton and headed for the stairs, slipping his shirt over his head as he went. "Tibbs!" he shouted, "Tibbs, I need my riding gear!"

Horace Tibbs, his eyes heavy with sleep, blinked drowsily in his small room next to the earl's chambers, where he had already put himself to bed. He fumbled to find his tinderbox and fumbled again to find the candle. The sound of footsteps pounding down the hall proclaimed that he had not dreamed the earl's voice, and he stumbled hurriedly into his lordship's chambers. "Wh-what is it, my lord?" he stammered, tugging the nightcap from his head and hiding it behind his back.

Wright took a long look at the figure in the white-and-black-striped nightshirt and grinned broadly. "You were asleep. I'm sorry, Tibbs. I did not think."

Tibbs, who had had charge of dressing Wright since the earl was ten, was inclined to mention that the earl very rarely thought before he acted, but he held his peace. "What was it you desired, my lord?"

"Riding gear, Tibbs."

"Your lordship cannot mean to ride off at this time of the night. It is—it must be—"

"It is just after midnight, Tibbs," supplied the earl, rifling through a chest of drawers and at last seizing upon a black twill shirt. "I thought perhaps you had not brought this," he added, pulling on the garment. "My doeskins? Are they here?"

"Yes, m'lord, but I cannot condone—"

"Bosh and fustian, Tibbs. Give 'em to me. If you could not condone them, you'd not have brought 'em, and that's a fact."

Tibbs sighed but retrieved the black doeskin breeches from the clothes press and, tossing them nonchalantly in Wright's direction, walked regally into the adjoining antechamber and returned with a pair of high-topped black boots and a set of silver spurs. "You will need a greatcoat. I have brought the surtout. It is in the downstairs hall beneath the stairs," he announced, waiting patiently for Wright to get his breeches laced before helping him to pull on the boots and strap on the spurs. "And if you find it necessary to wear that dreadful hat, it is beneath the stairs as well. I expect you intend to ride out sans coat, sans waistcoat, sans collar, et cetera."

"Yes, Tibbs, I do," agreed Wright, buckling a rapier around his waist and stuffing a horse pistol into his belt.

"May I inquire, Master Jocelyn, where you are bound?"

"Master Jocelyn, is it? I'm sorry, Tibbs. I know you don't approve, but that is only because you think I'm mad."

"Never!" declared Tibbs, his face drawing into a scowl.

"Yes, you do, but I know how Jenny was taken, you see, and I don't wish to waste the night."

Tibbs's eyes lit with sudden enthusiasm. "You know who has taken her?"

"Well, no, I don't know that."

"But you know where she is!"

"Not exactly, Tibbs. But I know why no one has been able to discover her trail. Glenby Oakes drove past the St. Swithin's turnoff. Either he was accosted south of Dorset and forced to take the Great North Road, or he drove north to escape whoever followed, thinking to turn back at Moorland Place." The earl tied a black scarf roguishly around his neck and then put his arm around the little valet's shoulders. "I shall ride north, Tibbs, and pound at every door I must until I have word of her."

Tibbs nodded. "But you will take Harry Cross with you. The roads are dreadful, and north they will be much worse."

"I shall take Harry Cross and I will trust you and the others to watch over Jess. And do not, Tibbs, no matter what, tell Martin Howard where I've gone. I do not trust the man as far as I can spit."

Harry Cross and Wright reached St. Swithin's by one-thirty and the Great North Road fifteen minutes later. A steady rain had once again begun to fall, signaling a storm to follow and slowing them to a canter. At three-thirty they came upon one of the few tollgates that the government had been audacious enough to establish along this wild stretch. Wright dismounted and kicked his boot against the door of the gatekeeper's cottage with a good deal of energy. He's bursting wi' excitement, Harry Cross thought, watching from his saddle in the chill drizzle. Knows he's right. The gatekeeper, having thrown himself into his breeches and only halfway into his shirt, answered the door with a long rifle in one hand and a lantern in the other.

Cross could hear neither the earl's words nor the gatekeeper's response. He noticed, however, that gold changed hands and the frown on the gatekeeper's grizzled visage faded into a smile and the earl smiled as well as he remounted. "He remembers seeing them, Harry! Hard to forget Glenby Oakes. Says it was the only time he ever saw a pirate driving a coach and four." A bit of a frown darkened the smile for a moment. "Said they paid the toll as far as Winnow Mills—two women inside, two men on the box and two outriders. Exactly as they should be. No one extra—unless, of course, Nelson and Gregory and Carson had been replaced by the kidnappers. Glenby obviously was not." Pulling the collar of his surtout tighter about his neck and the wide-brimmed black hat he had rescued from his great-grandfather's trunks farther down over his brow, Wright urged his horse northward into the approaching gale.

In almost total darkness, Harry Cross held his position alongside. They would not get very far, he knew, once the gale hit full-force, and he cudgeled his mind to remember where they might find shelter ahead. It was Wright, however, once the thunder rumbled over their heads, the wind roared around their ears, the frigid rain whipped into their faces and their mounts slushed through mud as high as their fetlocks and as thick as bread pudding, who turned off into the woods and within minutes brought them to an abandoned barn.

"We'll have to make do with this, Harry," he called, ducking under the doorframe as he rode Tugforth into the shelter. "Thought we might get as far as Lower Bite and the Huston's, but it's getting too strong." The earl dismounted and dug his flint box from his pocket. By its flicker he searched the building until in a far corner he discovered a lantern with a bit of oil in the base. He lit it and, coming back to where Cross fumbled to un-saddle the horses, cleared a space for it on the dirt floor.

At a loss for something with which to rub down the horses, Cross cursed under his breath. Wright chuckled. "The thing is, Harry, you're spoiled. You've been living in civilization much too long." So saying, he doffed his hat and surtout, pulled off his shirt and began to dry Tugforth with it. Cross, muttering that his lordship had spent too little time in civilization, fol-lowed suit. When at last the two men huddled together in a pile of straw to sleep, shirts hung over what remained of a single stall to dry and greatcoats draped over the horses to keep the animals from the chill, the sky was just beginning to lighten in the east, though one could barely tell, since dark clouds hung so thickly over the horizon.

Eleanor woke as usual at eight o'clock, the lack of sunlight in her chamber alerting her to the likelihood of a dismal day.

Though the fire in her room had already been laid and lit, she hurried nonetheless to dress in her warmest gown and draw a shawl about her shoulders. Really, she thought, Dorset must be the worst place in all of England once winter arrives. It is so cold now and only coming on the end of November. She reached the breakfast table to find her brother already begun upon shirred eggs and ham, a thin volume opened beside his plate and an extremely serious scowl upon his countenance. "Good morning, Martin," she said softly, helping herself to some eggs and ham as well. She poured herself a cup of tea and smiled across at him. "What is it has you scowling?"

"Oh, Ellie, good morning. Did you know that Wright had written a book?"

"Lord Wright? Are you sure? Perhaps his father."

"No, it's Wright. Extraordinary."

"What is it about, Martin?"

"Huh? Oh, nothing you would be interested in, m'dear. The ramblings of a madman—consign class distinction to the devil, educate the poor, give women the vote."

Give women the vote? Eleanor's mind reeled at such a ridiculous idea. And to destroy the distinction between the classes—the man was indeed mad. But educating the poor—well, perhaps one might teach them some little of reading and writing. That would be a nice thing to do. Certainly he could not mean to teach them more than that. Martin's attention went back to the page. She watched him curiously as she ate.

"Well, I'll be," he muttered once and then again. "Who would have thought it?"

Eleanor finished her breakfast listening to cryptic comments and studying her brother. Martin was truly a handsome gentleman. His dusty blond hair and wide-set brown eyes added to the appeal of a high forehead, a classical nose and a strong jaw. When he scowled, as he was doing now, a tiny vertical line scrolled between his eyes just at the bridge of his nose. She tried to remember whether the earl had such a line when he scowled but recalled instead deep indentations at each corner of his mouth when he grinned. She thought it odd in herself to be comparing Martin and Lord Wright but then acknowledged that perhaps it was not. After all, she had never truly noticed gentlemen at all until Jocelyn Elders had appeared that evening in the nursery. He had looked so strong, his shoulders so broad, his waist so trim—a giant, scooping little Jessie into his arms. Her glance appraised Martin. His shoulders were just as broad as the earl's. "How old is Lord Wright?" she asked abruptly, shocking herself.

"What? Wright? Don't know, exactly, Ellie. Near twenty-eight, I expect. Why?"

"I was just thinking how—how alike you are."

Howard snapped the volume closed and stared across at her. "Alike? Legion and I? Alike?"

"I only meant in—in form, Martin. You are built alike, strong and powerful and—and—"

"What has come over you?" Howard asked with a note of astonishment in his voice. "Since when have you taken to studying men's forms, Ellie?"

"I have not—not exactly—it is only—it is hard not to notice the earl—the way he is put together, I mean. Oh, dear, I am not saying this right at all." Eleanor sighed, reddening as her brother's eyebrows rose. "I only meant that he is quite handsome, Martin, and so are you, and I thought that you must be quite the same age as well."

"I have brought him to the forefront of your mind by mentioning this dreadful volume. The fault is mine. I will warn you again, Eleanor. The man is anathema, an obscenity. He belongs in Bedlam and shall be put there, too, one day. I know what it is, Ellie: You are grown gently and innocently into womanhood and the man has aroused instincts in you better left undisturbed until nurtured to fruition by your husband."

Eleanor glared angrily and rose to her feet. "Don't be absurd, Martin. The man has done nothing. It is certainly not his fault that my eyes see what stands before me!" Although, she added silently, Lord Wright really should not have appeared in public in those gorgeous white whipcord breeches. She tried to imagine Martin in such clothes and her glare changed abruptly to a small giggle. "Truly, Martin," she smiled, "there is not the least thing to worry about. I only wondered whether your being of an age and built so much alike did not have something to do with the enmity between you. I thought you had once been rivals for some debutante's hand."

"Oh," Howard sighed, crossing to her and escorting her from the room. "I cannot imagine what put such a thing into your head. I am a man of the cloth, Ellie, and the women I might court, if I so desired, would be of no interest to Wright. His interests lie in another direction entirely."

"What direction, Martin?"

"I—that is to say—a gentleman does not—not mention such in the presence of his sister, my dear."

"Oh!" Eleanor breathed on a little gasp. "You mean to say he has mistresses!"

Martin Howard seated his sister on the green silk divan in the back parlor and stood looking down at her with a perplexed countenance. "No," he said at last, "I don't mean to say that at all, Ellie, though it's true. I mean to say he is a hellion and a libertine and a scoundrel, and that he is not to be trusted in the company of gently bred women. Nor does he seek or encourage the interest of gently bred women, and that is the *only* thing I have ever found to respect in him. What a dismal day we appear to have in front of us," he added, walking to one of the windows. "I wonder if there has been any word of the duchess?"

"No," Eleanor sighed. "Not since the first ransom note."

"The what?"

"The first ransom note. They have been waiting, you know, for a second, saying where the money is to be delivered, but there has not been one as yet."

"Eleanor, what are you saying?"

Eleanor's hands went to her reddening cheeks as she recalled that Martin knew nothing of the business, that she had learned all from the earl last evening and that Martin had not the least idea Lord Wright had been anywhere near Mrs. Dish's cottage. "I, ah, learned of it at Mrs. Dish's. Mr. Kinsley delivered a note to the earl just after your altercation but has delivered nothing since." Eleanor's hands twisted nervously in her lap. She could not believe that she had just omitted all reference to her dinner with Lord Wright. She had never before felt the necessity to withhold information of any type from her brother, but she knew, absolutely knew, she should not mention that the earl had dined with herself and Mrs. Dish. Much less should she mention that she had enjoyed the evening a great deal. She looked up to see Martin tugging at the bellpull and listened in silence as he sent word to have the coach put-to. "Where are you going, Martin?" she asked in a tiny voice.

"Willowset. If what you say is true and not merely country gossip, a firm hand and a sound mind will be needed there."

"But surely, Martin, the earl may be trusted to act in the best interests of his own sister."

"Never! He's a barbarian—born and bred in a nest of barbarians. I wouldn't trust the man's judgment as far as I can spit! Excuse me, my dear. I apologize for my language, but I am that put out!"

"Then I am going with you. Perhaps I may be of help with little Jessie. Bowey and Shepard will both be at wits end with worry over her grace."

Martin Howard glanced at his sister with a rather suspicious eye, but seeing nothing in her countenance to indicate a desire for an encounter with the Earl of Wright, he shrugged his shoulders and nodded his consent. She would, of course, be welcomed heartily by the little duke's nanny and valet, especially if the tale of kidnapping proved to be true.

At Willowset the stir caused by Howard's obvious knowledge of the ransom note was exceeded only by his request to speak directly with the Earl of Wright. Though Howard chose to overlook the apparent distress in Burton's eyes as that stalwart of the Duke of Ware's household escorted them into the long drawing room, Eleanor conceived a distinct sympathy for the aging butler. He knows the earl will fly up into the boughs again, she thought, and is dreading it, poor man. "May I go up to the nursery, Burton?" she asked with an encouraging smile. "I should so like to visit his grace for a while."

"Indeed, Miss Howard, Master Jessie has been wishing for you. I will have Logan take you up."

The formality of being escorted by a footman to the third floor was not lost on Eleanor. Before Lord Wright's arrival she would have been allowed to make her own way to the nursery, much like a member of the household. Logan's presence made her feel much more a guest, and she could not like the difference. Nor could she help but wonder if the formality were a result of Lord Wright's orders or an attempt by Burton to protect her from an accidental confrontation with the man. Mrs. Bowers, however, greeted her with a bright smile, and Jessie raced into her arms with all his usual enthusiasm. "I knowed you would come, Ellie. I gaved Uncle Josh a terr'ble scold for frighting you away, an' he said he would 'pologize 'mediately. Can you stay an' play with me? Please?"

"Yes, of course. What are you playing, your grace?"

"We are playin' Spinach!" cried the little duke, jumping up and down excitedly. "I am the Spinach an' Bowey an' Colly are bein' ever'one else! I am the verimost best at bein' the Spinach. Even Uncle Josh says so!"

Eleanor glanced, bemused, at a chuckling Mrs. Bowers. "Spinach?" she asked.

" 'Tis a game the earl taught him. I suspect his lordship invented it on the spur of the moment."

"No, he dinit," Jessie protested with a serious shake of his golden curls. "He maded it up when he was little, an' my mama an' him was used to play it all the time. Uncle Josh said so."

"Aye, so he did," Colly Shepard confirmed as he entered the nursery from the adjoining chamber, his arms filled with fresh linen. "Heard him say so myself. But you must explain to Miss Howard how to play, your grace."

Eleanor's eyes lit with mirth as the little duke, hopping from one foot to another, then spinning in a circle, then plopping upon the floor and popping back up and skipping from one corner of the huge chamber to the other, related the most outrageous rules she had ever heard for what amounted to a game of tag. The delightfully bizarre explanations that accompanied the rules, which took into consideration that farmers planted spinach, hares nibbled it and most rational people attempted to avoid eating it, sent her into giggles. By the time Jessie had finished she could not doubt that the Earl of Wright had been an amazingly funny and ingenious child. How I should have liked to have known him then, she found herself thinking as she took up her part in the game.

It was Horace Tibbs who came to stand composedly before Howard in the long drawing room and explain succinctly that his lordship had been called away on business very early that morning and had not left word when he would return. Tibbs acknowledged that a ransom note had been received, since it was apparent Howard already knew of the thing, but denied that the earl had any idea of where it had come from. "No, sir," he lied readily in response to Howard's question, "I cannot show you the note. It lies still in his lordship's pocket. But we expect to receive another soon, since there were no instructions as to where the ransom should be delivered."

"And you have no idea where Wright has gone? Has he gone to collect the money, perhaps?"

"I cannot say, sir. His lordship did not confide in me."

Howard, who doubted that Wright confided anything in anyone, informed Tibbs that since Wright had abandoned the staff in such a precarious situation, he, himself, would remain at Willowset until the earl returned. This slight on the capabilities of the staff caused Tibbs's nose to rise higher into the air than usual, but the valet made no reply other than to bow and leave the reverend's presence and relay the unwelcome information to the rest of the servants at Willowset.

Five

The skies over Elders Rise were clear for the second day in a row when Glenby Oakes at last agreed that a return south might be attempted. He did not, however, agree that the Marquis di Roche might ride inside the coach, and so the marquis rode one of Wright's hunters, a roan gelding named Herod, who was fresh and eager and tried the marquis's patience immediately by preferring to jump the wall at the bottom of the drive rather than exit via the open gate. Tynesbury was compelled to agree with the duchess that the marquis clung to the saddle well, but she was finding it difficult not to laugh at the odd vision the little Italian presented, wrapped in an assortment of clothing gleaned from Wright's wardrobe. Still, she had to admit that even in baggy pantaloons, oversized boots and a greatcoat in which he could turn around completely without unbuttoning one button, the marquis managed to remain handsome. "You realize, your grace, that you must tell Lord Wright the truth when we reach Willowset. We cannot go on pretending to have been kidnapped."

"But we must, Peggy! Don't you see? Everything is working out perfectly. Francesco will be a hero when he brings me home. Joshie will get down on his knees and thank him."

"I do not think so, your grace." Tynesbury smiled, unable to picture the earl in such a posture. "And I do think your brother will notice that the marquis wears his clothes."

"Well, as for that, we shall simply stop at the Gander's Neck and Francesco will change into his own garments before we continue on to Willowset. His man awaits him there, you know."

"No, I did not know." Tynesbury grinned with a little shake of her head at the great thought that the two innocents had put into this endeavor. The Gander's Neck was a posting house that lay several miles northwest of St. Swithin's and within easy reach of Willowset, but a place Wright generally avoided when visiting because it catered to the local squires, whom he detested. "Well, I will not betray you, but you must, I think, hold conference with Oakes and Nelson and Gregory and Carson, all of whom will need to devise some story as to how they were taken and not one of them wounded in the process. They will not wish to appear cowards in his lordship's eyes."

"Oh, I had not thought. Oakes will not like Josh to think he was easily taken, will he?"

"No, your grace, Oakes will not. Nor none of the others. They are proud men, all of them. And they will not like the earl to think it took the likes of your little marquis to rescue them either, unless you can provide them with a very good tale."

Jenny's cherubic face took on a most becoming frown, which Tynesbury had always found endearing. She remembered how the Earl of Wright had chuckled when he had explained that it was meant to display to the world in general that his sister was giving a matter her deepest concentration. "I taught her, Tynesbury, to frown like that when she was three. It has been known to hold people at bay for ten minutes or more. Not, I think, because they believe she is pondering anything seriously, but because she does it so charmingly." Wright would never, Peggy thought, believe that the Marquis di Roche had rescued them all from abductors, but he might, if his sister's story proved fanciful enough, elect not to contradict her in the matter. And Oakes and the others could be persuaded not to tell him the truth of it until he was in a good humor. Peggy was just about to set these particular thoughts before the duchess when the coach came to a swaying halt.

"Tarnation!" Oakes muttered, handing the reins to Nelson and swinging down from the box. He walked slowly to the back of the vehicle, rubbed one large hand against the back of his neck and sighed. "Mind the team, Nelson," he called as Gregory and Carson rode up and dismounted beside him. "We've a wheel mired in this muck. Didn't I know this was gonna 'appen!"

"Want to try rockin' 'er out, Glenby?" Carson asked.

"Aye, reckon so. Here, you, m'lordship," Oakes shouted, waving the marquis to him. "You see kin ye find us a decent-sized rock ta put beneath this wheel. Gregory, help 'er grace an' Peggy out o' the coach. Ain't right they should be jostled aroun' like their gonna be if they stay inside."

"Help them where, Oakes? The ladies can't be standin' in this muck."

"Set 'em up on yer horses, then," muttered Oakes, walking up to look at the right front wheel. The sound of his boots sucking up out of the mire with every step did not bother him. He had grown used to much worse on the Peninsula. The marquis, however, shuddered and decided he would locate the rock they needed from Herod's back.

Unfortunately, though he located it from there, he had to dismount to collect it. This he did very gingerly, hoping to keep as much mud away from himself as possible. But the moment his boot struck the ground it sank into the mire. When he brought his other foot down it did likewise. He groaned, but bent forward to pick up the rock, and then found that he must dig down beneath it because it, too, had sunk a bit. He gritted his teeth and stuck his gloved fingers under the thing and pried upward. It came loose easily and he heaved a sigh of relief. He turned to climb with his prize back into Herod's saddle and found that though his foot had come free of the bog, his boot had not. A flood of Italian raked the wind as he stood wobbling on one leg, clutching tightly to the rock with both hands and attempting to keep his stockinged foot in the air.

In a fit of compassion, well disguised behind a wide grin,

Carson mounted his horse, rode to where the marquis stood and took the rock, resting it before him on the saddle. Then he leaned downward, put an arm around the marquis's chest and pulled him upward, straight out of his remaining boot—or rather, the earl's remaining boot—and transferred him across his own mount and onto Herod's back. Then he handed the rock to Francesco, jumped down and pulled the boots out of the mud. "Ride back and give the rock to Gregory," he instructed the marquis. "I'll bring the boots and you may try putting them on without dismounting."

This the marquis did with a great feeling of relief, but his relief was not to be long-lasting. In the end he was forced to dismount and lay his shoulder to the back of the coach along with Carson, Gregory and Nelson, while Oakes urged the team of bays forward, brought them back and bid them forward again, rocking the heavy vehicle until the wheel exploded out of the mudhole, liberally splattering everyone at the back of the coach with cold, wet muck. All of them, servants and marquis alike, groaned and backed away, instinctively brushing at the stuff, which only served to cover them more thoroughly with the disgusting sludge. Oakes, the only one of them not encased in muck, lifted the ladies' back into the coach; the men remounted and they resumed their journey.

Oakes was pessimistic about their chances of advancing farther than the village of John's Glen by nightfall. The team would be ragged even before then, swamped and hampered as they were with each step. He had no intention of pushing his horses beyond their limit. There was no posting house where he might exchange teams until they reached the outskirts of Dorset and civilization. His mind wandered to Willowset, and he wondered what Legion was doing about their supposed abduction. " 'Sblood!" he exclaimed suddenly, pulling back on the reins with one powerful hand and clutching at the side of the box with the other. The coach wheels skimmed over a deep layer of slime; the vehicle slued across the surface of the road and plummeted into a ditch.

* * *

Wright's boots squelched ankle deep in mud as he dismounted in the inn yard and handed Tugforth's reins to one of the hostlers. He struggled wearily through the sucking mire toward the wooden porch, Harry Cross just behind him. Several sets of eyebrows rose as they entered the building, including the landlord's. Wright sighed. His silver spurs were as brown and slimy as his boots; his breeches and surtout were spattered with grime; his hat brim dipped at odd angles from the thorough soaking it had taken; and he smelled exceeding like horse. He could feel the encrusted dirt crack on his face as he attempted to grin at the man behind the counter. "Afternoon, Allerby. Wouldn't happen to have an empty room or two, would you?"

"Well, I'll be hornswaggled! That you under all that filth, Wright? And Harry—Harry Cross! Well, I'll be danged! Course I got rooms. Only fools travelin' far in this weather." The landlord gazed mirthfully at both of them.

"I would take offense, Allerby," Wright drawled, "if I did not stand here proving your point."

The landlord chuckled. "I'll send a boy for your luggage, m'lord. Left it in the stables, did you?"

"No."

"Ah, you were planning on making it all the way to the Rise before sunset."

"Sounds likely."

Allerby's eyebrows rose a bit more, but an almost imperceptible shake of Harry Cross's head made him bite his tongue and lead the men up the stairwell to adjoining chambers. "I shall send hot water and the hip bath as soon as possible," he assured them. "When your clothes dry one of the boys can attempt to brush off the dirt. That's the best I can promise."

"It'll do," Wright muttered, shrugging out of his surtout as Allerby lit a fire in the hearth. "Allerby, you have not, perchance, had sight of my sister recently?"

"Ain't her grace at the Rise, m'lord? Thomas Grant was sayin' as how Mr. and Mrs. Simon were that astonished to be expecting company up there this time of the year."

Wright's incredible eyes, or at least as much as Allerby could see of them through the grime, lit with a sudden flame. "Mrs. Simon was expecting company?"

"Well, she sent Casper to Grant's for extra vittles, my lord, when she got your note."

"Of course," Wright nodded, "I had forgotten the—note." He dismissed Allerby, who wandered through the connecting door, lit the fire in Cross's room and then took himself back downstairs.

"The note, m'lord?" Cross asked, shrugging out of his coat.

"I haven't a clue, Harry, but we've come as far as John's Glen. Won't hurt to go on to the Rise to see if the Simons have heard from the kidnappers. Obviously they've heard from someone."

Mr. Michael Paxton of Grimsby, Paxton and Brookes heaved a great sigh as he followed Burton to the Willowset library, which chamber, it appeared, Howard had appropriated for his office. Paxton was not looking forward to an interview with the gentleman. The breeze Howard's unexpected and scathing letter had raised in the London office had resulted in a worried discussion centered upon the firm's responsibility in the guardianship of the little Duke of Ware, and whether or not either Howard or Wright might be trusted to see to the duke's best interests. Paxton, however, was friend to both men and well aware of the enmity between them, and he had agreed to undertake the task of setting all to right. "Am I to understand, Burton, that Wright has departed the premises?" he asked now, as he followed the butler down the first-floor hall.

"Yes, sir," Burton replied.

"And Reverend Howard has moved in?"

"Yes, sir, he and Miss Howard, who is more than welcome."

Paxton sighed again. "Well, now you have me for a few days as well. I expect Wright intends to return?"

"Indeed, sir," murmured Burton, knocking upon the library door and then opening it. "Mr. Paxton," he announced in grave tones; then, bowing the gentleman into Howard's presence, he closed the door upon the two and disappeared into the rear of the house.

"Paxton! Come in! You will not believe what has been happening in this house!"

Paxton, taking a seat before the fire and warming his hands at the blaze, heard the library door open once more behind him, and watched in silence as a footman carried in a tray containing a silver coffee urn, two Dresden cups and saucers, a pitcher of cream, a sugar bowl and a dish of scones. Thank you, Burton, he thought, pouring himself a cup of the steaming liquid. One could never fault the service at any of the Duke of Ware's establishments, which was the only thing that might make this particular visit bearable.

"So," he began, sipping at the coffee, "what goes on, Howard? Am I to understand that her grace has run off? And what exactly has Wright done to deserve such a disparaging review of his mental faculties as you sent us?" Paxton, knowing that his luggage was being carefully unpacked in one of the guest chambers and his cattle being equally cared for in the stables, sat back and crossed one leg over the other, a cup of coffee in his right hand, a scone in his left, prepared to listen with skepticism to the tirade he knew would come.

By the time Howard sputtered to a stop the scones had disappeared, the coffee urn had been drained and Paxton had developed a gigantic headache. "I'll tell you what, Howard," he offered, his eyes narrowing in pain. "When Wright reappears I shall have a talk with him. But I doubt he has gone as far around the bend as you fear. It's worry over the duchess that shortens his temper and increases his rage. I will, however, speak with him. Now, if you'll excuse me, Howard, I should like to lie down for a bit. My head, for some reason, is pounding."

Paxton knew exactly why his head was pounding, but one could not simply say to a gentleman of the cloth that his sermonizing gave you a blinding headache. Burton, awaiting Paxton's reappearance in the hall, directed the first footman to deliver Mr. Paxton safely to the Buttercup guest chambers and, recognizing the strained look on that gentleman's countenance, sent the second footman running up after them, headache powders in his hands. He then straightened his shoulders, lifted his chin, and strolled into the library.

"I beg pardon, sir," he began, facing Howard squarely.

"Well, what is it, Burton?"

"I did not wish to disturb your discussion with Mr. Paxton, sir, but it appears the earl has invited guests."

Martin Howard stared at the man. "What, Burton? Someone else has arrived with Paxton?"

"No, sir. Not with Mr. Paxton. Shortly following Mr. Paxton, sir. Arrived in a hired coach with all their luggage, intending to spend some time with his lordship. We have, of course, provided both ladies with chambers in the guest wing. And we have established the child in the nursery."

The Reverend Howard's eyebrows wiggled. "Child? What child, Burton?"

"A very small girl, sir. Her name, I believe, is Joyce."

Her name, indeed, was Joyce, and a very fetching little china doll she was. With hair coaxed into dusky, bouncing curls and deep brown eyes that seemed burned into the whiteness of her skin, Eleanor thought she had never seen a child as appealing. If only I had shown such promise as a babe, she thought, I might have grown into a diamond of the first water.

His Grace, the Duke of Ware was at that moment glaring suspiciously at the potential diamond as they stood in the center of the nursery floor. He bent down and stared unabashedly up into the china doll face. The young lady, who had turned three only a month before, proved equally unabashed and tangled her hand in his grace's enticing golden curls and yanked fiercely. His grace punched her. Joyce let go her grip and kicked the little duke in the shin. Jessie was just about to kick back when Bowey's hands came down upon his shoulders and the child's mama knelt behind the little girl, encircling her in her arms. "It is not nice, Joyce, to kick the duke. Nor to pull his hair. He will not want to play with you if you continue to do so."

"Oh," said the child, her eyes pinned upon Jessie.

"And you, young man," declared Bowey, "must never, never hit a young lady, for any reason, do you understand?"

Jessie nodded, but Eleanor could very well see that his hands remained balled into fists. "That's a girl, ain't she," mumbled the duke, glaring.

"Indeed, your grace, and a very pretty little girl."

"Pooh," muttered Jessie. "Who needs a ol' girl? They ain't any fun." Jessie was fairly positive this was correct. His cousin, Henry, had a sister and she was a girl and she was never any fun at all.

Joyce's mother giggled and gave her daughter a quick hug. "I believe you are out there, your grace. Joyce knows all kinds of fun things to do. She can play Spinach."

"She cannot," declared Jessie roundly. "That is my game and she don't know it."

"Oh, but she does, though she is not nearly as good as you at being the Spinach, his lordship says. And she knows how to play highwaymen, too, and hare and hounds, and duck, duck, goose. And she can paint with her fingers and play spillikins— almost."

"Who teached 'er?"

"Uncle Josh!" replied Joyce, jumping up and down within the circle of her mother's arms. "My uncle Josh!"

The duke's little jaw dropped in disbelief. "He is *my* uncle Josh," he shouted.

"My uncle Josh," taunted the intrepid young lady with a stamp of her foot.

Bowey released the duke with a pat on his bottom and told him that his uncle Josh might be uncle to Miss Joyce if he wanted to be, and that he had best take Miss Joyce and show her around the third floor so that she would not get lost. "For you are the oldest and must take care of her, Master Jessie. I am certain his lordship will expect it of you."

Once the children had gone Eleanor introduced herself and Mrs. Bowers and learned that the child's mother was called Mrs. Hampton and that she was employed by the Earl of Wright as his secretary. Mary, as she asked to be called, then startled them both by bursting into tears. Though they lasted barely a minute, the glistening droplets aroused a good deal of protectiveness in Eleanor's breast. Bowey was equally aroused, and between them, they led Mary to a window seat, Eleanor sitting beside her and Mrs. Bowers going to ring for tea.

"Oh, I am behaving so stupidly," Mary sighed, dabbing at her eyes with a small lace handkerchief. "But I was so counting on his lordship, and now—now he has run off again. Lily assured me he had come to Willowset."

"Well, and he has, Mary," replied Eleanor, taking Mary's hands into her own. "I have no idea where he has gone from here, but he will surely return."

"He has gone in search of her grace. It came to him why no one had been able to discover her trail and he and Harry Cross set out to see if his ideas were correct," Bowey explained to them both. "I assume they were, or else he would certainly have returned by now."

Eleanor stared questioningly at the nanny. "You knew where he had gone? Does all of the staff know? But why did no one tell Martin when he asked?"

Bowey had the good grace to look shamefaced. "It was the earl's wish, Miss Howard. He does not—that is to say—he asked his valet, Mr. Tibbs, to hold his tongue where Reverend Howard is concerned. He said he did not trust the reverend as far as he could spit."

Mary gurgled wetly. "Oh, dear, and here come I forcing you to say so in front of Mr. Howard's sister. How gauche. But you must not feel badly, Eleanor, for I expect your brother does not trust his lordship quite as far as he can spit either, does he?"

Eleanor laughed. "You are exactly right. I do recall hearing words to that effect escape my brother's lips. Can you not tell us what has made you cry? Perhaps Bowey or I may help?"

"No, only Josh—I mean, his lordship—" The very alluring wide eyes gazed shyly down at the floor and then back up at Eleanor. "It is—it is something quite personal in which I require his—advice."

Toddy Grimes had been a hostler at the Broken Wing in John's Glen for well over five years, and as soon as he rushed out into the courtyard and saw the Duke of Ware's crest on the coach coming to a halt and Glenby Oakes upon the box, a huge cloud of confusion rushed over him. Instead of taking the team, Grimes wobbled his way through the sucking mud up to the side of the box and placed a boot on the wheel, pulling himself up beside Oakes, forcing Nelson and Oakes both to slide over to one side.

"Toddy, what the devil d'ye think ye're doin'?" growled Oakes. "Git down an' see ta m'horses."

"Aye, an' tha' I will—but I thin' I ought ta be a warnin' of ye. 'Is lor'ship be in there."

"What lordship?" Oakes growled.

"His lor'ship the Earl o' Wright, and right fratched he looked, too, when I takes 'is horse. Covered wi' mud he were, lookin' like he'd rode ferever."

Oakes stared at Nelson; Nelson scrambled down and opened the coach door. "Pardon me, your grace, but it appears Lord Wright is here."

"Joshie?"

"Yes, your grace. We thought you would like to know."

"Oh, dear! Well, but we cannot go farther; the sun is nearly down and the horses are very tired."

"Not to mention that it would be unthinkable to allow his lordship to go on believing you to be in danger for one moment longer than necessary," prompted Tynesbury.

"Oh, yes, that, too. Oh, whatever are we going to tell him? Francesco," she called as that gentleman rode forward, "we must all know what to say to Joshie. He is here at this inn."

"Santa Maria," sighed that mud-encrusted gentleman. "How he knowing, these one, to coming here?"

"Don't matter far as I kin see," growled Oakes, leaping from the box and sending Toddy Grimes to the horses's heads. "I hope ye got a tale worth tellin', signor, 'cause we're all o' us about ta need one."

The riders and outriders gathered around, suggesting and protesting and arguing and at last agreeing as the sun set over the inn yard. Oakes swept the duchess and then Tynesbury up into his arms and struggled with them across the muddy inn yard to the wooden porch, where he set them safely upon their feet. "We shall go in first, then," Peggy said softly, "and the marquis will follow. Perhaps we shall be lucky and Lord Wright is asleep already in one of the rooms. Surely if he has ridden all the way from Willowset he will be exhausted."

They were not lucky. The earl, in breeches and shirt borrowed from Allerby and stockinged feet, was just descending the staircase. He stopped midway and his eyes lit with relief at the sight of his sister and her abigail. "Jenny!" he called, taking the rest of the stairs at a run and catching the little duchess up in a great hug. "I have been out of mind with worry," he sighed into one shell-like ear. "Are you all right? Truly? Who was it took you? Where are Oakes and the others? Were they taken captive as well, or are they—dead? How did you escape?"

"I—we—oh, Josh, it was so frightening," murmured the duchess, hiding her face in the folds of his shirt. "I thought we should all be killed. Truly, I did. If it had not been for—for Francesco—I am sure that is exactly what would have happened."

Tynesbury met the earl's eyes over his sister's head. It never ceased to amaze her how talented was the duchess when it came to role-playing. Even she would have believed at the moment that they had all been captured and held for ransom.

"Are you well, Peggy?" the earl asked. "You were not harmed?"

"No, your lordship, we have all survived quite nicely, thank you. The Marquis di Roche proved a most happy rescuer."

"Di Roche?"

"Yes, m'lord."

"Oh, Joshie, he was so wonderful!" cried the beguiling little creature in his arms, peering up at him through misty blue eyes, "so brave and decisive!"

"Di Roche?" The earl looked searchingly into his sister's lovely face and then over her head at Tynesbury. "That fop?"

Peggy took a very deep breath, attempted to ignore the worried eyes that made her wish to tell him the truth and nodded. "Indeed, he came to our rescue in the very nick of time."

The story that trailed from his sister's and Tynesbury's lips as Wright settled them before the public room fire and urged brandy upon them to take away the chill while their trunks were taken above, resulted in a vague uneasiness of mind that he could not resolve. The sight of di Roche, who appeared in all his mud just as the duchess came to the end of her tale, brought a low growl and a shake of his tousled curls. He noted the ill-fitting clothes, though he did not recognize them as his own, and the weariness, and the odd way the marquis's eyes did not quite meet his own. "I believe, di Roche, that I owe you my gratitude," Wright mumbled, moving toward the man and offering his hand. "You are responsible for my sister's rescue, and Miss Tynesbury's as well. I thank you."

"*Si,* you welcome," Di Roche nodded, removing his gloves and shaking the earl's hand. "These I doing for so lovely ladies as best I can. Excusing me. I am all over the dirt, *signor.*"

"Yes, of course, but you shall join us for dinner and explain to me the details of this adventure, shall you not?"

Francesco nodded and then he left, wearily climbing the stairs to a chamber above.

Six

Dinner at Willowset piqued Eleanor's curiosity, from the turtle soup straight through to the last comfit. Over the turtle soup she determined that Mary, with her dusky hair swept into a Grecian knot and long curls brushing her clear, smooth cheeks, was one of the most beautiful women she had ever seen and pondered how such a one came to be secretary to the Earl of Wright. Perhaps her husband had been one of the earl's great friends and had died, leaving his wife penniless, and the earl had taken pity upon her? Eleanor gave her head a shake at the thought. Lord Wright? To do such a thing? Martin would have laughed the idea to scorn. Over the pheasant à la orange and the seared halibut and the new potatoes and the peas, which had been cooked in an excellent cream sauce, she noted that Mary's companion, Miss Lipton, with her short-cropped golden curls, her pert, upturned nose and wide blue eyes, and her perfect bow lips, was equally beautiful. But then, why would they not both be lovely? Lord Wright would not surround himself with ugly women or even ordinary-looking ones. He was so very handsome himself, he must certainly have his pick of all of the beauties of London, she thought drearily.

Mr. Paxton and Martin appeared extremely attracted to the visitors, and the conversation flowed around the table with good cheer. Miss Lipton's most expressive eyes fell often upon the Reverend Howard, who sat to her left, and Eleanor was surprised to notice a becoming blush rise to her brother's cheeks when Miss Lipton declared that he was the most learned and interesting gentleman she had ever met. "And to think," she sighed in her husky voice, "that you have buried yourself away in the country and deprived all of London of your great knowledge. And it is just like Lord Wright to keep you a secret. Do you never come to London, Reverend Howard?"

"Seldom, Miss Lipton. I have my flock to care for, you know. And since his grace was taken so suddenly from us, someone must care for the Willowset tenants."

"And you have accepted that responsibility?" asked Mary Hampton with a slight frown. "I would think looking after their souls responsibility enough. Is there no estate manager?"

"Well, yes, of course, Mrs. Hampton, but—"

"I think it is remarkably kind of you," inserted Miss Lipton, pouting prettily.

"Why, thank you, ma'am," replied Howard with the most idiotic look upon his face that Eleanor had ever seen. Mr. Paxton caught Miss Howard's eye and winked at her.

"Do not be distraught, Miss Howard," he whispered. "Miss Lipton has scaled higher walls than your brother and imprinted similar looks of idiocy upon equally unsuspecting brows."

Eleanor giggled and Mr. Paxton smiled. "That is much better," he said. "I was beginning to fear your eyebrows might grow together in that frown. Do you know that Mrs. Hampton is Wright's secretary? It caused quite a stir when it was first discovered. The *ton* believed her to be his mistress, you know, and the tale of a secretary merely a sham."

"But it was not a sham?"

"Not a bit of it. She is his secretary in every sense. She has even written some of his speeches for Lords."

The idea of Lord Wright speaking in the House of Lords had never occurred to Eleanor, and she turned the thought over curiously in her mind. What would such a man wish to say before what must be a most austere assemblage? And how would his words be accepted? Did his peers think of him as Martin did? She wondered if Mr. Paxton would know, if he had ever listened to one of the earl's speeches or perhaps read one of them. Thinking it unlikely, however, she asked instead about Mary. "Do you know, sir, what made the earl decide to hire a woman as secretary?"

"Well, Mrs. Hampton had a child to support and no hope of obtaining a suitable position, so Wright made one for her. He intended, I believe, to provide Mrs. Hampton with confidence in her abilities and to provide himself with the aid he required."

"But how did he know what her abilities were?"

"He asked, Miss Howard." Paxton grinned. "He asks people the most outrageous questions. You do not know him well, do you?"

"No, not at all. We have only just met, and my brother is not fond of him."

Paxton nodded. "You must not think Wright as black as your brother paints him, Miss Howard. That would be extremely unfair. But he does have an odd kick in his gallop."

Eleanor's eyes were drawn by husky laughter to Lily's lovely face, and she found the wide blue eyes staring at her. "You have the wittiest brother, Miss Howard," Lily smiled. "I shall wish for Lord Wright to be gone another day so that Reverend Howard and I might get to know each other better."

Eleanor's eyebrows rose as her brother glanced sheepishly from beneath lowered lids at the incredibly gorgeous blond with the hourglass figure that plumped to perfection in a low-cut, high-waisted gown of sapphire blue silk. Never before had Eleanor seen such a look on Martin's face. It puzzled her, because she could not grasp the significance of it. Paxton, however, had no such problem and welcomed the trays of comfits with a decidedly wicked gleam in his eyes. He had come to Willowset prepared for an endless round of arguments, but his chances of being merrily entertained instead were definitely improving. There was every appearance that Wright's mistress had decided to toss her cap at the unsuspecting Howard—a delightful notion. What a pity, Paxton thought gleefully, that Legion is not here to witness it.

Eleanor, however, was there to witness it and grew more and

more amazed. When the ladies withdrew from table the gentlemen turned down their port and joined them immediately. Miss Lipton settled herself at the pianoforte and Martin sat beside her to turn the pages as she played. Miss Lipton expressed a desire to view the gallery, and Martin volunteered to escort her. Upon their return, Miss Lipton wished to play a game of piquet—and Martin brought out the card table. And when Miss Lipton thought it must be very near time for tea Martin tugged the bellpull and requested it.

"But he disapproves of cards thoroughly," Eleanor said, perplexed, as she accompanied Mary Hampton to the nursery to say good night to the children. "He never plays at home and does not like me to play either."

Mary smiled and put her arm through Eleanor's as they ascended to the third floor. "You must not expect your brother to act normally in Lily's presence, Eleanor. She is a captivating minx and has a remarkable effect upon most gentlemen. But she is the kindest, sweetest person in the entire world and your brother is quite safe with her. She will do nothing to jeopardize her relationship with Josh."

"Her—relationship? Her friendship, you mean?"

"It is a good deal more than friendship," Mary smiled. "I expect I ought not to tell you. In fact, I know I ought not."

"Tell me what? Oh, how unfair, to make me curious and then to withdraw so quickly! Do you mean to say that Miss Lipton and Lord Wright are relatives?"

Mary's laughter was as enchanting as her countenance. "Oh," she said, catching her breath, "Josh will shoot me, but I feel I must tell you. You must promise not to tell your brother. Can you do that?"

"Well, of course I can," declared Eleanor, though she had never agreed to keep a secret from Martin before in her life. "I will not say a word to him."

"Lily is under Lord Wright's protection."

"Under his protection?"

"Oh, dear, you are an innocent, are you not? Almost as innocent as I once was. She is the earl's mistress, Eleanor, and has been for years."

Eleanor felt her cheeks flame and raised her hands to them, coming to an abrupt halt in the third-floor hallway. "His—his—mistress? Miss Lipton? But—but how could she come here and behave as if—as if—"

"She belonged? Quite easily. Josh has taught her to speak and act and present herself as a lady. She has been most everywhere in London with him—even to dine at Carlton House with the Prince Regent—and never once has anyone thought to turn her away or call him upon it, even though everyone knows he plucked her from the alleys of Covent Garden. So, of course, when I said I intended to visit him here but must have a traveling companion, Lily offered immediately. She has been here before, you know, and assumed she would be welcomed again, and, of course, were the earl in residence, she would have thought rightly. He would never turn her away, nor would Jenny. But I beg you will not tell your brother—for I think he might very well send her packing, and that would be cruel."

Eleanor's mind reeled. The enchanting Lily, Lord Wright's mistress? Oh, indeed, and why should she not have expected as much? She knew he would have an opera dancer or an actress or someone. And why not someone as charming and beautiful as Lily Lipton? And why should it matter to her at all? She had nothing to do with the man. Whatever he did, with whomever he did it, it was certainly no concern of hers.

But Eleanor's mind was not to be so easily mollified, as she discovered when she had kissed the little duke good night and made her way to her own chambers. She struggled out of her dress and into her nightgown without summoning the aid of the chambermaid who usually assisted her, and snuggled down under the feather ticking, hoping to fall directly to sleep. Instead, Wright's finely sculpted face appeared before her, his eyes filled with mirth as he dried the dishes in Mrs. Dish's kitchen and mentioned off-handedly that he supposed *her* father had never had an affair with the cook. Eleanor's eyes flew open and she glared at the ceiling. "Go away," she whispered. "You are a rake and a libertine and I am *not* supposed to think of you at all!" But when she closed her eyes again he reappeared, dressed in the wonderful white whipcord breeches, laughing silently down at her. "Oh!" she muttered, turning over and pulling the pillow over her head. "You are the most abominable person in the entire world! Do go away!"

"Now," murmured Wright, as he watched his sister and Miss Tynesbury safely up the stairs, his arm possessively around the marquis's shoulders, "you and I, di Roche, shall adjourn to the public room, shall we?" Not waiting for an answer, the earl strolled off, pulling di Roche along with him. "Oakes! Do not run off!" Wright called as they entered. "Sit back down, and Nelson, you will do likewise. Rack punch, Allerby. I dare say that will satisfy everyone. Where are Carson and Gregory?"

"Gone to bed, m'lord," muttered Oakes, "which is where I be bound."

"But not yet, Glenby. Sit."

Oakes and Nelson returned to the table where they and Gregory and Carson had dined. Wright and the marquis joined them. "So, Glenby, how's your arm? In much pain are you?" Wright stared at the sling made from the hem of Tynesbury's petticoat. "Ought to get a physician to look at that, and your head as well, Nelson. Allerby?" he asked as the landlord brought the punch and glasses to the table. "Dr. Syles still about, is he?"

"Aye, m'lord. I can send Toddy for him."

"No," groaned Oakes. "Nothin' but a sprain is all. Been gettin' better all along."

"Yes? And Nelson's head is sprained as well?" Wright's eyes fell on the footman, who twisted uncomfortably in his chair.

"Y-yes, sir, m'lord. I m-mean, no, sir. Hit on the head, I was. Knocked unconscious. The duchess was kind enough to bind it up for me, m'lord."

"And Gregory? Does he bear the scars of battle as well?"

"Aye, an' Carson. Gone up ta bed they are."

"Yes, so you have told me, Oakes. And they, I expect, do not desire a physician's services either?"

"We 'ad two weeks or there 'bouts ta heal, m'lord. There ain't a one o' us took bad from it. Jus' a bit sore is all."

"I am surprised you could drive the duchess here, Glenby, with your arm bound up like that." Wright's eyes glittered ominously in the firelight. The silver specks floating on irises so blue as to be black sent a series of apprehensive shivers down Oakes's back. "Tell me, Glenby, how came you to be ambushed?" A hand quickly raised silenced the marquis, his anxious words dying on his lips. "I have heard your version and Jenny's, di Roche. Now I should like to hear Oakes's. I never thought you a bufflehead, Glenby. Had you no warning? Certainly one out of the four of you must have had an inkling of their approach. What? Had no one thought to load the weapons? Were any shots at all fired? Come, Glenby," murmured the earl, grinding lemon rinds into the punch and smiling coldly, "enlighten me. How many villains did it take to conquer four of Ware's finest men?" The earl filled the cups and passed them around the table.

"These is most embarrassing, no?" asked the marquis hesitantly. "But I am seeing as these thing it happens and they are all of thems most brave in defending the most beautiful Jenny and the Miss Tynesburries."

The corners of Wright's mouth quivered. "Ah, you were there at the start, then, di Roche? You did not tell me that. I assumed you came upon the scene only after these fine gentlemen had been vanquished. Tell me, Oakes, how it happened. I suspect you sprang the horses in an attempt to outrun the villains. Where did they overtake you? How many of them were there? Did you recognize any of them?" Wright's gaze pinned the unhappy coachman to his chair.

Glenby Oakes squirmed. He opened his mouth, then closed it again. He stretched out his legs beneath the table. He looked at Wright and then at di Roche, then back at Wright again. "I reckon as I don't 'member the whole o' it, m'lord. That upset I was over the thing. Took us on the Blacklow Heath, they did, an' forced us past St. Swithin's. Near ten of 'em, I reckon. Masked."

"Masked, Glenby? For two whole weeks? Surely you saw one face in that time. And where, by the way, were you held?"

Oakes's eyes glanced quickly toward di Roche. At least he had the correct answer to that one. "At the mill, m'lord, in the Miller's Wood."

Wright's eyebrow cocked. "So Jenny informed me. Bound and gagged the four of you, and she and Tynesbury locked in the upper room, and the marquis here at wit's end, puzzling over how to save the lot of you. So puzzled, in fact, it took him two whole weeks to bring the thing about. Never once thought to inform a constable of the situation. Never thought to come and tell me about it either. Odd, don't you think?"

"Aye, but who's ta tell how furriners does things, m'lord? Likely as 'e don't know nothin' 'bout constables. An' jus' as likely 'e feared ta leave us and ride all the way ta London ta git ye."

"Odd, too," mused Wright, pouring himself a second glass of rack punch, "that Mr. and Mrs. Simon should let on they were expecting company at the Rise at precisely the time you were abducted. Even Allerby came by the news that the Simons were preparing for visitors. You don't think, do you, Glenby, that Casper Simon and his wife were in league with the villains?"

Oakes's wide eyes blinked spastically. "Never!" he declared. "Not Casper, m'lord. Why, he's been lookin' after the Rise since before I ever knew ye. Why, he'd die ta pertect ye, m'lord. Ye know that!"

"Yes, well, I thought I did, Glenby; but then, I have been wrong before," murmured Wright, allowing his gaze to roam away from the man, staring instead at the hearth across the room. "It never occurred to me, you know, that your loyalties could be called into question either—or Nelson's, for that matter."

Oakes straightened in his chair. Nelson gasped. Di Roche's high, classical brow furrowed in bewilderment. "You things these ones betrayaled you? These is great insultment!"

"Do you know," Wright mused, ignoring all of their reactions and gazing steadily into the fire, "I have been giving it a good deal of thought, and it appears to me that a goodly portion of the details in this tale are confused. Were not the coachman and the outriders killed and the young lady and her companion whisked off to a mill on the Rhine? And the companion, I believe, was stabbed through the heart in defense of her charge's virtue. Yes, I am sure of it, though I am equally certain that Tynesbury's heart beat as steadily as ever at dinner. And the villain, Manfred something or other, was not his mind set upon destroying the young lady's lover?"

Oakes's mouth fell open. Nelson groaned. Di Roche's eyes blinked twice and his nose twitched nervously.

"What, di Roche? Do you not think that Englishmen read such hogwash from time to time? Gothic novels run rampant upon our shores, I assure you. Even I have not managed to avoid *The Abduction*. Jenny abandoned it in my townhouse and I read the thing. Your fearless rescue of my sister is almost word-for-word Valdarian's rescue of Ophelia. Come, Glenby," Wright added, his attention returning to the coachman, "I didn't mean to insult you or Nelson. I admire your loyalty to Jenny. But now you will humor me, will you not? You ain't hurt, Glenby. Take your arm from that confounded sling and open the door to the courtyard."

"M'lord?"

"The marquis, Glenby, is leaving us."

Di Roche opened his mouth to protest that he had not the least intention of leaving the shelter of the inn, but before he could utter a sound Wright seized him by the back of his coat collar and stood the astounded marquis upon his feet. Kicking a series of chairs out of his way, the earl marched di Roche—

the little Italian barely managing to touch his toes to the floor—
directly across the lobby to the front entrance.

"But m'lord," Oakes protested, hurriedly disentangling his
arm from the sling, "you don't want ta do that!"

"I don't?" the earl purred softly, giving the protesting marquis several quick shakes to silence him. "Why don't I, Oakes?
Enlighten me."

"Because those clothes he's wearin' are yours, m'lord," Nelson provided. "And if you toss him out into that courtyard, it's
your own wardrobe you'll be destroying."

"Exactly!" agreed Oakes thankfully, because for the life of
him, he hadn't been able to think of one reason why the earl
should not sling the little furriner out into the mud.

"There now," sighed Wright, "I thought there was something
familiar about the gentleman's over-large kit. Well, you are
right, Oakes, after all. I don't want to toss the little bastard out
into the courtyard—not in my gear, I don't. You will have to
take it off, di Roche."

"C-como?" stuttered the marquis, his teeth rattling as Wright
shook him once more and then with a quick shove sent him
wheeling spastically against the door.

"I said, you will have to take it off," drawled Wright, the
blade of a small dagger suddenly glittering in his palm. "Now."

"I—I—but, *signor,* ees not—"

"Nelson will help you, won't you, Neville? It's no wonder
nothing fits him. I wondered how such a strange fashion had
caught on—but then I thought, Italy, you know, and was prone
to accept it."

The blade of the dagger waved languidly beneath the marquis's startled eyes as Wright's right hand began to untie the
nondescript knot that held di Roche's neckcloth tidily in place.
Nelson, not unacquainted with the languorous tone of the earl's
voice and the seeming lethargy behind the partially lowered
eyelids and the bored drawl, rushed to the marquis, spun him
from against the door and jerked the coat off the gentleman.

"The waistcoat as well, di Roche," droned the earl, unbuttoning the waistcoat buttons with one hand and then undoing di Roche's shirtfront. "And now the boots and breeches."

"*Santa Maria!*" di Roche muttered, fumbling with the buttons of his breeches as the dagger tickled beneath his chin.

"I doubt that *Santa Maria* will be interested," Wright sighed. "You have, I'm afraid, played a game with my sister of which I cannot approve, and not one of all the saints in heaven will venture down to assist you. The small clothes."

"Oh, no, m'lord," whispered Nelson, tugging off one of di Roche's boots as the man balanced precariously on the other, still fumbling with his breeches.

"No?" Wright asked. "Why not, Nelson? They are mine as well, are they not?"

"Yes, m'lord, but—but—"

"But if ye strip the gen'leman buck naked," provided Oakes, with a sense of triumph in his own ingenuity, "you won't have nothin' to hold on to so you can fling 'im out the door proper like."

"Indeed." Wright nodded, the corner of his lip quivering. "Quite right, Glenby. I hadn't thought of that. Leave the small clothes then."

Di Roche, his face growing ashen as the blade fell from beneath his chin to draw a fine, invisible line toward more vital regions, struggled quickly to refasten the too-large breeches, tripping as he did so directly into the earl, who caught him with one hand, spun him around and, ordering Oakes to open the damnable door, flung the terrified young nobleman out into the night so hard that he missed the boarded porch completely and landed with a wet, sucking smack in the courtyard muck.

"You may close the door now, Oakes. I believe the entertainment is over for this evening."

"Yes, m'lord." The coachman grinned, shoving the door shut.

"And wipe that grin from your face, Glenby. You and the others are not out of the brambles yet. Harry Cross and I have ridden through storms, slept with the cattle and been doused with globs of muck, all the while imagining the lot of you at the mercy of highwaymen. I want the truth of it, and I want it now." Shepherding Nelson and Oakes back to the table and the rack punch, the earl spent another hour listening to their explanations and questioning them until he was satisfied he had achieved a full view of the incident. "I shall be forced to confront Jenny over it, I expect," he sighed over his fifth glass of punch. He leaned his chair back against the wall, put his feet up on the table and sighed again. Oakes and Nelson, watching the peculiar eyes close wearily, suggested that perhaps his lordship ought to seek his bed. Wright sought another glass of punch instead, dismissing the two of them with a listless wave of his hand. He sat alone in the public room, watching the fire die and the embers dissolve into ash.

What he would say to Jenny he could not imagine, but it must be something to the point so she would never agree to such an escapade again. Still, it was not her fault, he told himself sullenly. She could not help that she had hatched out a wet goose. Beautiful, yes, and charming, and gentle, but birdwitted? Lord, he had never met a chit as birdwitted as his sister! If only, he thought wistfully, the Good Lord had seen fit to give him a sibling with even half a mind—but no, he could not have been that lucky. He was never lucky. People like Martin Howard had all the luck. Why the deuce did Howard deserve to have a sister like Eleanor? That stiff-rumped, self-righteous, overbearing prig had everything!

Wright downed the rest of the punch and closed his eyes, envisioning Miss Howard in the soggy white apron. He saw her eyes, wide and apprehensive as she had rushed into the Willowset library at Howard's call and again, glowing golden with laughter in Mrs. Dish's kitchen. Miss Howard had an inquiring, if innocent, mind. She could hold a decent conversation and understand a man's ideas. A man could say things to a sister like that, he mused, without having to plan them out word-for-word. Then he gave himself a mental kick, put his feet upon the floor and, standing, placed his empty glass upon the table. Obviously di Roche was not planning to confront him over his treatment tonight, else he'd have stormed back inside by now. He supposed he might as well retire. He was foxed anyway, he thought, noticing that the public room had developed a distinct tilt downward and to the left, which made strolling toward the stairs a bit of a problem. He would strive to be in a better humor in the morning before he spoke to Jenny. He could certainly not face her as blue-deviled as he was at the moment.

Wright had never been able to bear the slight quivering of his sister's lower lip, the slow fade of color from the bright blue eyes, the delicate little hand that fluttered to her breast— all of which always preceded her collapse into tears at having displeased him. He had, therefore, frequently overlooked her lapses from propriety, her tendency to be drawn in by every hoax that came her way, and even her wide-eyed romantical notions. He damned his late brother-in-law for dying as he threw himself fully dressed upon the alien bed, and in the last seconds before he lost consciousness saw, as he always did, his mother falling from the tower window at the Rise. He shuddered, inhaled stertorously, and then passed out.

The Marquis di Roche, whom Allerby had smuggled back into the inn through the kitchen door, sat wrapped in blankets by the kitchen fire, his eyes pinned upon the door to the lobby. He sipped at a cup of tea and shivered. The innkeeper had gone to be sure the way to the marquis's room, a hot bath and a warm bed was clear. "He's drunk himself into oblivion," drawled Allerby, returning to stand before his much abused guest. "Won't be no bother to ye for the rest o' the night. Ye are not planning upon murdering the lad in his bed, are ye? 'Cause if ye are, I ought to warn ye that Harry Cross sleeps in the adjoining chamber an' will come to his aid at the first sound of an altercation, as will I an' every other Yorkshireman in the establishment."

Di Roche looked up from beneath long, light lashes and then shook his head. "These thing I would not doing, *signor,* to my beloved's most foul-headed brother."

"Good, 'cause one of us, he is, born and bred. Knowed him since he was a babe. What was it ye done to set him off? Do ye even know?"

Di Roche nodded wearily.

"Ye ain't figuring on challenging him to a duel? 'Cause if that be the case, I ought to warn ye that he's killed his man three times I know of—though we covered it up like. The world be well rid o' the scum he done away with, too, which made us all feel better like for not reportin' it."

"To duel with these one I am not so mad," muttered di Roche. "Besides which do I killing him, the most beautiful Jenny forgives me never."

"Well, that's true enough," agreed Allerby. "In love with the little duchess, are ye?"

Di Roche nodded. "Ees most dangerous thing to be, no?"

Seven

The storms that had raged over the north country earlier in the week were as nothing to the storm that confronted the Earl of Wright at breakfast the next morning and continued to break over him at odd moments during the entire journey back to Willowset. Tynesbury did her best to reassure Jenny that the Marquis di Roche stood in no danger from her brother's sword, that Wright had no intention of shooting the man and that di Roche was not going to succumb to an inflammation of the lungs because of the earl's ill-treatment.

But Jenny could not be reassured completely. Each time they stopped for refreshment, her pretty lower lip would begin to quiver and the color fade from the enormous blue eyes. A single tear would begin its crystalline descent down one feverishly pink cheek. These were merely the rising winds signaling the approach of the thunder and lightning and heavy rain on the horizon, and Wright read the warnings well, sending out innkeepers with ratafia and biscuits for the ladies and keeping out of sight himself until the teams had been changed and the journey once again commenced. Still, when he did appear to ride beside the coach, Jenny's wistful little sobs echoed in his ears, and at the sight of him she would burst into wails of agony. Truly, he longed to take her into his arms and assure her that she had done him no disservice—that he had been pleased to worry himself to distraction over her whereabouts, to ride night and day soaked to the skin, covered in mud and smelling of horse in the grim hope of finding her alive, that he condoned the plan she and the marquis had hatched between them, and that he was not in the least opposed to their making a match of it. But even Wright was not so good a liar as all that, so he suffered the lightning and thunder and cloudbursts of his sister's emotional storms in silence.

Once or twice he glimpsed the sympathetic smile that Tynesbury aimed in his direction and was grateful for it, but most of the time he rode out the storms feeling alone and powerless and a great bully into the bargain. He let down the coach steps himself before Willowset and offered his arm to Jenny with all the appearance of an ordinary gentleman returning from town with his sister.

Their appearance brought Burton running to the front door, relief for the duchess obvious on his face. "Reverend Howard, Miss Howard, Mr. Paxton, Mrs. Hampton, and Miss Lipton have just sat down to dinner, your grace, your lordship. Shall you wish to join them?"

Wright, taken aback at the list of names, gave a curt shake of his head. "The duchess is exhausted, Burton, as am I. We shall dine in our chambers once we have divested ourselves of this dirt. Is Jessie asleep?"

"No, your lordship. Nursery hours have been moved back since the little miss came to visit. I believe Bowey is even now in the midst of a bedtime story."

"Joyce is here?"

"Indeed, my lord."

"Well, we will go straight up to the nursery, eh, Jenny? Give the children a hug and assure them we are home safely?"

The Earl of Wright, cleaned and dressed very properly in white knee breeches and a wine red velvet coat, entered the drawing room long after dinner, but only minutes after the tea tray that evening. His extraordinary eyes appraised the company in silence. Howard was in the midst of carrying a steaming cup of tea to Lily; Paxton was seated comfortably beside

Mrs. Hampton on the small silver brocade sofa; and Eleanor was poised regally upon the gold divan pouring out. "Might I have a cup as well, Miss Howard?" he asked softly, immediately gaining everyone's attention. "Paxton," he drawled, with a curt nod in that gentleman's direction. "Howard," he added, acknowledging the reverend's presence as well. "You will both be pleased to know that the Duchess of Ware has returned safely and is snug in her own bed. Mary," he added with what Eleanor, studying very closely the planes of his face, thought to be lines of worry creasing his brow, "I am amazed to see you. You will join me later in the library, will you not? We shall indulge in a bit of conversation." He strolled forward, accepted the cup Eleanor held out to him and smiled down at her. "How good of you, Miss Howard, to assume the role of hostess in my sister's absence."

Eleanor opened her lips to assure him that she had not the least intention of usurping the duchess's role, but his hand brushed hers as he accepted the teacup and one long, delicate finger stroked the inside of her wrist very intentionally. The silver specks that lit his eyes floated upon a sea of silent laughter. "Do not look so frightened, goose," he murmured as he settled himself on the divan beside her. "I am pleased you assumed the responsibility since there was no one else to do so. Lily, what brings you to Willowset?"

"Mary could not travel without a companion. It would have been most exceptional, especially since she must stay overnight at an inn."

"Some people, Wright, have a concern for propriety," declared Howard.

"Indeed."

"But how is the duchess?" Eleanor asked quickly, sensing a sermon upon her brother's lips. "She was not harmed?"

"No one came to any harm."

"You know who abducted her, Wright?" Paxton queried with a sidelong glance at Mary.

"Yes, as a matter of fact, but it is over and done with. Let it lie, Paxton. It will not occur again."

There was such deadly finality in his tone that Eleanor's imagination quickly provided her visions of villains hanging by their thumbs from tree limbs and lying headless upon the ground. Involuntarily she gave a little gulp.

Wright grinned. He wondered what Miss Howard had envisioned just then to bring about that little sound. She is, he thought, fighting to keep his hand from patting the young lady's knee reassuringly, the most innocent little chit. Gazing down upon her, he found an odd lump beginning to form in his throat, and promptly drank down the remainder of his tea. The lump did not diminish and he concluded he was due for a putrid sore throat thanks to the horrendous conditions under which he had ridden the past week. The mere thought of falling ill at this juncture made him sigh and brought Miss Howard's lovely eyes upon him, lit with compassion. "You are exhausted, my lord. It is thoughtless of us to keep you from your bed."

"Indeed," agreed Paxton. "Go up, Wright. Do not stand upon ceremony with us. We shall go on quite well without you."

"As you have been doing in my absence? But then, you are planning to go up yourselves shortly, are you not?" Receiving a nod from Paxton and Mary as well, he set his cup back upon the tea tray and stood. "Then, if you will forgive me, I rather think I will take Miss Howard's advice and retire. Mary? Will you spend a moment with me in the library?"

Mrs. Hampton took the arm he offered and the two departed in silence, Mary's apricot satin gown swishing down the long hallway. As soon as the library door closed behind them, Mary's palm went to the back of the earl's neck and settled for a moment among the dark curls. "You are feverish," she declared. "Does your head ache? You must send Tibbs to fetch some powders from the still room. I am sure Mrs. Hornby has something there will do you good."

"Enough, vixen," Wright growled playfully, removing the hand and tugging her to an armchair before the hearth. "Sit and tell me what brought you to Willowset. Does your aunt know you have come? Have you taken Joyce to see her?"

"N-no. I thought to find you here, Jocelyn, and when I did not, I could not think but it might be unwise to visit Aunt Euphegenia without you. I had a letter two days after you left London—from Arthur." She looked up at him where he stood solemnly, his arm resting along the mantelpiece. "I know it was f-foolish of me to become so upset, but—oh, Josh, he frightens me so!"

"Did you bring the letter?"

"Upstairs."

"What does he say?"

"He threatens you and claims he will see you dead and says he will have his property returned to him without delay—me, he means. But it is all so disjointed and unreasoning."

"I should have killed him and had done with it," muttered the earl, running the fingers of one hand through his curls. "So, he is back. Will he come to St. Swithin's?"

"I have not the least idea. I have warned the staff in London not to betray our whereabouts—simply to say you and I are both from town."

Wright slumped into a chair beside her and stared into the blaze that sizzled and hissed and puffed smoke as a draft fought its way down the chimney. "I think we must expect him regardless, Mary. Hampton Hall is not far from here, and we cannot depend upon his having forgotten your aunt lives in St. Swithin's and my sister nearby."

"I am sorry to be such a bother," Mary sighed. "I have done nothing but cut up your peace from the very moment we met."

"True," Wright laughed, his eyes lighting with amusement. "Cut up my peace; cut up my draperies; cut up my house."

"Well, but I could not stand those draperies, and I did not wish to make your entire house into a nursery," Mary giggled, her worried frown disappearing for a moment. "And do not forget that we also cut up your sheets to make Joycie's first nappies."

"Oh, I have not forgotten." Wright chuckled, covering her hand with his own. "We were inept, were we not?"

"Had your servants not returned when they did, we should have been in very deep waters."

"Do not be afraid, Mary," Wright murmured. "Hampton will not harm you or Joyce, I promise you. And if he has the audacity to take up residence at Hampton Hall, I shall cut up *his* peace no end. There is some excellent cognac on the second shelf there," he added, pointing. "Will you join me in a glass?"

"No, and I shall not pour you one either. You are beginning to look distinctly unwell, Jocelyn. Let us go up to bed."

Wright raised an inquiring eyebrow and she laughed. "No, my dear. I meant that I shall go to my bed and you shall go to yours, as you very well know."

"And it has ever been so," drawled the earl with a forlorn shake of his head, which made her giggle.

Eleanor had already slipped into her nightdress when she heard the door to Mary's chamber open and close across the way. She wondered if the earl had, indeed, been able to put the young lady's fears to rest. Though Mary had not made any further reference to the tears she had cried that first night, Eleanor was certain that whatever had caused them had been the object of the private discussion in the library. Martin, of course, had been all for following the pair and demanding he be allowed to chaperon—and he would have done so, too, if Mr. Paxton and Miss Lipton had not both succumbed to hilarity the moment he voiced the thought.

A soft scratching at her sitting room door interrupted Eleanor's musings.

She climbed down from the high old four-poster, drew her wrapper around her and hurried into her slippers. She opened the door and stepped back agog to discover instead the Earl of Wright leaning against her door frame. "May I have a word with you, Miss Howard?" he drawled languidly, his eyes roaming over her in what she felt to be a most unnerving fashion.

"It is the middle of the night!"

"Well, no, actually it is merely eleven."

"But I am not—most certainly even you must know a gentleman does not—oh! Go away."

"I did not come to ravish you, m'dear, if that is what you're thinking."

His dark, sparkling eyes seized her own and held them, and they stood speechless for what seemed an eternity. Eleanor felt her heart leap in her breast, and it pounded so loudly that she thought surely it must echo all the way down the corridor. She knew at last that she must tear her gaze from his or sink down into his very soul. "Please," she gasped, a maddening warmth rushing over her.

"What a shy little mouse you are," he whispered, raising one hand and tucking a stray wisp of hair behind her ear with two amazingly gentle fingers. "I do not wish to come into your chamber, Miss Howard, only to beg you will not leave us now I am returned. Word among the staff has it that you intend to accompany your brother back to the vicarage first thing tomorrow."

"Y-yes—there is no reason for us to remain now that you and the duchess are in residence."

"No reason for Howard to remain, no. But I have mucked things up so badly that Jenny cannot speak to me. She is in dire need of someone with good sense, and Mary has too much upon her mind at the moment to fill that position. Lily might, but she is likely not sensible enough. And Tynesbury, upon whom I may usually depend without fail, has come home to word that her sister is gravely ill, and so she must depart again in the morning. If I can convince you to remain and give my sister some sound advice about—about the situation in which she finds herself—I shall invite your brother to stay a few more days. I won't be pleased to do it. Still, I cannot expect him to go merrily off and leave you in the clutches of a looney and a lawyer. That would be wishing for the impossible, would it not?"

His eyes overflowed with a quiet mirth, and the corners of Eleanor's mouth rose upward in response.

"Good girl," he murmured. "I knew you would see clear to help. I have been cruel to Jenny, you know. That is why she breaks into tears at sight of me and then cannot speak. If you will only venture to talk sensibly to her and hear her out and give her your advice, I shall be extremely grateful."

His eyes at last freed her, and Eleanor, feeling her pulses throbbing in her wrists and at her throat and even in her ears, took one small step farther back into the room. "I—I shall do my best, my lord," she said, stuttering only once.

"Thank you, Miss Howard. You cannot imagine how much I appreciate your generosity. Good night, then, my dear, and may your dreams be—exciting."

Eleanor looked up, startled. "Exciting?"

He winked at her and wandered off down the corridor in the direction of the south wing where, Eleanor had learned, his sister and brother-in-law had provided him with his own set of chambers, including besides a bedchamber and sitting room, a study, a library and a private dining room, and a chamber that housed a varied collection of musical instruments, some dating as far back as the fourteenth century and come from as far away as Calcutta and Asia Minor and the hinterlands of Greece. Mr. Paxton had told her this and even offered to escort her to see them if she liked. And she would indeed have liked, but Martin had frowned at her in such a way that she knew she should not accept, and so she had forfeited her opportunity.

Tibbs was even now rushing, arms filled with clothes, from one wing of the house to the other. His attempt, however, to arrive in the chambers of the south wing ahead of his master failed entirely as Wright met him at the French doors that opened onto the sitting room and took the apparel from him. "Forgot, did you, Tibbs? I expect I should have mentioned it while I was dressing to go down to tea."

"No, your lordship. Certainly I should have known you would not wish to reside in the main building once her grace had returned, and especially not now Mrs. Hampton and Miss Lipton have arrived. I was not thinking."

"You are always thinking, Tibbs." The earl laid the articles of clothing upon the great oak bed and began to put them away one by one. Tibbs, watching a linen shirt crumpled into the clothes press and a marvel of a riding coat shoved in atop it, hesitated only momentarily before relieving his master of the breeches he had plucked nonchalantly from the quilt. "I admit," chuckled the earl, "that I do not stow them precisely as you would deem proper, Tibbs, but I am only attempting to help."

"You would be more help, my lord, if you'd settle into one of them chairs in the study with a good book upon your lap."

"You have been saying that same thing, Tibbs, for the last twenty years."

"And it has been true for the last twenty years."

"Perhaps," the earl grinned. "But I don't feel much like reading tonight. Can you not just move the rest of my gear in the morning? I am wretchedly tired, Tibbs, and have not much patience for all this nonsense."

Tibbs, his nose twitching much like a hound upon the fox's scent, came to a halt with his hands upon his hips and stared up into the earl's face. "I expect you do not require any brandy be poured either, my lord?"

"Well, no—not really. Why? Would you like some, Tibbs?"

"I would not. Turn about and let me free you from this coat. You're feeling badly, aren't you?"

"No, Tibbs, I am not. I am tired is all."

"Yes, and caught a chill or something more dreadful from sleeping in stables and wearing shirts covered with horse."

Wright laughed. "Been talking to Harry Cross, have you?"

"And rightly so—I never heard such nonsense as he told me." Tibbs hung the coat in the clothespress and deftly continued to undress his charge as though he were still ten and only half awake. "Riding through acres of mud and sleeping in barns and never once being truly dry or eating a decent meal until you reached the inn at John's Glen. A travesty, I call it."

"Harry Cross has an enormous mouth," muttered Wright. "Did he tell you everything?"

Tibbs, coming to a halt before the beautifully lacquered chest of drawers, smiled contentedly. "Yes," he murmured. "Everything. Even what you did to the little marquis, though it was Glenby Oakes told Harry Cross about that because Harry had missed it, you know."

"Well, do not scold me now, Tibbs. I shall meet your wrath in the morning, eh?" Wright, naked, slipped between the sheets and was asleep before Tibbs had hung up his breeches. Which is why he was so thoroughly groggy five minutes after Tibbs departed when Lily, in a dressing gown of rose silk and little else, stole quietly into his bedchamber, climbed upon the bed and nibbled vexingly at his ear. He was not, however, so groggy as not to recognize the identity of the vixen beside him, and he stared up at her wearily. "What?" he groaned, blinking slowly. "Lily, you cannot possibly think I am in the mood for mischief tonight."

"Grumpy-grouch." The beauty smiled. "Are you suddenly become an old sober-sides?"

"No, Lily, I am suddenly become exhausted."

"Well, and no wonder, traipsing off all over the country. I shan't keep you long, Josh. I promise. I only wish to ask you something."

Wright groaned again, rolled over and punched his pillow into some degree of sturdiness and slapped it up against the headboard. Struggling a bit, he then maneuvered himself into a semiupright position. Lily snuggled into his waiting arms and he held her lazily, bestowing a chaste kiss upon her brow. "What is it, Lilliputian?" he asked.

"You will think I'm silly."

"I already think you're silly. What do you need to know so much that you think nothing of disturbing my sleep?"

"It is about—about—Mr. Reverend Howard."

"Reverend Mr. Howard."

"Reverend Mr. Howard. Are you certain that is correct? It does not sound so."

"Take my word, Lily. What about him?"

"He thinks I am a gentlewoman."

"I have gone to great lengths to teach you to be a gentlewoman."

"Yes, but, Josh, he thinks I am a *real* gentlewoman, and he wishes to drive me about the neighborhood and show me his church and his vicarage—with Miss Howard as chaperon."

"So, minx?"

"Well, but, if I accept his invitation, he will take it as a sign of encouragement."

"Encouragement? Lily, are you telling me that Howard is—interested—in you?"

The little blond head nodded. "I th-think so, Josh. At first I set out only to flatter him. He is very handsome, you know. But he pays me a great deal of attention and wishes to know my thoughts on everything, and—and—"

"And what, Lily?"

"And he has asked if—if my heart is free."

Wright chuckled. "If your heart is free? How very proper."

"He is very proper, Josh," she said, looking up at him with large, awe-filled eyes, "and so serious. He is not at all like any of your other friends."

"That, my dear, is because he is not my friend."

"But I thought—well, I won't accept his invitation then."

"Lily," the earl yawned, tightening his arms around her and planting a kiss upon one shell-like ear, "do you wish to go driving about the neighborhood with that—with Howard? Tell the truth. I will know if you tell me a bouncer."

"Y-yes, I would like to, but not if you do not wish it."

"Lilliputian, are you—has Howard—" The earl made a sound somewhere between a sigh and a chuckle and began again. "Are you falling in love with Martin Howard, Lily?"

"I have not the least idea," replied the husky voice thoughtfully. "I have never been in love. Have you, Josh?"

"No, not since I was eleven or so. I think, dear heart, that you had best go driving with him. It can't hurt, Lily."

"And you will not be angry?"

"Not at all, my dear. In fact—would you like me to go with you? I shall give Howard the loan of my curricle, and Miss Howard and I shall ride beside you. That, I think, will suit his notions of propriety and save Miss Howard from playing the role of spinster sister."

"Oh, yes, Josh," cried the lovely Lily with a clap of her hands. "It would be ever so much fun!"

"Indeed. Now slip off to your own bed, woman, and let me have some peace."

The earl's peace, however, was long in coming. He attempted, with the pillow over his head, not to imagine what had occurred between Howard and Lily in his absence, but images of the two of them filled his mind and set him to laughing. He clumped up the pillow, threw it across the room and flopped flat on his back, only to have Miss Howard's shy little face peer down at him from the dark ceiling. He rolled on his side and stared into the grate, where the fire had long ceased blazing and now merely winked at him through the ash, and saw Mary's beautiful brow furrowed with suppressed fear. He pulled the covers up over his head and sighed and thought finally he had found peace—when his sister's lips came to tremble before him and he could not help but see the tears glistening in her eyes. Cursing, he stumbled from the bed, retrieved his pillow and flopped back between the sheets onto his stomach, only to be visited by memories of an excited Joyce launching herself into his arms in the nursery. "Devil!" he mumbled. "Women everywhere! I may as well be headmaster at Longley's Academy for Young Ladies!"

Eight

Arturo Francesco Luciano Tivoli, Marquis di Roche, sighed with relief as he wiggled under the covers of his bed at the Gander's Neck. He was clean; he was warm; he was comfortable; and his own clothes were close to hand, as was his man, Nicco. The long ride over rough roads in a ragtag conglomeration of borrowed clothing he set aside as something to be laughed over with his beloved when they had grown old. It never occurred to the little marquis to doubt that he and his beloved would marry. Their love, he knew, was destined to survive even so great and dangerous a peril as the Earl of Wright. His eyes were slowly closing, his handsome face resplendent in repose, when the door to his chamber burst open and Nicco skidded to a stop beside his bed. A wild string of Italian burst into the space between them, causing Francesco to sit straight up and stare unbelievingly at his valet. "Inglese," the marquis mumbled distractedly—not forgetting his desire that his most trusted servant should understand and converse in the language they would adopt as their own because Jenny did not speak or understand one word of Italian. "These person, he below remaining still?"

Nicco nodded excitedly, his robust stomach bouncing with excitement.

"And you being certain what he saying to other gentleman?"

Nicco nodded again.

"Then must I to the down-the-stairs going, Nicco, and you with me. Ees my duty to protecting my Jenny's brother!"

It took Francesco less than ten minutes to dress and descend the staircase and hurry into the public room, Nicco on his heels. His classically handsome face assumed a pleasant demeanor as Nicco murmured in Italian that the man they sought was seated in an armchair before the hearth. The marquis took the armchair which sat directly beside his quarry and settled into it with a happy sigh. "Ees good to being warm again. You allow I interduce to you myself, *signor?* Arturo Francesco Luciano Tivoli, Marquis di Roche."

"Hampton," the gentleman responded.

"You will drinking with me, *Signor* Ham'ton? Nicco, go. Fetch for me these thin' the landslord calling hees con-cock-tion. Ees most wonderful drink, *signor,* much like in my homeland."

Hampton studied the little foreigner. "What brings you to England, di Roche? And to such a dismal part of it?"

"Ees necessarily I coming." Di Roche shrugged, crossing one leg over the other and fiddling off-handedly with his cravat. "Ees a private matter being. Ees business. Ah! Nicco comes!"

Nicco did indeed come, carrying a pitcher filled with a clear liquid and two glasses. Setting the tray on the small, round table between the two gentlemen, he bowed and took himself off to a back table and a glass of ale. Di Roche, grinning, filled both glasses to the brim, gave one to Hampton and sipped at the other speculatively. Declaring it to be "most excelling," he took a long swallow and snuggled deeper into the chair. Hampton sipped tentatively, grinned and took a larger gulp. "Damned if it ain't Blue Ruin." He chuckled. "This reminds you of a drink from your homeland?"

"Indeed, *signor,* ees much as my papa making upon his own fires."

Hampton blinked uncomprehendingly, then shrugged and took another swallow. He had a strong liking for gin. This particular stuff had been mixed with something else, but his palate could not distinguish the ingredients. He would need to ask old Crenshaw about it. Between them, di Roche and Hampton whiled away the time and the gin over a lazy conversation of sailing vessels, English roads and English weather. When the first pitcher had been emptied Nicco appeared instantly with a second. It was midway through that one that di Roche judged Hampton to be thoroughly foxed. He, himself, was a bit tipsy, but he had learned to drink well and with grace early in life and was not near as disguised as his quarry. "I am to you the lie giving." He sighed dramatically, raising his forearm to his brow in a gesture of remorse. "I am to these place coming not for business, but for revenge."

Hampton's eyes narrowed. "You don't say?"

"Yes, I do saying. I coming to revenge upon a devil be. These devil, he killing my brother—my—" The marquis, who was an only child, found himself stuck for a brother's name but recovered nicely by seizing a hero from one of his favorite romances. "—my Umberto. Ees shooting with the pistol."

"The man who did this is here?"

"I following from London. Ees at a place—Willow sets. Ees coming to keel him, me."

"What? Willowset? Not Wright? You ain't come here to kill the Earl of Wright?" Hampton's rugged countenance creased in dissipated laughter.

"Shhh," warned di Roche, wagging a finger before his lips. "Ees being called Legion these one, yes?"

"Aye," Hampton chuckled. "Wright is the one they call Legion. I'll be damned!"

"Why?"

"Because I have a great yearning to kill Wright myself. You have not challenged him to a duel, have you?"

"No. I am not yet meeting these devil."

"Well, don't. He'll pick you up in one hand and run you through with a butter knife before you finish speakin'."

"These likewise is opinion of all I asking about these man. Ees why, when Nicco telling me of you, I coming back the stairs down. My Nicco, he overhearing you and other gentleman, and to me he rushing to tell all."

Hampton's drunken gaze cleared for a moment and he began to stand, but the marquis simply leaned forward and patted the gentleman's knee. "Ees not to worrying. Ees to helping each other, I theenk we should, *signor.* I wishing to offer you my own assistance."

Hampton, stunned, not only that his hiring of a ruffian known as the Sneezing Fiend had been overheard but also that this Italian marquis appeared to be offering his talents in the effort as well, drained his glass and slumped farther down in his chair. "Well now, and ain't this a fortunate happenstance then?" Already completely disguised, Hampton's guard was down. He was less suspicious than amazed. It took the marquis only a few more deftly composed sentences muttered in correct dramatic style to convince Hampton that he was not only willing but eager to play a part in the man's plan. By the time they had finished the second pitcher of Crenshaw's famous concoction and had slipped halfway through a third, the marquis had made himself a confidante of Hampton, agreed to meet him on the morrow and watched quietly as the man slumped into oblivion.

Breakfast at Willowset the next morning proved intimidating. All the house guests had risen at a similar hour and all sat down together in the breakfast room under the gaze of a tragic Jenny, whose obvious despair effectively quelled conversation. Eleanor noted in chagrin that the only member of the party not present was the one she especially desired to see. "I do hope," she said hesitantly, "that the earl has not fallen ill. He did not look quite the thing last evening."

The duchess's wide blue eyes looked up, startled. "Oh, no," she replied in a quavering voice, one delicate hand going to her breast. "Oh, that cannot be. If I have made him ill, then I am the most deplorable sister on the face of the earth. How I could have been so thoughtless—" The duchess did not finish her sentence but instead looked down at her plate of shirred eggs, teardrops coursing slowly down her pretty, pale cheeks.

"It is Wright that has been thoughtless, your grace" Howard said. "Though we are all most grateful he rescued you, I expect he did so with some violence and no consideration at all to your sensibilities. It is obvious that this ordeal has taken a toll upon you, and I fear his actions may have added to it."

Eleanor noticed how Mr. Paxton frowned at her brother's words and noticed as well the sympathy that filled Mary Hampton's eyes as she glanced at the duchess. The only one who seemed unconcerned over the duchess's state of mind appeared to be Miss Lipton, who nibbled daintily at her buttered toast and said not a word. Perhaps Lord Wright has been taken ill, Eleanor thought, and he will not appear to invite Martin to remain. Though she could very well see that Wright's request of last evening had been founded in a correct reading of his sister's upset, and though she sincerely wished to accommodate him, she could not possibly remain under this roof if Martin returned home. She was just thinking to excuse herself and hurry upstairs to pack her bags when one of the footmen appeared beside Martin's chair and handed him a note.

"Well," her brother muttered, studying the paper in his hand. "Well, I do not know. Eleanor? Wright requests that we remain at Willowset until the end of the week. I can see no reason to deny him. However, if you do not wish to do so—"

"I should be pleased to remain. How kind of him. But perhaps the duchess would prefer—"

Jenny looked up from her eggs and smiled weakly. "I should like your company of all things, Miss Howard," she murmured, though Eleanor had the impression the words were spoken in deference to Wright's wishes and did not express the duchess's thoughts at all.

"Oh, do say you will stay," cried Miss Lipton softly, her gaze resting hopefully upon Howard.

Paxton gazed quizzically at Mary Hampton, who gave a little shake of her head, as if to discourage him from any comment.

"I must admit I did not expect it, but I do not see why we may not," Howard murmured. "I shall be obliged to prepare my sermon, of course, and to return to St. Swithin's for services. But now the roads are more solid, it will be no hardship." Howard thence sent the footman to assure the earl that he and Miss Howard would remain.

"Ha! So there!" Wright croaked the instant the footman had exited. "You see, Tibbs, he will stay."

"Yes, your lordship. Correct as usual," responded Tibbs, stowing the remainder of Wright's apparel safely away in the clothespress. "Do not dare," he added in his most threatening tone, "rise from that bed."

Wright, who was already doing so, slipped on his robe and made his way to the washstand. "I shall not be bullied into playing the invalid, Tibbs. I am merely a bit hoarse."

"You sound like a bullfrog and you have a fever as well."

"No, I do not. Cease playing nanny, Tibbs, or take yourself off to the nursery where you may tower over his grace with impunity. If you care to remain here," he added, carefully applying a straight razor to his lathered cheeks, "you may lay out something suitable for riding. Anything your heart desires as long as it is serviceable. I have promised to accompany a certain young lady on a drive this morning."

Tibbs, wasting his most reproachful look upon a gentleman who was clearly not attending to him, muttered under his breath and took himself to stand in contemplation before the antique armoire, which had been carted all the way from Elders Rise to fill the very particular space it did.

"And do not look so dour, Tibbs," Wright grinned. "I shall do very nicely on a leisurely ride. I am not dying."

"No," Tibbs muttered, "not yet."

"What, Tibbs?"

"I said you are not dying yet, Master Jocelyn, though lord knows why."

"Because I am too evil to die, Tibbs. I am cruel to my sister and unbearable to my acquaintances and a threat to womankind. The Good Lord will not have me and He don't want me loose in hell to influence the devil; that's why."

The earl peered carefully into the looking glass and discovered happily that his observation had wiped the worry from Tibbs's face and replaced it with a wide grin.

When at last Wright appeared in the breakfast room only Paxton remained lingering over his coffee and obviously pondering some problem. "What? I have not put that look upon your face, have I, Michael? I have been a virtual saint from the very beginning of this affair."

Paxton laughed. "No, it ain't you, Josh."

"Well, what is it then? No, Carson, go away. I shall serve myself, thank you. Have you noticed, Michael, how very much food appears on this board each morning?"

"Only when you're in residence, I think. Not that the Willowset staff does not always supply whatever is needed with great generosity. But Charlie was used to confess that every time you appeared under his roof, his chef appeared to go mad."

"I miss Charlie," Wright replied mournfully, carrying a plate of cold roast beef and a glass of ale to the table. "Do you remember how he used to sing those dreadful songs at breakfast?"

"Appalling behavior," Paxton laughed. "The very first time I heard him do so I thought I should be forced to retreat with my coffee to my own chambers."

"He only did it to set Jenny to laughing. He could set Jenny to laughing at any moment he chose. I wish he were here now."

"She is very sad, your sister. Tell me what happened."

"No. She's safe and won't be abducted again, I promise you."

"Yes, but how was she abducted? And who did the deed?"

Wright, distractedly cutting pieces of beef and using them to divide his plate into neat sections, eyed Paxton warily.

"Come, Josh. I thought that under Charlie's auspices we had

become friends. I'll not speak of it to anyone, you know, if you don't wish it."

The earl sighed and pushed his glass of ale in slow circles on the tabletop. "No," he said at last, "I know you will not, Michael." Then, with some hesitation, he laid the tale of Jenny's abduction before Paxton, who had to bite back his laughter upon discovering that the duchess and her party had kidnapped themselves—and so adroitly, too.

"Don't laugh either," the earl warned, seeing Paxton fighting to hold a sober countenance. "I am nearly certain that this escapade would sink her beyond redemption if it became scandal broth for the *ton*. And she would be devastated were that to happen. I mean, it cannot be acceptable, can it, to run off and pretend to be kidnapped in order that a gentleman should pretend to rescue you? I think it must be nearly as improper as running off to be married over the anvil or something like."

Michael Paxton watched in fascination as Wright began to shred a biscuit into tiny pieces and stack them atop and around the pieces of roast beef he had arranged with such nicety. "I shouldn't concern myself over it, Wright," he replied at length. "It never will be carried farther than this household, so it cannot possibly become scandal broth. Certainly the staff will not gossip about it. And I shall keep it well buried. Are you going to eat that rather artistic mess eventually?"

"Huh? Oh, no, I expect I'm not hungry. It was most inconsiderate of Charlie to succumb to some stupid fever and leave me to begin over again with Jenny. I must find her another husband, I expect, else I shall be forever on edge about her."

"Well, but obviously she has found a candidate for that position, Josh."

"What? The little Italian fribble?"

"But if she cares for him and wishes to marry him?"

"That's not the problem, Michael. The problem is, will he still want her once they are married and he discovers what a priceless piece of rumcake she actually is? And how can I trust such a—a—fool—to look after her?"

Paxton sighed, went to the sideboard and poured himself another cup of coffee, and poured one for the earl as well. As unobtrusively as possible, he removed the untouched ale and set the bone china cup in its place. Then he removed the plate of roast beef and biscuits and set a strawberry tart before the man. "And do not tear that into bits," he ordered, returning to his own seat. "Strawberry tarts are incredibly hard to come by at this time of year, especially in Dorset."

Eleanor induced the duchess to show her about the Willowset gallery and was staring in wonder at a childhood portrait of that lady and her brother when the duchess unceremoniously plunked herself down upon a bench and began to sob quietly. "I—I am sorry, Miss Howard. It is just—I am so unhappy."

"Is there nothing I may do to help?"

"Nothing," sobbed her grace despairingly. "It is I who must do something, but I cannot think what. It's Joshie, you see. I have made him so very angry that he wishes never to speak to me again. I—I have—have lost him. He sa-said I am a selfish little beast and he wants nothing more to do with me. And—and he meant it, too."

"Oh, but he cannot have meant such a thing! You are his only sister!"

Jenny's pretty lower lip quivered. "If I t-tell you what happened," she whispered plaintively, "will you help me to think how to mend things with him?"

Eleanor, finding herself much affected by the quivering lower lip and the beseeching eyes, took Jenny's hands in both of her own and begged that the duchess confide in her completely. By the end of the story she could not decide whether to laugh or cry. "Oh, dearest," she said on a sniff, "I am sure you and the Marquis di Roche did not mean to set up the earl's back, but, oh my, what an escapade! You must not tell anyone else of it," she added after brief thought.

"I must not?"

"No, I do not think so. Some people would find it very scandalous."

"The Reverend Mr. Howard?"

"Yes, I am afraid my brother is one of them."

"That is exactly what Joshie said—that I must not let it come to Mr. Howard's ears because he thought our family infamous enough already. But—but—what am I to do, Eleanor? I have made Joshie hate me and I cannot bear it!"

Eleanor knew perfectly well that the earl did not hate his sister. But no matter how she struggled to reassure the duchess, Jenny would continue to have it that she had alienated Wright's affections forever. When at last Mary Hampton arrived and sent Eleanor off to accompany the reverend and Miss Lipton upon their drive Eleanor was completely out of sympathy for the earl.

She met Wright in the hall and scowled at him. "How you could have been so inconsiderate is quite beyond me," she grumbled, facing him squarely. "You have made the duchess believe that she has lost your affections forever. I grant that you had every right to be upset with her, but need you have shouted so and said such abominable things? You have crushed her. Do not grin at me, your lordship. I find nothing at all amusing about it."

Wright attempted to cease grinning, but the angry flush upon Miss Howard's face and the way her eyes had turned a rich golden brown and the way her fists were balled upon her hips, forced his lips upward in rugged admiration. "I was extremely angry, Miss Howard," he croaked hoarsely, and then coughed. "Pardon me. I only shouted a bit, and I didn't say anything abominable that I can remember."

"You called her a selfish little beast and swore you would have nothing more to do with her."

"I said she was selfish to have brought Tynesbury and Oakes and the others into such a scheme and that if it occurred again, I would not come to her rescue."

"Are you telling me that the duchess is a liar, sir?"

Wright noted the frustrated tone and fought his lips back into a straight line. "Not at all, Miss Howard. I tell you only that Jenny perceives things differently from rational human beings—and sometimes she pretends. But she does not lie."

"Are you suggesting that your sister is irrational?"

Wright struggled manfully to maintain a sober countenance in the face of Eleanor's disapproval but could not withstand the piquant and zesty look of Eleanor in such a temper and broke into outright laughter, which sent him into a fit of coughing that caused him to gasp for breath. "N-no," he finally managed to say. "I am only t-telling you that Jenny is a wet goose. I am sorry, Miss Howard. I do not mean to laugh, b-but you look so like a little bantam preparing to fling itself into battle." Wright dissolved into another fit of coughing, for which Eleanor was grateful because she could not decide whether she had just been insulted and so did not know how to respond, though she had a distinct urge to slap him for comparing her to a fighting cock.

His coughing at an end, he stared down at her through tear-filled eyes and sniffed into his handkerchief. "W-when I asked you to advise her I did not mean for you to take *me* in aversion. Cry *pax*, Miss Howard, and ride with me."

"Now?" she asked.

"Yes."

"I am sorry, but I cannot. I have promised to accompany Martin and Miss Lipton upon a drive."

"No, Miss Howard. You deserve much better than the position of chaperon. Ride with me instead."

"I am afraid not. Martin cannot drive out in a closed carriage with an unmarried woman."

"I shall loan your brother my curricle and we will stay within sight of them. Go don your riding habit, and by the time you are down all will be right with your brother. You do have a habit, do you not?"

"Yes."

"Then be a good girl and run put it on while I send word around to the stables."

When Eleanor appeared, riding crop in hand, to meet the other three members of the party at the front door she was well aware of the amazed look upon the earl's face, though he hurried to change it to one of impartial geniality. In a velvet habit of deep rust color that brought out the red highlights in her hair and changed her hazel eyes to burning brown, she knew she looked a deal more handsome than he had expected. The habit was attractive, with a high, stand-up collar and black braiding, and a proper little hat of like velvet sat upon her tightly knotted hair. He offered her his arm and they followed her brother and Miss Lipton out to the circular drive where the curricle waited. Beside it stood the same gelding Wright had ridden into St. Swithin's days earlier.

Eleanor's gloved hand went up to stroke the shining black nose. "He is magnificent, my lord," she murmured. "I meant to tell you so before. What is his name?"

"Tugforth."

"Tugforth? Not Midnight Magician or Moonrider's Dream?"

"No, Miss Howard. Just Tugforth."

"A good many gentlemen give their cattle romantic names. And he is a most romantic-looking steed."

Wright chuckled and reached up to pull the horse's ear. "He is the most unromantic creature ever born, Miss Howard. His name is Tugforth because when he was young that is exactly what one had to do with him: Tug him forth out of the stall, tug him forth out of the stable, tug him forth out of the paddock—I rather thought him to be three-quarters mule and one-quarter sheer rebellion. But you are a bit more cooperative now, ain't you, Tug?" he added, giving the satiny neck a pat. "And this is Megrims," he said, leading her to her own mount. "She is Jenny's favorite."

"Megrims because she is constantly in low spirits?" asked Eleanor with a lifted eyebrow.

"No," Wright grinned. "Megrims because she will fall into

them if not constantly praised and catered to and given tidbits."
He put one hand into the pocket of his riding coat and produced
a lump of sugar, which he offered to Eleanor. "Go on, Miss
Howard, give it to her. She will be exceedingly pleased with
you for doing so and pleased with herself for having gotten it.
I think your brother is impatient for us to be off," the earl
murmured.

Howard, glaring at them from the seat of Wright's curricle,
was more than impatient; he was champing at the bit.

Nine

Wright rode beside the curricle, his eyes fastened upon Miss Lipton, and had not Eleanor challenged him to a race up the lane and urged Megrims immediately into a gallop before she had finished speaking, he might have ridden so all the way into St. Swithin's and back. But he responded to the challenge, though rather late, and Eleanor, arriving first at the finishing point, turned back to laugh at him, her face flushed with excitement. "You are beaten!" she laughed breathlessly as he drew rein beside her. "Admit it!"

"Never," declared Wright, grinning. "I shall swear I let you win or Tug and I will never live it down. Beaten by a preacher's daughter on a maggoty filly!"

"That is much better," Eleanor smiled.

"What is much better?"

"You. You are actually smiling. Would you care to race again? This time Megrims and I shall give you a head start."

Wright laughed and Eleanor decided that he was the most enchanting man she had ever met. Why Martin was so determined that she believe the earl to be evil she could not understand.

"Has anyone ever told you, Miss Howard, that you are a scamp?"

"No, sir, not that I recall—though someone did compare me to a bantam rooster a short while back."

"Ah, but you did not find that a compliment, I think. Still, it was intended as such."

"You bestow compliments oddly, my lord."

"I bestow everything oddly," Wright shrugged, turning to watch the curricle's approach. "It comes of being raised among barbarians and without a mother's careful guidance."

"Oh, I did not know. I am so sorry."

"Why?"

"That you—that your mother—"

"My mother died when I was nine, Miss Howard. I barely remember her. No, that is not true. I remember her well—every night, in fact."

"In your prayers," nodded Eleanor knowingly, and the earl inhaled a chuckle, gasped and began to cough wildly, sending Tugforth to prancing uneasily beneath him.

"Oh, Josh," cried Lily as the curricle came to a halt beside him. "You sound dreadful. You should not have come."

"You do sound dreadful," the Reverend Howard conceded handsomely. "Perhaps you ought to go back. I am quite able to look after Miss Lipton and Eleanor."

"No. Thank you for your consideration, Howard, but I have engaged to ride with Miss Howard and I shall continue to do so until we have reached our destination and returned."

"I was merely thinking of your health, Wright," Howard said with a shake of his head. "If you are not concerned then we shall go forward as we intended."

"Ffff-fine!" Wright sneezed into a handkerchief he tugged hurriedly out of his boot top.

Eleanor and Lily giggled to see it, and even Howard chuckled.

"What?" the earl asked.

"I doubt anyone ever thought to carry a handkerchief precisely there, Josh," Lily grinned.

"But it is a prodigious good idea," added Eleanor. "One does not need to search through all one's pockets for it."

Bob Kinsley was not an unreasonable man. When his father had died five years ago he had inherited the Crossroads Inn and he had run it with all the care and propriety his father had done before him. He supported his wife and three children, saw to the needs of his patrons, enjoyed a drink or two whenever he was invited and attended church on Sunday when he could not find an excuse to remain at home. He was unassuming, generally filled with good cheer and willing to help out another human being when he could. But he was not at all sure what he was doing at the moment was reasonable. He knew, of course, that the message he had delivered to the Earl of Wright at Willowset previously had been a ransom note. The message he carried now had arrived in an equally suspicious manner—having been discovered beneath a serving dish on one of the tables in the public room. It, too, was addressed to the Earl of Wright. To deliver two such messages into Legion's hands within the space of a se'ennite was like to lead to one's hasty demise. But then again, to withhold a message of any import from the man was to tempt fate as well. Kinsley gulped, his prominent Adam's apple bobbing beneath his cravat. He gave a tug at the little cart horse's reins and brought his gig to a stop at the side of the road to think the thing through one more time.

Mrs. Dish had often assured him that the earl was a fine chap. And Legion proved generally approachable whenever he came visiting the duchess and happened to enter the Crossroads. And he had been as pleasant as any man might be when he had come asking questions of the staff about that first note. But certain rumors and bits of gossip nagged at the back of Kinsley's mind. St. Swithin's was not so far from Elders Rise, and tales of Legion's exploits filtered down to them. It was that little tale about the earl's having cut off the messenger's ear with his rapier upon receiving word of his father's death that banged at Kinsley the most. Of course it was all a hum. Not even at the Broken Wing in John's Glen would a room full of men sit by and allow such a thing to go forward. Still, you never knew. The best of them in the hinterlands were only a peg or two above savages. Kinsley had all but decided to turn

the gig about and send one of the barmaids with the message—
even Legion would not harm a woman—when a voice he recognized well called him from his reverie and he looked up to
find the Reverend Mr. Howard, accompanied by an amazingly
fine-looking young lady, reining a curricle up beside him.

"Kinsley, well-met," Howard smiled. "May I make you
known to Miss Lipton? Miss Lipton, this is the landlord of our
inn, the Crossroads, Mr. Robert Kinsley."

Kinsley bowed in the young woman's direction and had just
opened his mouth to suggest that perhaps the reverend would
not mind delivering a message to the Earl of Wright when that
very gentleman rode up accompanied by Miss Howard.

"Kinsley." The earl nodded. "Out for a breath of fresh air?"

Bob Kinsley shook his head negatively while at the same
time attempting to acknowledge Miss Howard's presence. "On
m' way to Willowset," he murmured. "A m-message for you,
m'lord."

"For me? Well, hand it over," the earl muttered, taking the
paper from Kinsley's hand as Tugforth carried him in an impatient circle beside the gig. For a moment, as he unsealed the
message he faced away from Eleanor. But as Tugforth continued to turn and brought the face Eleanor was beginning to like
very much back into her sight, she noticed a frown develop
between Wright's finely drawn brows. "How did you come by
this, Kinsley?"

"One of the waiters found it under a serving plate, my lord."
The frown on the earl's face did not bode well. Thank goodness
the reverend was near.

"Well," mumbled Wright; and then, recalling himself to his
surroundings, he gave Kinsley a curt nod and thanked him for
taking the trouble to deliver the thing. "Will you drive back
into St. Swithin's with us, Bob?" he added, stuffing the note
into his coat pocket. "I expect the ladies might do with a
nuncheon, and I'd like to share a bit of ale with you if you
wouldn't mind."

"I—I don't know who left the thing," Kinsley blurted out in a shaky voice, which surprised all of the party except Wright.

"Heard about the ear, did you, Kinsley?" The earl grinned. "I am amazed you came at all. The duchess, by the way, is safely returned to us."

"Thank God," sighed Kinsley.

"Yes, well, God had very little to do with it, although I expect He was thoroughly amused. I didn't do it, you know."

"My lord?"

"The ear, Kinsley. It's a great clanker."

"Yes, my lord."

"So, will you drive back with us?"

"Yes, my lord. Be glad for the company." Kinsley pulled the little gig back onto the road just behind the Reverend Howard's curricle and gave his horse the office to proceed.

"We are becoming a parade," observed Eleanor as she fell in beside Wright. "I hope your message was not disturbing."

For a very long moment Wright's eyes searched her own. "I do not know you well, Miss Howard," he said, "but I think you are possessed of a good deal of sense. Are you?"

"Why, I—Mr. Paxton did say you asked the oddest questions of people. I think I am a person of good sense, yes."

"Then ride ahead with me. I have something to discuss with you that I do not wish to share with the rest of our party." Before she could even agree to do so the earl had urged Tugforth into the middle of the road and passed the two vehicles. Eleanor, perplexed, set out after him. She did not come up with him, however, until he had halted well beyond a turning in the lane that hid them from the view of the others.

"What is it, your lordship?" Eleanor asked.

"I—I—"

"Has it something to do with the note, my lord?"

The earl nodded in the midst of a sneeze.

"Perhaps if I were to read it?"

Wright fished in his pockets, produced the missive and passed it to her. Eleanor, thinking that the earl's cough, which had followed immediately upon his sneezing, was growing steadily worse, studied the handwriting. Her eyes grew larger with each word and having reached the end of the message she stared up at Wright, her lips parted, her eyes round and fearful.

Sniffing and tucking his handkerchief back into his boot, Wright held out a hand for the paper and stuffed it back into his pocket. "I cannot think," he croaked, "what is best to do. I know what your brother would suggest, but there are reasons I don't like to call upon the constable."

"B-but someone means to kill you!" Eleanor cried excitedly, and he put a finger to his lips to shush her.

"What I wonder is whether or not the message is to be believed, Miss Howard. Is there such a person, do you think, as the Sneezing Fiend? Besides myself, I mean," he added with a smile. "And where exactly is Cutter's Hook?"

"It's what they call the gully in Willowset's east pasture."

"Charlie was used to call that the gap."

"Yes, but the villager's call it Cutter's Hook. You will not go?"

"I haven't been asked to as yet, Miss Howard. But if I do not go, they will not be able to entrap me, and will possibly search for another way to put a period to my existence. You don't think I should ride to meet them?"

Eleanor could not believe she was having this conversation. He looked at her, his nose slowly growing red from so many meetings with his handkerchief, his intriguing eyes puffy around the edges and his face flushed with fever. She could discover no fear in his aspect, no agitation, only a serene bewilderment.

"The thing of it is, Miss Howard, that if I am to believe this missive, then I must believe that one of those involved wishes for some reason to preserve my obnoxious self. On the other hand, this may be some trick, hoping to—well, I am not sure what anyone would hope to do by it. To keep me holed up inside Willowset?"

"Why should anyone wish that?"

"I can't imagine. But then again, I cannot imagine who would send a note to save me while being a part of the plot to do me in. However, since the message was left at the Crossroads, it's likely, don't you think, that whoever it is resides somewhere in St. Swithin's?"

"Certainly none of the villagers holds such a grudge against you. We must ask if there are any newcomers about town," Eleanor said hurriedly, hearing the vehicles approach.

"Ask whom, Miss Howard?"

"Everyone we possibly can. Mrs. Dish to be sure, and the staff at the inn, and Lily and I shall make discreet inquiries among the shopkeepers—except you and Howard must stop at Mr. Coddlington's Hardware and the blacksmith's, for we cannot go there without raising a breeze."

"You must not tell your brother, Miss Howard."

"Oh, but why not? Martin could be a great help. The church members often share their gossip with him."

"Because he'll urge me to speak to the constable, and when I decline he will say I endanger Jenny and Jessie and must go back to London for their sakes."

"You don't think they would harm Jessie or the duchess?"

"No, Miss Howard. If I am correct, mine is the only life sought, but perhaps I am mistaken about who it is threatens me."

Eleanor's brow furrowed in puzzlement, but she was forbidden any more questions by the arrival of the gig and the curricle, and once again she and the earl joined the small parade toward St. Swithin's.

The em'netly infamous and 'stremely ferocious highwayman, Six String Jack—looking remarkably like the little Duke of Ware—and his equally ruthless assoc'ate, Ghastly Gus—much resembling Joycie dressed in his grace's castoffs—grinned widely over their 'scape from the hor'ble Newgate and hurried as quickly as their legs would carry them toward their hideout on Houndslow's Heath. Beside them their faithful protector, the gigantical and savaging Siberian wolfdog, Blaze, who a half hour before had been romping with the rest of Maizie's litter in the stableyard, kept pace. "We's almos' there!" announced Jack proudly. "We's just gotta slip down this here place an' climb up behin' that rock. I'll go firs'. You hol' on to Blaze till I gets to the bottom."

Ghastly Gus nodded, toddling back to seize the mighty wolfdog in both her arms and lug him, hindquarters wiggling in midair, to the verimost edge of the dang'rous cliff. Confident in his associate's ability to control the savaging beast, Six String Jack sat down upon the slope, pushed off with both hands, and skidded perilously on the seat of his breeches down into the gully at the end of the east pasture. Successfully reaching bottom, he peered about cautiously, checking for the presence of Bow Street Runners, then turned and announced to his associate that all was clear. Ghastly Gus, not nearly so good at sliding down hillsides and encumbered by the struggling Blaze, plopped down upon the ground and edged carefully toward the very lip of the sliding place. As soon as gravity took hold, she closed her eyes, clung tightly to Blaze and careened in a rain of mud and gravel toward the little highwayman below. She scraped her elbow upon a rock and bumped her bottom hard when she landed in the gully, but Ghastly Gus was brave as she could stare and did not make the least complaint. The mighty Blaze leaped free of her arms and chased about in happy circles as Gus stood and brushed herself off. Six String Jack added a pat or two to help knock the dirt from her backside. "This way," he instructed. "Follow me. We gots to reach the cave b'fore the Runners finds us." Jack led the way between two rocks, climbed gingerly up a pocked boulder and sniggled into the midst of a growth of blackberry tangles now nearly leafless.

"Wait!" Ghastly Gus protested behind him. "Blaze can't climb this here wock. You gots to help us!"

Six String Jack sniggled back through the blackberry tangle

and scrambled down to help. He got his face thoroughly washed by a wet puppy tongue for his efforts and giggled. When at last he managed to get both Blaze and Gus into the hideout, he was much gratified by their reactions. Ghastly Gus jumped up and down and clapped her hands, and the savaging Blaze plopped down upon the damp floor and rolled on his back.

"Aye," Jack grunted proudly, extracting his uncle's flints from a pocket. "An' now we'll builded us a fire an' make our nefar'ous plot for robbin' the Bristol Mail!"

Mrs. Dish threw a questioning look at Eleanor, drew the earl into her parlor and pushed him down into a chair. Before he could protest she placed a hand upon his brow and then ordered him not to move an inch until she returned. When she did return it was with a pot of tea brewed from fresh catnip, dried wild cherry bark and blackstrap molasses. Expecting, from the stubborn look on the handsome but feverish face, to meet with strong protest, Mrs. Dish brought along a bottle of Scotch whiskey as well and made a great show of mixing it into the pot. "Now," she declared, filling a mug to the brim and handing it to Wright, "I expect you to drink every bit of this, and you shall have a second cup as well. Do not protest, Josh. I will not have you dying upon my doorstep."

Wright smiled. "I have not the least intention of dying upon your doorstep, Melinda. It would be most unmannerly of me." He raised the cup to his lips, sipped at it and sighed. "Well, it ain't as horrible as I feared. Melinda, I wish you will do me a very great favor."

"And what is that?" asked the elderly lady, sitting next to Eleanor upon the couch and pouring tea for herself and the young woman from a pot quite separate from the earl's.

"I wish you will pack a trunk and come to Willowset for a while. I'll send Oakes with the coach later this afternoon to fetch you."

"Good heavens," gasped Mrs. Dish, "has something terrible happened to her grace?"

"What? Oh, no, Jenny is safe and sound, Melinda. She wasn't kidnapped after all. I expect I misread the note. At any rate, my wanting you to visit has nothing at all to do with Jenny. Mary has come to Willowset and brought Joyce with her."

"Oh!" cried Mrs. Dish, nearly spilling her tea. "Oh, my lord!"

"Yes, I rather thought you would like to spend a few days with your niece—and finally make Joyce's acquaintance."

Mrs. Dish's eyes began to fill with tears. "Oh," she sniffed, "I can barely believe it! My Mary! My darling Mary!" She wiped her handkerchief across her eyes and strove to control herself, but the tears would not be held back and began to trail down her cheeks. Wright set his teacup down and went to her, pulling her up into his arms in a great hug and rubbing her back as she sobbed.

"You're being a great baby," he whispered into her ear. "One would guess I had proposed a tremendous hardship."

"Oh, no!" sobbed Mrs. Dish. "Oh, my lord, it's so very wonderful! I am so—so—happy!"

"If you get much happier, my dear, I shall take a chill riding home in damp clothes," Wright laughed, winking at Eleanor over the good lady's shoulder.

Mrs. Dish pulled away to look up at him. Her eyes danced with joy behind the teardrops. "When I think of all you have done, and now you have given Mary courage enough to see me! You are a miracle worker!"

"Of c-c-course," the earl answered, sneezing mightily.

Mrs. Dish pushed him hurriedly toward his chair and placed his mug back into his hands. "Drink it before it cools," she ordered. "Oh, my, Eleanor, what a great to-do we are making, and you all unknowing."

"So, will you come?" the earl interrupted.

"Of course I shall come, Josh! Drink your tea!"

Eleanor, agog with the revelation that the beautiful Mary Hampton was Mrs. Dish's niece, fought down her curiosity and concentrated instead on village gossip, hoping to hear that a stranger had come to St. Swithin's and that Mrs. Dish knew who the man was and where he was to be found.

The Reverend Mr. Howard, meanwhile, was proudly escorting Miss Lipton about the town. They had parted from Wright and Eleanor shortly after enjoying a nuncheon at the inn, and Miss Lipton, having spoken privately with Eleanor before setting off, had taken it upon herself to discover whether anyone suspicious lurked about St. Swithin's. She did this by directing her attentions to particular shops and shopkeepers who might be expected to notice unfamiliar persons such as herself. While Mr. Howard might wonder at the peculiar tack of her conversation as she placed a charming little cottage bonnet upon her golden hair and struck a most becoming pose, or sniffed daintily at a crystal atomizer filled with attar of roses, or sighed over a cute little china pug dog and pondered whether she had an appropriate place to set it, he simply accepted her curious questioning of the shopkeepers as an adorable part of her personality. In fact, he found her interest in his little parish heartening, for he had all but decided that this glorious woman was to become the object of his very honorable and most sincere attentions. He escorted her proudly from shop to shop upon his arm, introducing her politely, smiling at every word, watching over her protectively. "Have you ever thought, Miss Lipton," he asked finally, escorting her into his church to view the bright sunlight through the stained-glass windows. "Have you ever thought of living in such a small village? That is, you seem so much at home here—not at all like a Londoner."

Lily glanced up at him. "I am not fond of London," she murmured. "If it were not for Josh, I should not be able to bear living in the city at all."

"But surely, Miss Lipton, your family does not force you to remain there? Have they no other residences?"

"I am without family, Mr. Howard," replied Lily, her blue

eyes searching his brown ones for a sign of understanding. "I am dependent upon his lordship."

"Upon Wright?" Howard stared aghast. His obvious horror at her words was all too clear. He had caught her meaning and could not abide the thought. Lily turned slowly and walked in silence out of the church and into the sunlight.

Howard, recovering from the horrid realization that some misguided gentleman besides Charlie had granted Wright custody over his child—and that child a young lady—raced after her. "Miss Lipton," he cried, seizing one gloved hand in his own, "surely there is someone else your father placed over you? Some barrister, perhaps? He cannot have been so thoughtless as to trust your welfare to Wright alone."

Lily looked up, puzzled. "My father?"

"Yes, certainly in his will he gave at least partial guardianship to some other? Perhaps there is an elderly relative? I cannot credit that he would have left all power over your future to such a—a rapscallion—as Wright!"

Lily's perfect bow lips formed a little *oh,* amazed. Mr. Howard thought her Wright's ward, not his mistress! She ought to explain it more thoroughly to him. And she would, too. Soon. As soon as she had talked to Josh about—about—things. She accepted Mr. Howard's proffered arm and allowed him to lead her back toward the village, where they had left the curricle.

"I hope you will forgive me, Miss Lipton," Howard said at last. "I should not have permitted myself such an outburst. It is only that—that I cannot conceive why anyone of sense should make that barbarian, Wright, guardian over innocents. I could not comprehend why my cousin, the duke, had done so—though at least he did not leave the man in sole charge— and I cannot understand why your father should do so either."

Howard felt Lily's hand tremble upon his arm and patted it consolingly. "Do not fear, Miss Lipton. I shall speak to Wright directly. If you are so very unhappy in the city, certainly other arrangements can be made."

Lily's hand pulled back from under his comforting pat and she came to a halt beside him. "Josh is not a barbarian."

"Pardon me?"

"You said that Josh is a barbarian. He is not."

"Well, perhaps not quite, Miss Lipton, but he is certainly a rake and a rapscallion and a libertine."

Lily opened her mouth and closed it again without another word. She had been ready to spring to Wright's defense, but it occurred to her that perhaps Josh did not wish to be defended. She determined to ask him first so as not to make a great mistake. "May we please not speak of it more?" she asked, slipping her hand back into the crook of Howard's arm. "Josh has been extremely kind to me and I do not wish to hear ill of him."

Howard nodded in agreement, and they set off in the direction of Mrs. Dish's in an agreeable discussion of the homey and pleasant atmosphere that encompassed the village of St. Swithin's. The Reverend Mr. Howard, however, determined in his heart to have a serious talk with Wright concerning the young lady's welfare and her professed distaste for London.

They found Eleanor helping Mrs. Dish to pack some of her clothes into a small trunk so that she might be ready when the coach from Willowset arrived. Wright they discovered asleep in the parlor before the fire, his long legs stretched comfortably out before him. All of the women were loathe to wake him, but the Reverend Howard was not the least disinclined to do so, for he wished to arrive back at Willowset in time to allow for his having a private discussion with the earl about Miss Lipton's future before the dinner gong chimed.

Their journey back from St. Swithin's was as enjoyable to Howard as the journey there had been. The sun shone brightly; the air was brisk and clean; the horses were sweetgoers; and Miss Lipton sat beside him, her delectable lips and innocent eyes and radical little nose all paying strict and admiring attention to his every word. Eleanor watched, bemused. Her lips tilted upward, thinking how handsome and debonair her brother appeared beside this particular young lady. And what a lovely couple the two of them made. And how remarkably enthralled Martin seemed with the young woman's every word. And then she noticed a bleary-eyed Wright scowling at the two on the box and gave a little gasp. Good heavens, she thought, I am riding along pondering a match between my brother and the Earl of Wright's mistress!

Ten

The Reverend Mr. Howard's hopes for a private audience with Wright were dashed, however, when they were greeted in the Willowset courtyard by Harry Cross and John Whitson, a disturbed Colly Shepard and a tearful Mrs. Bowers. Wright had no sooner dismounted than his sister came flying out of the front door, tears streaming from her eyes, followed immediately by Mr. Paxton, Mrs. Hampton and Burton. Jenny threw herself into Wright's arms and wailed that her precious son was most probably dead and it was all her fault. Eleanor noticed the earl's arms tighten about the duchess. He rocked her gently against his chest, his bewildered eyes seeking some sort of explanation from those gathered about. It was Shepard who provided it, his own arm lending Mrs. Bowers support.

"Well, the rascals have gone on holiday is all," the earl murmured, bestowing a kiss upon his sister's golden curls. "Did not one of you see them leave?"

"No," gasped Mrs. Bowers on a sob. "I left them painting pictures in the nursery. I only meant to be gone a moment."

"I called her away," cried the duchess. "It is all my fault, Joshie. I wished Bowey to help me with my stitchery and did not once think about the children!"

Wright continued to hold her and brushed a soft kiss against her cheek. "Don't be such a watering pot, chick. They have only sneaked out to play and will be home shortly."

"So I thought, but they are nowhere near," Mary sighed,

leaning upon Paxton's arm. "Colly and Harry Cross and Whitson have all searched for them and they cannot be found."

"They've taken one o' Maizie's pups with 'em," announced
Oakes, strolling around the side of the building from the stables. "Gone off on an adventure," he added, seeing his lordship
had arrived.

"More than likely," Wright nodded. "Glenby, hitch up the
traveling coach and drive into St. Swithin's. Mrs. Dish comes
to visit for a few days."

Paxton felt Mary tremble at the words and stared at her,
perplexed.

"Burton, see chambers are ready to receive the lady." The
earl, bestowing a glance of apology upon Miss Howard, swept
his sister up into his arms and strolled with her into the house,
carrying her as far as the small drawing room and setting her
down upon a chaise longue. He spent another few moments
kneeling upon the floor beside her and whispering into her ear,
and Eleanor, who had followed in his wake as had everyone
else, was thoroughly amazed to see the fear vanish from her
grace's lovely face, the tears dry up and a dimple appear in
one cheek. She was more amazed to hear the duchess giggle.

"Where did you go, Howard, when you and Charlie played
hereabouts?" Wright asked, standing.

"Well, I—I did not come here so very often—"

"Oh, Martin, do try and think," Eleanor urged. "There must
have been some favorite spot."

"There is the cave at Cutter's Hook," Howard mumbled, re-
minding his sister abruptly of the message the earl had shared
with her. "But we did not discover that until we were ten."

"A cave?" Wright asked.

"A very small one. I do not remember exactly where it is."

"Whitson," Wright ordered, pausing to break into a series
of sneezes, "take the grooms to search the park and the woods
again. Colly, you and Tibbs will explore the stables and the
barns, and do not forget the haylofts. Paxton? Would you object

to a sojourn down in the cellars with Howard? Some of them are ancient and the stairs not terribly dependable, but—"

"Martin and I shall scour them thoroughly," Paxton replied, giving Mary's hand a reassuring pat.

"And since I am already dressed for it, I will take Tug and see can I discover this cave. Don't worry, Mary; we will find the scamps playing at highwayman or some such, shan't we, Jenny?"

The duchess nodded, her trust in her elder brother evident to all. Wright bestowed a last kiss upon her brow, then strolled from the room. Eleanor heard his boots pound down the front staircase, glanced at her brother and declared that the earl was not well and should not ride out alone and since she, too, was already dressed for it, she would accompany him. Her tone left no doubt in Howard's mind that protest would be useless.

The Marquis di Roche took his mount carefully down into the gully behind Hampton and the Sneezing Fiend. Clouds boiled on the horizon as they gazed warily about. "These being the Cutter's Hook?" asked di Roche.

"Aye, and once we lure Wright into it, we cannot allow him to escape alive," Hampton growled, dismounting and tying his horse to a shrub.

"We shooting him?"

"No, we make his death appear accidental. He'll enter as we did, but the ground will give way under him tomorrow and send his horse plummeting. The beast'll roll over on him, or kick him in the head."

Di Roche looked about him amazedly. "Here, *signor?* These being not so steep as to plummet making ones."

The Fiend snorted. " 'Is freakin' lor'ship'll plummet oncet we loose that boulder at the top."

"We dig enough earth from under it and the slightest weight will send it crashing," explained Hampton, untying three shovels from his saddle. "And if his horse don't roll on him or kick him in the head by the time he reaches bottom, then one of ours will. I shall see to it."

Di Roche looked up. Covered by a layer of soil, weeds and shrubs at the top, the place of easiest descent had seemed solid ground, but from below he could see it was a large boulder balanced upon a foundation of smaller rocks and stones. Praying the earl would heed his hastily written warning, di Roche pondered how he might foil this plan if Wright did not and rode into Cutter's Hook on the morrow.

Midway up the rock face Six String Jack and Ghastly Gus peeked gleefully through the blackberry tangle at the three gentlemen below. "Bow Street Runners," hissed Jack, crawling back into the cave. "We have gots to be verimost quiet."

Ghastly Gus nodded, her dark ringlets bouncing cheerily about her grimy face. "Bostweet Wunners," she agreed. "We better gets awe pisto's." Unfortunately the savaging and gigantical Siberian wolfdog, Blaze, had not known the difference between their pistols and the other sticks in the cavern and had chewed them to pieces, setting the fierce an' 'str'ordinary highwaymen to scrambling about in search of new weapons. When at last they crawled, fully armed, back to the mouth of the cave, the dense clouds, heavy with rain, hid the sun and a slow drizzle fell. Below them, Hampton, di Roche and the very thin and deceptively frail-looking man known as the Sneezing Fiend, dug carefully into the cliffside.

Eleanor had expected some protest from the earl when she had ridden up beside him, but he had said nothing. For a full five minutes they rode in silence, Eleanor unable to think of what to say and the earl, apparently, not caring to say anything at all. "Are—are you all right?" Eleanor asked finally. "You are so very quiet."

"I am fine, Miss Howard."

The tone of his voice indicated otherwise, and Eleanor studied his dark, handsome profile with concern. "You do not sound fine, my lord. You sound as if you are dreaming."

"Dreaming?" The earl turned in the saddle to look straight at her. "Can people actually sound as if they are dreaming? I feel as though I am. It is this stupid cold and Mrs. Dish's tea, I think, and the whiskey. It is very much as if I were floating through a landscape that exists only in my mind."

"Oh, dear, you should have asked Martin to ride to Cutter's Hook. I knew you should have. But I did not think it my place to oppose you."

"No, it was not your place. Jessie is my nephew and Joyce—Joyce is my responsibility as well. And I am perfectly—perfectly—capable—" Wright snatched the handkerchief from his boot and halted Tugforth in the very nick of time to catch a long series of sneezes.

"I am amazed you do not sneeze yourself right off Tug's back," observed Eleanor when he had finished.

The comment brought a vague smile to his lips.

"Do you really believe the children are simply playing somewhere, my lord?"

"Of course. Did you not sneak off to play in the woods or the fields when you were young? Come, Miss Howard, even you and Martin cannot have been such perfect children as never to escape your keepers and take a holiday?"

"No," laughed Eleanor, "not even Martin and I were as perfect as all that. Oh, dear, it is starting to drizzle."

"It would," muttered Wright, tapping the heels of his boots against Tug's side and sending the horse into a gallop.

They stopped again as they neared the end of the field, and Wright swiped his coat sleeve across his forehead. "It is just beyond those trees, is it not?" he asked. "Damn but it's growing dim. I hope the urchins are hiding in the cellars and not here at all. They'll be frightened else, when it begins to storm." Thunder erupted upon his final words and Eleanor shivered.

"Are you cold, Miss Howard? Here, take my coat. It will make you a bit warmer and keep some of the rain at bay."

"No, thank you, my lord. You are the one already ill."

"I am not ill," protested Wright, having already shrugged out of his caped greatcoat and now holding Tug beside her mare as he arranged it over Eleanor's shoulders. "Besides, I'm boiling hot and the rain feels wonderful. Put your arms in the sleeves, Miss Howard. There is plenty of room."

Eleanor did as he said, and though grateful for the extra warmth, she eyed him worriedly. If he was indeed so very hot, then his fever had worsened and he might be gravely ill by morning. She told him so, hoping to make him take the coat back, but he only shrugged and replied amid a number of sneezes that a bit of rainwater was not like to make the difference between his life and death.

In Cutter's Hook a bright flash of lightning and the rumble of thunder close over their heads had magically transformed the stal'art an' bully highwaymen back into children and sent them scurrying into the center of the cave, where they had gathered a large pile of twigs. Joyce plopped cross-legged upon the damp limestone floor and gathered the no longer gigantical, no longer savaging, no longer even Siberian wolfdog into her arms and hugged the wiggling puppy tightly. "I'm afwaid," she mumbled into the tiny hound's fur. "I wanna go home now."

"As soon as them men leave," whispered Jessie, who had not the least intention of announcing to strangers that they had been spied upon. "Don't cry, Joycie."

"Not cwying. Not no baby," protested Joyce, biting her lip to keep her tears from falling. The lightning sizzled and the thunder roared again, louder and closer, and Joyce shuddered. "It too vewy dawk in here, Jessie. Makes are fiwere."

Jessie fished his uncle's tinderbox from his pocket. On the fourth try he succeeded in setting alight the pile of twigs the two had gathered earlier. "There," he said triumphantly. "I knowed I could. You stay right here, Joycie," he added, giving her head a pat. "I'm gonna see is them men gone yet."

The Sneezing Fiend, thoroughly drenched and living up to his name by letting out a series of sneezes almost as explosive as the thunder, stood staring up at the now barely balanced boulder. Di Roche stood side by side with the man and shook his head. "How *we* climbing out?" he asked.

"We lead the bloody horses up the far side and ride to Hampton Hall," Hampton answered, pulling his hat down farther over his brow to keep the rain from his eyes. "Ain't nobody been there in years, but—what's that?"

"Wha—t's what?" sneezed the Fiend and heard a sneeze echo back at him from above.

"Someone she comings!" exclaimed di Roche. *"Santa Maria* these persons will all our entrapping make a ruin."

Hampton, frowning, put a finger to his lips and drew the other men and the horses away from the trap and beneath the overhang of the cliff farther down.

Eleanor had ridden ahead of Wright, who had been slowed by a series of sneezes, and had brought Megrims to a halt on the undermined boulder. She felt a vague shifting of ground and an odd wobble and looked around, puzzled. And suddenly Wright was shouting her name and charging Tug at full speed directly at her. She gasped in fear, thinking him run mad, and attempted to turn Megrims on the instant, but the mare shied and fought her. And then Wright was upon her. He seized her by the folds of the greatcoat he had hung around her, tore her from the saddle and hurled her straight across Tugforth and back into the path from which they had just emerged. She attempted to rise on the instant, thinking to run, to get away from this lunatic, and then screamed as she saw Wright plummet downward in a jumble of rock, mud and slashing hooves.

Astounded that their trap had been sprung so unexpectedly, and by their quarry, Hampton, di Roche and the Sneezing Fiend stood frozen, mouths open, eyes staring wide through the dim light. "Devil if it ain't Wright!" hissed Hampton at last, moving toward the bedlam of kicking, shrieking horses. He seized a heavy rock from the muddy ground as he went. The Sneezing Fiend made ready to follow, but di Roche placed a booted foot in the way and sent the Fiend plopping face-downward into the muck. Then he dashed after Hampton and grasped him by the elbow, tugging the man with both hands back toward the place they had hidden. Hampton wheeled about in protest, threatening to bring the rock down upon di Roche, when the little marquis pointed excitedly. "There lady being with him. Hide! Hide!" he hissed as Eleanor, unaware of them, concentrated on making her way down into the gully. Hampton dropped the rock and motioned to the angrily rising Fiend, and the three men scrambled for cover. *"Santa Maria!"* whispered di Roche, "these lady she almost sees you killing him!"

"Then we kill 'er as well," muttered the Fiend, brushing at his breeches. "Ain't no reason to git in a dither."

"Already he dying, not?" whispered di Roche. "See, he lying very still. These lady will truly say how being an accidental and all believing her."

The three men watched as a terrified Eleanor stumbled toward Wright's inert form.

At the mouth of the cave Jessie peered out, awed into silence by the screaming and plunging of the horses amid the rock slide. Beside him, Joyce stared agog. "It's Uncle Josh," she gasped at last, tugging at Jessie's sleeve. "It's Tug an' Uncle Josh."

"An' Ellie!" cried Jessie, pointing. The two little ones, forgetting the strange men, the thunder and lightning, their fire and even the puppy, scrambled from the cave through the blackberry tangle and down the rocks. "Uncle Josh! Ellie!" they yelled, rushing toward the spot where Eleanor struggled to bring the injured, frightened horses under control and draw them and their murderous, iron-shod hooves away from the earl.

Hampton cursed under his breath. "Now where the devil did those brats come from?"

The Sneezing Fiend muttered that children could be killed just as easily as swatting flies or drowning kittens, but Hampton's exasperated glare silenced those observations and the three men, di Roche in the rear, quietly led their fidgeting mounts out of sight of the growing crowd. "This way," Hampton called over the rising wind as di Roche hesitated.

"I thinking I returning to these accidental," called back the marquis. "I making of me one helping passingbyer, not? These way we knowing the Legion being truly dead. And if he being not, I learning of it."

Hampton, after rapid consideration, nodded his approval. "An' if he ain't dead, you will have made yourself a hero and will be welcomed into the household, where you may see to it that we have ample opportunity to finish him off."

The marquis smiled gleefully, nodding, and led his horse back toward the sprung trap.

Eleanor, trembling with shock, had managed to lead both horses away from Wright and had knelt down beside him.

"Uncle Josh, wakes up!" shouted Joyce, running across the uneven ground to where he lay. "You can'ts sleep out here. It's waining!"

"Shhh, darling." Eleanor caught the imp in her arms and hugged her tightly. "He cannot hear you. Wherever have you been? Jessie!"

"Is—is he d-dead?" gulped Jessie, moving next to Joyce inside the comforting circle of Eleanor's arms. "He falled a awful long ways." Eleanor did not answer; but she released them both and attempted to roll Wright carefully onto his back. No sooner had she succeeded than the puppy dashed madly toward them and bounded onto the earl's chest. Jessie tugged it off and, staring at the blood that streamed from his uncle's forehead, sniffed back tears and cradled the pup in his arms.

"Jessie, you must give me your handkerchief to tie around your uncle's brow to stop the bleeding; his own will not do at all," Eleanor said on a sob.

"I don't gots one," mumbled Jessie. "I forgotted it."

"Meselfs the hankeringchiefs having," offered di Roche, leading his horse toward the sodden little gathering. He handed his reins to Jessie, gave Joyce a pat on the head and placed a large square of linen into Eleanor's hands. "I being the Marquis di Roche," he offered by way of introduction.

Eleanor, biting her lip to keep her tears at bay, bound the linen as tightly as possible about the earl's brow. His wicked, wonderful eyes opened, but she read no recognition of herself in them, and he mumbled disjointedly words she could not make sense of. Di Roche sighed and knelt beside her. "Ees bad hurting. Ees breaking arm and maybe leg, you seeing? Is breaking possible inside as well. You taking my horse and going for help, yes? I not knowing fastest way. Say must having men to carrying up and wagon for to taking home."

Eleanor was about to protest the plan, wishing to remain with Wright and the children and send di Roche instead, when Wright coughed and blood gushed from his nose and bubbled from between his lips. Gasping, Eleanor's face grew even more pale. "Very well, but you must get my saddle. I cannot ride astride in this habit. And we must attempt to move him out of this rain before I go. He will die of a congestion of the lung else. Do you think between us we can carry him?"

The little marquis shook his head gravely. "He being much too big. You must going now, quickly."

"Ellie! Ellie!" The little duke's voice sliced into Eleanor's panic-driven thoughts. "There's peoples comin'! I can hear 'em. Listen!"

Eleanor and di Roche both listened and heard the pounding of hooves from above. In a matter of seconds, Harry Cross, John Whitson and three of the duke's grooms had dismounted and were sliding down into the gully. " 'Twas the smoke upon the air brought us," Harry Cross explained, pointing to where a wide, billowing gray cloud floated out of the mouth of the children's cave and up into the darkening sky. "Whitson thought it might be a lightning strike and ye caught in it."

"Oh-oh," murmured Joyce, looking guiltily at Jessie.

"It's our fire," confessed Jessie, standing dejectedly before Whitson. Di Roche raised an eyebrow. Harry Cross took off at a run, struggled up the side of the cliff and into the cave.

The children and the puppy were then passed up the side of the gully—Jessie placed safely before Whitson; Joyce settled in one of the lower groom's arms; and Blaze, wet and tired, asleep inside another of the lower groom's jackets.

Harry Cross emerged from the cave and waved. "Out!" he shouted. "Go!" And immediately the men turned their horses's heads toward Willowset.

Eleanor sat upon the cold, wet ground and cradled the earl's head in her lap. Di Roche stripped off his own caped greatcoat and wrapped it carefully around the gentleman. Harry Cross used his coat to raise the earl's left arm, which lay at an awkward angle, out of the mud. All three then sat silently. No one could think of anything at all to say.

"Tug!" Wright shouted after a long period of stillness, his eyes fluttering open.

"Hush," Eleanor murmured. "Tugforth is fine, and we shall be back at Willowset within the hour." She was not at all sure of either thing, but she dared not tell him so.

"Jenny?" he asked huskily.

"No, it is Miss Eleanor," mumbled Cross, "and you are both safe. Now close your eyes, my lord, and rest."

The eyelids did flutter closed, but then they fluttered open again. "It ain't Jenny's fault," the earl mumbled petulantly.

Eleanor stared down, surprised. Di Roche nodded at her to answer the man. "What is not Jenny's fault?"

"Nothin'."

"I see," answered Eleanor in a hushed voice. He is in a delirium, she thought, tears beginning to trail down her cheeks despite her best intentions. She trembled in the chill damp. The moon was rising full and she looked down to find the nearly black, silver-flecked eyes blinking up at her, perplexed.

"It cannot be Heaven," the bloodied lips whispered. "Are you a *fallen* angel?"

"A fallen angel?" Eleanor was stunned by the question.

"I shall not mind Hell if you are with me."

"Do not speak so," Eleanor ordered him with as much

authority as she could muster. "You are not dead, much less gone to Hades."

"A man don't need to die to go to Hades," mumbled Wright.

"You are not well, my lord," whispered Eleanor. "Close your eyes and you will be better soon."

The earl groaned and gave way, gasping in pain, to a spasm of coughing.

Harry Cross handed Eleanor a handkerchief, and she gently wiped the blood from Wright's bruised and battered face. Would the wagon never come? She had never been so frightened for anyone in her entire life.

Eleven

The group gathered in the music room of the Earl of Wright's private suite at Willowset was silent. Even the Reverend Mr. Howard found nothing to say as he sat fidgeting next to Miss Lipton. Eleanor, clean and dry, one ankle bound in fresh linen and resting upon a footstool, thought she would go mad with waiting. Directly across from her upon a puce divan, Jenny waited as well, tears welling in her great blue eyes and rolling slowly down her perfect pink-and-white cheeks. Behind her the Marquis di Roche, once again clean and dry himself, stood with hands clutching the back of the divan so tightly that his knuckles had gone white. Mary Hampton paced the room, her hands clasped at her bosom, her face by turns pale and flushed with anger. Paxton's eyes never once left that lady as he stood with one arm resting upon the fireplace mantel, his hand formed into a tight fist.

"He is going to die," murmured the little duchess abruptly.

"No, he is not going to die," hissed Mary angrily. "Do not say such nonsensical things."

The anger in Mary's voice frightened Jenny into loud sobs, and di Roche moved quickly to comfort her.

Mr. Paxton hurried to Mary's side and drew her hand through his arm, whispering into her ear. Eleanor, watching, longed for someone to comfort her as well. Her clear hazel eyes glanced hopefully at her brother, but he had sat upon the arm of Miss Lipton's chair and was awkwardly patting that young woman's shoulder as she clutched a crumpled handkerchief to her lips.

Feeling completely alone, tears started to Eleanor's eyes and she stood and hobbled from the room in an effort to keep them from being seen. In all her life she had never felt so outcast, so alone. Everyone had someone to comfort them, but not she—she must suffer the fear, the dread alone. There was sympathy for Jenny and Mary and even Lily—but Eleanor had been the one who witnessed his fall; he had endangered himself for her sake; she carried the heaviest guilt in her heart; yet no one came to hold her hand or give her shoulder a comforting pat. "Oh, dearest God," she murmured, "how can I do this? How can I feel sorry for myself when he is the one who suffers? I am selfish beyond belief!"

Her steps took her through the dining room of the earl's suite and past the sitting room. She paused to glance hesitantly into the sitting room at the door to the earl's bedchamber, which lay beyond, and behind which Dr. MacGregor and Tibbs and Colly Shepard and, at the surgeon's request, Mrs. Dish, at present attended to Wright's needs. Tears brimming over, she edged indecisively into the room, crossed it with tiny, halting steps and put her ear to the bedchamber door. A deep voice spoke within and was answered petulantly by a voice Eleanor knew to be the earl's. She swiped at her tears and took a very deep breath, the mere sound of him making her heart leap for joy. She realized at that very moment how terrible had been her fear as she had held him in the farm wagon that he would not live another hour. He had lain so still, even his delusional mutterings silenced.

"Eleanor, what on earth?" cried Mrs. Dish as she opened the door and Eleanor fell into her arms. "Good heavens, child. Are you all right?"

"Eleanor?" Wright's voice reached her clearly, though he was hidden from her by Dr. MacGregor's broad back.

"I expect Reverend Howard would not at all approve of your entering a gentleman's bedchamber," mused Mrs. Dish, her eyes twinkling as she took Eleanor's hand and led her toward the bed. "But this particular gentleman has been most recalcitrant, and I am sure your influence can do nothing but good."

"So, this is Wright's angel of mercy, is it?" asked MacGregor, rising to take Eleanor's hand in his own huge paw. "He swears, you know, that it was you kept him clinging to life until I appeared. I, of course, am to take the blame for all his aches and pains—his fall having had nothing at all to do with it."

"I never said so," muttered Wright. "But if you lay your damnable healing hands upon me one more time, I'll draw your cork."

"Master Jocelyn, cease immediately. Such language in Miss Howard's presence!" Tibbs attempted to frown around a relieved smile but could not quite do so.

"Miss Howard don't care," muttered Wright. His eyes, which Eleanor now saw were an impossibly dark blue and not black at all, peered solemnly up at her as MacGregor led her to his bedside. "You don't mind, do you, Ellie?"

Eleanor shook her head and smoothed the tumbled black curls from his freshly bandaged brow. She trailed her fingers slowly down his cheek, noticing for the first time the great bruises on his cheekbone and at the base of his stubborn jaw.

"My poor Miss Ellie," Wright murmured, his eyelids fluttering sleepily. He reached to take her hand and held it, stroking the back of it with his thumb.

Colly Shepard seized a rail-backed chair from across the room and carried it to the bedside so that Eleanor might sit comfortably beside the earl, who seemed unlikely to release her hand at any time soon. MacGregor grinned and nodded. " 'Tis the greatest impropriety, Miss Howard, that you should be here, but 'tis also the first civilized and rational response we have been able to gain from him."

"Go away, you great lout," groaned Wright. "I don't want you here."

"I am most cognizant of that, milord," laughed MacGregor,

"and as soon as you allow yourself to fall asleep, I shall depart—but not until."

"Will you sleep if I stay with you?" Eleanor asked quietly. "You must only promise to do that and Dr. MacGregor will be satisfied."

"I need to speak to you, Eleanor."

"Yes, but you must rest first, my lord."

"No, you don't understand."

"I understand that you frightened me exceedingly a mere three hours ago by falling into a delirium and then passing out completely, and that whatever you wish to say to me may be said equally well after you have slept." Eleanor gave the hand that held hers a reassuring squeeze. "I shall be right here when you awake, you know. I give you my word." Eleanor breathed a silent sigh of relief to see the long, curling lashes brush against his pale cheeks as the earl ceased fighting to keep himself awake. In a matter of moments his grip upon her hand slackened and he began to breathe less stertorously.

"At last," murmured MacGregor. "You are a blessing, Miss Howard. I believe I must speak to your brother and request that he allow you to visit this gentleman's bedchamber from time to time, or we shall lose him."

"Lose him?" Eleanor gasped, quickly meeting the surgeon's eyes. "You cannot mean—" She was interrupted by a low, tortured moan from the earl's lips and his sudden thrashing between the sheets.

"Hush," whispered Tibbs, hurrying to the opposite side of the ancient canopied monstrosity and tucking a pillow back into place beneath Wright's left arm, which Eleanor now saw was splinted. " 'Tis only a bad dream, your lordship. 'Tis not real."

"What is not real?" MacGregor asked.

Tibbs eyed the stocky surgeon warily, and Eleanor knew on the instant that it was something of which Tibbs did not wish to speak. "You said you thought to lose him," she whispered, taking the surgeon's attention from Tibbs. "Is he so gravely injured?"

"He is bruised and battered and broken from head to toe, Miss Howard. Between the horses kicking and the rocks sliding and himself falling, he has come very near killing himself. And how he continues to breathe with three ribs staved in and his lungs severely congested besides, I cannot begin to guess. 'Tis lucky he was born a northern barbarian like myself. The injury to his head alone would have taken off any more civilized human being. Well, I shall leave him in capable hands until morning," MacGregor said, acknowledging Tibbs, Mrs. Dish, Shepard and Burton, as he gathered his things. He left a bottle of laudanum drops on the washstand and handed Colly Shepard a recipe to be prepared from the herbs in the Willowset still-room, and assured them that he himself would stop at the apothecary's before returning in the morning. "The duchess is in the music room?" he asked Eleanor quietly.

Eleanor nodded.

"I shall stop and speak with her. Do you remain with Wright?"

"I promised him."

"Yes, well, he will most likely not know, my dear, whether you keep your promise or not. He is like to slip back into delirium, as feverish as he is and with such a blow to his skull. I'll tell your brother, however, that your presence in this chamber is indispensable to Wright's well-being. But you must not overdo either, Miss Howard. You have had a bad time of it yourself. When you feel tired you must take yourself off to bed. These good people are quite capable of attending to his lordship's needs."

Arthur Hampton paced the front parlor of the south wing of Hampton Hall by the light of three tallow candles and a recalcitrant blaze in the old grate. From time to time his cool glance fell upon the Sneezing Fiend, who sat uncomfortably in a lumpy armchair from which most of the stuffing had been removed and sold years earlier. The Fiend sipped from a bottle of French cabernet rescued from the cellars and uncorked with the point of a ten-penny blade. Both of the men shivered from time to time as the wind whipped in through the chinks around the ancient windows and down the sooty old chimney.

"I cannot believe," growled Hampton finally, "that there ain't another halfway habitable room left in this ugly pile of stone. I ain't been gone from England but three years."

"Aye, but were it 'abitable when ye left?" muttered the Fiend, a spark of curiosity in his mud-brown eyes.

"Not all of it. But certainly more than one room. 'Tis this vicious weather done it. Took the tiles clean off the roof."

"Aye, an' the birds nestin' up on the chimbleys don't be helpin', guv'nor, nor the windowglass fallin' out an' the stones crumblin'. A property like this—man's gotta look af'er it."

Hampton grabbed the bottle from the Fiend's hands and took a long swallow. "Why haven't we heard from di Roche?" he grumbled. "What in the name of the devil is the man doing? It is less than ten miles overland from Willowset to here and he cannot send us word on Wright in well over four hours?"

"P'rhaps 'e misunderstood ye, guv'nor, an' sent word ta the Gander's Neck."

"A pox on him! Probably sittin' in the public room right now all cozy and warm and sipping his brandy!"

"I could ride over there an' check inta it."

"Go!" replied Hampton in extreme annoyance. "Damn foreigner is most likely lookin' all over the inn for us! You can't trust 'em, foreigners—never get anything right!" Hampton pulled his greatcoat more tightly about him and dropped down to sit upon the moth-eaten carpeting before the grate, hoping to soak up more heat from the piddling little fire. "Do ye find him, you bring him back here with you, understand?"

"Aye." The Fiend nodded, elated at the opportunity to exchange the decay that surrounded him for the camaraderie of the Gander's Neck. "Though I doubt as if we'll gi' back 'ere afore termorra."

Hampton dismissed the man with a disgusted wave of his gloved hand. "Miserable wretch," he mumbled, raising the bottle of wine to his lips. "Calls himself a fiend an' he can't even abide a bit of hardship!"

There had been a time when Arthur Reginald Hampton, the only son of Baron Reginald Hampton, would not willingly have abided hardship himself. Pampered and spoiled most of his young life, Hampton had inherited at the age of nineteen an estate worth well over one hundred thousand pounds. He had run through most of it by the age of twenty-two. With no head for farming and an innate dislike of the country, he had stripped Hampton Hall of all the monies it could produce without re-investing a cent of it. He had raped the land, sent the tenants scurrying for other estates, sold everything of value that Hampton Hall had held—including the stuffing in the furniture—and at the last had been forced to worm his way into the heart of a little heiress—Miss Mary Farmington—in order to save himself from drowning in the River Tick. Not that he had found the young woman distasteful. No, that was not it at all. She had been—was—one of the most beautiful women he had ever seen. But he had never intended to wed the chit.

Hampton took another swallow of wine and inched closer to the fire. He'd cajoled the innocent, trusting Mary into thinking herself in love with him, convinced her that their only opportunity lay in an elopement and secretly left behind a message for her guardian that he would ruin the girl if his monetary demands were not met. And it damn well would have worked if Legion had not got involved in it. What business had it been of his—devil! Hampton had gotten the money, had raped and abandoned an hysterical Mary at some godforsaken north country inn and had been planning to board a ship bound for Vienna almost three months later when the intimidating figure of the Earl of Wright astride that damnable black horse had overtaken Hampton's curricle on the way to Portsmouth, dragged him into the road and beaten him calmly and ruthlessly to a pulp. Hampton's hatred flared again at the memory of it. That devil, that barbarian, that savage, had then commandeered the curricle, driven him unconscious to Gretna Green and forced him to marry the girl over the anvil. And then the madman had beaten him again, stuffed him into a Scottish hack and sent him to the coast, vowing to kill him should he set eyes on him ever again. Hampton pounded his fist into the carpeting and a great cloud of dust rose into the air. "We shall see who kills whom, my dear Wright," he coughed, attempting to wave the dust away. "If you are not dead already—I promise you will be soon—quite soon!"

Mary, with Paxton close on her heels, had gone up to the third floor, relieved somewhat by the appearance of optimism Dr. MacGregor had assumed for Jenny's benefit. "For he would not speak so confidently, do you think, Mr. Paxton, if the earl were in grave danger?"

Paxton—who would have spoken in terms equally as optimistic had Legion been lying dead at his feet if faced with Jenny's tears—told a great clanker and assured Mary that the surgeon would surely not have spoken so confidently had the earl been in grave danger. "You must not worry, m'dear," he said, stunned by his own cowardice. "Josh will be ordering everyone about and pouting at having to stay in bed by tomorrow morning."

"I hope you're right," sighed Mary, "for I shan't be easy until I hear his opinion of this—accident. Look there," she added in a whisper as they entered the nursery. "Are they not the sweetest little scamps you have ever seen?"

"Mrs. Hampton," said Bowey, looking up from her knitting. "They have survived their adventures without the least harm—though I expect one or both may succumb to a case of the sniffles in the morning. Have you news of his lordship?"

"He will survive nicely as well, Bowey," Mary smiled,

smoothing Joyce's dusky curls away from her round little face. "Were the children not frightened for him?"

"Oh, no. I gather that once Miss Eleanor assured them he was not dead they had every confidence that all would be well. He is a great hero to Master Jessie, you know, and quite above needing to be worried about if he is not dead."

"He is a great hero to Joyce, as well," Mary nodded.

"And a hero to you?" Paxton asked as they bid Bowey good night and wandered back toward the staircase.

"And a hero to me," Mary said softly, her great brown eyes peeping doelike up at him from beneath long, curling lashes. She allowed him to escort her as far as the door to the chambers that had been prepared for Mrs. Dish and then sent him off to his own bed. "Aunt Euphegenia?" she called, scratching lightly upon the door.

"Mary!" cried that lady, tugging the door open. Swathed from head to toe in an enormous cotton nightgown, with a very pretty lace nightcap upon her silvered hair, Mrs. Dish led Mary into her sitting room and settled her with a cup of tea before the fire. "I thought at first it was Burton come to call me down to his lordship," she said, patting the back of Mary's hand as she sat beside her. "Oh, my dearest girl, I am so very pleased to see you at last. It has been so long. I thought you never would come to St. Swithin's again."

"I—I could not, Aunt. I was so—so ashamed. To have ruined myself, and then to discover myself increasing—I thought surely no one would wish to see my face ever again."

Mrs. Dish put one arm reassuringly about Mary's shoulders and nodded. "That wretched Roger made you think that—he and that nodcock Lucy."

"I am certain they were quite correct, Aunt, to turn their backs upon me after all the disgrace I had brought upon them."

"Nonsense! If Roger were not my own nephew, I should have told Josh to run him through—yes, and Lucille, too. You were in their charge and they ought to have protected you! But no more—I have longed to see you and that darling child, and here you are! Am I not the luckiest old woman alive?"

Mary smiled and bestowed a kiss upon the sweetly aging cheek. "Josh said all along that you would never turn me away, but I could not make myself believe it. You are the very best aunt in the entire world! Was it you sent him to find me after I ran away with Hampton?"

"No my dear. He found you quite accidentally. I did barely know the gentleman. He seldom came to St. Swithin's except in the company of the duke and duchess. And I do not remember him doing aught but nod in my direction at church until the night he came pounding upon my door, demanding to know was I acquainted with a Miss Mary Farmington."

"Oh, what a bouncer he told me! He said he had come to rescue me. That a dear friend of his and relative of mine had sent him. And I knew it could not have been Uncle Roger, and so, of course, I asked him if it were you. And he sat there with me sobbing against his chest and whispered that of course it was! Oh, Aunt, he must have been at the Rise and just stopped at the Broken Wing for a glass of ale and the innkeeper enlisted his aid. And I to swallow such a whopper! To believe that you might command an earl to ride to my rescue—and I have believed it nearly four years, too!"

Mrs. Dish chuckled and sipped her tea. "You gave him a terrible start when you refused to come to me or to return to London. Did you know that?"

Mary shook her head, wide-eyed. "He never said a word. Only agreed that I should not be further humiliated. He settled me at Elders Rise in Mr. and Mrs. Simpson's care. And then, when I discovered—when Mrs. Simpson wrote him that I was—well, increasing—he came storming back with Hampton in tow. I had been thinking then to simply kill myself and put an end to my degradation. Oh, I was very wrong, of course, Aunt, but I was so terribly depressed and it seemed such a simple answer to all my problems."

"And now look at you," murmured Mrs. Dish tenderly. "You

are beautiful and wise and a loving mother with years of happiness ahead."

Mary stared into her teacup pensively. "Did—did Josh not explain why he wished you to stay here for a time?"

"Why, to visit with you and little Joyce!"

"Yes, of course—and—and to protect you, Aunt."

"Protect me?" asked that lady with a frown.

"Hampton has returned to England and swears he will kill Josh and take me for his own. We feared he might remember you, Aunt, and seek to harm you in some way."

Eleanor looked up from her needlepoint to meet her brother's solemn gaze. "I agreed you might visit him from time to time, Ellie, but you cannot spend the entire night at his bedside. Go up to your own bed, now. I will sit with him until Tibbs returns."

"I promised to be here when he woke, Martin. I gave him my word."

"I am sure he will forgive you for not keeping it."

"No, he will not—for I do not intend to break it. I said I would stay until he woke and I will."

Howard muttered something under his breath, pulled a chair from across the room up beside his sister's and sat down. "Ellie, you are not becoming enamored of this—this—madman?"

"He saved my life, Martin!"

"Yes, I realize that, my dear, and I am cognizant of the debt I owe him, but he would have reacted similarly no matter who had been with him. What I am saying, Ellie, is that he would have done the same for Oakes or Tibbs or anyone. You must not refine too much upon it."

Eleanor jabbed her needle into her work and left it there. "Well, I do refine upon it, Martin! I have been refining upon it from the moment I saw him crashing down that hillside amid rocks, mud and flailing horses! I refined upon it when he lay bleeding in my lap. I refined upon it when I held him steady in the farm wagon. And I am refining upon it at this moment. And I shall not leave him, do you understand?"

Howard stared at his sister agog. He opened his mouth and closed it again. He shook his head and ran his fingers through his dark brown hair. He fiddled at his collar with one finger, stood up and then sat back down. "I—I—you cannot mean you intend to—to—encourage a—a—serious relationship?"

"Oh, Martin," Eleanor sighed, exasperated. "You are such a gudgeon! How can you think for one moment that someone like Lord Wright would be interested in me? Are you blind? Do you not see the beautiful women who surround him? No, I have not the least hope of a relationship as you think of it, but I intend to pursue a serious friendship, and if you cannot support me in that, then you may— you may—"

"Go to the devil," mumbled Wright.

Eleanor literally jumped up at the sound of his voice.

"Go to the devil," he said again, more clearly, his eyes seeking her in the candlelight.

"Yes," she agreed, taking his hand into hers. "Martin may go to the devil if he cannot like us to be friends. No, do not attempt to sit up, my lord. You cannot do it on your own. Your left arm is broken and your ankle, and your ribs."

A smile crept across the earl's face as she spoke and ended in a deep chuckle, followed by an obviously painful bout of coughing. "I g-gather I am rapidly f-falling apart."

"Rapidly," drawled Howard. "And I have not the least intention of going to the devil. I shall go into the sitting room, however, if you wish to speak privately with Ellie."

Wright's dark curls moved restlessly against the pillow. "Yes, go," he said after a moment. Eleanor noticed the remarkable eyes narrow in pain and noticed, too, how Martin hesitated when he saw them do so.

"Did MacGregor not leave some laudanum for him?" Howard asked, glancing about the room. His gaze fell upon the bottle on the washstand and he crossed to fetch it. "I shall get some cool water," he announced, peering at MacGregor's instructions. "And when I return you shall take this medicine, Wright."

Eleanor watched him go, then seated herself upon the edge of the bed. "Now, you must tell me what troubles you," she said softly.

"Is Melinda here?"

"Yes, indeed. She helped tend to you. Do you not remember?"

"N-no. She s-stays?"

"Yes. You asked her to stay, my lord. You sent Oakes to fetch her. Do you not remember?"

"I—y-yes, but I d-did not know if—Eleanor, I cannot b-be in such q-queer st-stirrups now."

The discouragement in his tone tugged at Eleanor's heart. "It cannot be helped, dearest," she murmured tenderly, smoothing the counterpane across his chest just as she would have done had it been Jessie in the bed. "Surely there is nothing requires your attention that one of your friends may not do for you."

"I d-don't have any f-friends," rasped Wright distractedly.

"Oh, bosh. Who is Mrs. Dish if she is not your friend? And Mr. Paxton, and Mrs. Hampton, and Miss Lipton? Not to mention your sister and the Marquis di Roche, and Tibbs and Oakes and Harry Cross. Yes, and Burton and Bowey and Colly Shepard, too. They will all be pleased to help you if only you tell them what must be done."

"Di Roche? Di Roche, Eleanor?"

"Why, yes. I know you are not quite pleased with him because of his silly escapade with the duchess, but—"

"He is here?"

"Do you not remember that either? He came to the Hook just after you fell. 'Twas he who first came to our aid. He has sent to the Gander's Neck for his things and has promised the duchess to remain here until you are on the mend. And Martin will stand your friend as well," she added. "I know you do not like each other, but truly, he is a most dependable person, and he feels himself in your debt." Eleanor pressed the back of her hand against his cheek and the heat of it frightened her. "You must rest now," she told him. "Martin will be here in a moment with your medicine."

"Eleanor," Wright groaned, "what was di Roche doing at the Hook? Was it he wrote the note?"

"Oh!" gasped Eleanor, the note warning the earl to beware of Cutter's Hook having fled her mind completely until this moment. "Oh, Jocelyn, it was not an accident!"

"I don't know." The earl coughed. "But you m-must watch over Mary and J-Joyce for me. It is H-Hampton w-wants my life and he w-will harm them if he can."

Eleanor's eyes opened wide. Hampton? Mary's Hampton? All this time she had thought Mrs. Hampton a widow. And she had thought, too, that Wright had not the least idea who wished to kill him. She began to demand some explanation when she noticed that his eyes no longer focused upon her and that his good hand flailed at the counterpane, attempting to throw it off.

"He has slipped away, Ellie," Howard observed, setting a pitcher upon the washstand and carrying a glass of water to her. "I have put the laudanum drops into it already. Let me support him, and you get him to swallow some. It will ease a good deal of the pain and let him sleep."

Twelve

Di Roche's message having conveyed the extremity of the earl's injuries, as well as the fact that they would now reside at Willowset, Nicco stopped at the apothecary's shop in St. Swithin's to procure a singular mixture of herbs by which his mother swore and the recipe of which he had memorized long ago. "Well, if ye're bound for Willowset," Dr. MacGregor, who was himself waiting for a prescription to be filled, smiled, "I shall see ye again shortly. Come to have medicine made up for Wright, myself. Accident. Got himself caught up in a rock slide. Richard, what's taking so long? That mixture ain't so complicated."

"C-c-coming!" the apothecary sneezed. "Here ye are, MacGregor. Here ye a-a-are!"

"It's that catskin waistcoat keeps ye sneezing," sighed MacGregor, taking the medicine. "Rid y'rself of it and see, why don't you? It's certainly worth a try."

"Someday, some d-d-day!" Hobbins sneezed again. "But it's me favorite, an' I can't bear the thought o' losin' it as yet."

MacGregor laughed, bid Nicco farewell, and departed the shop. Nicco, his eyes wide, recognized the Sneezing Fiend immediately. But did the Fiend recognize him? Had he even noticed Nicco eavesdropping in the public room at the Gander's Neck that evening? Most likely not, Nicco decided. Hampton hadn't. He drew himself up to his full five foot three inches and requested the medicine he had come for.

"Sure'n I kin mix it fer ye," Hobbins nodded. "New in these parts ain't ye? Foreigner?"

"I am coming to visiting my grandmama," murmured Nicco. "I am thinking how thankful she being I have stop and bringing to her these medicine."

"She live hereabouts?"

"No, no, *signor.* She living in Dither-on-moor, but there they have not the apothecary."

"No," Hobbins grinned, busily mixing up Nicco's request. "They ain't got much of nothin'. Here ye go, bucko."

Nicco crossed the Fiend's palm with gold and left the establishment. Packing the medicine carefully into the rented gig that carried his and di Roche's belongings, he tossed two coins to the boy who had held his horse, took the reins and drove off toward the high road. He did not turn toward Willowset until he was certain he was not being followed.

Di Roche sat up in bed, a magnificent striped nightcap clinging drunkenly to his thick mop of golden hair. "Are you being positive, Nicco?"

Nicco nodded, handing him a cup of hot chocolate. "I seeing meselves. These one the 'pothecary being."

Di Roche set the cup on the bedside table and crawled hurriedly from beneath the covers. "Ees must rushing be, Nicco. Ees already the big MacGregor with the earl. These medicine may poison being!"

MacGregor stared openmouthed at the marquis as di Roche, hastily thrown into his clothes, cornered him in the earl's bedchamber and attempted to explain that the medicine Richard Hobbins had given him might be poisoned. The surgeon's head shook in disbelief. "Hobbins, a murderer? I think not, m'lord. Of course, ye might taste the stuff and see does it make you ill. That might convince me otherwise."

Di Roche declined the privilege with a shake of his head.

"Well, then, he must have it," MacGregor mused. "He may well die without it. His fever is worse this morning."

"These you giving his lordship," urged Nicco, holding out an apothecary's bottle. "Fiend ees making for my fishtishing grandmama. Ees safe."

"For your what grandmama?" Tibbs, his eyebrows drawn together in puzzlement, had moved from the earl's bedside to the spot where the gentlemen conversed in whispers across the room.

"Mees fishtishing grandmama."

"He meaning his grandmama being not real," explained di Roche impatiently. "Ees fishtishing."

"Ah," nodded Tibbs, "fictitious."

"*Si,* yes," Nicco nodded. "You must not giving his lordship the medicine these Fiend knowing meant for him."

Tibbs scowled. "Here, what's wrong with the medicine?"

Once again di Roche muddled through the explanation and Tibbs gasped. "Devil if I have not already given him some!" he cried, rushing back to where the earl lay mumbling in the bed.

"Ye can't have," MacGregor growled. "I just arrived."

"Yes, and left a bottle of the stuff standing right there, saying his lordship ought to have a spoonful of it. And then you wandered off to fetch a cup of coffee!" exclaimed Tibbs. "And so I gave it to him. Master Josh," he cried, seizing the earl's shoulder and giving him a shake, "speak to me! Tell me who I am!"

"T-tibbs?" asked Wright, his eyelids fluttering open. "I—I think I'm going to—"

Nicco dove for the chamber pot in the very nick of time.

Lured from a solitary breakfast by the sound of banging doors, exclamations and a muffled cry from belowstairs, Eleanor found her way down into the kitchen, where the news that the earl had been poisoned had arrived on the heels of Dr. MacGregor's mad rush to the stillroom. Eleanor hurried to Wright's chambers, and one glance at the painfully retching figure surrounded by grim, determined faces sent her weakly into a chair in Wright's sitting room, where she determinedly put her head down between her knees and told herself over and over that now was most certainly not an acceptable time to faint. It was the little marquis who at last knelt before her and asked in broken English where he might find the "smelly things ladies using." Eleanor lifted her head and sighed. "I do not need help, my lord," she murmured distractedly. "I only felt a bit faint, but I am fine now." She saw MacGregor and then Tibbs and then Nicco emerge from the sickroom, and her face paled considerably. "He is not—he is not dead?" she asked hoarsely.

"No, Miss Howard," MacGregor sighed, collapsing into a chair across from her. "Though I expect another dose or two would have done the trick and I not likely to have suspected. When I get my hands on Hobbins I shall throttle him."

"Hobbins? Mr. Hobbins, the apothecary?"

"Yes, 'twas he poisoned the medicine. Nicco, here, says Richard Hobbins and another man are out to put an end to Wright."

Nicco nodded excitedly.

"And di Roche, here, he says Wright's accident was an accident, all right—but only because Legion arrived at the spot a day early."

Eleanor gazed at the marquis, who had moved from before her to perch upon one of the window seats. "H-how—how do you know this?" she asked.

By the time di Roche had finished his story, from Nicco's overhearing of the plot at the Gander's Neck to the unlooked-for arrival of Eleanor and Wright at Cutter's Hook, his entire audience was staring at him in disbelief. Tibbs shook his hoary head disgustedly and stomped back into the earl's bedchamber without a word.

"Was it you wrote the note, my lord?" Eleanor asked quietly.

Di Roche nodded. "I not wish to seeing my beloved's brother harmed being. I am think to spying upon these men and to keeping them from the earl. It ees not working."

"But you could do nothing more," Eleanor sighed. "And if it had not been for your valet, Lord Wright might well have been poisoned without any of us the wiser."

"Well, I'm the wiser now," growled MacGregor, one huge fist pounding down upon the chair arm, "and Richard Hobbins is about to receive a visit from myself and Constable Perkins."

The Reverend Mr. Howard scowled disbelievingly at his sister over the remains of his breakfast an hour later. "Richard Hobbins and one of the Hamptons? I cannot believe it, Ellie. Hobbins has been in the village over a year and attends services every Sunday, and none of the Hamptons have been in the neighborhood for well over four years. Besides, what possible reason could they have to assault Wright? No, it is too unbelievable. Some sort of mistake, likely. Foreigners, you know. Got something quite mixed up."

"Do you think that simply because Mr. Hobbins attends services, Martin, he cannot have attempted to murder his lordship?" asked Eleanor with a frown.

"My father attended services at St. Paul's every Sunday," remarked Miss Lipton, her kissable lips formed into a pretty pout. "And then he came home and said and did dreadful things."

Howard's eyebrows rose appreciatively.

"I only mean to say," continued Miss Lipton, addressing her remarks to the large piece of beefsteak upon her plate, "that a person may pretend to be proper and yet be quite improper. We all wish to present a good appearance in public. Except Josh. He does not care what anyone thinks of him."

"He does care, Lily," Mary sighed. "He cares very much. But he hasn't the least idea how to go on in any other way. He is most envious of Reverend Howard, you know, but cannot understand what he must do to be more like him."

"Wright envies Howard?" asked Paxton, a glimmer of subdued mirth in his eyes. "Mrs. Hampton, what a bouncer!"

"It is not a bouncer," declared Mary. "He envies Mr. Howard his self-confidence and his friendship with the villagers and his quiet way of life, and he says everyone respects Mr. Howard and not one person thinks him a villain. And he wishes he knew how to go about being more like Mr. Howard, but he cannot do it because his temper always gets the best of him and he is forever compelled to do things of which people don't approve."

The Reverend Howard's eyes widened considerably.

"Well, you must understand," offered Mrs. Dish, placing a plate of eggs and toast upon the table and taking a seat beside Mary, "the earl and Mr. Howard are much alike at heart, but their backgrounds and experiences are very different. I do not find it odd at all that Josh should envy Mr. Howard. I suspect that were he to admit it, Mr. Howard envies Josh some things as well."

Howard opened his mouth to protest vociferously but closed it again at the sight of the tears springing to Miss Lipton's eyes. "Miss Lipton, what is it?" he asked solicitously instead.

"I do not wish to talk about Josh anymore. Please may we not? He is so ill and cannot be here to defend himself and—"

"Oh, my child," Mrs. Dish said, pushing her plate from her and standing. "Come with me this moment. All this time you have been worried to death about the gentleman and not one of us thought to allow you to visit him." Taking Miss Lipton's hand in her own, Mrs. Dish led Lily off toward the south wing.

"I hope poor Wright has finished casting up his accounts," mumbled Paxton, lifting his coffee cup to his lips and blowing at the hot liquid.

Mary smiled wanly and kicked him under the table.

"Well, but, it's Lily," Paxton murmured. "I should feel privileged were you to hold my head while I was retching my guts out, m'dear, but to appear in such a state and so totally helpless in front of Lily? I think not."

"He will not be helpless, and if he is retching, he will cease to do so on the instant because Lily has tears in her eyes and he will do anything to make them go away. Lily is correct; he cannot be anyone but himself and himself will suffer death in silence if it will keep Lily from crying." Mary smiled and stood. "Eleanor," she said, "shall we look in on the children? I am positive Bowey is having a terrible time with them. They are both longing to see their Uncle Josh and do not understand why they cannot simply come down and jump upon his bed and cuddle with him. And perhaps we ought to stop and see if the duchess is presentable? I do not think, however," she added, as they left the gentlemen behind, "that we ought to tell her about the poison."

"Would he—would he truly suffer death in silence just to keep Lily from crying?" Eleanor asked haltingly, her face aflame.

"There, I knew I should not have spoken so outrageously in front of you and your brother. It is just that Lord Wright cannot bear tears, my dear. His first instinct is to do anything possible to turn them into smiles. That, I think, is part of the reason Jenny is so spoilt."

"Do you think she is spoilt?"

"Very. When first we met I thought she ran roughshod over Josh and terribly neglected Jessie and ought to be called to account for it. But one cannot."

"Well, I expect it was hardly your place to do so."

"Oh, it was not the thought of that kept me from it. It was—well, one just cannot. Jenny does not understand what you are speaking of when you attempt to point out to her the errors of her ways," Mary grinned. "She simply does not see things in an ordinary way. She is nearly as exceptional a person as Josh, and I should like to have known them as children, shouldn't you? Lily says that their father sounds to her like the blackest villain ever lived, but that Josh only ever speaks of him with fondness."

"Has Lily known his lordship for a very long time?" Eleanor asked as they climbed the stairs to the third floor.

"A very long time. Nearly five years."

* * *

In the south wing Lily sat upon the edge of the earl's bed tightly gripping his hand. "I shall never ever leave you," she whispered, leaning forward to bestow a chaste kiss upon his bandaged brow.

"Balderdash," muttered Wright, the dark eyes blinking open in his ashen face. "You know very well you are wishing to do just that, Lilliputian."

"No, never! You are the bravest, kindest gentleman in the entire world."

"Besides which, I am sick, eh? Come, Lily, I ain't going to die. Truth. Howard has won your heart. I watched how you doted on him all the way home in the curricle yesterday."

"He is nothing!" declared Lily with a stubborn pout. "He calls you a barbarian and he thinks he knows everything, but he does not. He doesn't know the least thing about people!"

"He calls me a barbarian because he don't like me, Lily. And you must teach him about people. He ain't had as many gadawful opportunities to experience people as you and I."

Lily's big blue eyes brimmed with tears. "I c-could, Josh. I c-could teach him, couldn't I? I do l-love him."

"Howard has no use for a mistress, you know. He will want you for his wife."

"But—but he is a gentleman. I c-cannot marry a gentleman."

"Why not? Oh, I know it ain't socially acceptable, Lily, but I would marry you if we loved each other like—like that. And I'm a gentleman."

Wright closed his eyes tightly as the urge to cascade all over the sheets swamped him. He fought it back and groaned.

"Oh, Josh, is there anything at all that I may do? Would you like some water or—or—"

The earl opened one eye to see Lily suddenly fluttering around the bed. He closed it and opened the other. Then he closed that, counted to five and opened both together. "Settle down, sweetings, do. You are making me exceedingly dizzy. Sit, Lil," he commanded.

Lily sat.

"Do you think, Lily, if I could arrange it, that you would like to marry the reverend?"

"Oh, yes!" breathed Lily, her gorgeous blue eyes lighting with hope. "Oh, Josh, thank you so very much!"

Mrs. Dish peered in through the doorway at that moment and noticed how the smile faltered on Wright's face. She announced then and there that the earl must rest if he was ever to get well and escorted Miss Lipton from the chamber. Tibbs, entering as they left, dashed to the bedside and seized the candle and candleholder from Wright's hand just before it could soar and crash against the opposite wall.

"Master Josh, whatever is wrong with you?"

"I am sure I don't know, Tibbs," muttered the earl. "I have a putrid sore throat; I cannot breathe; I am bound up in so many places and bruised in so many others that moving is agony; you have just finished poisoning me; and Lily has fallen in love—*in love,* Tibbs—with that sanctimonious, self-righteous bastard of a parson, Howard. And worse yet, I have given her hope that he will marry her!"

"Shhh," whispered Tibbs, setting the candle and holder out of reach and tucking Wright's good arm back under the counterpane. "You must not overexcite yourself, my lord. You will start to vomiting again and that will make your head ache ten times worse than it does already. And you are only making your fever worse, too, aren't you?"

Raising the earl gently with one arm and fluffing the pillows beneath his head, Tibbs suggested softly how pleasant it would be for the gentleman to forget everyone and everything and simply drift off to sleep. "And when you wake I shall see there is something nourishing awaits you, for you haven't eaten, you know, since yesterday morning." Pouring a glass of water and mixing three drops of laudanum into it, Tibbs returned to the bed, lifted Wright enough to get the liquid down him and then set the glass aside. He soaked a cloth in lavender water and placed it across the earl's aching eyes. "There now, that's a deal better, isn't it, Master Josh? We shall have you well in no time, and then you may deal with whatever crisis most appeals to you."

Paxton, who had wandered into the earl's suite to see how the madman was doing, stood watching silently outside the bedchamber door as Tibbs's ministrations eased Wright into unconsciousness. "I think he's well out of it, Tibbs," he commented at last. "If you've something needs doing, I'll be pleased to keep an eye on him for you."

"Mr. Paxton, sir," acknowledged Tibbs, taking the cloth from Wright's eyes, soaking it again and replacing it. "I thank you for the offer. There's clean sheets to see to, and his medicine, and I must consult with Aberdeen about something suitable to feed him when he wakes."

"I say, Tibbs, before you disappear—what crises are there he is to pick and choose among?"

Tibbs smiled and shook his head. "With his lordship there is always one crisis or another, sir. Born into the midst of them, he was, and has not the least idea how peaceful an earl's life ought to be. Was a moment there, when our little Jenny married the duke, that I had hopes he'd discover it, but—" Tibbs shrugged and took himself out of the chamber.

Paxton slouched into an armchair and sat staring at the figure in the bed. He ought to be on his way back to London by now, but he had not the least intention of undertaking that journey until Wright was on the mend. He had met the Earl of Wright on the eve of the Duke of Ware's marriage. He had heard of him, of course, before then, but it was the sight of those midnight blue, silver-flecked eyes burning into his own across a snifter of Charlie's finest brandy that had caused him for the first time to take seriously the heart-stopping tales of Legion that were whispered over dying embers and warm ale.

Charlie had read his thoughts instantly and laughed uproariously without offering explanation to any of his other guests, simply crossing the floor to clap Paxton on the back and whisper, "Indeed, Michael, he is everything you've heard and more, and I have made the devil's own bargain to get my Jenny from him." Those words had caused Paxton a deal of anxiety for the rest of the evening, until he had gotten Ware alone and forced him to reveal what bargain he had struck with the infamous devil. And then he had sunk into a chair—much like the one in which he lounged now—and stared in disbelief. "That's it?" he'd asked. "That's the bargain? No monies, no estates, no human sacrifices?"

"Only my soul," Charlie had grinned. "I am not even allowed the luxury of abandoning the dear girl in the country and loping off into town for a lark or two, Michael. I must always have her with me. I must watch over her and protect her and amuse her every moment of my life—or Legion'll see my life is over. And whatever her faults, I am sworn to overlook them and to abandon all hope of bringing her to understand and correct them. The thing is," Charlie had laughed, "it is the fact she is such a—a rumcake, Wright calls her—that makes me want to look after the girl the rest of my days. Smile, Paxton, it ain't a bad bargain—she's the love of my life, Jenny is, and I've sworn to keep it that way is all."

Paxton stirred in the chair, settling more comfortably. A bemused smile lit his eyes. "What bargain must I agree to, Legion, to take Mary and Joyce into my keeping?" he whispered softly. Wright moved uneasily upon the bed, groaning quietly with an unconscious effort to move the broken ankle. "Yes, well you might groan, devil. There's things I shall force you to tell me about Mary. Things she don't say. Is this Hampton who harries you some in-law of hers? What secrets do the two of you share that I know nothing of? I shall get it out of you, Legion. Yes, and I have no doubt 'twill prove to be another crisis for you."

Eleanor was surprised to discover Mr. Paxton bending carefully over Wright and attempting to cool the feverish gentleman with a cloth dipped in lavender water. "He is burning up again," Paxton murmured. "And whatever he dreams, I give thanks I do not share them."

"Give it to me, Michael," commanded Mary as she entered behind Eleanor. She held out her hand for the cloth and received it immediately. "Send someone to fetch Tibbs and—and Harry Cross, I think. And ask in the kitchen for them to send enough cool water to bathe him in. And tell my aunt Wright has need of her."

"Your aunt?"

"Mrs. Dish, Michael. Good heavens! I thought you knew. Mrs. Dish is my aunt."

Paxton nodded and left the room.

"Ellie, perhaps you had better not stay. He is grown much worse of a sudden."

As if to justify her cool assessment, Wright began to flail at the bedcovers and attempt to escape them. Eleanor flew to the opposite side of the bed and caught his splinted arm, holding it as still as possible. Cradling it upon the pillows Tibbs had set beneath it, she reached to stop the leg that sported the broken ankle from kicking.

"Do not, Jocelyn," Mary said in a low, clear voice. "You are only dreaming, love. Try and wake up, do. I shall give you a present if you will." Eleanor watched as Mary's deft hands pulled down the counterpane and began to untie Glenby Oakes's nightshirt, in which the earl had been swaddled. "He hates nightshirts," Mary murmured. "I bought him one once and he gave it to a hackney driver. They make him feel caught and tethered, he says, like a pig ready for roasting." She dipped the cloth back into the water and bathed his neck and chest as best she could, hampered by the bandages that held his ribs in place. "Oh, Josh, do stop fidgeting so. You will hurt yourself more and all for nothing. They are only dreams, dearest. They cannot harm you. Eleanor, tell him they are only dreams."

Eleanor stared at the young woman as though seeing her for the very first time. How could she have been so blind? Mary

Hampton thought nothing of undressing the earl, thought nothing of bathing him, had even, once, bought him a nightshirt. And Joyce—little Joyce, with her dusky curls and great dark eyes. She called him Uncle Josh, but he was not her uncle. He was her father surely. Why, even her name had been taken from his!

"Eleanor," Mary urged, "speak to him. Tell him he is here with you and that he must wake up now."

"I—I cannot—Your lordship, you are at Willowset with Jenny and Mary and Lily and—and me. Can you not wake up now? Please?"

"Please," mumbled Wright, his tossing slowly coming to a halt. "Please."

Mary laughed and planted a kiss directly upon his hot, dry lips as his eyelids fluttered upward. "Oh, Eleanor," she laughed, reaching across Wright's body to take one of Miss Howard's hands into her own. "You have shocked him back into reality. I do not believe anyone has ever said 'please' to him before in his entire life!"

Wright's eyes, dazed but searching, found Eleanor's. "Angel, I'm so damnably hot. Cannot you make the devil douse his fire?"

Thirteen

"You did what?" bellowed Arthur Hampton at the top of his lungs. His fine, sculpted hands, encased in buff kidskin gloves stained with mud, smoke and ashes, reached out ardently for the Fiend's long, skinny neck.

"Now, now, guv'nor," cried the Fiend, dodging to one side. "Only tryin' to help ye, I w—w-w-asscho! Ye said ye wanted him dead. Thought it a perfect time ta d-d-dooocho! ye a favor, don't ye know."

"A favor!" roared Hampton. "A favor! And is the devil dead, then? No! An' have we got a way to get to him? No! And is the whole county out looking for us? Yes!" Hampton's face, what could be seen of it between the collar of his greatcoat and the hat he had pulled down over his ears, began to turn a stunning purple. He lunged for the Fiend with both hands, got him this time and threw the unlucky villain clear across the room. The Fiend stumbled backward over a footstool, caught the heel of his boot in the fraying carpet and bounced into the parlor wall.

"Ooof!" exclaimed the Fiend as his unpadded posterior contacted the floor.

"Did you even ride to the Gander's Neck? Did you even bother to contact di Roche?"

"Weren't there, guv'nor. Not a sign of 'im. So's I jus' went on home, like, an' when MacGregor shows up upon m' doorstep this mornin' a wantin' medicine fer the earl, why I sees my chance, don't ye see. How he come ta figger out the stuff be poisoned is what perplexes me. I tell ye, guv'nor, it shoulda worked. It shoulda done the trick all nice an' quiet like. I kinnot figger out what went wrong."

"And now the constable is on your tail and you come flying here so that we may be hauled off to gaol together, is that it?"

"Aw, now, ain't nobody gonna come followin' me here," The Fiend sighed. "I skippered off fast-like. Soon's I see old MacGregor in company with Constable Perkins a crossin' toward the shop. Never laid eyes on me, they din't."

"Then how do you know Wright is not dead?"

"Why, he couldn't be—not so soon. They'd hafta give the bloke a whole bottle o' the stuff before he sunk right outta sight. Make 'im fade out slow so's it looked nat'ral, I figgered. I know ol' MacGregor did not pour an entire bottle o' the stuff down 'im in one mornin'."

"Dash an' blast it!" Hampton bellowed and threw the only decoration that remained in the room—a large putrid yellow snuff jar—against the wall above the Fiend's head, where it shattered into a thousand pieces, all of them seemingly bound for some part of the cringing Fiend's anatomy.

"Well, if yer gonna keep on about it," mumbled the Fiend, rising and brushing the shards and dust from himself, "I reckon I'll jus' be a goin' an' ye kin git on about the killin' wi'out me. I gots friends all up an' down the highway, I does, an' I ain't feared o' no Constable Perkins. No, an' I ain't looby enuf ta be spendin' my time freezin' ta death an' starvin' too in this sad excuse fer a hovel. Shudda knowed better'n ta git involved with a flash cove in the first place. I'll jus' go off on me way ta Lunnon, an' ye kin keep the rest o' yer blunt an' do the dirty work yerself."

Hampton, who, despite the intense hatred he carried for the earl, wanted nothing more at the moment than to be fed, dry and warm, stomped toward the Fiend. "I'm sorry," he muttered. "I should not have taken out my frustration on you. I expect it's not safe for you to return to the Gander's Neck, is it?"

"H-h-aaardlycho! But I reckon ain't nobody gonna remem-

ber us a meetin' in the public room tha' night, so as it'll be
safe fer ye to go back. Well, ye oughta go back, oughtn't ye?
All yer gear be stashed there."

"Yes. I tell you what, Hobbins. I shall go back, and you shall
go to wherever it is you desire, and we shall meet here tonight
to discuss what may be done. Wright's down, after all—he just
ain't out. What I am thinking is, there may be a way that we
may put an end to him tonight."

"What? Tonight? Yer barmy."

"No, no, I don't think so. I need to ponder for a while. Meet
me here tonight, about seven say, and we shall discuss it."

The Sneezing Fiend, a puddle of doubt in his mud brown
eyes, shrugged and nodded. Hampton's handsome but slowly
dissipating countenance broke into a smile. With a number of
reassurances that all was not as bleak as it looked and that they
were very near to accomplishing their goal, the two mounted
up and rode off in opposite directions. Hampton aimed directly
for the Gander's Neck; Hobbins wandered off in an alarmingly
aimless manner into the countryside. "Oughta have me mind
examined fer messin' aroun' wi' that flash cove," mumbled the
Fiend. "Me da taught me long ago they weren't a one o' 'em
ta be trusted. Always gotta do ever'thin' the hard way. Oughta
have me brain plucked ri' outta me head an' roasted."

Jenny, her eyes as blue and beautiful as country summer
skies, sat primly plying her needle in the long drawing room.
Dinner had been excellent as usual. The gentlemen were at
their port. And the ladies—all but Mrs. Dish, who had been
called to the south wing to persuade the earl to swallow whatever it was Aberdeen and Tibbs had cooked up between them
for his supper—sat silently in the modishly furnished room,
each attempting to appear composed. The logs on the grate
burned brightly and branches of candles clustered about the
room. With the blue velvet drapes drawn against the night and
a quiet warmth emanating from the soft colors in the candle-

light, Eleanor felt supremely cozy. Outside lightning cracked and thunder bellowed once again, but inside everything was snug and secure.

"I know no one chooses to do so," Jenny sighed softly, "but I do wish someone would tell me how Joshie goes on. Francesco will only say that I am not to worry, and Dr. MacGregor pats my hand and says Wright 'will do,' whatever that means. And your brother, Miss Howard, only murmurs distractedly under his breath and nods and smiles."

"Do call her Eleanor, Jenny," muttered Mary testily. "She has asked you to do so over and over again, and it is aggravating that you don't. She's your friend, you know, not some old maid come to scold you and see you tow the line."

"No, that's your job, isn't it?" hissed the duchess, and immediately tears flooded her eyes. "Oh, Mary, I did not mean to say that! T-truly I didn't! I am so very sorry!"

Eleanor, who had expected Mary to reply with some scathing remark, was surprised to see her cross hurriedly to the duchess and pull her up into a loving embrace. "Josh is doing much better, my dear, than anyone imagined he would. He will survive nicely, as he always does." Having hugged the duchess thoroughly and provided her a small lace handkerchief to dry her eyes, Mary led her to the divan upon which Eleanor sat. "We must none of us come apart simply because Jocelyn has been injured," she said, sitting down across from Eleanor and Jenny. "Lily, bring a chair and join us here. It is time we hold council among ourselves."

"Wh–what kind of council?" asked Jenny. "The k-kind Josh calls when he is angry?"

"Yes, in a way, because I am angry at what has happened to him and you are angry, too, Jenny. It is all my fault. Had I not been such a peagoose when I was younger none of this would be happening. Eleanor, it has been most polite of you and your brother not to ask, but this man, Hampton, is a—a relation—of mine, and he attacked Lord Wright because of me."

"Hampton!" cried Jenny. "Oh, Mary, he is not come back?"

"Indeed, though I hoped he would not come as far as St. Swithin's. Did not di Roche tell you how Hampton laid the trap for Josh in Cutter's Hook, Jenny?"

"No, not a word," the duchess frowned. "He told me 'twas an accident, and none of you have told me different until now."

"I expect the marquis did not want to distress you," offered Eleanor rather lamely.

"He loves you and could not bear for you to be distressed," Lily nodded. "He wished to keep you from worry."

"Bosh!" muttered the picture-pretty little duchess. "He was afraid I would fall into hysterics if I learned Joshie was threatened, and then *he* would not know what to do. Men are such babies!"

Lily gurgled wickedly, which brought a semblance of mirth to Mary's eyes and a distinct giggle from the duchess. Eleanor looked from one to the other of them with surprise.

"She is perfectly correct, you know, Ellie," Mary grinned. "Men are brave about a great many things, but they can none of them face an hysterical woman—and they expect we are all bordering on hysteria the moment anything exciting happens."

"Yes, and they are wrong," said Lily with a stubborn pout. "It is only upsets in love make one hysterical. What are we going to do about Hampton?"

"I think it is time for us to ride to Jocelyn's aid rather than the other way 'round," declared Mary. "Tomorrow we shall tell the gentlemen we are going on a jaunt without them, and we will ride to Hampton Hall and discover whether or not Arthur has taken up residence there."

"But suppose he has?" Eleanor asked worriedly. "Will he not seize you as he said? And how can Lily and I and Jenny keep him from doing so?"

"We will not ride directly up to the front door," offered the duchess, with a tiny frown to prove she was thinking very hard. "We shall circle around back, divide, sneak up and peer in the windows."

"Do you think so?" Lily frowned. "I had rather knock upon the front door and if he answers, shoot him where he stands."

"Lily, we cannot!"

"Why not?"

"Because then we shall be hauled off to gaol and dance upon the gibbet," Jenny sighed knowingly. "Even I know that. The gibbet is a very awful thing. I saw a man hanged once."

"You did?" asked Mary and Lily and Eleanor in one voice.

"Uh-huh. I thought he would die directly if he fell, but he did not. It took him ever so long to stop dancing and shaking about. Joshie said it was because his neck did not break as it should have and he had to swing until he choked to death."

"Ugh," cried Lily. "How hideous. Why did you go?"

"Because 'twas the villain who killed Mama, and so Papa took us."

"Oh, my poor dearest!" groaned Mary. "It must have been so terrible for you."

"Oh, no," announced Jenny brightly, "it was not terrible for me at all—only for the man on the gallows. I had a wonderful time because Papa and Joshie both held me and kissed me and explained what was happening and how we never need worry about that gentleman ever again. And we had a picnic lunch, too!"

Eleanor stared at the duchess aghast. "You—you liked it?"

Jenny nodded shyly. "But I should not like to swing upon the gallows myself."

"No, never!" exclaimed Lily. "But what shall we do if Hampton is there?"

"Capture him," suggested Mary.

"Yes, capture him," agreed Jenny enthusiastically.

"How?" Eleanor queried, her mind whirling at their audacity to plan to face such a villain at all, much less without the gentlemen's support.

"We shall entice him into the courtyard and then surround him, and Mary shall hold him at bay with Charlie's pistol while we three tie him up. I will bring a rope from the stables." The duchess looked proudly from one to the other of her guests. "Don't you think that is a good idea?" she asked artlessly.

The gentlemen, having finished their port, elected to tramp over to the south wing en masse to see how Wright fared before they joined the ladies in the drawing room. As they entered the suite of rooms, they were brought to an abrupt halt by a short scream from Mrs. Dish and the sound of a hubbub bursting out in the bedchamber. "Now what?" groaned Howard. "Cannot the man even be an invalid without raising a great breeze?"

Paxton rushed to the bedchamber doorway, took one look and rushed back into the sitting room. "Di Roche," he yelled, "pull that cord. We need a broom. Several, I should think."

The little marquis responded on the instant, quickly glancing back over his shoulder as Mrs. Dish came running into the sitting room, an apron thrown over her head, followed by an extremely agitated Colly Shepard. "A broom, a broom, we need a broom," cried Shepard, as one of the footmen came rushing in.

"More than one. As many as you can carry. But hurry," ordered Paxton. "Tibbs, come out here!"

"No, sir," called Tibbs from the confines of the earl's bedchamber. "I'll not be leaving his lordship to such a nasty fate all by his lonesome."

"Devil it, Tibbs, just get my pistols," brayed Wright hoarsely. "Better yet—" The congregation in the sitting room were then treated to the sound of pottery bursting against the walls of the chambers.

Mrs. Dish took the apron from her head and dashed back to the doorway. "Do not let him do that, Mr. Tibbs! Do not! He cannot possibly hit it with the crockery! Josh, cease and desist this moment! Oh! Oh! It is coming this way! Help! Someone help!" Mrs. Dish again threw the apron over her lovely gray hair and ran to the far side of the sitting room.

Paxton burst into laughter and went to the little woman's

side. "You must go up to the long drawing room, Mrs. Dish, with the other ladies. We gentlemen shall handle this in a moment, I assure you, just as soon as the brooms arrive."

The brooms at that moment arrived, eight of them in the hands of two footmen and Burton. "What is happening?" the butler queried as Paxton seized upon the brooms and passed one each to di Roche, Howard, and Shepard, and took two for himself—one to give to Tibbs.

"It's a bat loose in the bedchamber," Paxton grinned. "A great lout of a one! Follow me, gentlemen."

The line of huntsmen paraded into Wright's bedchamber and began to swing at the rather large black beast that fluttered excitedly about the room. They chased it against the drapes and beat several of the velvet hangings down onto the floor without success. They chased it atop the clothespress and behind the armoire. They swung at it in midair over the earl's bed, and Wright dodged brooms and bat, laughing and groaning simultaneously. The wretched thing flew in and out between the candelabras, hung from the top of the door frame, clung to the earl's bedclothes, scurried under the bed and out the other side. The gentlemen divided the room into four sections with two men stationed to a section in an effort to pound upon the bat and keep from pounding upon themselves. The bat chittered and squeaked shrilly and skittered from floor to wall to ceiling and finally on to the top of the canopy above the earl's head. "We've got it now," hissed Paxton. "Howard, move that chair over here for me to stand on."

"Oh, God," prayed Wright in a mournful voice loud enough to set Paxton's lips to quivering in delight, "guide thy servant's hand that he may strike down the interloper, but don't let him bring the entire canopy down on my skull, please?"

Howard held the chair steady; Paxton climbed upon it and raised the broom into the air; the rest of the men in the room held their breath.

"Damn but don't they look like little nuns when they're sitting still, Michael?" Wright murmured into the tense silence.

Paxton broke into whoops just as the broom descended; the bat soared as the broom missed it, and the hunt began anew. It was Tibbs who finally flattened the mammal against the fireplace bricks and then kicked it repeatedly with the heel of his boot. The men all stood around staring down at it for a full three minutes before one of the footmen, at last judging it to be dead, picked it up in gloved hands.

"Take it out and burn it, James," Burton ordered. "Can't be too careful with bats. Had a bit of the rabies, we have, this year."

James nodded and, holding the black body as far from himself as possible in both white-gloved hands, led the procession of footmen, followed by Burton, all with brooms shouldered like muskets, from the earl's chambers.

"What I want to know is how the wretched thing got in here," Colly Shepard sighed as he and Tibbs set about restoring the chamber to rights. "You all right, m'lord? Didn't bite you, did it? You ain't worn to a frazzle?"

"He's fine, Shepard," replied Paxton, righting a chair and sitting down in it beside the bed. "Needed a bit of excitement, no doubt."

"I say, Wright, thing didn't bite you, did it?" asked Howard, settling on the opposite side of the bed. "We have had a few rabid ones about this year. Took a number of the cattle."

Wright peered up at Howard. "And you came to do battle in spite of it? I am appropriately grateful, Howard. You were, I must say, magnificent. And you," he added with a glare at di Roche, "where did you learn to bat bats, *signor?* I cannot remember ever having seen more enthusiasm."

"I am pleesed to batting these animal," Di Roche grinned. "I would more pleesed to batting these villain what in these window stickied it."

"What? Somebody slipped it in through a window?" Paxton hurried to where di Roche stood, the casement wide open, an oil lamp held out into the night.

"There being the bag whatin they bringing," di Roche said,

pointing. "And these footprints not washing away yet. And these window being not shutted up, but standing open like so—" he demonstrated how he had found the thing. "Ees likely 'twas a batputer-inner, yes?"

Howard, who had gone to the casement as well, nodded silently, his eyes meeting Paxton's with a worried glance.

"Probably was rabid then, eh, di Roche? Appears your friend Hampton has had another try at me."

"Who is this Hampton?" Howard asked, crossing back, along with the other two gentlemen, to the bed. "Why is he trying to kill you?"

Wright's eyelids fluttered in an attempt to remain open.

"You are exhausted," Paxton growled compassionately. "Too much adventure for one night, especially after being poisoned this morning. Go to sleep, Josh. Won't be anyone attempting to stuff another one of those in your room tonight. I guarantee it."

The earl, surprising everyone, allowed Howard to lower him back down from a sitting position and arrange the pillows comfortably beneath his head, and then closed his eyes and fell soundly asleep without any argument at all.

"Who *is* this Hampton?" Paxton asked di Roche as the three gentlemen left Wright to Tibbs and Shepard and wandered out into the sitting room. "Do you know why he's trying to kill Wright?"

The marquis nodded energetically and explained all of which he was certain. Howard sat stunned. Paxton began to pace. "Her husband," he muttered. "That is why Mary feels so guilty. Damn the woman, why did she not tell me!"

In less than ten minutes Howard and Paxton between them had seen a guard mounted around Willowset—most especially around the earl's ground-floor suite. Oakes and Cross and Whitson roused the grooms and armed them; Burton and Shepard deployed the footmen, the gardeners and themselves. Di Roche went off to entertain the ladies while word of trespassers after the earl's life ran rampant among the staff belowstairs and

Howard and Paxton worked out a schedule to see Wright protected throughout the night. By the time they joined di Roche and the ladies in the long drawing room the tea things had already been brought and the ladies informed as calmly as possible what had gone forward. Mrs. Dish appeared the most upset of all, but then, Howard and Paxton both thought, she had had to face the bat and it had frightened her badly.

"Nothing to worry about now, though," Paxton asserted reassuringly. "No one will be able to come within a stone's throw of the place without being seen."

"But it is so dark outside, and the rain has not stopped completely. How will anyone know if a stranger walks among them?" asked the duchess with a shiver. "Oh, it so like a gothic novel, isn't it, Francesco? Almost like *The Castle of Doom*."

"*Si,* yes." Di Roche smiled, remembering the chills he'd gotten from those particular little volumes. "But ees not so bad as that, my Jenny. Here we having the magnificents peoples of Willowset to defending us."

Paxton longed for a moment alone with Mary and attempted to draw her off into a corner away from the others, but she would not come. Nor would she remain downstairs once the other ladies had expressed the desire to retire to their own chambers. Damn, he thought, are you avoiding me, Mary? Why? Do you think I hold you accountable for some rogue gentleman you may have *accidentally* married? And why did you marry the wretch? Were you forced into it, my girl? We shall talk about this, my dear, whether you wish it or not.

Howard sunk into a brown study rivaling Paxton's once the ladies had retired. His thoughts wove busily between Wright's growing acknowledgment of himself and Lily's puckered little brow when the earl's danger had been discussed. Certainly she is concerned about the man, he told himself. She's his ward, after all. And certainly she is distressed with all that has happened. But why attempt to defend him so at breakfast? And when Mrs. Dish had taken her to visit Wright, why had Lily come back a happy young woman? What had the devil said to her? What had he done? Why should Legion have the power to make Miss Lipton smile? Howard grunted and stared at the ormolu clock on the mantel.

"Ees late," murmured di Roche, following Howard's glance. "I, too, must saying goodnights."

"All of us, I think," muttered Paxton, rising.

Howard nodded, and the three gentlemen wandered up to the second floor together.

Beneath the dripping elms at the edge of the home woods on the west side of Willowset the Sneezing Fiend held one long, gloved finger under his nose and inhaled rapidly. Hampton glared at him. "You sneeze once, Hobbins, just once, and we are both dead men," he hissed. "Let's get out of here." They slunk silently through the mist and drizzle to the place where they had tied their cattle and, untying the horses, led them even farther from the edifice before they determined it was safe to mount.

"Gads!" exclaimed Hampton. "You release a bat into a room with a man who can't move but one arm and one leg, an old lady and two fuss-pot valets, and you would think the thing could find its target before anyone was the wiser! But no! No! An alarm gets raised; people come running from all over creation; the whole thing turns into a circus; and the damnable bat don't even take a nibble of Wright's ear. The man has got a guardian angel the size of Goliath! I'm telling you, Hobbins, I swear it on my father's grave! I shall get that devil! And when I do there won't be an angel or devil on the face of the earth or in the clouds of heaven will save him from me!"

The Sneezing Fiend sneezed. He shrugged his shoulders and wiped a forearm beneath his nose. "I gots to be goin,' guv'nor. That way like. Ye gets ta the Gander's Neck down that lane there. Does ye be wantin' o' me any time soon?"

"Tomorrow!" growled Hampton.

"Ah, guv'nor, give it a rest," the Fiend sighed. "It's us as is gonna die bein' things keeps up this way. Give 'em a week er two ta ferget. Time fer the guards ta disappear. Ye flash coves is too anxious, is what it is. That Legion o' yers, he ain't agoin' anywheres fer a good long whiles. Busted up, he is, real bad, an' goin' ta take months ta heal up all the way. Besides which, I seed that furriner fella inside there. Got hisself a good position, 'e does. Could be 'e'll finish the job fer ye."

"Tomorrow!" growled Hampton irrationally. "At Hampton Hall. Three o'clock. An' you had best be there, Hobbins. The price on Wright's hide has just gone up another thousand, an' if you don't want it, I'll wager there's plenty about who do."

The Fiend sneezed, nodded. "Three o'clock, then, guv'nor, or thereabouts, dependin' upon where I lays me head this night." He raised a hand in farewell and urged the cold, wet mare beneath him off into the night. Hampton watched him go, pulled the soggy beaver hat lower over his brow and spurred off down the lane that led in a roundabout way to the Gander's Neck. Hobbins was right: Di Roche had wormed his way into Willowset as he'd intended and might very likely accomplish the earl's death on his own. "Blast!" growled Hampton into the darkness. "I want that particular pleasure for myself!"

Fourteen

Wright, who had slept the rest of the night and all of the next morning, awoke to the inept but compassionate hands of Glenby Oakes and Harry Cross attempting to insert him into a freshly laundered nightshirt. He bit fiercely at his lip to keep from groaning and gave a sigh of relief when they had finally succeeded.

The Willowset cook, Aberdeen, actually appeared in person shortly thereafter and spooned an entire bowl of gruel into the earl's mouth before he had the least opportunity to object. This was followed by a glass of milk and a lecture on the necessity of taking adequate and correct nourishment in the face of illness. Wright would have protested that he was injured, not ill. All he had was a cold and a few broken bones and they would heal whether he ate gruel or oysters and he craved oysters, but he kept his mouth judiciously closed lest the giant Scotsman who ruled the kitchen should pour some other ghastly sort of nourishment down him.

Fast upon Aberdeen's assault came Dr. MacGregor, his round red face smiling, his gruff voice murmuring soothing nonwords as he obliged Oakes and Cross to lift and turn and trundle the earl into one position after another, each more painful than the last. Therefore, when Wright was at last alone and Mrs. Dish sneaked in to have a word with him, he was exceeding happy to see her and gave thanks when she did nothing at all but stand beside the bed and speak. But his heart lurched into his throat when her soft reassurances concerning his condition faltered to a halt and her bright eyes stared pleadingly down at him. "What?" he asked hoarsely. "Tell me, Melinda. Good God, Hampton has not harmed someone else?"

"No, Josh," murmured Mrs. Dish. "Oh, I am such an old fool. It is probably nothing at all. And what could you do about it? You cannot leave your bed, nor no one wouldn't expect you to, and besides, I am not at all certain."

"Certain of what? Melinda, don't make me guess. Get on with whatever you've come to say."

"It is merely that the young ladies have gone riding."

"Where to? With whom?"

"They have told the gentlemen that they go to view the ruins of Hoarsham Castle, but it is not true."

"It ain't?"

"No, I don't think so. The duchess slipped a blade into her riding boot when she thought I was not looking."

"Well, but she might, Melinda. She's an Elder, ain't she? She knows better'n to go traipsing about the countryside unprotected. They took some of the grooms with them, no?"

"Only Whitson, and only because he was adamant and totally ignored all their wishes. But they are not bound for the castle, Josh. I know there is something else afoot. I saw my Mary fetch dueling pistols and slip them beneath her cloak. And Miss Lipton sneaked into the stables and out again with a piece of rope. And Eleanor, she were deathly silent, my lord. Barely spoke a word when I asked did she never see the castle before. They were all of them acting most suspicious."

Wright nodded thoughtfully, the action sending an excruciating pain through the place behind his right eye. "And n-no one attempted to stop them?"

"All the gentlemen attempted to stop them. But the girls convinced them that they stood in not the least danger."

"Get Glenby and Harry Cross, Melinda. Hurry."

"I cannot, Josh. They have gone off with Constable Perkins and a group of the townsmen to search for Richard Hobbins."

"Damn! Then get Paxton or Howard—do not tell me they

have gone as well." He sighed as Mrs. Dish's eyes glanced worriedly away from him. "Where?" he asked quietly.

"To search for Hampton, my lord. Rode off to the Gander's Neck with the marquis to see if Hampton be stayin' there still."

"Uncle Josh! Uncle Josh!" screeched Jessie, bursting at that moment into the room. "Are you being all right? Are you? They wouldn't let us come an' cheer you up!" the little duke exclaimed, scrambling up onto the bed, followed instantly by Joyce. Mrs. Dish moved quickly to scoop them off as a groan escaped the earl's lips at the quick, unexpected jarring of his arm and ankle and ribs.

"No, Melinda, let them," he whispered on a quick intake of breath. "I am fine, rascals," he said, "but now you are up on my bed, you must not bounce around or wiggle too very much."

"Why?" asked Joyce, crawling over him to reach the other side of the bed because Jessie would not let her be the nearest to him.

Wright put his good arm around the little china doll and held her gingerly against himself. "Because parts of me are broken, sweetings, and when you bounce around they knock against each other and that hurts."

Joyce's wonderful dark eyes grew larger and rounder. "Oooh," she murmured.

"Noah an' Mark an' Mattie is got guns, Uncle Josh. They is outside walkin' aroun' wif guns! Real guns! Did you know?" asked Jessie excitedly.

"No," the earl said, looking appropriately amazed at the actions of the grooms. "Are you certain, Jess?"

"We seed 'em!"

"Uh-huh," agreed Joyce, leaning her dusky curls on the earl's shoulder. "We seed 'em."

"Oh, my goodness!" exclaimed Bowey, hurrying into the chamber. "I am sorry, my lord. I turned my back for a moment to fetch—"

"Don't matter, Bowey. I am pleased to see the scamps.

Bowey, the duchess did not, perchance, tell you where she was bound this afternoon, did she?"

"Mama's gone to Hampton Hall," announced Jessie before Bowey could speak. "She told *me!* She said we mus' be good an' not cause Bowey no trouble until she gits back."

Mrs. Dish gasped and Bowey stared wide-eyed at the earl.

"What?" asked Jessie. "Ain't she 'lowed to go there?"

"Your mama is a grown-up lady, Jess, and may go where she wishes," murmured the earl. "Melinda, I expect we are down to Tibbs and Shepard and Aberdeen. Will you fetch them for me?"

Mrs. Dish nodded and rushed from the room. Bowey took the chair beside the bed and stared worriedly at him, but he shook his head in warning, tugging at one of Joyce's curls.

"So, what is it you've been doing, varlets?" he asked, grinning. "I'll bet you ain't been picking roses."

"There ain't no roses in the wintertime, Uncle Josh," Jessie giggled. "You is a ter'ble safe better."

"Terrible safe," agreed the earl.

"We dwawed you pichers," announced Joyce, snuggling closer to him.

"Where are they?"

"In the nursery," explained Jessie. "We couldn't not sneaked out an' bringed the pichers, too."

"I see. And what are they pictures of?"

"Horses!" squealed Joyce.

"An' puppies!" exclaimed Jess. "You will like them very, very much!"

"I expect I shall. Will you go fetch them for me? Bowey will stay and keep me company until you come back."

"Yes!" shouted both children, beginning to bounce off the bed.

"Slowly," Wright implored.

"We almos' forgotted!" exclaimed Jess boisterously. "Climb down slow, Joycie. Don't rub Uncle Josh's parts together."

Bowey watched them run out and turned back to the earl

with a look of fright in her eyes. "This—this person, if he be there, he will not think to harm the duchess?"

"He will not have the opportunity, Bowey. Ah, Tibbs!"

Eleanor peered into one of the grimy main-floor windows at the rear of Hampton Hall and saw absolutely nothing. Beside her, Lily leaned her pretty little shoulders covered in blue velvet against the chill bricks of the house and tapped one boot-clad foot impatiently. "Do you see anyone?" she whispered.

"No one. I cannot see a thing. Lily, I cannot think we ought to be here. Surely we ought not."

Lily shrugged. "No one will see us, Ellie. The place is deserted. We have wasted our time, I think. Let us try the east side windows. Perhaps we shall have better luck there."

"Whitson must think we're mad," murmured Ellie, following the golden-haired beauty around the side of the building. "I cannot imagine what the duchess has told him."

"She has told him the truth, I expect. That we are come to be sure the Hall is secure and not occupied by that villain. Whitson is merely a groom, after all, and she a duchess. She need not extend herself to overcome his objections."

"But surely he must have attempted to dissuade her."

"Well, he could not possibly dissuade her." With a sigh, Lily rubbed at a grimy pane with a small linen handkerchief, and this time it was she who peered inside the veritable ruin of Hampton Hall. "Ellie," she hissed, "there is a fire burning in this room!"

Eleanor went quickly to peer in beside her. "We must tell the others at once, Lily," she hissed excitedly. "There is a gentleman's hat hanging upon the chair back!" With a great sense of urgency, Eleanor tugged Lily from the window and they went in search of the others who had proposed to peek into the windows at the front and west side of the house. The two had just turned the corner of the building when the sharp crack of a pistol, John Whitson's bellow, and then a groan brought them to an abrupt halt. The sound of scuffling and a scream cut short sent them scrambling back around the edifice. Another scream and more scuffling ensued, and then Eleanor and Lily heard very clearly the slamming of the front door. Wordlessly they crept to the window they had just abandoned and, crouching below it, huddled against the cold bricks, listening intently.

Hampton entered the parlor with an unconscious Mary thrown over one shoulder and dragging an equally unconscious Whitson by the coat collar. The Fiend followed, struggling with a silently determined duchess whom he pushed backward into a chair. "An' stay there!" he ordered, with a finger pointing straight at the earl's sister threateningly. "Else ye'll git the same as that lady there!"

"Bosh!" muttered Jenny, rubbing at one delicate wrist, which was already beginning to bruise from the man's grasp. "If you contemplate for one moment that I am frightened of you, you have stuffing for brains! You are the dreadful men have been plaguing Joshie, aren't you? You are the Sneezing Fiend," she accused, pointing. "And I know precisely who you are, Arthur Hampton. Have you no shame?"

"Shut up!" growled Hampton. "Tie her up and gag her, Hobbins!"

"W-w-w-achooo-ith what? We ain't got nothin' about ta do tha' wif."

Hampton stalked to the draperies at the window where Lily and Eleanor crouched and ripped the braided cords from the wall. He threw them at the Fiend in disgust. "Use your imagination, man. Tie her and stuff your handkerchief in her mouth."

"Do not you dare!" cried Jenny. "What a disgusting thought! You keep your filthy paws off of Mary!" she added, springing from the chair and hurling her little self upon Hampton as he bent over his wife, whom he had dumped on the carpet before the fire. Hampton turned to swat her away as he might a pesky insect. Jenny ducked under his swinging hand and stamped her booted foot with all her might upon his instep. Hampton was so surprised he stepped back, and Jenny kicked him flat in the kneecap. Hobbins caught her from behind and swung her back into the dusty old chair and sat on her.

"Now settle down, Missy," he ordered, "an' I'll git off ye. Lord, but I ain't never seen sich a feisty woman."

Eleanor, who could hear every word through the chinks in the window frame, peeked up to see what was happening just as Jenny pinched the Fiend ferociously upon his bottom and sent him soaring into the air. "And do never think to sit upon me again, you great lout!" Jenny yelled fiercely, "or you shall not be able to sit down for a week!"

"For gawd's sake shut the witch up, Hobbins!" shouted Hampton. He stamped forward, yanked Jenny from the chair with one hand and slammed the back of his other hand bruisingly across her face. On the floor behind him, Mary stirred. He heard her and released the duchess with a shove, sending her careening into the wall across the room. The Fiend jumped to seize her and Lily, who had found a loose brick close to hand, sent it crashing through the casement. Eleanor knocked the remaining shards of glass free with her riding whip, and both young ladies climbed screeching into the room. Hampton spun toward them; the Fiend spun toward them; Mary tugged the second dueling pistol from her cloak pocket, rose dizzily and brought its onyx and ivory butt smashing down upon the back of Hampton's skull; Jenny slipped the delicate Italian dagger from her boot, seized the Fiend by his coattails and pulled him against herself, holding the sleek, wavy blade just beneath his rib cage. "Do not move a muscle," she warned him in a calm, deadly voice. "Do not even twitch. I am an Elder and know how to gut a man like a mackerel with a twist of my wrist. An' I will do it without a moment's thought. I am Legion's sister and the daughter of the blackest villain ever breeched."

Eleanor, hearing every word, stared dumbfounded at the little duchess as Lily rushed, rope in hand, to tie up Hampton.

"Ellie, Ellie, take those drapery cords and tie up that fiend Jenny is holding. And tie him tightly, too. Do not be the least bit considerate," Lily commanded. "And then we must look to Mary and Whitson. They are both of them injured."

By the time the trio of Tibbs, Aberdeen and Shepard had coerced their mounts into carrying them to Hampton Hall—a process interrupted by Aberdeen's hack having frighted at a squirrel and dumped him summarily into a hawthorne, Tibbs having grazed his head upon the overhanging branch of an elm and Shepard having had to dismount and lead his steed the final mile because it would persist in turning toward home no matter in which direction Shepard pointed it—Mary was feeling a great deal recovered from the blow to the jaw Hampton had delivered her when she'd pointed the first of the dueling pistols at him, and Whitson's leg, which the ball from the pistol had grazed when it fell from her hand, was adequately bound and he himself returning from the other world into which a well-placed punch from the Fiend had sent him. The arrival of the three servants sent sighs of relief all 'round the horrible parlor, and though dusk was near, they agreed it best that the cook and the two valets remain at the Hall with Whitson and the prisoners while the ladies set out on their own for Willowset. "We will send Glenby Oakes back with the coach immediately," promised the little duchess prettily. "And you must not worry, Aberdeen. We ladies shall see to the making of dinner this evening."

Aberdeen's rugged countenance blanched at the words, but he only mumbled his thanks and went about breaking up an old ladder-backed chair he had discovered in the hall to feed into the dwindling fire.

"Mary, are you certain you should not remain and wait for the coach?" Eleanor inquired solicitously as Tibbs and Shepard assisted them to mount. "You do not look at all the thing."

"I shall at last give meaning to Josh's phrase," Mary replied.

"What phrase?"

"Why, I shall at last discover what it is to 'feel queer in the stirrups,' " Mary giggled groggily. "Oh, Eleanor, how I wish I had killed Hampton! Damn me for a fool that I could not pull the trigger when I had him standing right before me!"

"Is he truly your husband, Mary?"

"Yes, he is her husband, and the most wretched man on the face of the earth!" exclaimed Lily as she and the duchess rode up beside the two. "And he ought to be whipped like a cur and dragged naked through the streets of London."

"Oh, dear," squeaked the little duchess, "please do not say *that* in front of Joshie, Lily, or he will think to do it, and then they shall banter his name all over town again."

"They are always bantering his name all over town for one thing or another," Lily sighed. "I wish I understood the half of it."

"Has already," murmured Mary, holding tightly to her saddle.

"Has already what, dearest?" asked Eleanor, puzzled.

"Whipped Hampton like a cur—though I do not think Josh would ever whip a cur—unless 'twas a cur-mudgeon!" she giggled.

"They have gone where?" Howard's voice thundered through the earl's suite. "Damnation, Wright, why did you not send one of the grooms to fetch us? Surely someone knew we had gone to the Gander's Neck!"

"Stubble it, Howard," growled Paxton. "You know his brain's cloudy with laudanum and he ain't thinking as clearly as he ought. And you cannot possibly shuffle the blame onto his shoulders this time. 'Twas the three of us allowed them to ride off with naught but Whitson to lend them support. We were there. We bid them farewell. We countenanced the entire escapade, not Jocelyn. He was here in bed asleep, as I recall."

"Don't matter," mumbled the earl. "Tibbs, Shepard and Aberdeen have gone after 'em. Bring 'em back safe 'n sound."

"*Si,* these ees most likely, no?" di Roche nodded. "These Hampton he is staying still at the Goosie's Neck. Why then should he anywhere near this hall being?"

"Because that hall is his family estate, di Roche," Howard exclaimed impatiently. "And little more than ten miles from this house. I swear, Wright, if anything happens to my sister because of you—"

"It won't be because of him!" shouted Paxton, his head beginning to ache from Howard's bellowing. "You cannot blame Legion for everyone else's stupidity! He did not take the vixens at their word—we did. I shall wring Mary's neck if she don't come back in one piece," he added distractedly. "We shall get fresh horses and ride to Hampton Hall. At least I shall. Mayhap di Roche is correct and Hampton not gone near the place. Why should he, after all, ensconced so comfortably at the Gander's Neck as he appears to be?"

"I'll see one of the grooms brings 'em 'round," growled Howard, leaving the earl's bedchamber.

"Who is this Hampton?" Paxton asked, taking a seat in the chair beside the bed. Di Roche, who stood leaning his shoulders against the wall on the opposite side, listened interestedly for the answer.

"What do you mean, who is he?" Wright muttered.

"I mean, who is he, Jocelyn? I gather he is Mary's husband. But—but—where did he come from? Where has he been, and why?"

Wright, overwrought, attempted to move on the bed and cursed loudly as a series of sharp pains shot through his arm, ankle, ribs and head. He inhaled deeply and shoved the pain away as Paxton moved quickly to help him. "What, Josh? How do you want to be? You cannot do it yourself, you maggoty barbarian. Anyone would think you had windmills in your head." Arranging pillows, sheets and the earl into a more comfortable position, Paxton ignored the chair and sat on the edge of the ancient bed. "Why, if he's Mary's husband, does Mary live with you?"

The earl peered up at Paxton guardedly. "Paxton, you ain't in love with Mary, are you?"

"What?"

"What I mean to say is—you ain't looking to fix your interest with Mary?"

"I hardly think that possible without a great deal of influence now, Wright. Divorces are not easily come by—if she should even want a divorce."

"Oh, lord, you are looking to fix your interest with her!"

"Jocelyn," grumbled Paxton, somewhat red-faced, "why did you let me believe she was widowed?"

"I never said—you never asked—"

"No, but I assumed, Josh! She needed to make a way in the world for herself and Joyce. You took her into your town house and made her your secretary— Damn! I should like to throttle you!"

His interest attached, di Roche's shoulders slid soundlessly down the wall until he was sitting cross-legged upon the carpeting.

"I didn't know what else to do, Michael."

"What the devil does that mean?"

"You would not believe the state she was in. 'Twas the devil of a job to bring her out of despair after that bloody thatchgallows raped her, but then, when she found herself increasing—well, she came near to taking her life. So I collected the varlet and forced 'im to marry her over the anvil at Gretna Green."

All color drained from Paxton's face. "He—he raped her? He raped Mary? I shall kill the bastard with my own two hands!"

"Well, I wanted to, but Mary wanted Joyce to be born on the right side of the blanket and wouldn't let me kill 'im, so I beat 'im within an inch of his life and shipped him off to the Continent and threatened to gut him like a mackerel if he ever showed his face in England again."

Di Roche nodded his head silently. So, he thought, Legion being not only barbarous, but romantical. He rush to saving the lady like knight in the shining armor.

Paxton sat on the edge of the bed, his feet dangling, his eyes raking the carpet. He could think of nothing at all to say.

"Damnation, Michael!" Wright exclaimed. "How was I to know you would pop off into the clouds one day and come down wishing to marry her? How was she to know it? I shall fix it when I get back to London. I'll speak to Canterbury. He'll procure a divorce for her."

"You have influence with the archbishop? You, Josh?"

"He owes me, Michael. I pushed for his causes in Lords more than once. The gent owes me enormously!"

"Oh, Joshie, you will not believe what a splendid adventure we have had!" declared a rosy-cheeked Jenny, bursting in upon them just as Paxton's jaw dropped in astonishment. "Good evening, Mr. Paxton. How kind of you to sit with Joshie while we were gone. Oh, Francesco, my dearest!" she added, spying the quickly rising marquis and rushing excitedly to give him a peck upon his handsome cheek.

The three gentlemen stared at her agog. There was a great bruise growing upon her pretty little cheek, and ugly bruises showed at her wrists as she distractedly removed her riding gloves. Her puce velvet hat was wildly askew and its lone white plume hung limply from a broken stem.

"My dear duchess, what has happened?" asked Paxton, rising. "You are injured. You did not—that wretch Hampton—he was not at—"

"Yes, he most certainly was at the Hall, Mr. Paxton, just as we thought. And you shall not need to worry about him again, Joshie. Glenby Oakes is going to take him and that dreadful Sneezy person directly to the constable. And he is going to stop at Dr. MacGregor's so that the doctor may mend Whitson's leg."

"Mending Whitson's—" mumbled di Roche, bewitched and befuddled at one and the same time.

"Jenny, come here," the earl ordered softly.

She almost skipped around the bed to sit down beside him.

"Who hurt you, sweetings? Hampton?"

"Well, yes. Hampton and that Sneezy person, but Joshie, we fixed them good. Mary clouted Hampton upon the head with one of your dueling pistols and I threatened to gut that Sneezy person like a mackerel with my little Italian dagger. And I held it just like Papa taught me. Oh, you should have seen how much he shook."

"Mary clouted Hampton with a dueling pistol?" repeated Paxton, awestruck. "Mary?"

"Yes, and Eleanor and Lily were so very brave! They broke the windows and climbed into that dreadful parlor in the very nick of time, I tell you! Oh, they were wonderful to see!"

The Earl of Wright's lips quivered as he looked first to the marquis, then to Paxton, then back to his baby sister's flashing blue eyes. "Where are they, Jenny? They were not harmed?"

"Oh, well, that great clunch Hampton socked Mary in the jaw before she could shoot him and the pistol exploded when it dropped and the ball hit John Whitson in the leg and then that horrible Sneezy person hit him as well—but otherwise we are all fine."

"Exceeding fine," murmured Eleanor from the doorway. "I believe we shall all survive the experience quite nicely, my lord." She watched his eyes as his gaze roamed over her from head to foot, knowing she was smudged and disheveled and quite the most unappealing woman anyone could possibly imagine. Mary glided past her into the room and Paxton inhaled sharply at the sight of her damaged jaw. He stood and held his arms out to her and unthinkingly she slipped into them and rested her weary head upon his shoulder. Lily entered as well, tugging a totally confused Howard by the hand behind her. But Wright's eyes and all his attention remained focused upon the bedraggled Eleanor.

"May I ask, Miss Howard, how—how you are feeling?"

"Oh, quite exhilarated, my lord," replied Eleanor with a teasing smile. " 'Twas not so damp and muddy as tumbling down the side of a cliff, but quite as exciting." Her countenance assured him that she was, in fact, all right, and he visibly relaxed, but Howard's head jerked in her direction and his jaw dropped.

Fifteen

Not until the third quail had fallen from the spit into the fire, the peas had gone dry and blackened into hard little balls and the ingredients for a blancmange had inexplicably burst into flame upon a countertop, did Mrs. Dish take broom in hand and threaten to chase the young ladies from the kitchen.

"I assure you, Aunt," laughed Mary, raising her hands in surrender, "we did promise Aberdeen to see to dinner and have only the best intentions."

"Yes, but intentions are *not* edible," replied Mrs. Dish succinctly. "Off with the lot of you!"

Jenny giggled and wiped her hands upon the linen towel she had tied about her waist. "Even Joshie cooks better than we do. It's because he spent so much time in the kitchen with Mildred when we were growing up. He liked Mildred very much," she added with a thoughtful gaze at Eleanor.

"Was Mildred your cook?" Ellie grinned at Mary, who would not be persuaded to rest in her room, regardless of the bruise upon her jaw, and who was enjoying as much as anyone the tiny secrets that had begun to pop from between Jenny's pretty lips the moment they had set about making dinner.

"Oh, yes. Mildred was a wonderful cook, and Joshie wanted Papa to marry her."

"He did?" asked Eleanor. "Was she very pretty as well?"

"Pretty? No, not at all, but Joshie loved her. She was kind to us and never made a fuss over Papa's eccentricities."

"Was your papa very eccentric?" Mary queried, taking a seat at the kitchen table.

"I have not the faintest idea. He chopped a man's hand off once. Is that eccentric?"

"No, dear," declared Eleanor, doffing the apron she wore and taking a seat at the table as well, "that is barbaric!"

"Then I expect Papa was that more than the other. One time he tied a rope to a gentleman and forced him to run or be dragged behind his horse all the way to John's Glen. And another time he tossed a lady straight into one of the sloughs."

Lily slid into a chair and tugged the duchess into one beside her. "You are making Ellie very nervous, Jenny," she scolded with a smile.

"Why?"

"Say something good about your papa."

"Well, I told you last night. My papa caught the man who made Mama fall from her window and had him hung."

Lily looked helplessly at Eleanor. "Jenny does truly think that that was something good," she sighed.

"Well, of course it was!" Jenny looked from one to the other of them, perplexed. "Papa could have run him through on the spot, you know, but he wished for Joshie to see the man die, and Joshie was not there. So Papa locked the varlet up and sent to London for Joshie to come home at once."

"But why?" asked Eleanor in disbelief. "Why make any child watch such a thing?"

"Papa wanted to make Joshie's nightmares go away, and he thought that once Joshie saw the man hanged they would not bother him no more."

"It didn't work," asserted Lily and Mary as one.

"I should think not," declared Eleanor.

The memory of that conversation lingered as Eleanor sat in Wright's bedchamber later that evening, listening to her brother's fine baritone give life to the nefarious characters of

The Mysterious Freebooter. It amazed her that Martin had offered to read the notorious work to the earl, and that he read with such vigor and enthusiasm. His voice changed with each of the characters. He shrieked; he grumbled; he threatened; he snickered. Wright, his head resting upon the pillows, listened with eyes closed, the deep line above the bridge of his nose evidence of the pain he refused to acknowledge. He was breathing a good deal easier than he had in many days, and the news that Hampton had been captured, Eleanor thought, calmed him a great deal. When Martin halted at the end of a chapter and put a finger in the volume to mark his place, Wright's eyes opened and a smile touched his lips. "You astound me, Howard," he drawled languidly.

"Why?"

"Well, you cut up so stiff a while ago, I never thought to see you in here again."

"I was angry," muttered Howard.

"And now you ain't?"

"Well, not at you, Wright. I appreciate you did the best you could in the matter."

"An' you ain't angry at Eleanor either?"

Howard scowled at Wright's familiar use of his sister's name, but the scowl fled. "You're exhausted, Wright. I can hear it. Take your medicine and I'll read till you fall asleep."

"Uh-uh."

"No? Why not?"

"Hate it. Tastes like—like—"

"Like what?"

"Can't say in front of y'r sister."

Howard broke into laughter and Eleanor blushed. "Would you like me to leave, m'lord?" Eleanor asked.

"Uh-uh," he murmured. "Won't take the stuff if you leave."

Howard went to fetch one of the several bottles that had collected upon the earl's washstand and placed it and a clean spoon into Eleanor's hand. "Tibbs says he's to have two spoonsful, Ellie, before he falls asleep. I shall lift him a bit and you must get it down."

"Uh-uh," protested Wright. "I ain't about to f-fall asleep."

"Yes, sir, you are," declared Howard, raising the gentleman carefully by the shoulders. "Stop acting like an infant, Wright, and take the wretched stuff. Do you wish Ellie to think you are no older than Jess?"

Eleanor poured the evil-smelling liquid into the spoon and wrinkled her nose. "It does smell dreadful," she acknowledged with a shake of her head, "but it is good for you, my lord, and will make you feel better."

"Nothing," groaned the earl, "will make me f-feel better."

"Well, it will make you sleep so you won't feel anything at all," Howard sighed. "Honestly, you are worse than Jessie."

"Am not," mumbled Wright, and Eleanor slipped the spoonful of medicine into his mouth before he could close it again. He swallowed, making a face that sent Eleanor into giggles.

"Oh, it cannot possibly taste that bad," she said, pouring another spoonful. "Really, Jocelyn." Eleanor gave him the second spoonful without once noticing the reaction of either gentleman to her use of the earl's Christian name.

True to his word, Howard settled the earl back onto the pillows and continued with the astounding adventures of J. Tildon Dillsworthy, alias the Speckled Feather, whose generally rambunctious nature lay at the core of the mystery of *The Mysterious Freebooter.* Eleanor listened with pleasure to her brother's theatrics, but her gaze stayed fastened upon the earl. She watched him fight to keep his eyes open until at last he lost the battle. In less than a minute he began to worry the coverlets and mumble. Howard closed the volume; Eleanor went to sit upon the edge of the bed.

"What does he see when first he falls asleep?" Howard murmured.

"Something horrendous," replied Eleanor, reaching out to brush the unruly black curls from Wright's brow. "Jenny says he has had nightmares since he was a child. Did you know his mother fell from a window at the Rise and was killed? And that his father took him to see the man responsible hanged? Took Jenny, too. I cannot imagine such a thing!"

Howard's eyebrows rose as Eleanor tucked the earl's flailing hand back under the covers. "I had heard that once. I did not believe it—about the hanging, I mean. Certainly no educated gentleman would escort his children to such an event."

"He postponed the *event,* Martin, until Jocelyn could be fetched from school to see it!"

"Ellie, that's the second time you've called him Jocelyn. I won't have you doing so. 'Tis most improper."

"Oh, bosh, Martin. I shall call him Jocelyn if I please. Mary does."

"Mrs. Hampton is a young matron and stands in no jeopardy of losing her reputation because of it."

"No. I expect you think she has no reputation to lose, being long established in the earl's household."

"I never said—"

"But you think it! Well, she is not his mistress, Martin, if that is the conclusion you have drawn. And Joyce is not his child! I do not care how much the babe resembles him or that her name is taken from his—Mary is a gentlewoman, and if Jocelyn had gotten her with child, he would have married her!"

Howard stood openmouthed. "I n-never!" he exclaimed. "What on earth are you speaking of, Ellie? No such thoughts ever entered my mind—well, not about the child being his, at least. The babe is undoubtedly Hampton's."

"It is? She is? Undoubtedly?" Relief rushed through Eleanor at the nodding of her brother's head.

"Well, of course she is. I expect she is named for Wright because it was he who took Mrs. Hampton in even before the babe was born. I remember Charles came near to have an apoplexy over the thing. He wanted Wright to bring the girl here, where she might reside with propriety, but Mrs. Hampton would not come. Wright kept her at the Rise first and then took her to London. There was a great hubbub over it. I expect the scandalmongers dined out on the speculation for a month. Still, anyone who knows anything cannot deny the child's a Hampton. She's got the mark."

"What mark?" asked Eleanor breathlessly.

"Why, the Hampton birthmark. Every child in the family's had it. Right out upon their cheek where anyone may see it. 'Tis a strawberry mark in the shape of the Isle of Wight, though it's very tiny."

"Oh, Martin," gasped Eleanor, swiping at the sudden tears that had started to her eyes. "Oh, you are the very best brother in all the world!" And with no explanation whatever she threw herself upon him and hugged him as hard as she possibly could.

"Well, well," Martin spluttered, unsure what to do at such an inexplicable and unexpected show of affection. "I am sure you're a good puss, my dear, and a splendid sister as well."

All the ladies retiring soon after Eleanor and Howard had returned from the sickroom, the gentlemen were once again abandoned to their own resources. Over a fine French cabernet, they discussed the safe return of Oakes with Tibbs, Shepard, Aberdeen and Whitson; pondered what would be Hampton's fate; continued to be amazed at the bravery of the little band of ladies; and in the end decided that they had missed a grand show by not being present at the capture.

"Ees astonishing, no?" asked di Roche, his eyes beaming with a combination of pride and one glass of wine too many. "Ees my Jenny so impertinent being as to sticking a dagger in that Fiendish's ribs."

"Yes, exactly so," Paxton nodded, also a bit cheerier than usual. "To think—Jenny is such a delicate little thing and always so in need of protection and yet—a man can barely comprehend it. And Mary—I thought 'twould break my heart to see her bruised so badly, but not a word out of her except 'bout how she dealt the blackguard that quelling blow. Saved 'em all she did, by gathering her wits about her so quickly. Not sure

I'd have done the same, I tell you. And your sister, Howard, and Miss Lipton—to endanger themselves so readily with not the least thought but to rescue the others. Certainly you cannot help but be bursting with pride."

Howard, who had not drunk quite as much as the other two, sat for a moment in contemplation. "I can't help but think that somehow Wright instigated the thing," he muttered finally. "I know he didn't," he added, raising his hand to silence Paxton's expected protest. "I know he didn't say a word that could be construed as sending the ladies out, but I can't think they'd have done so had we been the object of Hampton's threats, can you?"

"Well, but of course—" Paxton began, and then stopped. "You know, Howard, you may be right. 'Course, we are all up and about and quite able to defend ourselves."

"Si," nodded di Roche. "Whereas the Legion himself cannot protecting. He ees most imcom—uncon—incompatipated."

"Incapacitated, di Roche. Incapacitated."

"Si, incompatipated." Di Roche poured more wine all around and slumped down into a chair before the fire. "Ees most romantical, Legion. Ees most appealing to the female hearts. Ees a prince of romance."

Paxton roared with laughter. "Legion? You have had a great deal too much to drink, di Roche. Legion? A prince of romance?"

"The man's demented beyond belief!" cried Howard with a glint in his eyes.

"Is that why you have been caring for him so tenderly, Howard?" Paxton grinned.

"I am a man of God, Paxton. It's my duty to aid those in need, to bring comfort to the suffering."

"Yes, well, Josh is certainly suffering at the moment. But how will you reconcile him to accepting his normal treatment at your hands once he is well again?"

"His normal treatment at my hands?"

"Si," nodded di Roche. "My Jenny, she telling me of your hatred for her brother."

"Nonsense. I don't hate anyone. It is his—his—sins I detest, and his villainy."

"Balderdash," hiccoughed Paxton. "You're envious of him is what it is, Howard. 'Tis just as Mrs. Dish implied." He hiccoughed again and set di Roche to chuckling. "Never seen the like—you envious of Legion and he fit to chew wormwood over wantin' to be you."

"Surely you jest, Paxton. The devil don't stand a chance of being me."

"No, and don't he know it, and don't it turn him green."

"Really?"

"Yes, really. I swear, Howard, at times you are the greatest clunch! Can't you think what it must be like to be Josh? To have such a family as he has had? To be always under scrutiny—always aware that everyone expects you to do something totally mad, and that they will come down upon you instantly when you do? Why would he not sometimes long to have your exceeding pleasant existence?"

"I had not thought," murmured Howard.

"No, and you never chafed at always being expected to be perfect, did you? You have never longed to experience even one of Josh's escapades?"

"Well, now that you mention it," sighed Howard, his eyes cast downward at the Persian carpeting, "there were perhaps a few times I had wondered how it might feel to be—to be—"

"Less stiffly rumped!" inserted di Roche triumphantly. His eyes glowed with pride that he had followed the entire conversation and understood exactly to what Paxton referred.

Eleanor paced the floor of her sitting room. She could not sleep. She could hear the gentlemen prattling away in the drawing room below, but their voices were quite faint, and it was not them kept her awake. Coming at last to a determination, she slipped out into the hall and scratched upon the door opposite her own. Mary answered in an instant.

"I am very sorry to get you from your bed," Eleanor murmured, "but I must speak with you, Mary."

"Come in, goose. If I had been snug in bed, do you think I should have answered your summons so quickly? I have been walking the floorboards for this past quarter hour."

The two young women in flannel nightdresses and woolen robes, warmly knit slippers upon their feet, settled on a gold velvet couch before the grate. Curled up into opposite corners, they smiled shyly at each other. "I had almost decided to knock upon *your* door," Mary said. "Aunt Euphegenia and I had a rather long discussion last evening and much of it concerned you."

"Me?" Eleanor was startled at the thought. "Why on earth would you be discussing me? And you will pardon me for asking, but why do you call Mrs. Dish 'Aunt Euphegenia'?"

"Because that is her name."

"I thought her name was Melinda."

"Melinda? Now, where on earth—"

"Lord Wright calls her so."

Mary smiled at the seriousness of Eleanor's countenance. "Do not look so very grave, Ellie," she urged. " 'Twas only Jocelyn granting wishes again. He is like a great lout of a leprechaun sometimes and will grant a person their heart's dearest desire. My aunt has no greater desire, I think, than to be someone other than Euphegenia, and so he has made her Melinda."

"Oh, most surely she has greater desires than that—to see you and Joyce, for one."

"No, I do not think that desire so great as the first—for she has wanted to be other than Euphegenia all her life. But even so, he granted her one and then the other, for at last he has got us together again."

"Why were you discussing me?" Eleanor asked, feeling herself terribly bold to do so, but exceedingly curious.

"Because my aunt is much taken with you and wondered how I liked you. I said that I liked you very well. And she asked if I thought you would do for Josh."

"No! She never did!" cried Eleanor, her hands going to her suddenly flaming cheeks. "Whatever possessed her?"

"She told me of your rabbit dinner and how Josh entertained you. He wouldn't have shrugged off his sulk if you hadn't been present, Ellie. He often sits before her kitchen fire for hours, she says, and will not even eat when she has put his dinner directly beside him. Jocelyn, my dear, is taken with you."

"But why?" asked Eleanor, startled. "There is nothing about me bears looking at twice, and I am Martin's sister besides. And he and Martin cannot bear each other."

Mary shook her head slowly from side to side. "Tell me," she said quietly, "why did you scratch upon my door?"

"Because I wished to ask you something about—about his lordship. You have known him a long time, have you not?"

"Not so very long—"

"But when you speak, you seem to know everything about him. Well, perhaps not everything, but so very much."

"Not nearly so much as Lily," Mary replied with a grin.

"Do you know what it is he dreams, Mary, when first he falls asleep? It is very bad, I think, and perhaps, if I knew what 'twas, I might find some way to—"

"That is why." Mary smiled, reaching to take one of Eleanor's hands into her own. "Did you not hear Jenny speak of Mildred tonight—how Jocelyn loved her and wished for his papa to marry her—it is her same compassion that fills your heart and climbs straight into your eyes that calls to him. It is this that attracts him. Oh, Ellie, he truly is a wonderful gentleman and deserves to be loved by someone decent and kind and good."

A rush of sympathy and then hope swept through Eleanor. "I knew," she said. "I knew he was not the devil Martin said!"

"Jocelyn is nowhere near a devil! But he is strong and passionate and impetuous. And he is most powerful, Ellie, in

Lords. Since he is loyal to neither Whig nor Tory, he is courted wildly by both sides. If ever you heard him take the floor, you would understand. They all say he is mad, but he is a compelling speaker, and his arguments are always sound and often irrefutable and his opinion holds sway more often than not."

"You admire him very much, do you not?" Eleanor asked, noting the light that sparked in Mary's eyes when she spoke.

"Oh, incredibly much. He is brilliant and exciting and passionate. I never thought to meet such a man in my life."

"Are you—in love with him, then?"

Mary burst into laughter. "No, you silly goose. I am in love with Michael Paxton."

"You are?"

"Indeed, though nothing will come of it, for I am married to Hampton and cannot undo that deed. Yet, at the time, it was all in the world that I wanted—to be married to Joyce's father before she was born. Which makes me think Jocelyn even more brilliant, for he attempted to convince me that what we want most when we are young often turns out to be the thing we most despise in later years. And if now I could take back those marriage vows, I should be the happiest woman on earth. But enough! You wished to know about Jocelyn's bad dreams. There are a great many of them, actually. But when first he drifts off he sees his mother falling. Sometimes he cries out for her, but most often he stops himself and wakes up and then sets out to sleep again. I think it is the medicine makes him so much worse at present."

"And his mother fell from a window?"

"Yes," Mary nodded sadly. "I cannot think what it must have been like for him. Jenny told me once that he screamed and screamed for days after it happened. He was only eight."

"What had this man—this man he was forced to see hang—to do with it?"

" 'Twas a man called Alex Clearmonte. Led a pack of cutthroats to Elders Rise while the earl was in London. Killed all of the stablehands but Harry Cross, who was only twelve and hid in the hayloft. Killed the gardener and the butler and the three footmen as well. Jenny's nurse bundled her off into the night and hid on the moors, along with the other women servants. But the countess was in the tower of the east wing with Jocelyn and did not know of the attack until the beast appeared before her. The blackguard seized Josh and went to throw him from the tower window. The countess fought to save her son and in the process fell to the cobbles herself, three stories below. Jocelyn grabbed a branch of candles and set Clearmonte afire, but not soon enough to save his mama. Then he ran and hid, and Clearmonte and his band destroyed nearly everything in the Rise searching for him. When they could not find the boy they set the Rise afire and rode off."

"But why? Why?" gasped Eleanor, horrified.

"Because Clearmonte's son had waylaid the earl's coach a month before upon the Great North Road and the earl had shot the young man to death and left his body to rot at the side of the highway. Clearmonte intended to kill the earl's son in return." Mary sighed and gave Eleanor's hand a squeeze. "You cannot in the least understand it, Ellie. I have attempted to do so over and over. Persons such as ourselves are never subjected to such brutality and cannot possibly tolerate it. Jocelyn, however, sees it as nothing exceptional. He protests long and loudly in Lords that it is they and all who think themselves most civilized who are the true barbarians."

"But how can he think so?"

"You must ask him," Mary smiled encouragingly. "He will tell you—and convincingly, too. I have come to believe he has the right of it. But I do not think, Ellie, that you may do anything to stop his nightmares. No one has been able to do so for all these years—and Jenny says a great many people have attempted it, including the sainted Mildred."

In Wright's suite the sainted Mildred had come to play a role in the earl's opiate-confused dreams, and her name rising in a hoarse whisper from his lips roused a drowsy Tibbs and brought him to the earl's bedside. The elderly valet untangled covers and sheets and rearranged pillows in an attempt to make Wright more comfortable and prayed silently that the long-departed cook's whispered name would not this time be prelude to a night of fever, aberrations and ancient fears. "For she wouldn't like it one bit," he murmured, bathing Wright's face with cool water. "Mildred would be most upset, Master Josh, to think herself connected in your mind with such night terrors. That she would."

"Who would what?" asked Burton's hushed voice. "How is he tonight, Horace?" More stunning than usual in a cherry red smoking jacket with a sparkling white silk cloth tucked about his neck, Burton's face wreathed in smiles as Tibbs made a great show of studying his garb.

"Do not tell me," Tibbs grinned. "I have a faint memory of gifts in silver paper."

"Indeed—last Christmas, and well you know it. Though why his lordship should think a hoary old butler in need of a cherry red smoking jacket and silk cravat I still cannot grasp. I begin to fear what I shall find awaiting me this year."

"And well you should, Burtie," Tibbs chuckled. "Well you should, for I have seen it. All bought and paid for months ago."

Burton sighed dramatically, raising the back of his hand to his brow, and both old men fell into soft laughter. "I'll stay with you awhile, eh, Horace? Harry Cross intends to relieve you about three o'clock I hear."

Tibbs nodded. "Honored by your company, Burtie."

"Tell me something," asked the Willowset butler, settling into one of the chairs. "Why is it Harry Cross and never just Cross or just Harry?"

Tibbs smiled. "I cannot tell you. I doubt Harry Cross can tell you. When I came to wait upon that young gentleman," he nodded toward Wright, " 'twas how he referred to the other boy every time. 'Twas Harry Cross this and Harry Cross that, and so everyone did likewise. Now it is most awkward to refer to Harry Cross in any other way."

"When you came? I thought you had always waited upon his lordship, Tibbs."

"No. Enlisted, I did, in the forces of the old earl when his lordship was a twig of eight and Miss Jenny a prattling little maid of three or so."

"Should have thought the earl'd have sent the boy off to school by then."

"Did the following year, but by then, of course, I had grown to be indispensable."

Burton's eyebrow cocked, his intelligent gray eyes filled with mirth. "All Yorkshire servants become indispensable, do they not, three days after they are hired?"

"Exactly! 'Twas the luckiest day of my life when I arrived at that ruin of a castle and was immediately set upon by Master Josh, demanding to know was I goin' to be a glim-flashy ol' curmudgeon like Harry Cross said or was I goin' to let 'im keep his ol' nankeen breeches even if they stinked a bit."

"Stinked a bit?" Burton chuckled.

Tibbs nodded. "Came into very close contact with a polecat, they did. Apparently Master Josh had been in them at the time. I, of course, made the desired response and found myself a home, though it took a good week's worth of effort to save those breeches. By the end of that week, Burtie, I'd not have left the lad had he gone and caught himself a polecat all over again."

Sixteen

Constable Perkins and several of the men of St. Swithin's had escorted Hampton and the Sneezing Fiend safely to Dorset, where the two would writhe in frustrated anger in gaol until the next assizes. Constable Perkins himself stopped at Willowset on his return to assure the earl that all was well, and that if anyone in the household need appear at the court they would be adequately notified, but that his lordship would not be requested to do so and he need not bother his head about it. Eleanor, who had been present at this small exchange, had noted the combination of relief and wonder in Wright's eyes but kept silent on it.

Eleanor expected Martin to announce any day that they must return to St. Swithin's and the vicarage, but he neglected to mention it. Instead he worked upon his sermons in the Willowset library and took the duke's coach into the village to attend to his duties. The interminable rain began to change into snow, and still the diverse little group at Willowset remained together without anyone's mentioning that they ought to go home. It was Mrs. Dish who broached the subject first as she helped Wright to breakfast one morning.

"Do you want to go home, Melinda? There is certainly no reason you may not. You need only ask Oakes to drive you. Tibbs and MacGregor and Harry Cross shall torture me mercilessly once you have departed, of course, but that must not be your concern."

"Oh my, what a clanker!" Mrs. Dish laughed. "And so pitifully said!"

"But you do not wish to leave Mary and Joyce? Will you take them home with you, too?"

"Your lordship," Mrs. Dish said quite seriously, taking a spoon from his hand and replacing it with a cup of hot chocolate, "I have been here near a fortnight, and that is quite long enough to impose upon the duchess's hospitality."

"Has Jenny said something?"

"No, dear, she has not. She has been the most pleasant and entertaining of hostesses. But Christmas approaches, and most certainly the duchess expects guests."

"No she don't."

"Jocelyn, how do you know?"

"Well, because Jenny wanted to know did I wish to ask the London staff to come here for the duration, since no one else was coming. If you are worried about your cottage standing empty, I can send one of the servants to check upon it. Stay, Melinda. Please? You will want to spend Christmas with Mary and Joyce, and if you take them home with you, I—I—"

Eleanor, who had stood silently in the doorway on Howard's arm to keep from interrupting this conversation, felt her heart go out to the gentleman as he declined to finish the sentence. Mrs. Dish only smiled at him and shook her head. "You are the most practiced manipulator, y'r lordship. What a wretched woman I should be to deprive you of Mary and Joyce at Christmas time, after you have made them a part of your family for four whole years. Very well. I shall stay if the duchess approves, and I shall only ask Oakes to take me home to fetch more clothes and perhaps to stop at some of the shops."

In the end they were all of them invited to stay the holidays, and much to her surprise, Eleanor heard Martin accept the invitation willingly for both of them. She thought his acceptance had a good deal to do with the fact that Miss Lipton had also elected to remain, but she did not truly care why he had accepted—only that he had. "You will not mind, will you, Ellie?"

he asked her in the drawing room as they shared a brief moment together. "You certainly might go to Mama and Papa if you wish, though I have had a letter from Papa saying they intend to spend the holiday with Aunt Beth. Still, I expect Aunt Beth will be glad to have you."

Eleanor knew immediately what Martin was thinking. She had always spent the holidays in the bosom of her family—had never once in all her twenty-one years ventured off to a house party. "I am not as unadventurous as you assume, Martin," she murmured. "I shall like to spend Christmas here above all things."

Howard looked at her with surprise. He had expected a different answer, she thought, smiling gleefully up at him.

"It's Wright, ain't it?" he growled quietly. "I swear, Ellie, I do not know what to expect of you one moment to the next since you have come to make his acquaintance."

"Do you not wish me to remain, Martin?"

"Yes, of course I do, but I did not expect it."

Eleanor, her eyes shining in the candlelight, winked at him and turned away, taking Lily's arm just as she approached. "We ladies want you in this corner, Lily," she grinned. "Tonight the gentlemen must amuse themselves, for we have things to discuss."

"What things? Eleanor? Why are you smiling so deviously?"

"They expelled you from the drawing room?" Wright asked, sitting up in his bed and looking suspiciously healthy, a deep maroon smoking jacket buttoned around him to keep the chill away. "All of you?"

"Well, they are all of them huddled into a little group at one end of the room and paying us not the least attention," Paxton shrugged. "So we thought to come here and pester you. You, at least, do not mind if we smoke."

"Not at all if you mean to offer me one."

"It's a cheroot, Josh."

"Yes, exactly. You do mean to offer me one, do you not?"

Di Roche took one as well, and Howard, and by the time an hour had passed, the gentlemen were peering at each other through a dense fog.

"Open a window, Paxton," Howard urged. "It's getting thick in here."

"You open one, Howard. I produced the cheroots."

"I opening the window," di Roche offered jovially, for the gentlemen besides puffing on Paxton's cheroots had spent the last hour downing a goodly portion of Wright's brandy.

"I don't suppose Ware came by this wonderful liquid legally," Howard mused, sipping at his third.

"Charlie did not come by it at all, Howard. It's mine. I liberated it from the cellars at the Rise this past summer."

"Then I'm certain 'tis not legal," Howard muttered.

"No, it ain't," announced Wright, his smile of a moment before fading. "Came to my cellars duty free by way of the schooner *Argonaut*, over the cliffs and through the moors by donkey train, accompanied by brigands and villains each step of the way."

"Settle down, Wright," Paxton urged. "He only wondered is all. No need to take offense."

"I am not taking offense. I am merely explaining to Howard the facts of life. One does not buy brandy upon the open market unless one cares nothing for honor and guts and glory—"

"You're drunk," laughed Paxton, "and Tibbs will have our skins for even thinking to pour you a glass, much less three."

Howard's brow furrowed. "Honor and guts and glory?" he mused loudly. "Honor and guts and glory? What the devil is he talking about?"

"About the free-trading men," di Roche answered. "The bootmakers."

"The freebooters," Paxton laughed.

"Well, but I never heard those words connected with them before—at least, only in one of those deuced novels."

Wright's darkling eyes met Howard's stubborn ones. "I shall

explain it all to you one day, Howard—who 'tis smuggles brandy and how many families must depend upon the revenue it brings—and exactly how many lives have been lost in the delivery of it."

"Do not start, Josh!" grumbled Paxton. "You are not in Lords an' I ain't longing for a debate upon the blockade or the tax bills or nothing else."

The earl stared at him a moment, set his glass upon the bedside table, hiccoughed and grinned. "Sorry, Michael. I'm drunk."

"Yes, I know you are. You were near to drunk when we walked in, were you not?"

"Uh-huh."

"What?" Howard lurched from his chair, recovered his equilibrium and strolled cautiously toward the bed. "How? Where did you come by anything to drink?"

"Oakes brought cabernet this afternoon; Harry Cross brought port; Burton sneaked in with a bottle of French champagne and Tibbs relented and said I might have a glass of sherry or two with my dinner."

"By thunder, the man has been drinking for six hours straight!" roared Howard. "No wonder he looks so devilishly healthy!" And with that they all broke into whoops.

When the laughter finally died the gentlemen found themselves comfortably strewn about the room in a companionable silence. No one seemed inclined to disturb any of the others and all of them stared from one angle or another into the flames blazing away upon the grate. It was the earl who finally dispensed the stillness with a sigh. "I just wish you wasn't such a fop," he muttered.

"Huh? What?" asked Paxton, rising from dreams of Mary.

"Where in the world did that pop out of?" queried Howard, shaking Lily to the back of his mind. "Who do you wish was not a fop, Wright?"

"That little Italian one, leaning against the wall there by the window. Don't you ever sit down, di Roche? Don't they have chairs in Italy?"

Di Roche grinned. "Chairs they having, my lord, but to be sitting too much is to be creasing my verimost best of breeches for which Nicco he killing me."

"You oughtn't to call him a fop anyway, Wright. Man saved y'r life," mumbled Paxton.

"He did? When?"

"Well—well—it was he first warned you about Hampton."

"No, that was Mary."

"Well, he brought help after you took that tumble."

"Harry Cross said Jessie's fire brought them."

"Yes, well, how about the poison? He saved you from the poison, didn't he?"

"No, that being Nicco," offered di Roche with a smile. "I doing nothing much."

"You have been doing a great deal, di Roche. But ain't none of it had to do with saving my life," murmured the earl with an odd grin. "You have been quarting—courting—my sister every minute you've been under this roof."

"Not every minute," protested di Roche with a chuckle. "Only when I am waking. She being all things most beautiful, my Jenny."

"My Jenny, di Roche. She ain't yours as yet."

"Soon she being mine."

"What makes you think so?"

"Fonder and fonder of me you growing, *signor.* I seeing in your eyes. You even this moment calling of me fop."

"But a fop is not a good thing, di Roche," Howard explained. "To call you a fop is an insult."

"Until this evening he not calling to my face anything. Now I being notice of taken, *si?* Soon I being his brother-in-law."

Wright groaned loudly and tossed a pillow at di Roche's head. It went low and wide of the mark and plopped on top of the logs hissing on the grate. Paxton jumped to grab the thing off and, giving it a quick jerk to keep from burning his hand, tore the ticking open upon a sharp twig. Feathers bubbled and hissed. Di Roche dove for the chamber pot under the bed; Howard rushed for the water pitcher. "Use the tongs, Paxton, the tongs!" the reverend shouted, rushing back around the bed to fill the chamber pot with water and sloshing most of it over di Roche because both continued to move toward the fire. Paxton succeeded on the third try to emancipate the stinking thing and then tried to push it down into the chamber pot. It would not fit. Pieces of feathers sizzled and burped and went limp, but the fire smoldered relentlessly deeper. Di Roche rushed to the window, opened it wider and Paxton and Howard threw the unwieldy bundle, chamber pot and all, out into the frigid air.

"What is going on in here?" came Tibbs's voice, followed immediately by that stalwart individual. "Good heavens, such a smell! Phew! You have been burning feathers? Has his lordship fainted?" The worried little valet's gaze flew directly to the bed, where he noted that far from having fainted, Wright was roaring with laughter.

"I calling the Harry Cross, no?" di Roche chuckled, holding back the draperies casually with one hand and gazing with supreme innocence out into the yard. "Is fire outside. The Harry Cross will knowing where are buckets."

"A fire?" Tibbs looked from one gentleman to the other to the other. "A fire? Outside his lordship's window?"

"Well, it was inside before it was outside, Tibbs," Paxton grinned. "But not to worry."

"Not to worry?" echoed Tibbs. "Good heavens, at least close that window before you give him an inflammation of the lungs—again. It is blistering cold out there!"

"Yes, blistering cold," hiccoughed Wright, holding his ribs and trying to stop laughing.

"He's drunk," Howard informed Tibbs primly. "Ought to know better than to let the man have sherry with his dinner."

"Indeed," di Roche nodded with a wide smile.

"Don't mix well with the medicine he's taking," Paxton

added as the three inched past the valet and strolled hurriedly out of the room.

"What was that all about?" muttered Tibbs, turning to the earl. "Master Josh, cease giggling at once or you shall hurt one hundred times more in the morning than you do at the moment!"

"I—I'm trying, Tibbs. T-truly, I am. I—Tibbs?"

"Yes, m'lord?"

"T-tibbs, I am afraid I n-need a ch-chamber pot."

"Well, and there's nothing to be afraid of in that," murmured Tibbs, bending to look under the bed.

"No, T-tibbs, I m-mean a new chamber pot."

"But what's happened to this one, m'lord? There ain't a sign of it here."

"It's outside the window, Tibbs. Those three blackguards have stole it from me an' set it a-f-fire."

Eleanor looked over Mary's shoulder at the lists and grinned with satisfaction. "We shall be able to get everything we need without the least hardship in St. Swithin's," she said happily. "I love Christmas!"

"Well, and since we are combining our efforts, we shall get everything bought that must be bought and everything made we wish to make without the least rush," Mary smiled. "You will help us, Aunt, will you not? With our sewing and knitting, I mean. I have already begun the slippers for Mr. Paxton, but they do not look quite the thing."

"And I have almost finished Joshie's shirt," Jenny giggled, almost jumping up and down on the fainting couch but not quite. "I began on it last August. He will be so surprised! And we must plan for the balls as well!"

"The balls?" asked Eleanor.

"We always have two balls at Willowset over the Christmas season. One is for the staff and the other for the tenants and the people of St. Swithin's. They are called the little ball and the grand ball and they are so much fun."

"Must we write out invitations then?"

"Oh, no, everyone expects to come. We must only leave word at Mrs. Gresham's boutique and at the Crossroads as to the day and the time, and word will reach absolutely everyone. Have you had word from London, Mary? About the staff at Wright House?"

"They are all to have bonuses and the holidays off with pay. Josh instructed me to see to it last week. And Mr. Dunville proposes to join us here with Collen and Jamie on the twentieth. Josh has told Mr. Grimsby to hire a post chaise for them and to see them safely off."

"Oh, wonderful!" squeaked Lily, clapping her hands excitedly. "And Congreve is coming as well, with the presents I bought in London. It will be the most excellent Christmas."

"Mr. Dunville is his lordship's butler," Mary offered with a glance at Eleanor's confused countenance. "And Collen and Jamie are—well, they are not quite anything yet, though Josh says Collen shall be a coachman one day—"

"—and Jamie a valet," continued Lily with a wide smile. "Though I think Jamie's becoming a valet is only wishful thinking upon Josh's part. He is much more likely to become a burglar."

"They are two of the orphans," Jenny explained as Eleanor continued to look confused. "We must put them upon the list as well, Mary, and Dunville."

"Jocelyn has already provided for the three of them quite nicely." Mary grinned. "He has been buying Christmas presents since June, and Dunville will *need* a post chaise to carry them all. You will not believe what his lordship has bought for Burton. That gentleman will be stunned at it."

Mrs. Dish, who had been listening quietly to the young ladies as she plied her needle, chuckled. "I rather think several gentlemen will be stunned if you find everything upon your lists.

Ah, the tea things arrive, my dears, and I think the gentlemen are close behind. Is that not them laughing in the hall?"

Eleanor closed her eyes that night determined not to think of Wright at all. She was pleasantly excited at the prospects that lay before her in the coming weeks. And she was extremely happy to have found herself surrounded by such almost-sisters as Mary and Jenny and Lily had become. Eleanor had never been close to either of her sisters, they having married and moved away almost ten years before she left the schoolroom. The loving companionship among the ladies at Willowset that now included her as well, set her whole being aglow and gave her a self-confidence she had never known before. It no longer occurred to her at awkward moments that Lily was an unacceptable person, that Mary had sunk herself beyond repair, or that Jenny was a duchess and far above her reach. They were all her friends, her confidantes, and what's more, they had faced grave danger together. The bond forged among them by that adventure had every evidence of becoming a strong and lasting one. "I have never been so very happy," she whispered into the night.

Wright, meanwhile, had closed his eyes—several times—more than several times. He should rightfully have slipped immediately into slumber. He found he could not. He attempted with great fortitude to lie still so as not to bring his restlessness to Tibbs's attention, but his one good hand went unconsciously to pluck at the coverlet and his good leg began to jump regardless of how hard he strove to keep it from doing so. In a matter of five minutes Tibbs was sitting down upon the edge of the bed. "Too much wine and too much hilarity," the gentleman's gentleman murmured.

"No, it ain't that. I didn't mean to bring you to me, Tibbs."

"Don't I know that? But I am here regardless, my lord. So now you must tell me what keeps sleep at bay. Are you in pain?

I thought best not to give you the laudanum after all that wine; however—"

"No, no, I ain't in any great pain, Tibbs. I am well beyond pain. I am into extreme self-pity."

"Now, your lordship, that is inexcusable."

"Yes, I know, but I cannot seem to shake it off. I want to be up, Tibbs, and about, and doing things."

"Of course you do."

"Yes, and I do not want to be tended to and watched over as if I were some mindless infant."

"No, of course you don't."

"No, and I cannot understand why Ellie don't come to see me hardly at all anymore."

Tibbs's wrinkled face creased into a hopeful smile. "You must not bother about it, m'lord. She would come if she could. But you are out of danger now, and her presence is not so necessary to you as it was."

"And so she don't want to come?"

"I am quite certain Miss Eleanor would be most pleased to come, but she is a young unmarried woman, and it is most unacceptable for her to be visiting a gentleman in his bedchamber."

"But she did."

"Because you were so very ill, Master Josh, and her merest whisper seemed to quiet you and make you better, so the Reverend Mr. Howard allowed her to ignore propriety on your behalf."

"But now he won't?"

"Not except for a quick look-in, and then only if Mrs. Dish accompanies her." Tibbs brushed the unruly dark curls gently from the bandaged brow. "And it will do you not the least good to pout about it. Pouting is not the answer."

"What is the answer, Tibbs? I shall be stuck here in this bed forever—MacGregor says I may not walk until well after Christmas, nor I mayn't use this blasted arm until then either. I am going slowly mad. I can feel it. If I had not gotten so wonderfully foxed this evening, I should have completely lost my mind. I cannot bear it another day, Tibbs. And if she don't come to see me but once in a fortnight, I will never get the opportunity to—to—"

"To what, my lord," asked Tibbs quietly.

"Oh, nothing. My mind is numb. Do you think Miss Eleanor is pretty, Tibbs?"

"No, my lord."

"No, I expect you are right. Her face is plain—not like Lily's, for instance."

"Not like Lily's, my lord."

"No, and her hair is just plain brown, ain't it?"

"Yes, my lord."

"But her eyes, Tibbs. Her eyes are like honey."

"Like honey, my lord?"

"What? Do you not think so?"

"Oh, of course, my lord. Exactly like honey."

"Yes, and they speak to me, Tibbs. They tell much more than she wishes for me to know."

"Indeed, my lord. Miss Eleanor is everything kind and compassionate."

"And alluring."

Tibbs's mind jerked wildly at this and rushed about in great confusion, searching for anything at all the young woman had said or done or even anything in her appearance that would prompt such a word to be connected with her in his lordship's mind. He could find nothing. Distractedly he patted the back of Wright's hand as he would have done were the earl a child of nine. "Go to sleep, my lord. You will feel a good deal less maudlin in the morning."

"I cannot!" shouted Wright abruptly at the top of his lungs, nearly shattering Tibbs's eardrums and causing the elderly gentleman to leap to his feet. "I'm dreadfully sorry, Tibbs," he said immediately afterward in a much softer tone. "I am feeling as cantankerous as Jessie when he is forbidden to go outside."

"And responding exactly like," pronounced Tibbs with formidable forbearance. "You are more than five, your lordship."

"I feel like three," muttered Wright, beginning to move restlessly again. "By gawd, Tibbs, you would not be all patience and sufferance were you in my place."

"N-no, your lordship," Tibbs answered, the dire look deserting him and his lips beginning to quiver. "I should be at a dreadful loss were I unable to leave my bed. You have me there. But you have got to sleep," he added, "or you shall end by making yourself ill again."

"I want Ellie," mumbled Wright petulantly. "An' I want her now!"

"Your lordship, it is late and Miss Howard has retired. Do not be such a—"

"A what, Tibbs?"

"A jackanapes, your lordship."

"I am not a jackanapes. I am merely—rapidly—losing my mind!"

Tibbs walked to the washstand and returned armed with a newly filled bottle and a spoon. "In that case, Master Josh, since your mind is already leaving you, I shan't worry about giving you this." The liquid oozed into the spoon before his lordship's weary eyes and as Tibbs sat beside him and raised him enough to take the medicine, he wrinkled his nose and sighed. "It is all her fault," he muttered and then swallowed. "I should never be in half so bad a state if she had not gone Miss Propriety on me."

"Exactly so, my lord," mumbled Tibbs encouragingly as he poured another spoonful of the dreadful stuff.

"Exactly so," muttered Wright, accepting the second nauseating dose without argument. "Exactly so, Tibbs. She don't like me at all, prob'ly. Don't blame her. I'm maggoty."

"Yes, you are." Tibbs grinned, setting the medicine aside and easing the earl back down. "Maggoty, fanciful and capricious, a regular Spinach."

In her own chamber Eleanor tossed restlessly between the

sheets. She had been concentrating hard upon her newfound friendships, but in the end *he* had come sweeping into her mind without so much as a by-your-leave, scattering Jenny and Lily and even Mary to the winds. He of the midnight blue eyes flecked so stunningly with silver; he of the broad shoulders and slim waist, the white whipcord breeches and—"Oh for goodness sakes!" muttered Eleanor, slamming her fist into the pillow. "Anyone would think I had never seen a gentleman before in my life! And now what is this about orphans? What is wrong with the man? He goes about rescuing ravished maidens; he re-creates lightskirts into ladies; he nearly falls to his death to save me—me!—and now he keeps orphans at his home in London?"

Eleanor's fist beat at the pillow again, and then she rolled onto her back and stared up into the darkness. She had barely seen Wright in the last two weeks. He was on the mend, Martin had said, and her assistance was no longer necessary. And no, she might not spend any more evenings in the man's bedchamber no matter who accompanied her. "And perhaps Jocelyn does not even notice my absence," she mumbled forlornly. She sighed and rolled over to stare into the winking remains of the fire. She had not had a decent night's sleep since that man had come charging into the nursery and scooped Jessie up into his arms and mistaken her for a nursery maid. Always when her head touched the pillow visions of him came swooping out of nowhere to keep her awake for hours. And it was all his fault, too, that she had not gotten her breakfast before eleven o'clock any time these past two weeks and more. Well, he would not keep her up any longer tonight! She did not care in the least whether he kept orphans in his home in London or not. It certainly was no concern of hers. And she would not spend one more moment thinking about it—or him—or anything else either!

Seventeen

When Eleanor reached the breakfast room late the following morning she was surprised to find a bleary-eyed but grinning Tibbs lying in wait for her. "I have been entrusted with a message, Miss Howard," he told her as he accompanied her down the sideboard. He insisted upon holding her plate as she filled it and carrying it to the table for her. He then brought her a steaming cup of coffee and, concluding she was well settled, produced from his waistcoat pocket a many-folded sheet of paper. " 'Tis from his lordship," he announced.

"He has not taken a turn for the worse, Tibbs?"

"No, miss, but he awaits, most impatiently, an answer to this scribbling."

"It certainly is scribbling," Eleanor murmured, squinting her eyes in an attempt to decipher the scrawled characters.

"Yes, miss. 'Tis because he is forced to write right-handed, which he hasn't done since he left school. But he would not abide my writing it for him."

"He wishes me to visit him, Tibbs? Does he not understand that—in his music room? He wishes me to visit him in his music room? How can that be? I must be deciphering something wrongly."

"No, miss, that is exactly what he writes."

"He would not let you write for him, but you know exactly what he wrote?" Eleanor asked, smiling up at Tibbs.

"Well, miss, uncertain he was how to phrase it, seeing as

how he meant to be extremely proper. He is not always positive about propriety, but he tried extremely hard this morning."

"I see," Eleanor grinned. "But how does he propose to do this? You have not been forced to move his bed, Tibbs?"

"No, miss, simply himself. Deuce of a time we had of it, too. 'Twas an ordeal on everyone's part, especially his lordship's. But he is turned out right and proper, and Mr. Howard can have not the least objection. The other ladies have been invited as well."

"Well, then you must tell him I shall come as soon as I have finished my breakfast, Tibbs."

What Eleanor beheld upon entering the music room brought her to an abrupt halt. Joyce sat upon Mary's lap pounding the harpsichord keys with great enthusiasm. Jenny and Jessie giggled and jumped and stamped about the Turkish carpeting in broad imitation of a Scottish reel. Mrs. Dish and Mrs. Bowers huddled together in one corner, their needlework in their laps and their hands to their ears, laughing heartily. And on a high-backed divan near to the fire, one foot pillowed upon a footstool and one arm in a sling, the bandage gone from his brow, and scrubbed and shaved and combed and polished until he gleamed, the Earl of Wright sat and pounded with his good hand upon an odd little drum with feathers dangling from it. Never had she witnessed such a general and gleeful disregard for peace and quiet and decorous behavior. The sheer joy that filled the room overwhelmed her. So much so, in fact, that she did not at once notice when the pounding upon the drum ceased and the darkling eyes stared up at her with lavish good humor.

Wright saw his gaze went unnoticed and seized the opportunity to study Miss Howard intently. In an unadorned morning dress of checked muslin with long sleeves and high collar, a bright green woolen shawl about her shoulders and a matching ribbon of bright green threaded through the coronet of braids upon her head, she looked quite pretty. Tibbs had been wrong. Her face was not plain, but definitely attractive, though he could not quite put his finger upon what made it so. And her eyes *were* like honey; he had been correct about that. A warm golden brown, liquid and alluring. And her figure, plumper than Lily's or Mary's, made him ache to take her in his arms, to feel the softness of her against his own hard body.

Around him the room quieted as one by one the others noticed Eleanor's presence and his entrancement with her. Mary put her arms tightly about Joyce and whispered in her ear to keep the child from bouncing off the stool and running to greet Ellie. Jenny scooped Jessie up into her arms and spun him around in a great circle, all the while admonishing him to keep his peace for a moment, saying he might run to Ellie as soon as his uncle had welcomed her to their little party. Mrs. Dish and Mrs. Bowers took their hands from their ears and smothered their laughter. Eleanor, seeing the jollity come to an end, wondered if somehow she were the cause of its cessation and opened her mouth to protest that they need not cease because of her arrival, and then she noticed the beguiled look upon Wright's face and his total absorption in a study of herself. A flush rising to her cheeks, she stood her ground and stared directly back at him, thinking to give him a deserved setdown for such a lack of manners. But he did not notice. Though he was most certainly looking at her, he was not seeing her at all, or so she thought. His mind had wandered down some other path altogether.

"Josh," Mary's husky voice called from across the room after another moment, "do you not intend to say so much as 'good morning' to Miss Howard?"

"Huh?" The earl seemed to tumble all at once into awareness.

"You have been staring Ellie out of countenance for the last three minutes," Jenny giggled.

"I have? I do apologize, Miss Howard," he drawled, a twinkle in his eyes. "Abominable how my mind wanders lately. Come and join us. We are having dancing lessons, I think."

"Me the 'sician!" squealed Joyce, scrambling from her

mama's lap and running full tilt to be caught up into Eleanor's arms.

"An' I am the caperchant!" shouted Jessie. "An' Mama must do ever'thin' the way I say!"

"You are the what?" asked Wright.

"The caperchant! The caperchant! The caperchant!"

Eleanor, Joyce in her arms, watched enthralled as the earl's proud, fine lips began to quiver and twitch and a small dent at one side of his mouth made a gleeful appearance, and then, unable to resist, she burst into laughter with him.

"Well, what am I then?" demanded Jessie. Hands on hips, his feet spread wide and his curly head tilted upward, he gave every indication that he would one day become an engaging replica of his departed father.

"You are the caper merchant, Jess," chuckled Wright, "though you ought not say so. You must say you are the dancing master."

"Why?"

"Because gentlemen do not use cant terms in the presence of ladies."

"But it was Mama tol' me to be the caper—merchant."

"Yes," laughed Wright, "but your mama had the misfortune to have me for a brother. Miss Ellie would not have told you so."

"You wouldn't, Ellie?" The little duke cocked his eyebrow at her in direct imitation of his uncle.

"I—I do not think so," Eleanor chuckled. "I have never heard a dancing master called so before, my dear. But I cannot think there is a great deal of harm in it. You may certainly be a caper merchant in my presence if you wish."

"Do not encourage him, Miss Howard, or you will find yourself leaping about the Turkish carpeting," Wright grinned. "Will you sit and visit for awhile?"

"I should be delighted, your lordship." Eleanor looked about for a chair and selected one near a casement on the opposite side of the room.

"No, not way over there," Wright sighed. "There is room beside me here on the divan. I do not bite, Miss Howard."

"Uh-huh!" squealed Joyce, wriggling out of Eleanor's arms. "Uh-huh! Mama, Mama," she giggled, running back to Mary. "Uncle Josh gonna bite Ellie!"

"Oh, I do not think so," Mary laughed.

"Uh-huh!" The dusky curls bounced enthusiastically as she nodded, her gaze pinned expectantly upon the earl.

"I amend my statement, Miss Howard. I do not bite young ladies beyond the age of six."

"And you do bite them until then?" Eleanor asked, sitting primly down beside him on the very edge of the divan.

"Well, I find I have a distinct tendency to nibble upon their fingers and toes when I have an urge to make them giggle." He grinned engagingly. "I thought never to see you again, Ellie. Tibbs said you could not visit my chamber unless I were near to sticking my spoon in the wall."

"Near to what?"

"Dying, my dear."

"Oh—I—I have never heard it put quite that way before."

"Has no one ever spoken cant to you? Not even your father's grooms?"

"No one. I—my mother would never allow it, your lordship."

"Why do you sit as if you will leap straight into the air at any moment? Sit back, Miss Howard, and be comfortable. I shall not suddenly spring at you across the seat. I shan't likely be in springing form for at least another two months, MacGregor says. He is the most obstinate old Scot in the entire world."

"Does he know you have left your bed, my lord?"

"Yes, and has thrown dire threats at me for doing so. There is such a list of things I have promised him to do and not to do that I can't remember a one of them."

"One of them, my dear," inserted Mary lightly, carrying a white wicker chair to face the divan, "is to leave that pillow you are fiddling with alone, or else Dr. MacGregor will not be responsible for the sorry state of your ribs. It is there to support your back."

"It is there to annoy me—and doing a d-deuced good job of it, too. Where's our vixen gone?"

"She was disappointed you did not bite Ellie and so has run off with Jessie somewhere on a secret mission."

"Yes, and we are all going to discover what it is and be total flabbergasted," added Jenny, pulling a chair she had scavenged from the bedchamber up beside Mary's. "That is what Jessie informed me—'total flabbergasted:' He is the funniest little boy, nearly as funny as you was used to be, Joshie."

"Do you know Lily has gone with Reverend Howard to cut ivy and holly branches for the church?" Mary asked nonchalantly, her bright eyes discreetly awaiting the earl's reaction.

"No, has she? I assume they are properly chaperoned," Wright drawled.

"No," Jenny giggled. "Though Mr. Howard looked a bit guilty. I convinced him, you know, no one would object, since all knew her to be quite safe in a vicar's company."

"Especially Howard's," droned the earl. "You are quite sure they are gone, Jenny?"

"Oh, yes, quite sure. And Francesco and Mr. Paxton have gone riding. They would not say where—only that they wished to get in a ride before the snow melted or turned into rain again. Do you like Francesco yet?"

Eleanor caught the look of glee in Mary's eyes. They had spent a number of hours one afternoon discussing the likelihood of a successful alliance between Jenny and the marquis. "You will see," Mary had said at last. "Jocelyn will be forced to give his blessing to the two. He is a great stubborn lout and will stand firm upon his opinions until doomsday in the House of Lords, but Jenny will shake the ground beneath his feet until he is forced to give in to her."

"No," Wright replied with an obstinate set to his jaw, "I do not like him yet. He is a complete dandy, Jenny. How can you possibly find anything to like in the man?"

"There, you are relenting already. I knew you would once you came to know him."

"Relenting?"

"Well, you used to call him a fribble in London, and then he said you called him a fop, and now he is a dandy—you are liking him better and better!"

Wright rolled his eyes toward heaven in obvious supplication, which made Eleanor laugh.

"No, but 'tis true," Jenny declared. "You used to call Charlie a fribble as well, when first we met."

"I was exceeding wrong about Charlie."

"You are exceeding wrong about Francesco as well. He is handsome and kind and brave and romantic."

"Indeed—and is he rich as well?"

"Oh, rich as Croesus."

"Well," Wright grinned with a twinkle in his eyes, "that's a point in his favor. Will he give me a loan, do you think?"

"A loan for what?" Mary asked.

"That is none of your business, my dear."

"Oh? I will remind you that I know more about your finances, my lord, than you do yourself. You have not taken up another lost cause, have you, Jocelyn?"

"I do not take up lost causes," stated the earl smugly. "Perhaps I have lost money from time to time, but I have never lost a cause."

This time Mary rolled her eyes toward heaven and Jenny burst into giggles.

"That's it. Off with the both of you at once," growled Wright. "Go see what sort of bumble bath your rascals are getting into and cease plaguing me."

To Eleanor's amazement, both ladies rose without the least objection and strolled from the room arm in arm.

"At last we are alone," Wright said wickedly when they had disappeared.

Eleanor started, then caught the gleam in his eyes and heard Mrs. Bowers cough.

"Oh, we are not," she grinned. "Mrs. Bowers and Mrs. Dish are right over there."

"They don't count, Ellie. They're on my side."

"On your side? Whatever do you mean?"

"I mean they're here to play propriety, but they have agreed not to save you from me."

Eleanor's eyes opened wide. "Will I need to be saved, sir?"

"Damned if I know." Wright's fingers went to run distractedly through his artfully arranged locks and set the curls free to fall helter-skelter, in the process uncovering the lingering bruise upon his forehead and the forming scar where MacGregor had stitched the wound closed.

Eleanor gasped at the sight of it, and her fingers went to caress the injury. The earl flinched. "Does it still hurt, then?"

"A bit. I don't know why I cannot leave my hair where it belongs. Tibbs spent forever getting it to lie down and behave, and now I've gone and messed it up again, ain't I? He'll ring a peal over me for it."

"Oh, bosh."

"No, he will. He's angry with me already."

"Why?"

"Because I insisted upon getting dressed. He was all for carrying me in here, you understand, but he had some fool idea that I should appear in robe and slippers like a blasted invalid. Come to think of it, I rather believe that was one of the things I promised MacGregor."

"To appear a blasted invalid?" Eleanor queried with a smile.

"Uh-huh. But I could not, you see, because—"

"Because why?"

"Well, because you might find something improper about my being in robe and slippers and not come. I couldn't take such a risk. And now I'm relieved I have not suffered for nothing."

"Suffered?"

"It is fierce embarrassing to be scrubbed and dressed like a babe, Miss Howard, and worse to have it take Tibbs *and* Burton *and* Colly Shepard to get one into one's breeches."

"It took all three of them?"

"In the end it did, because every time we attempted to—never mind, you do not need to know—but I did not hit anyone and I only cursed a little."

Eleanor realized for the first time how painful it must have been to have his battered body forced into the tight-fitting garments and experienced an odd sense of pleasure to think that he had done so for her sake. "I think," she murmured shyly, "that you did not suffer so for me alone. You found remaining in your bed extremely tiresome, did you not, sir?"

"Yes, but I'd not thought to leave it till Tibbs explained."

"Explained?"

"About your visiting me any more being improper. I can't see it, myself. What am I like to do bound up in bandages from top to toe? Ravish you? I rather think not. You might fight me off with one finger if you wished." Eleanor gave a little gulp as for the first time in her experience the earl's eyes gazed pleadingly into hers, without arrogance, without mirth, without even the mesmeric quality she thought they inevitably possessed. "I am not familiar with all the rules of propriety, Miss Howard. But I wish you will understand that I am attempting to do everything properly. I—I find I like you."

"You like me, my lord?"

"Very much. And I have missed you, you know. And I've determined to abide by the rules of propriety, so that your brother mayn't always be keeping you away from me. Only I never have paid a great deal of attention to propriety—so you must tell me how to go about it. Do you think me a fool, Miss Howard?" This last he added with a sadness in his eyes that made Eleanor wish to hold him tightly in her arms and reassure him that he was brave and kind and good and she was proud to be liked by him, did he know how to behave with propriety or not.

"Of course you are not a fool, my lord," she whispered, taking his hand, which had balled into a fist, and massaging the tension from it. "You are a gentleman of the first order and I am proud to be your friend."

"You are?"

"Indeed."

Running feet sounded from the hall, and Jessie and Joyce erupted into the room. With all the self-centeredness of childhood, the two squiggled up on to the divan between Eleanor and Wright, forcing Eleanor to let go his hand. Jessie, gaining his knees on the seat, reached down to pull up a burlap sack he had left on the floor. "We gots the most 'mazin' thing, Uncle Josh. Me and Joycie founded it on our roun's."

"On your what?" asked the earl, resting his good arm along both slim sets of shoulders. His eyes strayed to Eleanor's.

"On our woun's, Uncle Josh," repeated Joyce impatiently. Ever' day we goes on our woun's jus' like Mr. Pewcavill."

"Oh, I see. Mr. Perciville is the groundskeeper," he explained to Eleanor. "And what is this amazin' thing you found? May I see it?"

"Uh-huh," Joyce nodded. "But you must be vewy quiet."

"Quiet?"

"Uh-huh," Jess nodded. " 'Stremely quiet. It likes ever'one to be quiet." As Joyce watched with wide eyes and little hands waving excitedly in the air, Jessie opened the sack and reached down into it with both hands. Whatever it was inside, he could not seem to quite get hold of it, so he stuck his head inside the sack as well and wiggled down as far as his shoulders.

Eleanor could not guess what to expect. She glanced questioningly at Wright, but he was focused on Jessie and did not notice.

"Your grace," he asked pleasantly, "is this amazin' thing alive in there?"

"It was yes'erday," called back Jessie, muffled.

"Good lord, you do not mean to tell me you have kept something alive in that sack since yesterday?"

"We letted it out in the stables. Mattie maked a place for it. But it's hard to carry wifout a sack. I gots it, Uncle Josh!"

"Good. Now come up for air."

"I cannot gets out."

Joyce bounced from the divan and grabbed the bottom of the sack and pulled with all her might. So hard, in fact, that she fell backward onto her bottom. Eleanor expected the tiny child to cry, but though her face screwed into a pout, no tears came, and the pout faded into a grin under the earl's scrutiny. "That's my girl," he declared enthusiastically. "You ain't hurt, are you? And you have rescued Jessie and his—lord, Jess, that's a kit."

"Uh-huh! That's what Mr. Percavill saided too. What's a kit, Uncle Josh?"

The earl touched the feathery fur coat with one long finger and stroked it gently. Two great brown eyes stared up at him from behind a pointed little nose. "A baby fox, Jess."

"I thoughted it wased a kit-ten," cried Joyce, scrambling over to lean on the earl's knee and stare at the creature.

"Foxes is bad," Jessie sighed, attempting to keep the frightened creature from scrambling away. "We can't keep it if it's a fox, Joycie." Discouraged, the little duke went to put the kit back into the sack. The kit scrabbled madly, slipped from Jessie's grasp and rushed into the first dark space it could find— the earl's sling.

Eleanor gasped and reached toward him around Jessie, then noticed the bemused look on Wright's face and giggled. "It is not biting you, I take it?"

"I think I've just been wet upon," drawled the earl. "Yes, definitely. And now I'm being licked. No, don't try to get it out yet, Jess. It's frightened. Give it a chance to settle down."

"But it's on your hurted arm, Uncle Josh."

"It's much too small to make my arm ache. It don't weigh no more than a feather. And it thinks it is safe in a little cave."

"I din't know it was a fox." The look on Jessie's face was so forlorn that Eleanor moved closer, put both arms around him and pulled him onto her lap. Joyce climbed up to take his place beside the earl and peeked hesitantly into the sling.

"We gots to drown it, I 'spect," moaned the little duke, big blue eyes awash with unshed tears.

Eleanor kissed the top of the curly blond head and glanced beseechingly at Wright, who shook his head and grinned. "Foxes are not bad, Jessie," he said softly. "You must not think that."

"But they eats peoples's chickens an' ever'one hates 'em!"

"Well, I do not hate them."

"You doesn't?"

"No. I'm becoming rather fond of foxes, as a matter of fact."

"You are?"

"Uh-huh. And I believe Joycie is as well. Do you like this kit, Joyce?"

"Uh-huh," answered Joycie, carefully inserting her finger into the earl's sling. "What's dwown?"

"Nothing you need to know about at the moment, sweetings. Do you wish to make a pet of this kit, Jess?"

"Y-yes," answered the duke with a quivering lip, "but no one will lets me now it is a fox."

"I will let you."

"You will?"

"Indeed. But you must treat it very kindly and take excellent care of it and not let it anywhere near the hounds."

"I'll keep it upstairs." Jess nodded soberly. "An' me an' Joycie will feed it an' pet it an' ever'thin'."

"Yes, well, I'll see can I talk Bowey and Colly into it." The earl grinned with a glance across the room at an overtly inattentive Mrs. Bowers. "Ow!" he added with a chuckle. "Jessie, come and take this critter. I think it's hungry. No, I shall fish it out of the sling myself, but you must carry it in both hands, and Joycie must take the sack. You will frighten it all over again if you put it back *in* the sack." Wright lifted the tiny ball of reddish brown fluff in one hand and placed it into Jessie's outstretched, anxious ones. "Now hold it close against you, Jess. It is being close against you will make it feel safe."

"Bowey, Bowey," called the duke in a tiny whisper, so as not to scare his new pet, "come'n see what we gots."

"I know what you have, Master Jess," replied Bowey, setting aside her needlework and crossing to where the children stood. "And I shall tell you this—when the thing needs to go outside, it won't be your Uncle Josh as will see to it."

"No, and it won't be you either, Bowey. I promise," the earl grinned boyishly. "I shall consult with Colly and Harry Cross and we will see to its keeping."

"I expect you had better consult with Tibbs first, your lordship," Mrs. Bowers smiled. "Your sling appears to be—damp." Putting a hand on each of the children's shoulders, she shepherded them from the room.

"Very neatly done, my dear," declared Mrs. Dish. "I should very much like to hear how you are going to convince Colly Shepard and Harry Cross to become nursemaids to a fox. It will not die, will it? It is so very tiny."

"And come at the wrong time of year. Extraordinary they should find the thing alive at all, Melinda. Makes one think Jessie must be fated to raise it."

"Balderdash! If his grace did not want it, you would take it and raise it yourself."

"Would you?" Eleanor asked.

Wright nodded. "Well, I could never bring myself to drown the thing, and it would be dreadful cruel to let it starve to death or put it outside to freeze," he added defensively. "Besides, we do not hunt foxes at the Rise, and if it does not come up tame, I shall set it free there. There are a great many scavengers it may feed upon in the home woods without once making contact with anyone's chickens."

"Is the Rise your main residence?" Eleanor queried, thinking how surprised her brother would be to hear that his demon of a man could not even stomach the eradication of one tiny fox.

"Yes. No. It was the main seat while my father lived, but I have closed it up and moved to London."

"Oh. I am so very sorry. I had not thought."

"Not thought what?" asked Wright, puzzled.

"That naturally you would not wish to—to—go on living at that particular place."

"What particular place?"

"Why, the place where your mother died, of course."

"You know about that? I spoke of it when I was half out of my mind, no doubt. It is just the Rise overwhelms me when I must face it alone, Ellie. There is no way to explain it rationally. I went to winter there once after m'father died and I found I couldn't, so I hired Mr. and Mrs. Simon as caretakers, found other places for the tenants and staff and went back to town. Charlie built this suite for me when Jenny told him about how I could not stand the Rise, and he brought most of my favorite things to fill it with. But I could not bring myself to stay here much either. A duke ought not have to contend with his brother-in-law's presence in his own home day after day."

"But I expect his grace had come to like you."

"It's kind of you to think so. I came to like him. But still, a man ought not impose upon someone else's family for his own comfort. I attempt to spend a month or two at the Rise from time to time, but it is always the same. One or two weeks and I am blue-deviled beyond endurance, totally foxed from sunup to sunset, and all my neighbors are begging me to be gone."

Eighteen

Lily placed the last holly branch upon the base of the crèche and turned, smiling, to see if her decoration of the Nativity scene met with Mr. Howard's approval. In the softly tinted sunlight she took on an ethereal hue and an enchanting tenderness Howard had thought never to see until he had died and gone to heaven. He inhaled a quiet gasp at the sight of that lovely, appealing, adoring face.

"Do you like it?" Lily asked worriedly when he said nothing at all about her handiwork. "If you don't, I can arrange it some other way. You must only tell me what is wrong."

"Nothing. It's perfect," murmured Howard. "Miss Lipton, come sit here beside me. There's something I must say to you."

"What?" asked Lily, settling herself upon the pew next to him, her wonderful blue eyes searching his apprehensively, her pretty porcelain cheeks tinted pink with cold and her golden curls sparkling and glinting in the rainbowed sunlight.

"I have—you are—I cannot—" Howard cleared his throat, stared for a moment at the flagstone floor and then looked back into her sweet face and began again. "Miss Lipton, Lily, I must speak with Wright. I dread the thought of it, but I must do so."

Lily stared at him, perplexed.

"I must speak with Wright about—about paying my addresses to you, dearest."

Howard paused at the extraordinary expression on her face. He could not tell whether she were pleased or frightened. He hoped and prayed the expression was one of surprised delight.

"I expect I should not say so much at this moment, Miss—Lily—for I have no idea what nonsense Wright might see fit to put me through, but I can no longer continue to—oh, tarnation, Lily! I am madly in love with you. It must be apparent to all who look upon me. My heart has been hanging upon my sleeve since first I saw you. I want you to be my wife."

Lily's perfect bow lips opened and closed in silence. Her eyes left Howard's and studied the flagstones at her feet. The pink tinge in her cheeks widened and grew darker and even more alluring. For the longest time she made no sound at all, and Howard felt his heart sinking. When at last she looked at him again the pretty blue eyes had filled with tears. She tugged her hands free of his gentle grasp and rose and ran from the little church. Howard, in a sudden panic, sat frozen and watched her leave, and then rushed after her, his boots echoing through the church. As he burst through the doors, she had just run down the final step and turned toward the little cluster of houses at the bottom of the hill. He caught her in five long strides, clutching at her red velvet cloak and swinging her around and into his arms. Lily buried her face in the deep folds of his open greatcoat and sobbed loudly. Totally nonplussed, the Reverend Howard held her in the cold, brittle sunlight until the sobs faded into a series of hiccoughs and then into a deep breath.

"I am such a fool," he whispered into the adorable, shell-like ear that peeked out from beneath the dark fur hat he had knocked askew. "I should not have spoken so soon. I should have waited and asked Wright to prepare you somehow."

"N-nooo!" moaned Lily against his chest.

"No? Do you abhor me, then? Have I no hope to ever win your heart?" Howard thought he would be violently ill right there if she told him it were so. Whatever he had done, whatever it was that had made her run from him, it could—it must—be undone. He could not bear to live another moment without Lily as his wife. "I shall do whatever you wish, Lily. Anything. Only tell me how I may gain your love."

"I do love you," sobbed Lily. "I love you with all my whole h-heart. You are the m-most wonderful m-man I have ever known!"

Howard felt relief flood over him. "I am?" he asked quietly.

"Oh, yes! B-but I cannot m-marry you."

"Do you not want to marry me?"

"Oh, yes! I w-want to marry you ever so much, but I c-cannot, no matter w-what Josh says."

Howard put one long gloved finger beneath her chin and lifted it until she was looking into his eyes. "Why can you not?" he asked softly, choosing to ignore the mention of Wright's name.

"Because I am not who you think I am."

"You are not Miss Lily Lipton?" Howard asked, beginning to smile at what he thought must be some silly womanly nonsense.

"No, I mean, yes, but I am not—not a gentlewoman, and—and—you will not want nothing to do with me anymore!"

"Lily," Howard sighed, his arms fitting themselves more tightly about her, "what sort of nonsense is this? Of course you are a gentlewoman. Have you no dowry? Is that it? But it does not make a bit of difference, my darling. I am hardly a poor country preacher. I have quite enough income to support us comfortably for the rest of our lives. Whatever you may think, my dear, I am not on the lookout for a rich wife."

"No, I know you are not, Mr. Howard, but—" Lily's hand came up to touch Howard's cheek tentatively, and she stared at him as if to memorize each line of his face. "I don't know any other way to tell you than to say it straight out," she said at last, her voice wavering. "My father was a wastrel and an idler, Mr. Howard, and my mother a Covent Garden whore."

Howard paled, but she was no longer looking at him. Her eyes were glazed and her lips trembled and her hands, no bigger than a child's, pushed against him as if to tear herself from his embrace. "And I am a whore, too. At twelve my mama put me upon the streets and I earned my bread there until the night

Josh took me into his carriage and—and—into his bed." She pushed him as hard as she could and gave a quick twist and broke free of his encircling arms. With a rattling gasp she dashed across the frozen ground, down the hill and into the village of St. Swithin's.

The Reverend Martin Howard stared after her, dumbfounded, his arms hanging limply at his sides. He stared numbly for what seemed like hours, until he could no longer see her bright red velvet cloak, until the tipsy little fur hat disappeared from his sight, until the sight and sound and smell of her faded completely away. Then he turned on his heel, stamped viciously back into his church and, seizing a branch of candles, hurled them violently at the pulpit.

Paxton and di Roche strolled companionably through the second floor of Hampton Hall. "A total ruin," Paxton muttered. "Best thing to do is tear it down."

"No, you thinking so?"

"It would cost a fortune to repair it, di Roche."

"But I a fortunes having."

Paxton smiled. "And you are just longing to find a bottom-less pit to dump it into, are you?"

Di Roche shook his head emphatically. "Looking I am for to making happy my Jenny."

"Well, but I haven't the vaguest idea why you think buying Hampton Hall would make Jenny happy, di Roche. Besides, I don't think it's for sale."

"No?"

"No. And we had best depart before someone discovers we have climbed in through that broken window and made our-selves to home. We are trespassing."

"No, looking only. Di Roche to buying wishes. Is perfect place once fixing is being done."

Paxton started down the main staircase. "Perfect for what, di Roche? I have always thought Wright was mad—now I'm beginning to think you are as well. Appear to be more madmen running loose in England than are locked carefully away."

Di Roche chuckled. "Is madman must being to marry the Legion's sister. So said my friend, Charlie, when first his bride he bringing to visit me."

"He may have been correct," Paxton nodded as they reached the first floor and started down to the ground level. "Charlie was always a bit maggoty, but once he decided he must have Lady Jenny for his wife he grew a great deal worse."

"But happier," Di Roche grinned.

"Oh, a good deal happier," agreed Paxton. "But madder."

"A good deal madder," Di Roche laughed. "These place I buying. Someone I thinking will selling to me. I giving very too much money for buying it."

"But what are you going to do with it? You have a villa on the sea at home."

"I not home going no more. Here I staying in this most damp and muddiest of countries. I am becoming step-papa to the most delightful Jessie and husband to my *bella* Jenny and brother-in-law to the incomparable Legion. And I am making for himself this house into the school he is wishing."

"A school?" Paxton halted abruptly on the bottom step and stared at di Roche in wonder. "Legion wants a school? No, you have got something wrong, di Roche."

"My Jenny she telling me."

"Then Jenny has got something wrong. Why the devil would Legion wish to build a school?"

"Ees a living-at school. A place for all the children. Ees fearing to do at Elder's Rise, but here ees good."

Paxton turned toward the parlor and the broken window, his hands thrust into his breeches' pockets, his thoughts churning. "Are you telling me that Josh was hoping to turn Elder's Rise into some sort of school, di Roche?"

"*Si*, but he ees fearing it. Ees bad place for the Legion. These saying my Jenny and he not money enough having to buying and fixing another place. Think he does to selling all his hold-ings not being entailed."

Paxton ducked through the window and out into the sunlight. Di Roche followed. They strolled toward the tethered horses in silence. Mounting, they turned the horses toward the pasture land behind the hall. "We looking at the lands," announced di Roche with authority. "Ees may be help to paying for these school, no? Ees may be farming some of these lands."

Lily ran blindly down the high street, tears chilling in the wind. She had not the least idea where she was bound. All she could think was to get as far from the Reverend Howard as she possibly could. All she wanted was to rush into Josh's arms and cry until there were no more tears left. She veritably flew past the chandler's and the green grocer's and the modiste's, slowing only as she came to the little park that sat directly in the center of the village and was frosted around the edges with snow. Her steps took her to the edge of a partially frozen pond that lay diamondlike in the sunlight and she stared down into it soberly. How long she stood, she had not the least idea. Her charming fur hat had fallen into a gutter during her flight, and her cloak had come undone, and after a long while she began to feel both cold and numb. She looked up from the pond and saw that the sun hung much lower in the sky and that heavy gray clouds were beginning to gather.

"Lost are ye?" whispered a heavy voice behind her. "How bleedin' sad." A hand seized her by the arm and a deep voice droned in her ear. "Don't make a sound, m'dear, or yer dead. It's a knife I've got in yer back an' I ain't afeared ta use it. Now, jus' turn aroun' nice an' walk wi' me real pleasant like."

Lily turned, startled, to see a heavily bearded giant of a ruf-fian glaring down at her. "Who—who are you?" she stam-mered as the hand on her arm urged her forward.

"Ain't none o' yer bidness, missy. Ye jus' do what I say."

The man had evidently slipped the knife into his coat pocket, but he had taken such a tight hold of Lily's arm that she could see no way to escape him. She would surely lose in an all-out struggle. She thought to scream for help, but as if he had read her thoughts, he hissed that one scream and she would be dead upon the ground before its echo died. With a string of dire threats he urged her beyond the park and into a stand of pines where a closed coach waited. Roughly he jerked open the carriage door, thrust her inside and slammed it closed after her. Lily banged roughly against the squabs and bounced from them onto her knees on the floor. She heard a rush of wind and jerked up quickly, but not quickly enough. A cudgel came swiftly down upon her golden curls, and in an instant she lay unmoving upon the floor of the coach.

"Yep, that's one of 'em, by gawd," muttered the Sneezing Fiend angrily. "Jerry, spring 'em, lad!" he shouted through the trap. "We daren't linger! We'll be catched sure as Hades!" The heavily bearded giant grunted and sent the four perfectly matched horses forward at a spanking pace—down the road, around the bend and racing toward the Guilder's Heath like lightning.

The sun had all but set by the time Howard, his cravat untied, his hat missing, his greatcoat flying in the breeze, reined in his blowing and exhausted horses at the front entrance of Willowset and jumped to the ground. He stormed into the hall past Burton without so much as a by-your-leave, bounded up the staircase and ran down the long corridor, where he took the stairs at a resounding pace down again to the ground floor and made his way with glaring rapidity to Wright's suite. He stalked through the music room with such haste that he saw neither his sister, Mrs. Dish, nor the Earl of Wright, all of whom stared after him astonished. He stormed through the small dining room, the sitting room and into the earl's bedchamber, where he let out a roar of epithets that reddened Eleanor's ears and made Mrs. Dish cringe. Spinning on his heel, he stalked back over the path he had just traced until he came eye to eye with Wright upon the divan near the fire, Eleanor beside him.

Howard swept his greatcoat from his shoulders and tossed it savagely toward a small cane chair, which it knocked over. Mrs. Dish, with a little squeak, rose and went to rescue it and was told to let the dashed thing be and get out.

"Martin!" Eleanor cried. "What is wrong with you? How dare you speak so to Mrs. Dish."

"You, too, Ellie! Leave us at once! I have words that are fit for Wright's ears alone. You bloody bastard!" he added, roaring again. "You filthy, unprincipled swine!"

"Martin!" Eleanor stood, her eyes flashing. "Stop! Have you lost your mind?"

"Get out!" yelled Howard, reaching down to snag Wright by the lapels of his coat and pulling him upward.

"Martin, no! Put him down! Put him down!" screamed Eleanor. "You will hurt him!"

Wright, who was having the devil of a time not to shriek in pain, kicked away the footstool that was twisting his leg around and in the process sent a shock wave through his entire left side which made him gasp and turn incredibly white. The gasp alone sent Eleanor scurrying for help. James, the first footman, just entering with the tea service on a large oval tray of beaten silver took a quick step to avoid Eleanor in the doorway and sent the china to rattling and himself to stumbling awkwardly. Eleanor's eyes blazed. She seized the tray from James's hands, sending teapot, cups, saucers, plates, scones and all soaring into the air around them. Then she swung around, raced to where Howard stood shaking the earl like a terrier with a rat and brought the tray slamming down upon the back of her brother's head. Stunned, Howard loosed his grip on Wright and crumbled to his knees. Mrs. Dish rushed forward and tugged the tray from Eleanor's hands while James ran for the bellpull, gave it two quick jerks and hurried back to the two men. The earl turned sideways on the divan, holding his ribs, drawing his knees up onto the seat as far as he was able. James recovered the footstool and attempted to get Wright to turn back around and rest his broken ankle back upon it. Useless. Wright had no intention of straightening out at that moment. He took a stertorous series of breaths, shook his head and mumbled, "Look to Howard, James."

Eleanor was beside Wright in an instant, brushing the dark curls from his eyes with one hand and rapidly unbuttoning his coat and waistcoat with the other. "Be still, darling," she murmured, as the waistcoat came undone and she began to untie his cravat. "Breathe evenly, Jocelyn." His neckcloth went flying over the back of the divan and both of her hands went to the task of unlacing his breeches.

Wright, groaning and laughing at once, muttered, "Ellie, I wish you wouldn't undress me in front of your brother. He's already powerful fratched at me about something. He sees one more lace undone and I'm a deadman."

Howard, stunned, found himself assisted into a chair by James and Mrs. Dish, the latter sending the second footman, who had answered the bell, off to the kitchen for something cold to place against the back of Mr. Howard's skull, upon which a bump was definitely rising. The second footman hurried out just as Tibbs raced in. "What on earth?" asked that imperturbable individual. Ignoring the spilt tea, the smashed scones and the pieces of china that littered the room, he went straight to the earl and stared gloweringly down upon him. "One would think we lived in some squalid hut on Petticoat Lane," Tibbs declared in stentorian tones. "Such behavior as must produce this result—its occurrence here is totally unacceptable."

Howard, his eyes just beginning to uncross, moved to stare up at the valet, but even that slight adjustment sent a wave of nausea through him, and he lowered his eyes quickly. The earl groaned as Eleanor touched his bandaged ribs. The groan brought Tibbs to his knees before the divan. "Miss Howard, if you will pardon us, I shall see to his lordship," he declared. "James, fetch someone to help carry my lord back to his bed.

How you could cause such chaos when you cannot even stand by yourself is beyond understanding, Master Josh," he added more softly. "You are the devil's own child, and that's a fact."

"I d-didn't do it," gasped Wright, amid pain and laughter. "Ellie hit Howard in the head with the t-tea tray."

"Miss Eleanor never did," declared Tibbs. "Don't you be laying blame upon that sweet young lady. 'Twas your own doing, I'll be bound. Though how you managed it, as strapped up as you are, and the vicar yet! You ought to be ashamed, Master Josh!"

Eleanor protested Wright's innocence and asserted that the fracas had all been her brother's fault and that he had deserved a tea tray upon his head and a good deal more besides for what he had done to Lord Wright. Tibbs, his fine gray eyes disbelieving, attempted to ease the earl's knees down and turn him around to face forward. "And don't be pushing me away, Master Josh. You are not such a weakling as to let a bit of pain frighten you."

"A bit of pain?" cried Eleanor. "He has been jerked up and shaken about and thrown down again like a piece of old muslin, and it is a wonder if he did not break his ribs and arm and ankle all over again—especially since his heel was caught upon the footstool and he had to kick it away or have his leg twisted completely around beneath him!"

"I shall twist his leg around his throat as soon as I can stand," mumbled Howard almost coherently.

"Shhh," said Mrs. Dish, taking the chunk of ice wrapped in a napkin that the second footman handed her and applying it to the back of the reverend's head.

"Ow!" Howard gasped. "Ellie, leave that fiend at once. Ow!" he said again as Mrs. Dish applied the ice more firmly.

"It's you are the fiend, Martin," Eleanor declared, putting her arm about the earl's shoulders and helping Tibbs to ease Wright into a straighter position. "Let Tibbs help you to straighten your knees, Josh. We cannot tell how badly you are injured if you will not let us look at you, my darling."

Tibbs fought not to look up in amazement as the "my darling" slipped from Miss Howard's lips, but he did conceive of a hopeful belief in miracles as he removed the studs from his lordship's shirt. Wright suppressed a series of groans as Tibbs's experienced fingers probed his ribs. "I expect you'll live, Master Josh," announced Tibbs, who went on to remove the earl's slipper and the stocking they had contrived to get him into earlier in the day. Both of the small splints that had held the ankle immobile had snapped in half and Tibbs unwound the bandages hurriedly. Eleanor gasped at the rapidly swelling injury. She held Wright more firmly against her, murmuring endearments and bestowing motherly kisses upon the soft curly head that rested beneath her chin. Tibbs pushed up the leg of Wright's breeches to discover, as he thought, that his lordship had also twisted his knee in the attempt to disentangle himself from the footstool. The knee was beginning to enlarge as well.

"Just chip off a piece of Howard's ice an' throw it on, Tibbs," mumbled the earl, not struggling in the least to remove himself from Miss Howard's embrace—which he would have done, thought Tibbs optimistically, had it been Mary or Jenny or even Lily, for Master Josh could never stand any lady to think him in need of coddling.

"No, he will not," answered Eleanor before Tibbs could reply. "We shall send for Dr. MacGregor immediately and it shall be attended to properly."

"I'll attend to him," growled Howard, making a move to stand but sitting back down hastily.

Wright wriggled carefully out of Eleanor's grasp, forbade Tibbs so much as to touch his arm, and stared puzzledly across the room at the reverend. Harry Cross and Glenby Oakes came tramping in at that moment, followed by the first footman and a number of maids. "Back to 'is bedchamber, eh?" asked Oakes.

"Yes," Tibbs nodded.

"No!" countermanded the earl. "Howard, what's got into you? You're being definitely less than perfect."

"Oh, don't bother about Martin, Jocelyn," Eleanor sighed. "You must get him safely to bed and someone must ride to fetch Dr. MacGregor," she added with a look of supplication at the large coachman and the earl's head groom.

Tibbs nodded at the men and took himself off to the earl's bedchamber to turn down the counterpane and then hurried out to fetch fresh water and clean bandages.

"Get your hands off," growled the earl as Oakes touched his shoulder. "Howard, are you deaf? What's got into you?"

"Send your bodyguards away an' I'll discuss it with you," hissed Howard. "Eleanor, I said to come away from him! Now!"

"Be quiet, Martin, or I shall hit you over the head again," replied Eleanor with a stubborn tilt to her chin.

"*You* hit me?" Howard asked, astonished. "You, Eleanor?"

"Indeed."

"Mrs. Dish," sighed the earl, "might I persuade you to clear this chamber of footmen, maids, Oakes and Harry Cross? Obviously things need discussing that had best be dealt with in private."

"Absolutely not," responded Mrs. Dish, with a hint of fire in her eyes. "If you think for one moment that I am going to allow you to face Mr. Howard alone—why, Mr. Tibbs would have a seizure at the mere thought of it."

"Mr. Tibbs? What has Tibbs to do with it? I shall handle Tibbs, Melinda; just please be off somewhere and take all these people with you."

"I am not going," Eleanor stated with a toss of her head. "You may send everyone else away, but I shall not budge."

"There, Melinda. I'll have a bodyguard. Howard will not dare attack again."

Mrs. Dish, bestowing a most oppressive glare upon the reverend, rose and shooed everyone, including Harry Cross and Glenby Oakes, out into the hall, closing the door behind her.

"Now," sighed Wright, resting his head against the back of

the divan and trying like the devil not to breathe too deeply or to jiggle any part of his body, "out with it, Howard."

"I cannot possibly tell you, you infidel, in front of my sister."

"Is it about Lily, then?"

Howard nodded.

"I know all about Lily, so you needn't worry my innocence shall be soiled." Eleanor lifted her chin defiantly, not even noting the amazement upon Wright's face as well as Howard's.

"You—you, know that Miss Lipton is his—his—" Howard's voice trembled. He sounded on the verge of tears.

"Ellie, go speak to him. Bring him here to sit with us," urged Wright in a whisper. "Get him to move his chair closer at least. He has had a terrible shock and needs you to help him."

Eleanor did exactly as Wright asked, convincing Howard softly that not only was she sorry she had hit him, but she was just as sorry that she knew what Lily was. She brought him to sit opposite Wright, who had waited silently with eyes closed. When the eyes opened there was a dullness in them that made Eleanor fear the earl even more injured than she and Tibbs suspected. But his voice was strong and he spoke without hesitation. "Lily told you the truth of the matter then, Howard. Why?"

"Not your business."

"It is my business. Did you propose to the chit?"

"Yes."

"And she said what?"

"That she is your mistress."

"Well, she ain't, not anymore, not since she came here and met you, Howard. She told you about her father? About her mother? About her circumstances before we met? She told you that she loved you with all her heart?"

"Yes."

"And you said what?"

"Nothing. I—I had no words. She ran away from me before I could think of anything at all to say."

"Well, but then you ran after her."

"N-no."

"Damnation, Howard, why not? The girl loved you so much that she told you the truth! Don't you know what such a confession cost her? Ain't you got any kind of a heart at all?" shouted the earl and then winced at the pain that shot through him. Eleanor, who was sitting on the arm of her brother's chair, made a move to go to Wright, but he shook his head. "When you finally went and fetched the chit and drove her back did you say nothing to her even then?"

Howard faced Wright's indignant frown. "When I—did she not return without me?"

"Without you? How should she return without you? You drove her to the place—who was there to drive her back?"

"I thought—I thought Kinsley or one of the men from the village. There was not a sign of her anywhere in St. Swithin's. I assumed she had caught a ride from someone."

"Ellie," Wright said urgently, "pull the cord. Get someone to discover whether Lily has returned. Damn you, Howard, if she is not here and safe, I'll have your lights an' your gizzard. I swear it. How can you have lived so long and not know what despair Lily suffered to see the look upon your face and to hear not a word from your lips when she loved you enough to tell the truth?"

Nineteen

Lily woke to a great aching in her head and a ringing in her ears. She was unsure at first what had happened, and then she remembered the fierce bearded man in the park and the waiting coach. Tentatively she raised her head to look about. Alarmed at first because she could see nothing, her aching eyes soon became accustomed to the darkness, and she discovered that she lay upon a cot in a tiny, shuttered room. One of the shutter boards apparently had been broken, for a dim sliver of moonlight filtered in to give her the merest bit of illumination. The damp, cold chamber contained only the cot upon which she lay, an old, chipped chamber pot, a ladder-backed chair with one broken leg and a broom. Lily groaned and lay her head back down. She closed her eyes and listened. A drone of voices reached her from somewhere below, and though she could tell they were male voices, she could not distinguish one from another and so was incapable of forming any concept of how many ruffians there might be. Two, at least—the bearded man and the Sneezing Fiend, whom she'd glimpsed only a second before she'd lost consciousness. But the Sneezing Fiend had been captured and taken to gaol in Dorset. Perhaps she had merely imagined it to be him.

An odd scent reached her nose then and she puzzled over it for a great while. If only her head would cease aching, she would be able to place that aroma. It was extremely familiar. Her thoughts began to wander, and Martin Howard's face came unbidden to her mind. He was smiling down upon her, explaining how he had come to be vicar at St. Swithin's, and the beguiled gleam in his eye was giving her hope—hope that Josh was right and that such a fine gentleman might love her enough to marry her. But then the scene outside the church slammed into her consciousness and tears started to her eyes. "Oh, Martin," she sobbed, "I should have known. I should have anticipated the horror I would see upon your countenance. I should never, never have told you the truth." But she knew she could never have deceived him. Too much of what Josh had unwittingly taught her—along with proper comportment and proper speech—depended upon truth and the courage to speak it. And now she would need a different courage. Sooner or later one or more of those villains would come to check upon her, and she must find pluck enough to face them down until someone came to her rescue. With a deep sigh and a small fidgeting, Lily at last fell asleep and the aching in her head lessened considerably.

Willowset was in turmoil. Howard, finding Lily had not returned, had set off in near panic for St. Swithin's. Paxton and di Roche, returning from their ride, rode off again at a spanking pace in Howard's wake. Jenny sent word to the kitchen to hold back dinner for two hours at the very least, which set Aberdeen on edge and the staff to buzzing. And shortly thereafter the first and second footmen informed everyone belowstairs of what had gone forward in the earl's music room and of Miss Lipton's possible peril. "She loved 'im, ye know," murmured James passionately. "A girl like that—as much hardship as she's had her whole life—wouldn't s'prise a person did she leap into the pond and drown herself."

Lettie, the littlest tweeny, fainted dead away at his words. Mrs. Bowers dropped the nursery plates. Broccoli, potatoes, lamb and shards of china skidded across the flagstone floor. Burton stalked into the kitchen to see why no bells were being answered, did not see the mess and skidded straight into Mrs. Hornby.

In Wright's suite things were no better. The earl was in high dudgeon. Each time someone thought they had silenced him, he turned out to be merely attempting to breathe more regularly and broke out again into angry invectives. Jenny pleaded with him to control himself; Mary demanded that he cease and desist his nonsense and allow himself to be tended to; Tibbs scowled down his nose and announced in stentorian tones that unless his lordship recovered his senses within the next two minutes, he was going to be dosed with every bit of laudanum left in the house; and Oakes and Harry Cross growled ferociously that the earl might act the mad king all he wished but in the end he would find himself in bed and strapped down the same as his bleedin' majesty at Windsor. It was Mrs. Dish who finally whispered in Eleanor's ear and gave her an encouraging pat on the shoulder.

"Do you think?" asked Eleanor.

"Indeed. I shall collect the others and then there will be no one for him to rail at except yourself—and I do not think he will choose to shout you down, my dear."

Mrs. Dish emptied the room of everyone simply by moving from person to person and whispering a brief word to each of them. When they had all disappeared Wright stuttered to a halt. He took an immensely deep breath, gasped at the pain it caused him and then glanced at Eleanor, who came and sat demurely beside him again. She took his hand in hers and stared into the fire.

"Are you not leaving as well, Miss Howard?"

"Is that your desire, my lord?"

He did not answer. Eleanor glanced out of the corner of her eye and saw that he was staring morosely at the hearth. She allowed him to do so for a full five minutes, gazing with like intensity at the leaping blaze. "I am certain they will find Lily safe," she said at last. "Lily is strong and brave and will not do anything foolish."

"I've made a complete muddle of it," Wright sighed. "I ought to have told Lilliputian straight out that Howard would not have her once he knew the truth. I was stupid to hope."

"Hoping is never stupid, my lord."

"Yes it is. People've been attemptin' to teach me that lesson since I was in leading strings, and still I can't seem to learn it. And now because I am such a dullard, I've hurt Lily somethin' terrible. But I thought—I thought—"

Eleanor waited for him to finish but he did not, only made an odd gulping sound in his throat.

"What did you think, my lord?"

"I don't know—that if Howard truly loved her, he would not care that—he would not quibble over—I cannot believe how stupid I am!"

"You are not stupid! Do not keep saying that. You're sweet and kind and good."

"No, I ain't. Everyone will tell you I ain't, too, even those as have known me all my life. Whenever I attempt to be good it don't work. I reckon I ain't made for it. I cannot even be around good people without breaking into a cold sweat."

Eleanor turned her gaze from the fire, put a finger under his chin and turned him to look at her. "This sounds highly suspicious, my lord. You break into a cold sweat when you are around good people? Are you sweating now?"

"No."

"Does that mean I am not a good person?"

"Well, of course you are. I ain't speaking of you."

"No? Explain then. I wish to hear."

"I'm wallowing in self-pity, ain't I, Ellie?"

"I cannot truly say, my lord," Eleanor grinned. "I have not heard enough to be certain. Do you break into a cold sweat in Mrs. Dish's presence? Or Mary's? Or Mr. Paxton's? They are considered good people, I believe. I know you don't do so in Martin's presence. What you break into in his presence is not near a cold sweat."

"It's because Howard is such a paragon, Ellie, that I'm always so fratched with 'im."

"Oh, what a clanker!"

"No, it's not. Your brother has got practically everything, Ellie, an' he ain't never had to suffer for any of it. And 'cause he ain't, he don't understand about people like Lily and—and me. He ain't got the least idea what it's like to have a father whip a man to death or—"

"Your father did that?"

"Well, yes, and more, though that's the thing they bring up whenever they wish to put me in my place."

"They who?"

"All of them as want to make me out a barbarian—Harrow and Chesterfield and Alvanley and Esterhazy and half of the House of Lords. And Howard don't once think what it's like to have Jenny for a sister, either. Oh, she's pluck to the backbone and as brave as she can stare, and will stand by a person no matter what, but she ain't bright, like you, Ellie, and she's wrapped about in romantical notions, and there's no denying her upper story's to let most of the time."

Eleanor, never having heard that particular expression before, giggled, and the flecks in Wright's midnight eyes burst into glistening silver.

"Yes, well, but it's true, Ellie. And all Howard needs to do is to call her a featherbrain and get on with his life—but I cannot, you know. I need to look after her no matter what. And besides, Howard is perfect and—and knows all the rules, and keeps them, too—which I don't and can't, Ellie, no matter how much I intend to do so. That is why Lily ran away."

"Why is why? I'm getting confused, my dear," Eleanor smiled, brushing his unruly locks back from his brow.

"Lily is hurt because *I* did not follow the rules."

"What rules did you not follow?"

"You know perfectly well," Wright sighed. "I ought not to've let Lily think it all right for her to come here and to comport herself as—a respectable young lady. I didn't have any right to teach her to be one in the first place. It's just that—that—"

"That you are as romantic as Jenny and wished with all your heart to save Lily from the squalor into which she was born, and give her happiness and love and self-respect. Do not look at me with your eyes so wide and disbelieving, Jocelyn. I have not lived in this house for so many weeks and not spoken with Lily and Jenny and Mary. I know more about you than you think I know."

"You do?"

"Indeed, sir, and I think you are more saint than demon."

"You do? But Ellie, that ain't so. Even Tibbs will tell you there ain't no saint in me at all."

Eleanor could not resist the completely bewildered look that confronted her and placed a whisper of a kiss upon the earl's cheek. "Tibbs thinks you are the finest, most noble gentleman in all of England and has told Mrs. Dish so. And Mrs. Dish agrees wholeheartedly."

"Ellie, you kissed me."

"I certainly did. I could not resist, you know, because you looked for a moment like a sweet, confused little boy. Are you calmer now, do you think?"

"Calmer?"

"Uh-huh. Will you let me call Tibbs and Oakes and Harry Cross so that they may put you to bed and tend to you properly?"

Wright grinned for the first time since he'd heard of Lily's flight. "Yes, if you'll come an' have your dinner with me. Will you, Ellie? Howard ain't here to say how improper it is, and I—no, you shan't break the rules on my account. I can't believe I haven't yet learned that lesson either."

"I shall come to visit you after dinner to see how you go on. Martin is sending Dr. MacGregor, you know, and you must allow him to see if you've been further harmed. Mary and Jenny and I shall all come once the doctor has gone, and then we shall all be in the brambles for sashaying about an unmarried gentleman's bedchamber, and we shall share in whatever peals are rung. But you must not fight with Tibbs anymore, or Oakes or Harry Cross, either. They only wish to help you, Jocelyn, and you must let them do so. That is part of your duty as a gentleman."

"It is?"

"Indeed." With a smile, Eleanor freed his hand, gave him a very sisterly kiss upon the brow and left the room to discover that the rest of the party waited in expectant silence on the stairs at the end of the hall. She sent the men to Wright, put one arm through Jenny's and the other through Mary's, gave Mrs. Dish a broad wink and led them up the stairs and back to the main part of the house.

Less than an hour later Howard, Paxton and di Roche returned without Lily, but accompanied by Constable Perkins and Dr. MacGregor. Mr. Quinn, the village haberdasher, had seen a young miss with bright yellow curls running full tilt down the high street, and Mrs. Abigail Land had found a most becoming fur hat lying inexplicably in the gutter, and the young lad who ran errands for Mr. Coggins had seen a beautiful lady standing in the middle of Hawk's park staring down into the pond. But no one had seen Lily after that, nor could Howard, Paxton or di Roche locate her even though they'd knocked upon every door in St. Swithin's. "She's dead," moaned Howard, gripping the adorable fur hat in both hands as if it, too, might run from him. "She has gone and drowned herself and it is all my fault. I am a worse villain than any man ever lived."

Eleanor sat on the arm of her brother's chair and put a consoling arm around his shoulders. "Nonsense, Martin; Lily would never think to drown herself. She is not such a coward."

"But Howard villain being," Di Roche, who had taken a seat beside Jenny on the small divan, nodded. "I am hearing all and I am thinking he ees rigidly posteriored beyond believing."

"He's what?" asked Constable Perkins, bewildered.

"Stiff-rumped beyond belief," interpreted Paxton with a self-satisfied nod. "I am better and better at understanding di Roche becoming."

Mary smiled at him and he took her hand. "Do not despair, my dearest girl," he assured her. "We haven't given up the pursuit. We'll find our Lily wherever she's gone. But we ran abreast of Constable Perkins, and there is news must be dealt with here at Willowset before we continue our search."

Thus invited to take the floor, Constable Perkins lurched uneasily into the sordid tale that had reached him from Dorset. "Three Bow Street Runners came up from London," he sighed, "with writs to take Hobbins and Hampton back to the city with 'em. Had a hired chaise an' four—everything. Took possession of the pris'ners and started back. Never made it. Found on the Great North Road—the coach in a ditch, the horses missin' and all three of them Runners stone cold dead. Shot they was. Highwaymen most likely. Not a sign, though, o' Hobbins an' Hampton. Gone."

"Oh!" Jenny squeaked, with a glance at Mary's pale face. "Oh, you don't suppose they intend to come back here?"

"Can't be sure, my lady," replied the constable. "I'll set a watch upon Hampton Hall, but since 'twas the earl they attempted to murder, I thought first to come an' warn his lordship."

Arthur Hampton huddled upon a three-legged stool in the bit of an office at the very rear of the abandoned factory. A lump of coal dwindled upon the grate. With a grunt, the Sneezing Fiend filled the coal scuttle and passed it to his cousin, Jerry. "Lay some o' that on, Jer, me lad. Freezin' we'll be erstwise. I wonder do the little piece o' muslin be warm enuf upstairs."

"Ye got ye a hankerin' fer that sweetpiece, Dicky? Purty bit she be."

"Aye, a eight-course dinner fer a man's eyes."

"And that is all," grumbled Hampton. "One of you lays a

hand upon her before we have heard from Wright and you shall be dead on the instant."

"What makes ye thin' we be goin' ta hear from 'is bleedin' lor'ship?" Jerry Worchester chuckled. "Come as 'ow he mi' be ri' tired o' tha' petticoat by this time an' more'n willin' ta be shed o' 'er."

Hampton shook his head. "He ain't one to offer up any chit in place of himself. We were extraordinarily lucky to come upon the girl like that—especially since we could not get old Euphegenia. Likely as not he's got the old bat at Willowset with him. But it don't matter now. That gel will do the trick for us. You're certain, Worchester, your brother knows what to do?"

"Aye, m'lor', Nate'll git the message through, 'e will. Straight inta the earl's own 'ands jis like ye tole 'im."

Hampton sighed and stood up, one hand rubbing at his aching back. "Going to check on our bait, gentlemen. Perhaps she has recovered enough by now to wish a bite to eat. Do you think? I shall take her something. A bit of bread and butter perhaps." Hampton bent to paw through a large wicker basket and stood triumphantly with a half loaf of bread and a crock of butter in his hands. He snatched a knife from the high writing desk where he had left it earlier and made his way up the narrow, rickety stairs at the back of the office.

Lily woke to a knocking sound in the chill darkness and tried to remember where she was and what had happened. The knocking persisted and she followed the sound to a door set in the wall across from her cot. "What?" she called hesitantly. "What is it you want?"

"I want you to open the bloody door, my sweet," called Hampton grouchily. "My hands are full."

"How?"

"Lift the latch, my dear. Don't require a deal of brains."

Lily felt around in the darkness until her hand met the latch. She opened the door slowly, afraid to meet the gentleman on the other side.

"Lord, ain't you got enough wits to light a candle?" grumbled Hampton, pushing past her into the room.

"I didn't know I had a candle," replied Lily, astonished to see the man dump something upon her cot and then move toward the window with the broken shutter.

"Well, you do. Whole branch of candles around here somewhere. No, wait—you're correct. They are in the hall." Hampton stalked back out through the open door, clattered about in the hallway for a moment and then reentered with a branch of candles lighting his way. "Close the door again; you're letting in the cold. Just a moment and I'll have a bit of a fire upon the grate. I've brought you a bite to eat. On the cot."

Lily stared disbelievingly at Hampton as he fiddled with the few lumps of coal on the grate. Then she stared at the bread and butter and especially the knife on the cot. Then she stared at the open door.

"Do not even think it, my pretty," hissed Hampton, without turning to look at her. "Not only would you quite probably break your lovely neck rushing down those practically unusable stairs, but if you did somehow get to the bottom alive, there are two ruffians immediately below who would like nothing more than to have their way with you. The door don't have a lock, but were I you, I should find myself something to put against it from the inside to keep the scum out."

"You—you're Arthur Hampton."

"And you're one of Legion's whores. Came bursting through the window at Hampton Hall. What's your name, gel?"

"Miss Lipton," replied Lily with a toss of her head that brought her recent encounter with a cudgel directly to mind. She gave a little gasp at the pain and abrupt dizziness, and made her way carefully to the cot.

"Yes, sit down, Miss Lipton, and have some bread and butter. I should apologize for such plain fare, but when one is forced into hiding, one has so little choice and must take what is given. The blade is dull, my dear. It will do you not the least bit of good to think of using it against me." Hampton pulled the old ladder-backed chair up close to the cot, straddled it and balanced it precariously on two legs. "Tell me, how does the earl go on? He has grown healthy again in my absence, no?"

Lily broke off a piece of the bread and smeared it thickly with butter, all the while taking stock of the man who faced her. In the flickering light of the candles, he seemed a devil. Unshaven, filthy, deep lines of dissipation shadowing the crevices of his face, his teeth showed long and yellowing as he grinned lasciviously at her. His hands were ungloved and as he watched her, his fingers flexed, then formed a fist, then flexed again, then formed a fist. His eyes raked her from head to toe, and he made her think of the men who had come to her in the alleys about Covent Garden, always hungry, always impatient, always foul in mind and body. She shivered and he guffawed.

"Oh, you're safe enough for now, vixen. No one will touch you as yet—not until we're sure of Wright. Once that interfering blackguard has met his death, however, you and all the rest of his harem shall discover what 'tis to belong to a real man. Don't feel alone, sweetpiece. That harridan Mary and her cronies will be joining you soon. Yes, even the devil's sister. She's just as saucy as the rest of you, but she'll come down off 'er high horse just as swiftly as will you and Mary and that other plain brown mouse came bolting at us out of nowhere."

"You shall be very sorry you ever thought to come back to England, Mr. Hampton," responded Lily smartly, chewing a bit of the bread. "Josh will hack off both your ears and give them to you to eat. See if he don't."

Hampton roared into laughter.

"Yes, you had best laugh now, because it will be no laughing matter at all when Josh discovers I've been abducted, I assure you." The room, her weariness and Hampton's very demeanor all combined to crush Lily with memories of her life before the earl. This man, like her father and so many others, would take her in a drunken rage, pummeling her, cursing her, beating her until she wished only to die and be set free. But the thought of Josh kept the old thieves' cant from her lips, kept her sitting straight and elegant upon the old cot and kept the trembling from her voice. She was no longer a cheap bit of muslin who belonged nowhere and deserved nothing. Josh had told her so and she knew it was true. She would never—never!—let this base, contemptible excuse for a human being drag her back down into the degradation from which she had fought so hard to rise.

Absolutely no one wished to inform Wright of Hampton's escape, and once Dr. MacGregor left they visited him, determined to ease his mind about Lily and equally determined to say nothing about the guard that had been set once again about Willowset. Burton himself saw to it that the drapes were tightly drawn across the casement windows of the earl's bedchamber so that the flaring torches the grooms carried toward the home woods and the flickering lanterns that accompanied the footmen as they trudged in set patterns around the grounds would not be noticed. Mary and Paxton and Mrs. Dish informed Wright that the search for Lily would begin again at daylight and that they thought she had most likely taken shelter at the Gander's Neck. "For I doubt she would think to stay at the Crossroads, my dear," added Mrs. Dish thoughtfully. "She does not wish to see or speak to Mr. Howard as yet and will not want him to find her. The gentlemen did not speak to Mr. Powell, you know, who is forever driving his gig back and forth between the two inns. He will have picked the child up and taken her with him."

"We'll check the Gander's Neck first thing in the morning, Josh," added Paxton, who had changed out of all his dirt for dinner and paced the small bedchamber looking as neat and proper as he usually did. "And if she ain't there—but I think she will be—we will extend our search to the outlying farms."

Mary smiled expressly for the benefit of the gentleman in the bed. "She will be home before any of you are awake. Lily is not a child and she will come roaring back to face the Reverend Howard just as soon as she has given herself a good talking to. She knows she is just as good a person as he, and she will tell him so in no uncertain terms!"

"She's a better person than he," Wright sighed, fidgeting. "She's overcome seventeen years of squalor, misery and shame, and he ain't overcome nothing."

"Not even his tendency toward pomposity," Paxton grinned.

Jenny, when she entered on di Roche's arm, brought him a cup of hot chocolate and told him all about the rumpus the kit was causing in the nursery as he sipped at it. "And Jessie has determined to sleep with it, too!" she added, knowing that her brother would have demanded the same when he'd been small and that the thought of it would make him grin. Di Roche watched the play of eyes and smiles between them and knew beyond doubt that Jenny had told him no lie. There would be no whisking away of the duchess to foreign shores. The sister would never abandon the brother nor the other way 'round. They were a matched pair and neither could survive if separated.

A repentant Howard was led into the chamber by a determined Eleanor, who glared at him until he stammered out a disjointed but sincere apology for setting Wright back a number of weeks in his recovery. "And you, sir, must apologize as well," she told Wright with a cocked eyebrow.

"I ain't sorry," mumbled the earl. "I didn't tell 'im to chase after the chit."

Eleanor nodded, but told him he must apologize nevertheless and that he must explain to her brother all he could about Lily's background and about why he had hoped Howard would overlook it and marry the girl. That bit of explanation, stumbled over in a haze of distraction as Eleanor sat beside him and held his hand, took the earl nearly an hour, at the end of which his eyes were fighting to close. "Damned Aberdeen put somethin' in the chocolate," he muttered. "Can't trust nobody."

Twenty

Nate Worchester was no more a fool than the next man, nor was he blind. He had recognized the guard set around Willowset and had taken shelter at the Crossroads until morning because of it. No use getting shot just to deliver the flash cove's note. Wait until morning, ride directly up to the front door and brazen it out with the butler. In his worn greatcoat, his refurbished beaver and his down-at-the-heel boots, he knew well enough he ought to go around to the rear entrance, but that wouldn't get the thing done. Message had to go directly into the earl's hands. Them was the directions the guv'nor had given. Deliver it personal. Worchester shuffled his feet on the top step. Burton eyed the man as he opened the door. The ruffian reeked of cunning and guile and old tallow, and the very smell of him caused Burton's nostrils to quiver and his hackles to rise. "Yes?" he asked with a disconcerting scowl.

"I got a message fer the Earl o' Wright."

"I shall be most happy to deliver it for you," scowled Burton, holding out his hand.

"Naw, guv, ye don't unnerstan'. It's got ta go direc'ly from me ta him. Tha's me orders."

"I see. Oblige me by waiting here," grumbled Burton, closing the door and leaving the odd-smelling personage upon the doorstep. With measured tread the elderly butler made his way toward the breakfast room. His entrance brought three eager men in riding dress to quick attention.

"Is it Lily?" asked Howard. "Has she returned?"

"Someone with word of her?" Paxton asked.

The Marquis di Roche only took another bite of an apple tart and waited to hear what Burton had to say.

" 'Tis a personage with a message for his lordship," announced Burton in tones betraying disgust. "Declares he must meet with him in person."

"You didn't take him to Wright?" Howard sputtered.

"Certainly not, sir. I have left him on the doorstep, where he even now adds unwanted flavor to this establishment."

"Anyone you recognize, Burton?" Paxton asked, wiping his mouth on a fine linen napkin. "Might he recognize Wright?"

"I think not, sir."

"Escort him into the front parlor, Burton," ordered Howard, standing. "I shall speak with the man. Does he be anyone from St. Swithin's, I'll be certain to recognize him."

"And if he ain't from St. Swithin's, you will assume Wright's character and accept the message in his place, will you, Howard?" Paxton stood as well, shoving his hands into the pockets of his riding breeches.

"Yes. And if he is from hereabouts and recognizes me, then you must be ready to step forward in Wright's shoes, Paxton."

As it turned out the only thing Nate Worchester knew about the Earl of Wright was that he ought to be tall, muscular and have dark hair. The Reverend Howard filled the bill well enough. Worchester passed the crumpled note into his hands, confident he had the correct person. "The guv'nor wants a answer, 'e does," grumbled Worchester, Howard's stature and pompous manner making him extremely uncomfortable but confirming in his mind that this indeed must be an earl.

"Yes, well, your guv'nor can wait a bit." Howard stared down at the spidery lines, attempting to digest the meaning of the missive. His heart pounded so violently within his chest, he thought it would etch a tattoo against his waistcoat. "Can you read?" he scowled down at the man. "What's this word here. I cannot make it out."

Nate Worchester shook his head. "Don't take wi' no readin' an' writin'."

"Well, where is this place he wishes to meet me? That is the word I cannot make out."

" 'Tis the cemet'ry what lies along nex' ta Fennel's Marsh. West o' here it be. I ben't knowin' the name o' it. I ain't come from aroun' here."

"No, well, I expect I shall find it. There is some sort of building there? A church of some kind?"

"No, guv, ain't no church what I knows of. Jus' wants ta meet ye in the cemet'ry, I thinks."

Howard's mind whirled. The note came from Hampton. It said only that he had taken Lily hostage and wished a meeting with Wright. It said nothing about getting Lily back.

At the end of the hall very near the servants' doorway, Paxton and Burton waited in grim silence, eyes focused on the archway into the front parlor. In the breakfast room di Roche wiped his fingers daintily, looked up and smiled at Jenny as she entered and gained his feet.

"Are you going already?" Jenny asked. "It is only eight."

"There ees coming a person to this house—a message carrying to Legion. I am thinking it being about Lily. I am thinking to follow these man."

"But perhaps his message is not about Lily and you will follow him for nothing."

"I think not, my love. Your Burton, suspicious he being. You will telling no one, Jenny. When I seeing does Lily be at the end of my ride, I sending word quickly."

Jenny nodded as the marquis struggled into his riding coat, perched a high beaver upon his fair curls and exited into the side yard through one of the French doors. Word having already reached the stables for each of the gentlemen's mounts to be saddled, di Roche reappeared within moments, tipped his hat gallantly to her and cantered off in the direction of the front gate. Jenny stared pensively after him.

Howard's first notion was to grab the messenger and shake

Lily's whereabouts out of the man, and without the least hesitation he tossed the note down upon a small cherrywood table, turned and reached out with both hands toward Worchester. Before he could even grab the ruffian's lapels, however, the muzzle end of a horse pistol abruptly pointed itself at his midsection.

"Aye, they said as ye'd be attackin' o' me did I not keep me peepers wide," Worchester grinned. "Ought not ta be a thinkin' o' sich thin's, guv'nr. Won't 'ave no little missy at all erstwise. If'n me own sainted person don't be appearin' in a perticuler place at a perticuler time, why this flash cove what writ to ye is gonna have 'is way wid the mort—an' then me brother and me cousin swears ta git in on the fun as well—an' then, o' course, we are gonna haf ta kill the darlin' girl, ain't we? Aye, tha's better, guv'nor. Ye jis do what it says in that message, an' I expect the chit won' have nothin' ta worry about. 'Tis ye the guv'nor's longin' ta meet wi', an' bein' real careful o' the petticoat 'e will till ye shows yerself."

"Get out," Howard growled, his hands forming into fists at his side. "Get out of my sight."

"Pleased ta oblige, y'lor'ship," Worchester grinned, showing a gap where his upper front teeth should have been. "Ain't no need ta call that prissy proper little butler o' yourn ta show me the way neither. I reckon I kin fine it on me own."

Howard, his face growing rapidly red with anger, went immediately to the bellpull. "If you believe I'll allow you to wander as far as the door without someone watching your every step, you're more of a fool than I suspect," he muttered. "Burton, escort this person from the premises."

Burton, who had run up the hallway, slid to a stop and sedately opened the parlor door, bowed Worchester out of the room, stalked disdainfully behind him to the front entrance, opened the front door and closed it vehemently behind the man. Howard was there when he turned around, and Paxton as well.

"Hampton has got Lily, Burton," the Reverend Howard

mumbled. "He requests Wright's presence at a cemetery somewhere near Fennel's Marsh at dusk."

"Do you know anything at all about the place?" queried Paxton as the three men started up the main stairway.

" 'Tis ancient and vile and not fit to be looked upon in the daylight," muttered Burton. " 'Twas a killing ground where persons suspected of witchcraft met their deaths, and 'tis fit for nothing but the spreading of disease and the frightening of bairns."

"The perfect spot for a private murder," Paxton sighed. "Kill Wright, toss his body into the marsh and—"

"And what, Paxton?" grumbled the reverend.

"I don't know. I know he wants Wright dead. I know he has certain goals in mind regarding Mary, but I cannot conceive that he should think his way clear at Willowset once Josh is gone—unless—unless—he intends to use Miss Lipton to lure us one by one onto the marsh and dispose of us?"

"Balderdash!" exclaimed Howard, turning on his heel into the breakfast room. "The man may be mad, Paxton, but even a Bedlamite like Wright would not think such a project practical."

"Speaking of whom—" added Paxton, with a glance at Burton.

"You may rest assured, Mr. Paxton, sir, that not one word of this shall reach his lordship's ears," stated Burton determinedly.

"What project would Joshie not think practical?" asked Jenny's sweet voice from the direction of the sideboard. "Burton, we are almost out of coffee and none of the ladies has yet eaten. Do you expect we might have more?"

"Immediately, your grace." Burton bowed and departed.

"I have heard there was a messenger come," continued Jenny. "Is it someone found Miss Lily?"

Paxton and Howard stared awkwardly at each other, neither certain just how much her grace had heard or ought to be told.

* * *

Di Roche waited behind the windbreak of pines at the edge

of the path until the grim-looking ruffian had passed by and taken the turning of the lane that led toward St. Swithin's. The marquis then gave a slight shake to the reins and urged his horse slowly forward in Worchester's wake. It was not going to be terribly difficult to follow a lone rider across the winter-barren landscape, especially when one had memorized exactly the color of his horse's tail, but it was going to be the devil of a thing to keep from being seen while doing it. Di Roche, woolgathering a bit, wished he might speak as clearly in English as he thought in Italian. If he did not make quite so many foolish mistakes, perhaps the Legion would learn to like him more quickly. He was having the devil of a time curbing his amorous tendencies toward Jenny. He had stolen a kiss from her in the second-floor hall and given her a squeeze in the main drawing room and held her tightly against him for an eternal moment, gazing down into the bottomless depths of those so captivating blue eyes on a freezing stroll through the frozen rose garden. *Santa Maria!* but he could not hold himself in check much longer. She was the most bewitching, beguiling, appealing, alluring lady he had ever met and his heart beat for her alone. He could hear it beating even now, loudly, in his ears, sounding—sounding almost like—di Roche spun around to stare over his shoulder at the bay approaching him from the rear. "Nicco?" he almost shouted as the round little rider approached. "Nicco, what brings you? There is happening nothing to my Jenny?"

Nicco shook his head as he came up beside his master. "I am coming to assisting you, yes? You the villain following and I following you. Ees good, no?"

Di Roche grinned at his valet. "You speaking true, Nicco. Ees good. Does finding the lovely Miss Lily, you shall ride to informing Paxton and Howard while I standing of the watch."

Nicco nodded, and together they rode in Worchester's wake.

* * *

Paxton was all for telling the ladies everything—but Howard

did not like it. Mrs. Hampton might indeed be entitled to the knowledge, but his sister, Eleanor, would more than likely cause a ruckus when she learned he intended to take Wright's place at the cemetery. And she might somehow slip and speak of the plan to Wright—which would bring everything down around their ears. Paxton agreed to that. If Wright were to learn that Lily was being held captive by Hampton, he would be on horseback in a matter of moments, injured or not. And he would like as well die from the effort. And that would likely get Lily killed. "All right. I agree," he murmured over a brightly painted china cup of coffee. "Jenny, I think Howard has the right of it. We must not let on to Mary and Miss Eleanor that the plot has thickened. Howard and I will work out what everyone must do and you must just say that we haven't word yet of Lily's whereabouts."

Jenny nodded. Then she stood and left the room. She had told them Francesco had been impatient and ridden toward the Great North Road to continue the search. They had accepted that explanation of his departure without question. She was not in the least worried that di Roche might come to harm. Her confidence in him had grown to be almost as great as her confidence in Wright. In her mind the little marquis was invincible, and he would rescue Lily without the least hesitation and then put a definite period to that hideous Mr. Hampton, after which Joshie could not fail to acknowledge Francesco's superior good qualities and would acquiesce to their marriage joyously. And she did so wish to marry the little marquis. He was a good deal like Charlie, whom she had loved with all her heart. He was funny and thoughtful and understood about Joshie and how she could never suffer herself to be divided from him. And he was willing to see that she never was. He had even whispered in her ear that he had sent one of the grooms with a message to his man of business in London that he wished to procure Hampton Hall and its environs, and that his man of business had already set about the purchase of the place from a cousin who had bought the property from Hampton himself after he had fled to the continent. And Francesco would be good to Jessie, too. Already he knew what entertained the child and did not mind playing with him and telling him stories. And he had even thrown his heart over the hurdle and learned to play Spinach!

"My goodness but you are deep in thought," Mary commented as she took a seat beside the duchess in the cozy back parlor. "Has something happened?"

"Yes," Jenny nodded. "Something enormous, but we must wait for Eleanor before we discuss it."

"No, you must not," replied Eleanor from the doorway, "for I am right behind Mary and have brought you a cup of coffee. What is it has happened, Jenny?"

Jenny, without the least hesitation, told them everything. "I did not promise not to tell," she added, "though your brother thought I did and so did Francesco. I have always found that it is better to nod at gentlemen when they are attempting to be valiant and then to do what one thinks best. My papa was used to be valiant sometimes. And Joshie is always valiant, though most often it don't occur to him that he is."

"But—but—Martin cannot possibly think to take Jocelyn's place at that cemetery!" exclaimed Eleanor. "It would be insane for any one of them to go alone. What if the fiend has laid an ambush for him?"

"Oh, he most likely will," agreed Mary. "Hampton would not stand a chance against Josh if they were to meet on equal terms."

"Yes, and so I told them," Jenny replied, "but we are not to worry. At this very moment they are planning an ambush of their own and will attempt to seize Hampton and his ruffians as they arrive at the place. They have gone out to the stables to consult with Glenby Oakes and Harry Cross and John. I think they plan to take every able-bodied man about Willowset with them."

"Oh," sighed Eleanor in relief. "That is much better. Then Martin will not be in such grave danger."

"Exactly, and Lily will not be in danger either once that

horrible person has led Francesco to the place they are keeping her," Jenny grinned. "Everything will work out wonderfully, and Joshie needn't know a thing."

"That's good," Mary nodded. "I hardly think Josh is up to handling any of this at the moment—though Dr. MacGregor did say that he hadn't rebroken his ankle, only twisted it badly and rebruised his ribs and sprained his knee. His arm, at least, is nearly healed. Your brother is terribly in love with Lily, isn't he?" she asked with a hopeful glance at Eleanor.

"I—yes, I expect he is, but—"

"But what?" Jenny's marvelous blue eyes were somewhat disconcerting, Eleanor found, when they were directed so ingenuously and expectantly at one.

"But I do n-not know if he will marry her. He has not said."

"He has already asked her to marry him!" declared the little duchess.

"Yes, Jenny, but that was before he discovered that Lily was not a member of the Polite World," Mary sighed.

"Oh, devil the Polite World! Lily loves him and he loves her. Joshie would most certainly marry her if he felt the same as the Reverend Howard does, and Joshie is an earl!"

"Yes, but he is not wrapped about in all the trappings of class and social acceptability that surround Mr. Howard. And besides, Josh has not the least understanding of what could be wrong with—with—"

Eleanor, seeing the look of complete incomprehension on Jenny's face that brought Mary to a stuttering halt, giggled at it. "I have come to think that there is a great deal to be said for being raised among the northern barbarians, Mary. Martin is not as free to marry where he will as Jocelyn, your grace. He must marry to please our parents and to set a good example among his parishioners, and he has always expected to do so— to marry a young lady of sterling qualities."

"Lily has sterling qualities. She is brave and honest and true and would lay down her life for him," Jenny proclaimed innocently. "What more sterling qualities does the man require?"

None at all. The Reverend Howard required no more sterling qualities whatever than those he knew his Lily already possessed. Involved in the planning of the ambush that would capture Hampton and set Lily free, the reverend could not keep from thoughts of that gloriously sweet and beautiful young woman. So what if she were not Quality? She looked like Quality. She spoke like Quality. Her every action evoked visions of a pampered and well-brought-up young lady. His parents, having been to London only once in the last fifteen years, would never have heard even rumors of Wright's mistress. He would simply say Lily was a gentlewoman who had been orphaned and had no family to attend the wedding—which they would hold in his father's little chapel at Irving-Kent. And since Howard had every intention of remaining in St. Swithin's, his wife and children securely about him until the day he died, surely no one who knew of Lily's background would ever have a chance to confront them—only those in this house who were her friends—and Wright. It was Wright stuck in his craw. Damn the man! He had not ruined the girl—Lily had already been upon the streets—but damn the man! How could he, Howard Martin, son of a gentleman and a vicar, accept the leavings of a demon like Wright? How could he take her into his home, make her his wife after Wright had had his way with her? Howard's conscience began to grind away at him then. Lily was a harlot, a fallen woman—and would he actually lie to his family and his parishioners in order to marry her? Was his character so weak, his commitment to goodness and virtue so minor?

"So, what do you think, Howard?" Paxton mumbled.

"Huh?"

"Of the plan. Are you satisfied with it? Perhaps we ought to lay the situation before Wright after all. He's more adept at this sort of thing than any of us."

"He's like as not gonna wanta be in on it if we do," Harry

Cross sighed, sipping from a mug of coffee. "Wouldn't let the reverend here take 'is place, that's a certainty. Want ta face up to Hampton hisself."

"He cannot possibly do so," declared Howard, his anger with Wright over Lily coloring all thought. "We shall do it as it stands. I shall be the bait and Wright shall know nothing of it. There can be very little danger provided we have gotten there and provided ourselves with cover before the villains arrive."

"True," muttered Glenby Oakes, "only we ain't much used to thinkin' like villains—not as used to it as his lor'ship, I mean. Not even me. Could be as there's somethin' we ain't seein' here. Something we oughta know but we don't."

"Wright is not the only gentleman in this establishment with a mind!" Howard exploded, slamming his fist down upon the rough-hewn table and then staring amazedly at his pain-filled hand, wondering why he had done such a thing.

"But Legion be the only gentleman with a twisted mind," John Whitson mumbled, "and we likely ought to take advantage of 'im."

They fell back into a discussion of all that might happen in the situation, and in the end Howard won out, for none of the men could think of any possibility they had not covered. Together, gentlemen and servants united to implement the plan, to capture Hampton and his ruffians and to rescue Miss Lily. At least an hour before the coming of dusk the cemetery at Fennel's Marsh would be alive with the able-bodied men of Willowset.

The gentleman whose opinion they had declined to ask was sitting up in his bed, vociferously denying that he ached anywhere at all, though his head was pounding and pain stabbed through his knee and ankle. "I am just as fit as I was yesterday, I tell you, Tibbs, and I want to be out of this chamber."

Tibbs, a bushy white eyebrow rising, snorted and turned to face him, noting with a tinge of pity the obvious anxiety upon the finely chiseled face. " 'Tis Miss Lily worries you. You expected to see her first thing this morning, did you not?"

"Yes, all right, I did, Tibbs. I expected her to come riding up in someone's gig at sunrise. There's something more happened than anyone's seen fit to tell me. Lily ain't a gudgeon and knows she can't run off to London or anywhere else without money. And she knows perfectly well that she need only ask and I will send her wherever she wishes. And—and—any of the people in the village would've gladly helped her to come back to Willowset. They would, wouldn't they, Tibbs?"

Tibbs's eyebrow rose a bit higher. "I am amazed you need to ask, my lord, after all the years we have visited here," he murmured, carrying one of the bottles MacGregor had left and a spoon toward the bed. "I had thought you would know."

"Well, I do know, Tibbs!" exploded the gentleman, pushing the medicine away. "They are kind and will help a fellow out."

"Then why, Master Josh, do you keep them at arm's length?"

"What?"

"You know precisely to what I refer. You have never once let down your guard. You are forever hiding from them."

"No, I ain't, Tibbs."

"Yes, you are, and do not think they don't know it, either."

"I am friends with Melinda."

"Yes, but only because of Mrs. Hampton. You could not hide behind your villainous mask after you had already gone to her niece's aid, could you? Mrs. Dish knew the truth at once."

"What truth?"

"That you are a good and honorable man, but you are frightened no one will accept you as such."

"I ain't frightened of nothing or no one!"

"No, of course you are not. Open your mouth and swallow this, Master Josh, or I shall forbid Miss Eleanor to see you when next she comes." Tibbs gave quick thanks under his breath for Miss Eleanor as the earl ceased arguing and swallowed the tonic. The valet's wise gray eyes shone with rapidly burgeoning belief that the earl at last had found a young woman for whose good opinion he would dare anything—even peace and respectability. "Now, if you will cease haranguing me and rest quietly for another hour or two, I shall think seriously about helping you to a chair before the fire in the sitting room." With deft hands and a heart swelling with hope that by the time the earl woke again Miss Lily would be rescued and Hampton back in gaol, Tibbs helped him back down between the sheets and waited until the medicine made the stubborn eyelids flutter. As soon as he was certain Wright slept, he set out to locate Burton and learn what plan had been decided upon and how it was to be carried out.

Mrs. Dish met Tibbs just outside the earl's suite. "You know, do you not, Horace, about the note?"

"All about it, my dear."

"You do not think we ought to tell Josh?"

Tibbs thought a moment, then shook his head. "I think not. There is nothing for him to do, you see. Could he swing up onto Tugforth's back and ride off to face Hampton, I would think differently. But he cannot. And for him to know and be unable to act—'twould be infinite torture to the lad."

Mrs. Dish nodded. "The gentlemen did not think fit to tell the young ladies, either. Only Jenny knows of it. They fear Miss Eleanor's reaction to Howard's proposal to play the earl."

"Bah," muttered Tibbs with a shake of his head. "They underestimate that young lady, they do—and the others."

Mrs. Dish could not help but smile. "I think, Mr. Tibbs, that there is a good deal of his lordship rubbed off upon you over the years."

"One cannot help it." Tibbs grinned. "He believes so strongly. He believes that Jenny is brave, and so she is; he believes that Mrs. Mary is strong and intelligent, and so she is; he believes that Miss Lily is sweet and innocent and his belief has made her so."

"And what does he believe of Miss Eleanor?"

Tibbs's eyes lit perceptibly. "I do not know, my dear, but I begin to hope that he believes her the young lady in all the world meant for him alone."

"I think he does, Horace." Mrs. Dish smiled, giving that gentleman's sleeve a pat.

"Do you, Melinda?"

"Yes. You will not go to the cemetery, will you, Mr. Tibbs?"

"If I am needed, my dear. But I rather think they will wish me to remain with his lordship. I expect Aberdeen and Burton will remain as well. I am off to discover what has been decided upon."

Mrs. Dish nodded, her cheeks dimpling as Tibbs took her hand into his own and patted it gently.

"Not to worry, Melinda. All will be well, I assure you."

"I shall sit with Josh, Horace, in case he awakens," she murmured, flushing like a schoolgirl beneath the tender gaze of his fine gray eyes.

"Do you know what Master Josh believes of you?" Tibbs asked, holding her hand in his own for much too long. "He believes you are beauty and stability and a fount of wisdom, compassion and understanding. He believes you are a woman 'twould be an honor to die for. And I—I believe the lad has the right of it."

Twenty-one

The Marquis di Roche and Nicco peered at the abandoned tallow factory from behind a large pile of rocks. "These place being what?" whispered Nicco, bewildered. "Ees burninged, no?"

The marquis nodded thoughtfully. "Ees factory, Nicco. Burning outted factory. I closer going."

"I, too."

"Very well. Going me firsts and you seconds over there," di Roche said, pointing to a clump of small pines near the large hole in the rock wall through which Nate Worchester had disappeared. Placing the reins of their mounts securely beneath a heavy rock, the two skittered quietly from one place of hiding to the next. Di Roche, wary of every sound and movement, waved the eager Nicco to remain hidden and to keep watch while he proceeded to explore what he could of the dilapidated building. Great chunks of stone had fallen. Charred rafters and remnants of beams pierced sky and ground at disturbing angles. Looking much like a gray, rotting whale, blackened bones piercing its hide and great chunks torn from the smooth flesh, the building sent chills down the marquis's backbone. When he reached the rear of the place and a sudden wind sent the sickening sweet smell from ancient boiling kettles into his aristocratic nostrils, bile rose and he gagged on the bitter, stinging substance, turned away from the building and retched. Recovering himself, he seized a large linen handkerchief from his breeches pocket, held it to his nose and proceeded on around the building, peering into one cavity after another, hoping for sight or sound of Lily. When at last he returned to Nicco he had decided that the only way to discover whether Lily were in the place was to go into the place himself. Nicco nodded. "Going too me," he murmured.

In the small office above the work floor, Nate Worchester shared a hot cup of tea with his brother, his cousin and Arthur Hampton. "You're sure he intends to meet me," Hampton asked, one booted foot resting on the seat of a chair.

"Aye, guv'nor."

"Good." Hampton grinned, took a sip from the mug he held and then nodded. "You didn't see a short blond foreigner about, did you? Little prissy-looking gentleman."

"Can't figger what happened ta that di Roche," mumbled the Fiend as Worchester shook his head negatively. "Ain't been a sign of 'im since we seed 'im helpin' ta chase that bat. Ye reckon they catched onto 'im, gov'nor?"

"Well, he didn't end in gaol in Dorset with us, Hobbins, and it appears Wright ain't dead. Reckon di Roche's body's likely buried somewhere around Willowset. Ain't worth worryin' about. Killed the brother—killed di Roche. Typical."

"Now we goes ta the graveyard an' lays a trap fer the earl?" asked the Fiend, rubbing at his whisker-speckled chin. "Ain't goin' ta show up alone, ye know. Puddin'-'eaded ta do that."

"Legion ain't pudding-headed. He'll bring every able-bodied man at Willowset if he's a mind to seize me alive and pry the gel's whereabouts out o' me. I am counting on it. What was that?" Hampton asked abruptly, turning toward the main section of the factory.

"Rat pro'bly. Lotsa rats about," grumbled the Sneezing Fiend, draining the last of his tea. "S'prised they ain't et all o' our provisions. Yer wants me ta take 'er 'ighness a bit o' bread an' butter, guv'nor?"

"No, I'll take it, Hobbins."

Nicco, eyes round with excitement, sighed quietly in relief and very slowly, very softly, lowered the loose board di Roche

had hit with his elbow the rest of the way to the floor. Di Roche
blew a wisp of blond hair silently out of his eyes. Together,
huddled behind an immense copper kettle turned dull green
with age and disuse, they watched as Hampton gathered bits
of food together and made his way to the rickety stairs at the
back of the office. Di Roche pointed upward with one long
finger and mouthed the words: *Miss Lily.* Nicco nodded.

Lily stuffed the pieces of shutter back into place and went
to stand the broom back in the corner as she heard Hampton's
boot kick against the bottom of the door. "I'm coming," she
called. "I did as you suggested," she murmured as she held
open the door for Hampton to enter. "I put the chair under the
latch."

"A very good idea," Hampton nodded, dropping the bread
and butter he cradled in one arm upon the cot and handing
Lily a chipped mug filled with tea. "I put sugar in it. Unfortunately we do not possess any cream. You found something
to feed the fire?"

"Some of the floorboards—from that corner—and paper
from the wall. I saved the rest of the coal until this morning."

"You are very efficient, Miss Lipton. I shall bring more coal
presently. We haven't much, but I should hate for you to freeze
to death, my dear. My plans do not in the least involve leaving
you here like a piece of frozen mutton, I assure you."

"Where is here, Mr. Hampton?" Lily asked, warming her
hands on the tea mug. "Are we still in St. Swithin's? I cannot
believe so. There is no place stinks like this in that lovely village."

Hampton chuckled, tore off a piece of bread for himself and
went to sit on the lip of the hearth, ignoring the dirt and ashes
that lingered there. " 'Tis a tallow factory, sweetness. Make
tallow much like they make glue, you know. Boil down—"

"I know what they do, Mr. Hampton," interrupted Lily. "I
do not wish a verbal picture of the operation. I'm surprised I
didn't recognize the smell."

"Aye, you ought to recognize it. I swear, Wright's done a

fine job on you, my dear. I would never suspect that you come from muck and misery."

"Well, I do," spluttered Lily around a piece of bread and butter, "and I am not ashamed of it, either. And it is not Josh made me into anything. I have stood up upon my own two feet and done what I needed to do to make myself a better person. It was I who did it. And Josh will tell you so, too."

"Amazing," murmured Hampton. "Took a sniveling, filthy, lying little harlot and infused her with pride. How'd he do that, my dear? Might I guess? Happen while he had you upon your back?"

Lily set the mug of tea upon the floor. Then she stood, walked quietly forward and, bending down, slammed the back of her hand across Hampton's face. Hampton seized her wrist and the toe of one of her half boots met solidly with his groin. He groaned and she pulled away and returned to her seat upon the cot. She lifted her mug from the floor and sipped the tea. "I need not listen to such lewdness from any man," she said calmly, her blue eyes wary. *"That* is one of the things Josh taught me."

Eleanor was surprised to find the earl seated on a chaise longue before the fire in his sitting room. In brocade dressing gown and woolen slippers, a blanket tucked securely 'round his long legs, he was attempting to read a thin leather-bound volume balanced on one knee, while beyond him in the bedchamber Tibbs and two chambermaids were busily changing sheets, cleaning out the hearth and dusting the heavy furniture. Wright did not hear her enter and she studied him affectionately. His curls were tousled. His incredible eyes squinted just a bit, causing his nose to wrinkle slightly. The fine slim hand that belonged to the arm in the sling kept creeping over to hold the other side of the book, but it could not quite reach and went back to rest inside its linen support between attempts. She almost laughed as she watched him try to turn the page one-handed, but did not and was glad she did not, for a most self-satisfied smile crept to his lips when he managed the thing without dropping the volume. She thought how he must have looked just so when he had been Jessie's age and accomplished a goal he had not thought he might. Between his lips the tiniest bit of his tongue showed as he concentrated. It was Tibbs who looked up and saw her from the bedchamber and smiled, waving her silently into the room. She nodded and crossed silently to Wright's side and stared down over his shoulder. "Is it very interesting, my lord?" she asked.

"Ellie!"

She seated herself in a chair beside him and peered down into the pages of the volume. "What on earth is it?"

"It's a volume on the raising of swine."

"Oh. And are you planning on raising swine, my lord?"

"Can I see a way to do it. People raise hogs in Yorkshire."

"They do?"

"Uh-huh. Well, some. I would raise cattle, but there ain't much pasture land at the Rise. Lily has not come back yet?"

Eleanor shook her head but smiled. "Not yet, but Martin and the others have learned she is at the Gander's Neck and have gone to fetch her. And since Martin and she will have a great deal to say to each other we need not expect to see any of them until dinner." She had thought at first that she could not possibly lie to him, but when she saw the sparkle of hope leap to his eyes a gentle fog settled over her conscience and eased her mind. Surely it could not be wrong to set his mind at rest. And with all of the men but di Roche, Burton, Tibbs and Aberdeen gone to entrap Hampton, the thing must be done quickly and Lily back safe by dinner time, and Jocelyn would be none the worse for not knowing.

"Does Howard truly wish to speak with her, Ellie? I mean, does he—has he—thought again about marrying her?"

"I believe he may have done so, my lord." Eleanor smiled, watching the volume slide unnoticed down his leg and onto the floor. "He is very much in love, you see."

"Well, yes, I thought so at first, too, but perhaps he is simply infatuated. Does Howard become infatuated with women?"

"I have no idea," Eleanor laughed. "I am merely his sister. He does not confide his tender feelings for other ladies in me."

"Oh."

"Do you discuss such things with the duchess?"

"No," sighed the earl, rubbing at his eyes, "but only because I don't appear to have tender feelings."

"Bosh!" Eleanor leaned down to rescue the forgotten volume and placed it upon the cherrywood table beside her chair. "Jenny and Mary and Mrs. Dish are bringing the tea things in a moment or two. It is early for tea, but we thought you might like some."

"I'd love some. Aberdeen and Tibbs are forever shoving milk at me as though I were a two-year-old. I hate milk!"

"Bowey is bringing the children to tea as well."

"Uncle Josh! Uncle Josh!" shouted two excited voices at that very moment, and Jessie and Joyce dashed into the room, the little fox cradled carefully in Jessie's arms and the gigantical and savaging Siberian wolfdog, Blaze, bounding merrily at Joycie's heels. "We have got Blaze an' Tarnation to be friends!"

"No, have you?" asked the earl.

"Yes," Jessie nodded enthusiastically, setting the kit upon his uncle's lap. Luckily the gentleman was quick enough to get a hand upon it before it scampered into his sling.

"And why is it called Tarnation?" he asked, gently stroking the soft red fur.

"Because that is what Bowey always says when she sees him. 'Tarnation! What's that beastie doin' 'pon my stitch'ry?' an' 'Tarnation! You git that thin' out of yer bed this very moment!' "

"Bowey is vewy funny," added Joyce with an enormous smile.

"Tarnation is a boy, Uncle Josh. Harry Cross said so."

"Well, an' Harry Cross would know," Wright grinned. "Are

you certain that puppy isn't going to scamper up here after Tarnation? I don't want to be trampled."

"Blaze an' him is fwiends," Joyce assured Wright, stooping a bit to pat the puppy's head. "We teached 'em."

Eleanor spied Jenny and Mary and Mrs. Dish at the door and went with Bowey to help with the tea things.

"Don't you think he is wonderful with the children, Eleanor?" asked Jenny in a whisper as she set her tray down upon a small card table. "He will make an excellent father, I think. You do want to have children, don't you? Joshie wants them with all his heart."

"Jenny!" Mary hissed. "Shush! You are incorrigible."

Eleanor grinned self-consciously at the two of them, her face reddening.

By the time the tea things had been laid out and chairs gathered 'round the chaise longue so that the earl would be in the midst of things, the children had pointed out all of the kit's most notable good points and managed to shove the puppy up onto Wright as well. The fact that the puppy lay panting, spread out across Wright's lap with the kit balanced complacently upon its back, and that the children were feeding them both pieces of macaroons, the crumbs scattering all over the earl, and that the fox drooled onto the puppy's head and the puppy drooled onto the earl's robe seemed to bother the gentleman not at all. His silver-flecked, darkling eyes danced with joy, and he included each of the children most seriously in his conversation. When tea was finished and the table and dishes cleared to the other side of the room Bowey produced a tiny music box from the pocket of her wide skirts and placed it upon the arm of her chair. "These moppets have made up a play for you, m'lord," she announced cheerily. "Are you ready then, Master Jessie? Miss Joyce? Hurry. Run and take your places."

Both children rushed to hide behind the big wing chair in which Bowey sat, and as she opened the music box Joyce skipped into the circle made by the adults. "This the stowy of

Bowey's hot potatows soup, Uncle Josh," she squeaked excitedly, "an' I am Bowey!" and then she did a charmingly inept little dance as she pretended to be the nanny making soup. Eleanor watched enraptured as the children giggled and stumbled and "oops-ed" their way through a tale in which Bowey must protect her soup from robbers and highwaymen and the Prince Regent—all characters portrayed with enthusiasm by Jessie—and even from the mighty wolfdog, Blaze—who was dragged from Wright's lap to play himself. At the end, of course, the Duke of Ware, in all his glory, stepped in to save the day—and the soup.

The delighted adults encouraged the little actors by "ohing" and "ahing" in all the appropriate places and gasping dramatically when it seemed called for. Wright fell into chuckles so often that his ribs began to ache. Shouts of "Bravo!" and enthusiastic applause erupted just as they should at the end. Giggling triumphantly, Jessie and Joyce rushed to Wright and scampered up onto him to plant wet kisses on his cheeks. Eleanor saw him pale as the children's weight and wiggles wrenched his aching bones, but the wide grin never left his face or his eyes, and the only protest he made was that they must not sit upon the little fox, who had climbed intelligently up onto his shoulder. After a few moments of boasting and bragging and giggling over their great success both little actors cuddled down atop the earl and the puppy curled up beneath the chaise and Wright's gaze roamed happily about the room until it alighted teasingly upon Eleanor's enraptured countenance, and he laughed again. "I think, Ellie, you have never made up a play of your very own, have you?"

"No," Eleanor replied softly.

"Never?" asked Jenny. "Not even when you were little?"

Eleanor shook her head.

"We were used to do so often, Jenny and I," mused the earl, his eyes sparkling with memories. "Sometimes Mother and Father would take part. And once Tibbs played the part of—"

"The knave of hearts!" Jenny giggled. "I remember!"

A groan from the doorway of the bedchamber, where Tibbs had stopped to watch, brought laughter to Mrs. Dish's eyes. "Oh, how I should like to have seen that," she chuckled.

"Perhaps you shall, Melinda," replied the earl. "One never knows what is like to happen during the Christmas season."

Every hack in the Willowset stable had been saddled and mounted, and the group that set off toward Fennel's Marsh and the small cemetery beside it looked to be a small army equipped with everything from long guns to swords, pitchforks and hoes. "Thank goodness Wright can't see us," murmured Paxton.

"Indeed," agreed Harry Cross. "We'll have enough explainin' to do does anyone return injured and he discover it, believe me."

Burton watched them go from the front steps, hope rising as he raised his hand in farewell. Certainly such a show of force would overwhelm Hampton and bring Miss Lily safely home. And perhaps the man at the head of the small army was not going to remain a pompous ass for the rest of his life, either. Might be the reverend would learn what 'twas like to be flawed and frightened and unsure of oneself.

The Reverend Mr. Howard was indeed learning what 'twas to be unsure of himself—a new experience and uncomfortable in the extreme. Though he professed great confidence in his plan, he could not believe that they would take Hampton without a struggle, nor could he be certain that Hampton had not already done Lily some great harm. I'll kill him, he thought grimly. If he has harmed Lily, I will kill the man with my own two hands. A small voice in the back of his mind berated him for allowing such a thought to surface, but he scoffed at it. What a fool he was. What a hypocrite. Had he ever once thought what life was like for such a young woman as Lily? Had he ever before opened his eyes and recognized the injustice and the evil that drove such men as Wright to violence?

Had he ever once attempted to understand anyone unlike himself? No. He had assumed that all should be exactly like himself. He had assumed that he was perfection and that they might be equally as perfect except for their own stubbornness. He had been a complete imbecile. Well, he knew now that he was not perfection, that he might sink to violence as readily as Wright, that his heart might be torn from his chest and pummeled into dust by remorse and uncertainty as easily as the next man's. He had opened his mind along with his heart now, and he was learning that *he* must fight for what he believed in and those he loved, that *his* was the responsibility to rescue those who could not rescue themselves, that the war between good and evil was not a thing to be preached from the pulpit, but a very real confrontation in which a man—if he were a man—must take a very real and personal part.

In the late afternoon light di Roche and Nicco sought shelter in the shadows beneath the office balcony. They had learned that Lily was to be left in the custody of only one man. The rest were even now preparing to leave. Di Roche and Nicco eyed each other with joy. There would be not the least need for Nicco to return to Willowset for help. Between the two of them they might easily overpower one ruffian and rescue the damsel.

No sooner had Hampton and the Fiend and Jerry Worchester stamped out into the rear yard and the sound of their horses' hooves echoed into the distance than di Roche and Nicco made their way cautiously back outside the factory and around to the front, behind the pile of rocks where their horses waited, so that they might discuss the situation without fear of being overheard. "We going straight up the stairs?" asked Nicco eagerly. "Easily we overpowering only one person."

"No; supposing a pistol these man having. Sneaking around we must. I not having a pistol, Nicco, only my sword. We going once more around these building and seeing how best we coming upon these villain unawares."

Nicco nodded. It would be best did they surprise the man if he had a pistol. Together the two set off, keeping out of sight as best they could. When they reached the rear of the factory di Roche came to an abrupt halt. He caught at Nicco's sleeve and pointed to his ear. Nicco listened and nodded. Both looked upward in an attempt to locate the creaking sound that had reached them.

On the second story of the tallow factory Lily had removed the pieces of shutter she had already pried from the broken window and once again forced the broomstick into the hole. She placed the broken leg from the chair between the broomstick and the shutter for leverage and pushed downward. The shutter creaked, then split. Lily pulled the loose wood away, and this time the hole was large enough to let her see down into the yard. Her eyes lit at the sight of di Roche and Nicco staring back up at her. A finger went to di Roche's lips, warning her not to give voice to her excitement. "If we could climbing in that window, Nicco, we could surprising that villain most assuredly."

Nicco spluttered into the forbidden Italian, and di Roche's countenance lightened considerably. He responded in Italian himself and Nicco hurried off. Within moments the valet returned carrying a partially burned wooden ladder. It held only a sprinkling of rungs and would offer a precarious climb, but di Roche was small and light and had not the least doubt that he could make the trip without incident. In less than five minutes di Roche and Lily between them had managed to remove the shutter and hand its remains down to Nicco to dispose of silently. Then di Roche climbed in through the window and gave Lily an enthusiastic hug. "You safe being now, Miss Lily," he whispered. "Nicco and I taking you home. But going down broken ladder in long skirts not being possible."

"I can do it, my lord. Honestly, I can."

"No, you falling perhaps. The Legion being most upset do

I bringing you home with neck broken. Nicco and me having plan."

Lily listened with great attention to di Roche's whispered words, and when he had finished she nodded and took a deep breath and then screamed at the top of her lungs as the little marquis drew his sword and flattened himself against the wall beside the door. There was no sound from below. Lily screamed again.

With a sigh, Nate Worchester ceased poking at the fire and made his way to the rickety stairs. "Wha' the devil ye hollerin' 'bout?" he called gruffly. "Ain't nothin' what kin hurt ye up there. All the thin's what kin hurt ye gone ridin' off," he added under his breath.

"Oh, help, help!" squealed Lily, flinging open the door to her chamber and running out to the top of the stairs, holding her skirts high. "Help me, please. There is a great, ugly animal up here, an' it is smelly and growls! Please come! Please!"

Nate Worchester, devoted to the wife he had left at home and therefore Hampton's choice to leave in charge of Lily, was not a great unfeeling lout. He had faced similar expressions of fear from his own Annie, and though he knew that the very most this animal might be was a rat, he shook his head and started carefully up the stairs. "I'm comin' then, missy. Got's ta take me time er I'll be fallin' ri' through the treads, I will. I ain't no lightweight." By the time he reached the landing he had taken the horse pistol from his belt. Taking Lily's arm with one meaty hand, he turned her back to the doorway and drew her along with him into the little room. "Now, ye show me where's this beastie an' we shall put an end to 'im."

"Dropping please these pistol," requested di Roche politely, the tip of his sword coming to rest against Worchester's back. "I these beastie being and I not wishing to killing you."

Worchester turned in a split second, pulled Lily in front of him and fired his pistol. Di Roche's sword clattered to the floor. Lily kicked the heel of her half boot into Worchester's kneecap, and the man grunted and shoved her from him, threw the now useless pistol aside and went after di Roche with his fists. He landed only one blow before Nicco brought a board down upon the back of his head.

"I thinking you falling through stairs," Di Roche grinned, wiping at the cut lip Worchester had given him.

"Are you not shot?" Lily asked, amazed.

"No, I am moving very fast aside."

"Why are you dropping sword?" asked Nicco, busily searching the room for something with which to tie up the villain.

"I am knowing you are coming, Nicco. His gun ees empty, yes? Why should I killing when he cannot harming us any longer? I not like sticking peoples with swords."

Nicco, grinning, took the sword into his own hands and slashed the coverlet upon the cot into strips with which to bind Worchester's hands and feet.

As the sun lowered in the western sky the men of Willowset took up stations throughout the neglected cemetery. They had searched thoroughly beforehand for some sign of Hampton and his henchmen but had found none. Paxton let a sigh of relief escape him as he took his own place behind a twisted and denuded oak. "You'll await them beside that stunted sycamore, right, Howard?" he asked. "In the open, where they may see you, but still somewhat in shadow, so Hampton will not realize immediately that you are not Wright. And so he won't have a clear shot at you."

"I have not the least intention of giving him a clear shot at me, Paxton. I'm not a fool."

"No, of course you ain't. But you are not used to dealing with villains, Howard. You cannot talk the man into surrendering, you know. He must be captured, and there will undoubtedly be a struggle. Shots will be fired."

"And you *are* used to dealing with villains, Paxton?" the reverend asked with a cocked eyebrow.

"No, Howard, I ain't, but I'm used to London footpads and

the need to defend myself. I don't mean to insult you, only to keep you from getting killed."

"I shall not get killed, Paxton," Howard said with a sudden grin. "I would not give Wright the satisfaction to say I was not up to the challenge."

Paxton watched the vicar take up his position beside the sycamore. Tugforth, pulled into service to further convince Hampton that Howard was indeed Wright, stood impatiently pawing the earth next to the reverend. All about the cemetery the sound of Willowset's soldiers settling themselves and readying their weapons whispered into the air, and then there was only silence.

Twenty-two

Eleanor sank onto the sofa in the long drawing room with a satisfied sigh and took up her knitting basket. She had already finished a bright-red-and-cream-striped scarf for Martin and had decided that she might with propriety knit a scarf for Wright as well. "Did you note, Mrs. Dish, that his lordship made not the least fuss about returning to his bed?"

Mrs. Dish, looking about her for her embroidery, smiled. "I think the children wore him out, Eleanor. But I will lay you odds, my dear, that he will be teasing Tibbs to let him up again by the time we dress for dinner."

"Oh, I hope Martin is safe," Eleanor murmured softly. "I cannot help but fear for him."

Mrs. Dish's eyes widened. "You know? My dear, you know where your brother has gone?"

Eleanor nodded, recalling too late that she was not supposed to know of the note or the plan or anything. "It is all right, Mrs. Dish. I have known all along. The duchess told Mary and me."

"Well, well, Mr. Howard and Lily will be home before dinner," stated Mrs. Dish. "I am certain of it."

"Who will be home by dinner?" asked Jenny, her dimples showing to perfection as she lit a taper at the hearth and proceeded to light the candles scattered about the room. "Dusk is coming and I cannot conceive how either of you can see well enough to know what you're doing. I hate stitchery."

"Truly?" asked Eleanor, a hint of laughter in her eyes.

"Oh, you know very well I'm a complete buffle-head when it comes to needles—my fingers are all thumbs. Do you know that one Christmas I made Joshie a handkerchief and embroidered his initial upon it and when he saw it he fell into whoops and it took a whole half hour to quieten him."

"What was wrong with it?" asked Eleanor, grinning.

"Nothing at all. It was a perfectly fine handkerchief—except that it was not exactly square."

"No?"

"No, it was—distinctly lopsided," Jenny giggled. "And Josh had to ask which of his initials I had put upon the thing. And when I told him, he—he held it up to the light and twisted it all about and said that, indeed, it was the most creative and imaginative *J* he'd ever seen and he was proud to own it."

Mrs. Dish and Eleanor and Jenny laughed heartily, but their laughter was interrupted by sounds of a scuffle and a scream.

"Take him," hissed Hampton, shoving Burton at the Fiend and Worchester and pounding up the staircase after Mary. "Not so fast, my gel," he drawled, catching her in the first-floor hall and jerking her around to face him. "I'm your husband, remember."

"Let go of me, Hampton!" Mary demanded, attempting to break free, but he yanked her into his arms and forced his lips down upon her own. The more she struggled, the more roughly he responded, bruising her lips and crushing the breath from her lungs. Fully occupied, he did not see Jenny's golden curls as she peeped out into the hall, inhaled abruptly, and turned back to the two ladies in the long drawing room.

"It's Hampton!" she whispered urgently. "Hampton is assaulting Mary in the hall!"

"Hampton?" gasped Mrs. Dish, her eyes round with disbelief.

"But he can't be here. Martin and the others await him at Fennel's Marsh!" cried Eleanor.

"Well, he is here and there are voices and sounds of a struggle below. I expect he has brought his blackguards with him

and they have taken Burton by surprise. Quickly, we must warn
the others. Mrs. Dish, you and Bowey must dress the children
warmly and take them down the servants' stairs and out into
the home woods to the gamekeeper's cottage. Bowey knows
where 'tis. Eleanor—go to Joshie. Tell him what has happened."

"But—but what are you going to do? Jenny, you cannot confront him."

"That's exactly what I shall do, Ellie. I shall turn him away
to face the staircase and then you must both run to the servants'
stairs." With a grim, determined look, the little duchess stalked
angrily into the first-floor hallway. This time Hampton did see
her and shouted, dragging a resisting Mary forward with him.
The duchess, however, brought him to a halt by not attempting
to run away at all. Instead she stamped toward him, a furious
scowl upon her lovely face, kicked him in the kneecap, stomped
with all her might upon his foot and slammed her knee into a
very tender portion of the man's anatomy, just as her father
and Joshie had taught her. Mary fought free of Hampton's grasp
as he leaned forward, groaning, and pummeled him mercilessly
about his ears. Jenny reached down and tugged the man by the
lapels of his greatcoat around toward the staircase, and watched
anxiously as Eleanor and Mrs. Dish flew toward the red baize
door that hid the servants' staircase. No sooner had the door
closed behind them and Jenny given a small sigh of relief, then
two sets of boots pounded up the stairs and Jenny was lifted
into the air by two strong arms, and Mary was taken as well,
though she landed a goodly number of blows upon Worchester's
face and body before he managed to subdue her.

"What about the butler?" Hampton groaned. "You ain't left
him alone down there?"

"Tied 'im up wif the drap'ry cords, guv," The Sneezing Fiend
chuckled, carrying a furiously kicking and punching Jenny toward the open door to the long drawing room. "Bloke ain't
goin' nowhere. You reckon there's anyone else about?"

"Yes," hissed Hampton, seizing Mary from Worchester,

throwing her down on a settee and smashing the back of his hand across her cheek. "There's another lady, ain't there, Mary?"

"No, there is not!" cried Jenny angrily before Mary could respond. "Eleanor and her brother have gone home. There are only the maids and Mrs. Bowers and Burton and Cook. But Joshie will be back soon and then you will regret having burst in upon us, Mr. Hampton. You will regret it with all your heart! And if you have hurt Burton, Joshie will kill you without the least hesitation."

Hampton, Worchester and the Fiend looked at each other and laughed. "Your brother, my dear, will not return for at least an hour, more likely two," sniggered Hampton, sinking down beside Mary on the settee and putting a heavily muscled arm around her rigid shoulders. "What a hero he has turned out to be, eh, Mary? Grown overconfident. I expected that. Did not even question why I should call him out to that infernal cemetery, did he?"

Mary's eyes met Jenny's. "He assumed you had called him out to kill him, Hampton. A logical assumption, was it not?"

"Oh, quite logical. And I *shall* kill him, my dear, but not until I have tortured him beyond bearing."

"And how do you intend to do that?" asked Jenny.

"Why, by destroying all his handiwork, my dear. You, and Mary, and that lovely creature I already hold. And I shall have the child too, Mary. I shall have it and I shall sell it to gypsies for the price of a decent horse. By the time I've finished all of you will be grateful to crawl off into the night and sell yourselves upon the street!"

Jenny's mouth opened in a small *oh,* and Mary groaned.

"Hobbins, Worchester, check the rest of this floor and the next. The child is about somewhere. Bring it here. And if there's a nanny or a nurse gives you trouble, shoot the witch. As soon as we have it, we leave this provincial palace aflame behind us."

"Oh!" gasped Jenny. "How dare you! This is my husband's home and you shall not set fire to it. I will not let you!"

Hampton chuckled. "You have not a word to say in the matter. You're as audacious as Legion, ain't you? Shameful he and I got off on such a wrong footing. I do admire the way he's trained his sister. Married you myself, I would have. Of course, soon I shall take the benefits of marriage without the obligation."

In the nursery Bowey and Mrs. Dish bundled the children into their warmest garments, explaining that they must be very, very quiet and do exactly as they were told. Bowey murmured breathlessly that they were all going on a great adventure, but the fear in her eyes and the worried look upon Mrs. Dish's face brought the little duke to a halt in the midst of donning his nankeen jacket. "That ain't the truth, Bowey," he stated with a stubborn pout. "I kin tell, you know. You are *worried.*"

"Awe you?" asked Joyce, her eyes growing round and large.

"Yes, I am," Bowey sighed. "We are in great danger, darlings, and must run to Mr. Plummer's as fast as we can."

"Mr. Plummer's in the woods?" asked Jessie.

"Exactly so, your grace."

"Is Mama an' Uncle Josh going wif us?"

"No, my dear," whispered Mrs. Dish, recognizing the extreme worry in his great blue eyes. "Your mama and Uncle Josh and Joyce's mama, too, and even Miss Ellie will follow us very soon. They stay here until they are certain we are safe. That is why we must hurry, so that they will have time to be safe, too."

"Oh," the duke nodded as Mrs. Dish buttoned up his jacket and helped him to pull on his gloves. "We mus' take Blaze and Tarnation wif us, then. An' Maizie and the puppies. An' Burtie."

"An' Tibbs!" added Joyce excitedly. "An' Abewdeen."

"Shhh! They will all come, darlings. But we must go first

and at once," explained Bowey, slipping into her own cape and helping Mrs. Dish to don another. "Burton will be sure to bring Tarnation and Blaze," she lied, hating herself for doing so, but realizing that she and Euphegenia stood not the least chance of gaining the gamekeeper's cottage if the little ones insisted upon carrying along the puppy and the fox. "Come now, down the back stairs as quietly as mice, and when we reach the kitchen door, we must flee like foxes through the garden and into the trees."

The unlikely foursome sneaked down the backstairs only seconds before Jerry Worchester and the Fiend gained the third-floor landing and began to open every door.

Eleanor, panic-stricken but striving to maintain an outward calm, entered the earl's suite and discovered Tibbs pressing one of his lordship's shirts in the sitting room. She waved him to accompany her back into the music room, from which chamber their conversation would be unlikely to wake the earl. Tibbs demanded to know if it was Hampton alone who had entered the house, but Eleanor could not be sure. "There were sounds of a struggle belowstairs," she answered thoughtfully. "We did not see anyone else; still there must be at least one other, don't you think? Burton must have been engaged in battle by someone while Hampton slipped up the stairs."

"Burton engaged in battle," Tibbs sighed woefully. "He is much too old for such nonsense and has undoubtedly been conquered. I knew we ought to have told Master Josh about the note. Well, we must tell him now, certainly."

The earl woke to two frightened faces gazing down at him and his mind sprang instantly to attention. "What is it? Tibbs? Eleanor? What has happened? It is not Lily? Lily is not—not—"

"No, no, no, Master Josh," Tibbs interrupted hastily. "It is nothing so bad as that." Between them, Eleanor and Tibbs enlightened his lordship about the note and the plan and the fact that Hampton and possibly his henchmen had entered Willowset, seized Mary and quite possibly the duchess by this time."

"Damn the man!" muttered Wright. "Tibbs, get me a shirt and breeches. Ellie, go to the window and see if there is any sight of Mrs. Dish and Bowey and the children. Hurry, Tibbs. I cannot take on Hampton from my bed, nor not dressed in a nightshirt neither. They'll need to cross the kitchen garden to reach the woods, Ellie. It is to your right."

"I see them," announced Eleanor a moment later. "Jessie and Joyce are beyond the garden—almost to the trees. Oh, and now Bowey and Mrs. Dish are coming into the garden themselves."

"Good," muttered the earl. "Keep watching, Ellie. You must tell me if anyone follows them."

The sound of sharply inhaled breaths and a stifled groan made Eleanor wish to go to Wright, but she held her position by the window. "They are all out of sight now," she said at last, "and no one has followed them."

"Excellent," declared Wright. "Come here, Ellie."

Eleanor turned and stared at the gentleman seated upon the edge of the bed donning, with Tibbs's help, a down-at-the-heel pair of riding boots. "You cannot possibly force your ankle into that," she protested. "You shall break it all over again."

"No, I don't think so. Tibbs has taken the bandages off and it ain't swollen half so bad as yesterday. An' the boots are too big, ain't they, Tibbs?"

"They have stretched a bit, your lordship. But I cannot imagine you shall be able to stand."

"I need to stand, Tibbs. How am I to face Hampton and his men if I cannot stand?"

"They ain't aware ye be anywhere about, yer lor'ship," mumbled Aberdeen, strolling hurriedly into the room. "Miz Dish tole us in the kitchen how thin's stood. I sent Miz Hamilton an' the maids to the stables jus' in case. 'Ere, lean on me an' we shall see if ye be standin' or no."

Eleanor held her breath as Wright put his good arm over

Aberdeen's shoulder and rose slowly to his feet. His face blanched pure white as he shifted his full weight to the injured ankle. She stared as he bit his lower lip, released his hold on Aberdeen's shoulders and took a step. With an impatient oath he tore at the sling that protected his broken arm. "Take it off, Tibbs! Take the damnable splints off as well. It is near enough healed to be of use. It will need to be of use. Aberdeen, on the top of my armoire are balls and powder. Fetch them. Eleanor, in my dining room is a china cabinet. See can you take a stool, my dear, and reach as high as the top shelf. My pistol case lies at the very back. You cannot see it, but you can feel it well enough. It lies on the side toward the windows. Fetch it down for me."

Eleanor was on her way before he had finished his sentence.

In the nursery Worchester and the Fiend had peered out the window just in time to catch sight of the children fleeing into the woods. They paused long enough to witness Mrs. Bowers and Mrs. Dish set off after the little ones, then pounded through the hall and down the servants' stairs, leaving doors wide open behind them. Nose twitching, ears kinked with curiosity, Blaze scurried from beneath a table and snuffled in the strange odor of the tallow factory that clung to the men's boots. With a series of excited woofs, the puppy scampered about in circles, undecided whether to follow the wonderfully outrageous smell or not. From behind the draperies the kit peered cautiously. It was not about to come out into the open until it was positive that the giants who made the gruff sounds had disappeared. Blaze saw the tiny pointed snout and went to give it an exuberant lick.

In the long drawing room Hampton toyed with a horse pistol and scowled. "Can't imagine what's keeping 'em. Who else has stayed behind, Mary?" he growled, pointing the muzzle of the pistol directly at her heart. "Who might come upon them?"

"No one," muttered Mary, pushing the muzzle aside and

rising. "You are too impatient just as you always were, Arthur. Do you expect that Joyce will run directly into their arms? She is not as trusting as all that, I assure you."

"Joyce? 'Tis a girl? And you had the audacity to name her after his bloody lordship?"

"Oh do be quiet, Hampton! Would you have had me call her after you? I think not! 'Twas Jocelyn kept me from taking my own life, and Jocelyn forced you to give her legitimacy, and Jocelyn paced the floorboards the night she was born. Therefore she is Joyce and proud of it!"

"You are a big, fat blackguard, Mr. Hampton," Jenny pouted, her lower lip protruding adorably. "It is a wonder someone has not murdered you before now. It is not fair, you know, to make Joshie do it. After everything he has done for you so far, you ought at least to be considerate enough to shoot yourself in the head and save him the trouble."

"And you, my dear, ought to learn to keep your comments to yourself—and you will learn it, too. I assure you. Your brother is an audacious, vicious, interfering fool, and you will be made to pay for it as well as he."

"Humph," mumbled Jenny, with a toss of her golden curls and a quick glance at Mary. "We shall see, shall we not, Mr. Hampton? Mary, bring me my sewing basket, will you please? It is there, just beside the hearth. You do not mind, do you, if I sew until your henchmen return?"

"Oh, for gawd's sake do whatever!" grumbled Hampton, rising and stuffing the totally ignored pistol into the pocket of his open greatcoat. "We shall be shed of this place as soon as Hobbins and Worchester return, at any rate."

Mary lifted Jenny's work basket from the floor and carried it to her. Jenny's bright blue eyes flashed excitedly. "Don't pace, Mary. Let that great, fierce villain pace, and you come and sit beside me. I'll show you Joshie's Christmas present."

Hampton groaned and turned away to peer out into the hall. Jenny reached down into her basket, seized a scissors lying there and plopped it into Mary's hand as she pulled that young woman down beside her. "Put them in the pocket of your skirt," Jenny whispered hurriedly. "And keep your hand upon them so that you may draw them out quickly. Your aunt has gotten the children safely away by now and Eleanor has gone to warn Joshie. When our opportunity to escape appears we must take it on the instant."

Hampton's head turned toward the whispering and Jenny immediately ceased to do so, holding up before herself and Mary the most atrocious excuse for a shirt Hampton had ever seen.

"And I am going to embroider his initials upon it, too," murmured Jenny, as though continuing a conversation. "Only I cannot decide just where to put them."

Hampton snorted and turned back toward the door.

With admirable deftness the little duchess reached again into the basket and pulled from it a slim silver dagger which she stuck into one sleeve of her dress. "Are they not coming?" she asked in a bright, teasing voice as she set the basket down upon the floor. "Perhaps Joyce has bitten them and they have run screaming into the night."

"It is not night," scowled Hampton. " 'Tis barely dusk, and the only screams that will be heard about this place will be yours if you do not close those adorable lips and cease plaguing me! Lord, I cannot imagine how Wright endures you!"

Wright, staring out his window as Tibbs loaded the pistols, was enduring at that moment a great deal of pain, apprehension and anger. "Damnation!" he snarled. "Aberdeen, Tibbs, two men are in the garden and heading for the trees after Bowey and Melinda and the children! Are the pistols loaded?"

"Yes, my lord," answered Tibbs, tamping the ball into the barrel of the second pistol. "Ready to go."

"Excellent. Give one to Aberdeen and you take the other and go after those scoundrels."

Tibbs raised a fine white eyebrow. "I think not, your lordship. Aberdeen and I shall certainly stop those brigands, but you will need your pistols. You are not likely to subdue Hampton with your fists or any swordplay—not in your condition."

"Leave me one, then. Take the other." Wright opened the casement windows and urged Aberdeen and Tibbs—carrying one of the prized Manton's—out into the yard. "Eleanor, carry the pistol for me, will you?" he asked, limping badly toward the door. "You think he is in the long drawing room?"

"Yes, that is where we left Jenny. He was just beyond in the hall, plaguing Mary."

"Well, it ain't me he wants," Wright sighed. "Not yet, at any rate. He would never have sent a message to draw me to Fennel's Marsh else. 'Tis Mary and Joyce he's after. That's why his men have followed the children into the woods. He'll not leave till he has the babe, I guess."

Eleanor watched in wonder as the scowl upon the earl's face deepened, then eased, then turned into a satisfied smile. "I'll lay odds Jenny and Mary ain't told him I'm here, no, nor you neither. We've that much to work with. He'll not expect any resistance. Now do I remember correctly, there is a way from the gallery to the long drawing room."

"No, there is not," murmured Eleanor. "One must descend from the gallery and climb the main staircase. I asked Jenny to show me the gallery the day you asked us to stay. I—I thought there might be a portrait of you."

The earl's lips twitched. "Did you find it?"

Eleanor gazed up at him, blushing, and nodded. "You were very young."

"Twelve—and Jenny five. Poor painter had the devil of a time to keep us still. Do not look quite so worried, my love. We shall stop Hampton, I promise you—but you must be very brave."

Eleanor nodded on a little gulp. The bravest she had ever been was when she had leapt through the window at Hampton Hall in Lily's wake and helped to subdue Hampton. She was not at all certain whether she could do such a thing again. But Wright gazed down at her with such a look of confidence that she set her mind to the task of conquering her own doubts and, urging him to lean upon her as much as need be, they set out for the main part of the house. "There's a passage from the gallery," Wright muttered. "Charlie showed it to me once. Now, please God, I will remember how to get into it."

"And it goes to the drawing room?" asked Eleanor, amazed.

"Oh, it goes everywhere, love. Duke of Buckingham drew up the plans for it during the Civil War. 'Tis a labyrinth, but one may find one's way if one knows the secret."

"And do you know the secret?" Eleanor put an arm around his waist as they reached the stairs and held him tightly as he attempted one painful step after another.

"No, but the Buck was equally as mad as I, love, or so I understand, and I think once I see it again I'll be able to decipher the thing."

Aberdeen and Tibbs, having the advantage of knowing exactly where the ladies and the children were headed, made a wide circle through the woods, coming up one on each side of Hampton's henchmen just as Worchester and the Fiend sprang for the old ladies and the children.

"Run, Jessie! Run, Joyce!" screamed Bowey as the Fiend's hand snatched hold of the hood upon her cape and with a quick twist and a toss, he sent the poor woman careening into the trunk of an oak tree. Bowey fell like a corpse to the ground.

Mrs. Dish spun about before Worchester could do her a like turn and sent a heavy skillet she had borrowed from the kitchen cracking into his chest. Worchester roared in pain and reeled away. The Fiend launched himself at her from the side and she swung the skillet again, pummeling his shoulder. Aberdeen sprang from the underbrush just as Worchester spun back into the fray and met the man face-to-face, swinging a long unused fist into Worchester's stomach and a second straight into the middle of his nose. Tibbs hurled himself at the Fiend and brought an elderly but determined fist crashing into the side of the Fiend's jaw. "Get clear, Melinda," he yelled, puffing.

Mrs. Dish did exactly that, and Tibbs ducked the Fiend's return blow, tugged his lordship's pistol into view and cocked the hammer. The Fiend, eyes wide, stopped in midswing. Worchester, hands over a broken nose that sent wide rivulets of blood streaming between his fingers, groaned and dropped to the ground.

"Melinda, are you all right?" Tibbs asked worriedly, his eyes and the muzzle of Wright's pistol staring directly at the two scoundrels. Mrs. Dish's soft lips upon his cheek were all the answer he required.

"Aberdeen and I shall look to Mrs. Bowers," she whispered softly in his ear. "You are so brave, my darling Horace. I do not know what we would have done without you."

Bowey being quite unconscious and seemingly intending to remain so, a decision was made to continue on to the gamekeeper's cottage where the children would be waiting and where Mrs. Bowers might lie comfortably upon a cot until a carriage could be fetched to carry her home. Aberdeen picked the unfortunate nanny up in his arms and led the way; Mrs. Dish with her skillet in hand and Tibbs flourishing the earl's pistol brought up the rear; and the Fiend, sneezing from high anxiety, and Worchester, moaning in pain, were sandwiched neatly in between. By the time they reached the modest bungalow that Duncan Plummer had made his home for over twenty years, it was full dusk, a chill wind had risen in the north and all of them, villains and heroes alike, longed for warmth. The cottage, however, stood cold, silent and empty. "I expect Plummer's gone wi' the others," mumbled Aberdeen as he carried Mrs. Bowers to the bedroom and set her down upon Plummer's cot. He covered the nanny with a feather ticking and strolled back into the main room.

"But where's the children?" breathed Mrs. Dish, looking worriedly about. "Jessemy, Joyce, are you hiding, my dears? Come out now. We are safe. Aberdeen and Mr. Tibbs have rescued us."

No excited voices responded to Mrs. Dish's words. No enthusiastic faces appeared before them. Not a blond head nor a dark one peeked out from behind or under any piece of furniture. The children had disappeared.

Twenty-three

The 'roic and indom'able Duke of Ware, curse of bla'g'ards, righter of wrongs, an' avengerer of innocents sneaked with amazin' little noise right into the anteroom where Burtie was tied up han' an' feets upon the floor. His loyal companion, Miss Joyce Ellen, only lady Bow Stweet Wunner, gave a tiny squeak and plopped down right nex' to Burtie an' gave the butler's head a consoling little pat. Burton, eyes wide, attempted to mumble something through the dirty kerchief tied around his mouth, but neither of the rescuers could understand a word of it. "Is you huwt, Buwtie?" asked Joyce, leaning forward to bestow a cold, wet kiss upon Burton's cheek.

"Don' worry, Burtie," whispered the Duke of Ware, plopping down beside him as well. "Me an' Joycie gonna save you."

"Uh-huh," agreed Miss Joyce Ellen with an enthusiastic nod.

Burton mumbled again, and with a deep scowl the little duke crawled around behind him and began to work at the knot that held the kerchief in place. "We can'ts unnerstan' you, Burtie," he whispered. "Wait." With amazin' delicatcy an' determ'nation, the 'roic Duke of Ware undone the tangled maze of knottin' an' tugged the cloth from Burtie's mouf.

"Master Jessie, Miss Joyce," hissed Burton. "Untie me, my dears. I must help the ladies."

"We comed to catch the bla'g'ards," explained the duke, crawling back to peer down into Burton's face. "Where's they?"

"You must untie me, Master Jessie, and then you and Miss Joyce must hide. There are very bad men here."

"We ain't 'fraid of no bad mens," declared the 'roic duke, divesting himself of his jacket and hat and tugging Joycie out of hers as well. He had a bit of trouble with one of Joycie's buttons, but he triumphed in the end and dropped the little coat on the floor beside him. "We's heroes, Burtie."

"Yes, Master Jess, indeed you are. And now untie me."

The Duke of Ware screwed up his eyes in deep contemplation. "No," he announced at last. "You are hurted, Burtie. You better stay ri' here. Your head is bleedin'."

Miss Joyce Ellen gazed at her companion, speechless.

"If we unties 'im, Joycie, he won' let us be rescuers," whispered the duke in her cold little ear. "I know. Burtie will makes us hide an' not come out till everthin' is over wif."

Burton, quite able to hear and understand every word, would gladly have kicked himself for being so stupid as to mention the children's hiding before he was untied. He opened his mouth to protest, but at that very moment Miss Joyce scampered away. She came back directly with a very pretty pillow from the front parlor and with the duke's help lay it lovingly under Burton's head. Then she gave him another pat and another kiss upon the cheek. "We be the wescuwers, Buwtie," she said. "Me an' Jessie go wescuw evewyones."

Eleanor held tightly to Wright's waist as the earl, a branch of candles in his hand, descended a short flight of stone steps. The passage was astoundingly clear of cobwebs and not once did the pitter-patter of rat feet send shivers down Eleanor's spine. It was, in fact, not at all what Eleanor had imagined a secret passage to be. Not damp, not filthy, not even smelling of must or decay—but it was immensely confusing. She had lost her sense of direction at the very first turning and could not have made her way back to the gallery without a great many mistakes. It therefore astonished her that after a matter of moments Wright knew exactly which turnings to take and which staircases to follow. In the flickering candlelight Eleanor's heart went out to the gentleman. Sweat streamed down his face in spite of the chill that surrounded them. Each step, she knew, was torturous, but he never once complained. His shirt clung wetly to him and his breath rattled against his bound ribs. Several times, if not for her support, he would have fallen and been quite unable to rise again. So she had kept her arm firmly about his waist until this very moment.

Now he handed her the candles and signaled her to set them down upon the steps behind them. "We are only a few steps from the long drawing room," he whispered when she had done so. He placed both her arms around his waist, enveloped her in his arms and hugged her solidly. She felt the breath of a kiss upon her brow and then his lips touched her cheek softly, like the whisper of flutterby wings. "I lied about not having tender feelings, Ellie," he murmured. "Even barbarians have tender feelings sometimes. You are fine and brave and exceeding patient, and I am come to love you with all my heart." He took a painful breath, and Eleanor's arms clasped more tightly around him and she rested her head upon his shoulder. "Will you kiss me, Ellie?" he whispered, his lips brushing her hair. "Before whatever happens, happens, will you kiss me?"

Eleanor felt the pricking of tears at the back of her eyes. His every word stirred long-damped fires in her soul, and she knew as clearly as she knew night from day that she could never, ever, bear to be parted from him. With a tilt of her head, she offered him her lips and gently, seductively, with the solemnity of a saint, the barbarian kissed her. Blood roared in her ears. Hunger for him cramped her stomach and she groaned as his tongue touched hers. Then, inexplicably, he pulled away, and one long, slim finger drew a delicate line down her flushed cheek. "Do you have the pistol, Eleanor? Give it to me."

On the opposite side of the wall Hampton had turned again to peer out into the hall. "Where the deuce have they got to?"

Jenny looked up from her sewing, which she had thought it

best to pretend to be doing, and shrugged her shoulders at him. "Perhaps they've found Joshie's jewelry and absconded with it," she offered nonchalantly.

Mary laughed. Hampton snorted. And Jenny's adorable blue eyes saw a tiny gap in one section of the wall paneling. She stood immediately and tugged Mary after her toward the far window. "I think I have hit upon the answer, Mr. Hampton," she said loudly. "Your fellows *have* found Joshie's stash and are even now on their way into the night. Come and see if you do not believe me."

Hampton, scowling, stalked angrily to the window. In the passage Eleanor watched a slow, admiring smile spread across the earl's face. "Good girl, Jenny," he breathed. And then he set Eleanor behind him, jerked open the hidden door and stepped silently into the room, his pistol pointed at Hampton's back. "Evening, Hampton," he muttered, and the sound of his voice caused the man to spin about.

But Arthur Hampton was not a fool. He knew on the instant he would turn to face pistol or sword, so he caught Jenny by the arm and jerked her around in front of him.

"Ought to learn to shoot people in the back, Wright," he hissed. "Neater and certainly won't destroy *your* reputation."

"Let Jenny go."

"Not on your life. Do you think I'm as mad as you? Lower the pistol, Wright, or I'll do the wench in." Hampton held a struggling Jenny tightly with one hand while he reached into his coat pocket with the other and produced his own pistol. "I'll shoot the gel, Wright. I swear it. Put the weapon down."

Eleanor bit at her lower lip as she watched the pistol in Wright's hand. It was shaking. Not very noticeably, but shaking all the same. And then she realized—it was in the wrong hand. He held it unsteadily in his right because his left arm was not yet strong enough to bear the pressure of firing the thing.

"Put it down," she whispered. "Jocelyn, you cannot possibly hit him without hitting Jenny as well. Put it down."

"I would have shot you in the back," Wright announced with

a charming grin, "but I was set upon Ellie's perceiving me to be an upright and honorable person. Here, have it then," and he set the pistol, still cocked, upon a small table.

As Hampton's eyes followed the earl's movements, Mary tugged the little scissors from her pocket and stabbed them forcibly into Hampton's shoulder. Hampton cried out and dropped his own pistol. With a flash and a roar and the smell of sulfur the thing exploded and sent a ball whizzing past Wright's knee. Jenny tore herself from Hampton's grasp, slid the little silver dagger into her hand and, tugging Mary, who had dropped the scissors in shock, behind her, ran to her brother's side. She slid the dagger into his hand just as Hampton fumbled a blade of his own from the depths of his greatcoat and flung himself at Wright.

The 'roic Duke of Ware and his loyal companion, Miss Joyce Ellen, had just reached the first-floor landing when Hampton's pistol exploded. Joycie put her hands over her ears and wrinkled her nose. Jessie seized her by one arm and swung her up against the wall. He pulled her hands away from her ears and, wrinkling his own nose at the smell of the gunpowder, explained that the noise had been a pistol shot. "You stay right here, Joycie," he ordered. "I'm gonna see what happened." He tiptoed toward the open door from which sounds of a fight clearly emanated.

Belowstairs di Roche, Lily and Nicco had just entered the front door as the pistol fired. Without pause, three pairs of legs rushed into Burton's view and then out of it and up the stairs, leaving the butler hurling expletives and struggling more violently against his bonds. Di Roche reached the upper landing first, spied Joyce pressed against the wall, grabbed the child up into his arms and handed her off to Nicco. Nicco carried her as far as Lily and passed the little girl into Miss Lipton's open arms. Lily hugged Joyce, murmured encouragingly in the tiny ear, then turned and carried her back down the stairs as the two men rushed toward the little duke, who was just then scurrying around the door frame and into the long drawing room.

"You stop right this minute!" yelled his grace, Charles Jocelyn Stuart Jessemy Brenford. Hands on hips, he scowled at the pile of people scrambling about on the floor, all of them, it appeared, including his very own mama, attempting to squash his Uncle Josh. "You leave my Uncle Josh alone!"

At the bottom of the pile, having managed before going down to knock the blade from Hampton's hand and lose his own dagger in the process, the earl was being viciously pummeled by Hampton, who in turn was being pummeled and pounded by Jenny, Mary and Eleanor. None of them heard Jessie's shout. The little duke, all pretense at being anyone but himself gone, spied his uncle's dueling pistol upon the table and ran to get it. Di Roche and Nicco spun into the room just as Jessie turned with the weapon in both hands and yelled again, tearfully, for everyone to get off of his uncle. "No!" di Roche shouted, hurling himself across the room. With a great roar the weapon misfired and di Roche crashed to the floor.

Nicco, following in his master's wake, swept Jessie up into his arms and attempted to smother the smoldering sleeves of the child's shirt. He ran for the hallway and the servants' stairs, thinking to carry the boy to the kitchen pump without delay. He jerked open the baize door and fled down the steps, not even noticing the puppy and the kit, who scampered down from the second floor toward him. Blaze, trembling with excitement, bounced first one way and then the other, unable to decide whether to follow the running man or investigate the entirely new smell from the first-floor hall. The smell won out and he padded, sniffing, through the open door, the kit staying cautiously behind him.

The second roar of a pistol had brought the ladies atop Hampton to a sudden halt, and the villain rose up from beneath them, sending them flying in all directions. With a final, vicious kick to Wright's ribs, Hampton seized Mary and dragged her biting and kicking into the hall. Eleanor dashed after them. She reached the hall in time to see Hampton tumble backward over the puppy and release Mary in an attempt to regain his balance. Blaze, unaccustomed to great clumsy feet stomping upon him, yelped, and the kit in response jumped to the highest place it could find—Hampton. Cursing, Hampton seized it by the scruff of the neck and flung it from him. The gesture got his boot heel twisted in the carpeting and he careened backward down the stairs, fetching up very still at the bottom just as Lily, with Joyce in her arms, and Burton rushed into the entryway and the front door crashed open and Paxton, Howard and the men came barreling in.

It was very late as once again a subdued group gathered fearfully in the earl's music room. Jessie, his hands and wrists bandaged, dozed fitfully upon his mama's lap as di Roche's arm remained protectively around them both. The little marquis's leg sported a bandage where the pistol ball had gone clear through his calf and MacGregor had ordered him to bed, but he had not listened. Howard, weary and relieved and worried all at the same time, sat silently upon the brocade settee, both arms around a bedraggled Lily, her lovely head resting upon his chest. Mary cuddled Joyce in both arms and Paxton cuddled Mary in a like manner. Mrs. Dish, who had seen Bowey tucked safely into bed with a bandage 'round her brow, sat on the arm of the wing chair in which Eleanor fidgeted and held that young lady's hand. Arthur Hampton would not threaten anyone anymore. His neck had broken in the fall.

"Any moment now," Mrs. Dish murmured, "Horace will emerge and tell us that Josh is giving Dr. MacGregor a very hard time and that you must go and calm him down at once, Eleanor. And you will find Harry Cross cursing beneath his breath and Glenby Oakes threatening to pummel the earl into submission."

Eleanor smiled at the thought. But she knew it was only wishful thinking. Jocelyn had neither moved nor made the least sound since the men had lifted him from the drawing-room floor and carried him to his bed.

"It is my fault, all of it," groaned the Reverend Howard from across the room. His eyes rested upon his sister's bruised face as his fingers stroked Lily's golden blond hair. "If I had been more a man and less a paragon—"

"No," Lily sighed. "It is not your fault, Martin. I should not have run from you. The man would have done nothing had I not delivered myself into his hands."

"You are mistaken there, my dear," offered Mary, bestowing a comforting kiss upon Joyce's brow. "He would have found a way, Lily, to continue his vendetta. It was not the fault of anyone present. Lay the blame where it belongs, upon Arthur Hampton."

Paxton kissed Mary's ear and then gave Joyce a loud, smacking one that made her giggle. "Enough sour faces and regrets," he said. "You are all safe now and the blackguard gone to his just reward. And Wright will recover, you know. Never would he succumb to such an indignity as dying in his own bed."

Jenny giggled at that and nodded. "He has always said he will die with a sword in one hand and a pistol in the other—or be trampled to death on the floor of the House of Lords."

"So there, you see," declared Paxton, "we are all of us in the sullens for no reason. In a moment Tibbs will appear just as Mrs. Dish has so wisely predicted and we must all decide what to tell him."

"What do you mean, decide what to tell him?" asked Mary wonderingly.

"Don't you think he will demand to know, my dear, if I am finally to become Joyce's father? *Am* I finally to become Joyce's father, Mary? There is nothing left to stand between us that I am aware of. I love you, Mary Hampton. I have loved you from the day I found you in Josh's study, tossing his account books about the room and cursing under your breath. Will you marry me?"

"I was not cursing!" Mary exclaimed. "But he had the most disorganized accounts I had ever seen. He is such a gudgeon and so full of unaccountable impulses. He has near spent himself into ruin, you know, over his orphans and his school. And yes, Michael, I will marry you, and not merely to have a decent father for Joycie neither."

Joyce, her eyes wide, reached up to pat Paxton's cheek.

"Would you like to have a papa, Joyce?" Paxton asked with a grin. "Would you like to have me for a papa?"

"Uh-huh," nodded the china doll, her dusky curls bouncing. "You an' Uncle Josh."

Di Roche laughed. "I expecting that is answer I getting from these child, if he awake being."

"Joshie must countenance our marriage now, don't you think?" asked Jenny, her brilliant blue eyes gazing into di Roche's above the little duke's golden curls.

"He being overwhelmed with my prowess when I telling him," Di Roche grinned. "No longer being I a fop. Now I must advancing to rank of buck, no?"

Howard sighed and held Lily more tightly against him. "And will you forgive me, Lily, for being such a pompous ass? You are my life, my love, and I do not care a fig for what anyone says. Will you marry me, darling?"

Lily sighed against him and nodded her head. "But only if you do not lie about me to your parents, Martin. If you are not willing to tell them the truth, then I shall always think that you are ashamed of me—and I could not bear for you to be ashamed of me."

"I am not ashamed of you in the least, precious. I am proud. You are strong and brave and loyal and everything wonderful, and so I shall tell my father and mother, I promise you."

Tears streamed down Eleanor's cheeks and she swiped at them with the back of her hand. She was happy for each of the couples, but would she ever hear a proposal from Wright's softly seductive lips? Would she ever again share a kiss with the man she loved? Or would she stand over his grave in a chill winter wind and bury her heart forever?

"Ellie!" came a familiar bellow just then. "Ellie!"

Eleanor sprang to her feet and ran through the music room and the sitting room and into the earl's bedchamber, where she came to an abrupt halt beside the bed. "Oh, there you are," the gentleman sighed, clasping her hand in his own and pulling her down beside him. "Make these dastardly villains go away, Ellie. They will not take me seriously as I cannot pummel them within an inch of their worthless lives at the moment."

Eleanor looked around her at a pensive Tibbs, a silent Harry Cross and a harassed Dr. MacGregor. She saw a crease in Aberdeen's brow, and Glenby Oakes took a deep breath. "Reckon I ought to tell Peggy ye be alive, then, yer lor'ship," the coachman muttered. "She come home jus' as we was carryin' ye from the drawin' room. Reckon she be a mite worried."

"Aye, an' the rest of them as well," agreed MacGregor, closing his bag. "We are none of us leaving, mind you, Wright. We shall return as soon as you have fallen under the spell of this young lady and are approachable again. You may count upon it."

Eleanor watched as they trailed from the room. Tibbs closed the door behind them and MacGregor eyed the valet censoriously.

"Well, but he's going to marry the girl," Tibbs murmured. " 'Tis no secret. 'Twas all he mumbled about when he was coming to his senses. A man ought to have a moment alone with the woman he's going to marry."

"Eleanor?" Wright was propped up among a nest of pillows, his face and body badly bruised, his ribs freshly bound and his left arm back in a sling. "Ellie, are you all right? They promised you were not hurt, but your cheek—" His hand went to the bruise and caressed it gently. "Oh, but I am a villain to have done this to you."

"You?" Eleanor's eyes opened wide. "You? 'Twas Hampton hit me when I attempted to pull him off of you."

The earl's darkling eyes flashed. "Do you mean that a parson's daughter and a vicar's sister is accustomed to roll about on the floor punching at blackguards and that my devilish influence had nothing at all to do with it?"

"Since you have come to Willowset I have done a great

many things I never thought to do before, my lord," Eleanor grinned.

"And I have thought a great many things, Ellie, that my mind has shied away from for years. I—I—" Wright's face, nearly as white as the sheets beneath him, twisted in pain, and he attempted to take a deep breath, bringing forth a muffled groan.

Eleanor put a hand on each of his pallid cheeks and kissed him very carefully and tenderly on his swollen lips.

"Ellie," he gasped as their lips parted. "Ellie, I—I—"

"Shhh," Eleanor murmured. "There is all the time in the world for us to talk, Jocelyn. Now you must rest. You must do as Dr. MacGregor tells you. Yes, and as Tibbs tells you, too."

MacGregor, true to his word, did not leave. He spent the night at Willowset and was again closeted with the earl the next morning. When at last he came into the breakfast room Eleanor had just sat down and he joined her.

"Is Josh—is his lordship better?" Eleanor asked worriedly. "What is it keeps you here?"

"Worry, Miss Howard. I'm an old man. I worry."

"But you said last evening that he would be all right."

"Indeed. And so he will be—but he'll never be the same as he was, my dear, and well the devil knows it. And *that* is what worries me. He didn't ask you to marry him, did he?"

Eleanor looked up from her muffin, startled.

"No, I thought not. When he began to regain his senses you were all he spoke of, Miss Howard. He feared for your life. He swore to protect ye. He begged ye to marry him. Ye were not there, of course. Do ye love the devil?"

Eleanor, flabbergasted at his directness, nodded.

"I hoped ye did. He needs you, Miss Howard, more than he has ever needed anyone. No one has told him yet all that has happened. He only remembers going down beneath Hampton's onslaught and a great deal of pain. I've added to the pain this morning by being brutally honest with him."

"Honest?"

"Yes, my dear, and now I will be so with you. Two of his ribs have been broken again. One of them has pierced his lung."

"Oh, no!"

"And his ankle has rebroken as well. I doubt he'll ever walk without a cane and a dreadful limp, if he walks at all. What I'm attempting to say, Miss Howard, is that Wright's rough and wild life has come to an abrupt halt. He ain't going to charge off on horseback across the country any longer, nor ride to hounds. Lucky he'll be to get from one room to another on his own."

Eleanor set the muffin back upon her plate and rose. MacGregor rose with her. "Do you go to him, Miss Howard?"

"Yes, immediately."

"Do not offer him pity, my dear. He won't want it and don't need it. 'Tis you he needs, and hope for a new way of life."

Eleanor burst into Wright's bedchamber without pausing to knock and discovered the earl alone, gazing out the window. He did not look at her as she sat down beside him on the big old bed. He did not even say "good morning." He simply sat and stared as he had long ago stared somberly into the fire in Mrs. Dish's kitchen. She took his hand in both of hers and gave it a reassuring squeeze. "It will not be so very bad, Jocelyn. You'll see. You may still attend Lords, you know, and stir them up as much as you like. We shall find a way to get you there. And—and—everyone who is anyone keeps their own carriage in London. No one will even notice you don't ride Tugforth anymore. And a great many gentlemen carry walking sticks, do they not? Lily told me once that some had ivory handles and even gold balls on the top. You will be right in the midst of fashion. And you don't need to be fighting anyone anymore, Josh. If you want, Martin will teach you how to talk your enemies to death."

"I rather think I resent *that* statement," growled her brother as he entered the chamber with Lily upon his arm. "I will, however, do so if you desire it, Wright. Apparently even my sister thinks I'm quite good at it."

"Josh," breathed Lily, the sadness in her great blue eyes betraying that she and Howard had also had conversation with Dr. MacGregor. "Would you not like to hear all that happened and how di Roche and Nicco came to my rescue?"

"No, Lily, go away."

Howard lifted an eyebrow and Eleanor inhaled a sob, but Lily only waved for Mary and Jenny and Paxton and di Roche to enter.

Jenny, supporting di Roche to a wicker chair near the washstand, sat down herself upon the Turkish carpeting at the side of her brother's bed. "Stop staring out that window this moment, Joshie. You are being a reg'lar curmudgeon and making Ellie cry," Jenny declared, her innocent eyes staring upward as his own turned down to meet them. "You are acting every bit as villainous to her as Papa did to Mildred. And that is why Mildred did not marry him, you know. A gentleman who will not share his deepest, darkest fears with a lady does not love her half as much as he thinks and is not worth the effort of marrying. That is precisely what Mildred told me."

Eleanor felt the earl's fingers entwine themselves among her own. "But I can't, Jenny."

"You can't share your fears with her?"

"No, rumcake, I cannot ask Ellie to marry a cripple. I could never dance with her, not even at our wedding. And if I could walk, I would have to limp around like some freak from a country fair. And I could not walk with her across the moors because I would start puffing like a ragged old goat and need to sit down for an hour before we had gotten anywhere. You know you would never wish to be married to someone like that. No, nor Mary nor Lily neither—nor any woman beneath the age of seventy."

"I am going to marry Francesco," stated Jenny. "And he is short and funny and Italian. And Mary is to marry Mr. Paxton, who can barely sit a horse and has his nose forever buried in someone else's business. And Lily has said yes to Mr. Howard, and we all know he is a dead bore. Ladies do not always want the same things in a gentleman. You are just being a big baby, Jocelyn Elders, and I shall tell Francesco not to give you Hampton Hall for Christmas if you do not cease sulking this very moment."

"Hampton Hall?"

"For your school—and we have already spoken to the people in St. Swithin's and they are not at all opposed to having London orphans in their midst—as long as you are in charge of them. Now, we're all going into the next room except Ellie, and I'm going to close the door behind us, and if you cannot do the proper thing, I shall take Ellie to London to find a proper beau and not bother about you anymore."

Eleanor, blushing a bright pink, watched as the parade of friends marched from the room. "Jenny does not mean a word of it," she murmured. "She and di Roche and Paxton have worked very hard to get title to Hampton Hall. They would not abandon it now. Nor would they ever abandon you."

Wright turned to look at her, his gaze as mesmerizing as that first night in the nursery. "I shan't stop being stubborn and maggoty, Ellie. And I shan't stop getting into trouble, and I shall probably complain a great deal more than I am used to do—which is a lot, I assure you—but I shan't be able to do all the things I wanted to do with you—all the things you deserve a husband to do with you."

Eleanor smoothed the curls from his brow and her fingers trailed softly down his cheek. "What makes you think I require dancing and walking the moors in a husband?" she asked with a smile. "And by the way, my darling, a limp will only make you more interesting and more dangerous to ladies' hearts."

"But if I cannot walk at all?"

"Oh, you will walk. I have not the least doubt. You are much too stubborn not to. Besides, how will you get up to the nursery to tease our children if you don't?"

"Our children?" The silver flecks in Wright's eyes burst into flames. "Our children, Ellie? You are not just being kind? You do wish to marry me?"

"Well, it would be nice to be married if we are to have children, don't you think? Of course, you ought to ask me properly. I rather think Jenny had that in mind when she led everyone from the room."

Wright chuckled. "Miss Eleanor Howard," he said, with a twinkle in his eyes that made her giggle, "I will make you a devil of a husband; I will try your patience no end with my queer starts and insane causes; and most likely I will drive you to drink by taking Jenny's advice and sharing with you all my deepest, darkest fears; but I love you from the top of your head to the tips of your toes, and I will treasure you until the day I die and do all in my power to keep that smile upon your sweet lips and your eyes shining like honey in the sunlight. Will you do me the honor to become my wife?"

"Yes," breathed Eleanor, sliding forward and kissing him carefully upon his bruised lips. "Yes, yes, yes!"

ZEBRA REGENCIES
ARE THE
TALK OF THE TON!

A REFORMED RAKE   (4499, $3.99)

by Jeanne Savery

After governess Harriet Cole helped her young charge flee to France—
and the designs of a despicable suitor, more trouble soon arrived in the
person of a London rake. Sir Frederick Carrington insisted on providing
safe escort back to England. Harriet deemed Carrington more dangerous than any band of brigands, but secretly relished matching wits with
him. But after being taken in his arms for a tender kiss, she found
herself wondering—*could* a lady find love with an irresistible rogue?

A SCANDALOUS PROPOSAL   (4504, $4.99)

by Teresa DesJardien

After only two weeks into the London season, Lady Pamela Premington
has already received her first offer of marriage. If only it hadn't come
from the *ton's* most notorious rake, Lord Marchmont. Pamela had already set her sights on the distinguished Lieutenant Penford, who had
the heroism and honor that made him the ideal match. Now she had to
keep from falling under the spell of the seductive Lord so she could
pursue the man more worthy of her love. Or was he?

A LADY'S CHAMPION   (4535, $3.99)

by Janice Bennett

Miss Daphne, art mistress of the Selwood Academy for Young Ladies,
greeted the notion of ghosts haunting the academy with skepticism.
However, to avoid rumors frightening off students, she found herself
turning to Mr. Adrian Carstairs, sent by her uncle to be her "protector"
against the "ghosts." Although, Daphne would accept no interference
in her life, she *would* accept aid in exposing any spectral spirits. What
she never expected was for Adrian to expose the secret wishes of her
hidden heart . . .

CHARITY'S GAMBIT   (4537, $3.99)

by Marcy Stewart

Charity Abercrombie reluctantly embarks on a London season in hopes
of making a suitable match. However she cannot forget the mysterious
Dominic Castille—and the kiss they shared—when he fell from a tree
as she strolled through the woods. Charity does not know that the dark
and dashing captain harbors a dangerous secret that will ensnare them
both in its web—leaving Charity to risk certain ruin and losing the man
she so passionately loves . . .

*Available wherever paperbacks are sold, or order direct from the
Publisher. Send cover price plus 50¢ per copy for mailing and
handling to Penguin USA, P.O. Box 999, c/o Dept. 17109,
Bergenfield, NJ 07621. Residents of New York and Tennessee
must include sales tax. DO NOT SEND CASH.*

**If you liked this book, be sure to look for others
in the *Denise Little Presents* line:**